NANNY RETURNS

ALSO BY EMMA McLAUGHLIN AND NICOLA KRAUS

The Nanny Diaries

Citizen Girl

Dedication

The Real Real

NANNY RETURNS

EMMA McLAUGHLIN

and

NICOLA KRAUS

SIMON & SCHUSTER

New York   London   Toronto   Sydney

Published in Great Britain by Simon & Schuster UK Ltd, 2010
A CBS COMPANY

Simon & Schuster UK Ltd
1st Floor, 222 Gray's Inn Road
London WC1X 8HB
www.simonandschuster.co.uk

Simon & Schuster Australia, Sydney

A Cataloguing-in-Publication record for this book is available from the British Library.
ISBN 978-1-84737-096-9

Cover illustration: Sarah Gibb
Art Direction: Lizzie Gardiner

Printed and bound in Australia by Griffin Press.

The paper used to produce this book is a natural, recyclable product made from wood
grown in sustainable plantation forests. The manufacturing processes conform to the
environmental regulations in the country of origin

10 9 8 7 6 5 4 3 2

To the children on their way—
we await you with arms and hearts open.

A NOTE TO READERS

Nanny Returns is a work of fiction. Names and characters are the product of the authors' imagination. Any resemblance to actual events or persons, living or dead, is coincidental. Although some real New York City institutions—schools, stores, businesses and the like—are mentioned, all are used fictitiously.

"Brooke Astor was always candid about the fact that she was not the motherly type."

New York Magazine, "The Family Astor,"
8/7/2006, Meryl Gordon

"And yet, for all his good works, Herman (Merkin) was a remote, withholding father. Short of not living at home he couldn't have been less involved."

New York Magazine, "The Monster Mensch,"
2/22/09, Steve Fishman

"The (Madoffs) have not spoken to their father since his confession to them . . . or to their mother, not because they think she was involved—they don't—but because they believe her tendency to side with him, no matter what . . . enabled his dirty deeds."

Vanity Fair, "Did the Madoff Sons Know?"
6/3/09, David Margolick

NANNY RETURNS

2008

1

"What're we doing?"

At the sound of my husband's voice I twist atop the ladder, where I'm attempting to jerry-rig a curtain panel to an ancient nail. He stands in the doorway of the otherwise empty room, wiping his flushed face with the bottom half of his damp Harvard T-shirt. "Hey, there," I say.

"Three weeks of living in a construction site and Mom's lost it already, Grace." Ryan addresses our twelve-year-old golden retriever as she tromps up the last few stairs to join us on the fourth floor of our new home. Beneath the stark light of the bulb jutting from the ceiling's plaster rosette, we watch as she promptly drops her throw rope at his sneakers for a treat. "Good girl." He ruffles her head and she saunters to the ladder to greet me, her paws grayed with the grit of Riverside Park.

"Did ya have a fun jog with Daddy?" I call as she trundles away to her water dish waiting in our bedroom next door. Loud lapping ensues.

"They're opening a Starbucks on the spot where that bodega burned down." He tugs his feet out of his Nikes and walks over in his socks.

"Then the drugstores, then the banks. We're ahead of the wave."

"So." He nuzzles my bare thigh with his sweaty brown hair before turning to peel off his shirt. "What *are* you doing?"

"I found the curtains!"

"So I see." He swipes up his sneakers on his way out.

I stretch to secure the other end of the cerulean linen fabric onto a second nail protruding from the fossilized wallpaper and, with a bracing hand on the cool metal, lean back to assess. Smoothing my palm along the crease from the last month the curtains have spent boxed, I remember scoring them at an Uppsala flea market two years ago to lift our flat from the Swedish winter blahs. Not that I'm complaining. After Ryan's position with the UN had relocated us from Haiti to southern Africa to northern Africa, I was just grateful to have seasons, even if three out of the four involved snow.

I adjust the cloth to hide the sea of sledgehammer dents where Steve, our contractor, "investigated" to see if it was feasible to install a window. Or if the openings had been bricked up sometime in the last century for a reason. Like the brownstone's back wall will collapse.

"Nan."

"Check out my window." I clamber down as he reappears in the doorway with a towel around his waist. "I'm going to put Grandma's old red desk under it and it's going to be my nook."

He comes over and wraps me in his arms, pulling me against his sweat-damp frame, the nubbly terry cloth brushing my legs. "We have over three thousand crumbling square feet—"

"Of potential."

"—of potential. You will have your nook and your window, and I have to ask if you are planning on wearing this to my parents' closing?" He slides up the sweater of his that I threw on in lieu of my still-missing robe. "Because I, for one, will find that distracting."

"I thought that's why I was coming, to distract you." I tug the towel free from his waist.

"To support me. And we're pushing the clock here." He grabs the towel back and snaps my ass as he strides out and down the short hallway to the one bathroom that functions in our over three thousand crumbling square feet. "I promised my dad he wouldn't have to give this closing a second thought. So fifteen minutes and we need to be walking out the door."

"Okay, but I need coffee first and the machine just conked," I update him from the doorway of my future office. "Another fuse blew in the kitchen."

"Bringing us to—"

"Three: the hall, the bedroom, and the bathroom. Any sign of Steve out front?"

"Not yet."

"It's almost nine. I should call him."

"You're stalling! You can call from the cab!" I hear the protesting shriek of the hot water being summoned. "And subtract five minutes for a pit stop if you want coffee!"

"I *want* a hit of the crack conveniently sold across the street!" I yell back, but he's already underwater. As I enter the bedroom, Grace raises her head from where she's flopped across our mattress, and I face the wall of wardrobe boxes. "You'd need crack, too, if he was making you go back to 721 Park."

A half hour later, the taxi jerks forward to traverse another halting increment of Park as all its lights turn green in unison, a municipal detail I always thought so perfectly fit the neighborhood's constricting mores—everyone on the avenue pressed to do the same thing at the same pace. I remember how much the unpropitious stop lights stressed me out when I worked here, now well over a decade ago. Placating some nap-deprived child squirming beside me on the backseat, I'd be breaking into a cold sweat over whether we'd be late for whatever the next bizarre assigned activity was—Flower Arranging for Four-Year-Olds or Tai Chi for Tots—and wishing the subway I rode to and from work with the rest of humanity was deemed safe for little Elspeth.

Below Ninety-sixth Street the meridians are blooming with lushly packed Easter tulips and I remember accompanying my grandmother, trowel in hand, to help plant the bulbs when I was a child. But by the time I grew up to work in the buildings flanking these flower beds, my employers had long since outsourced the duty to others for whom English was a second language, as was their predilection for any task requiring them to drop to their knees. We pass a limestone building I nannied in my first year at NYU, the one where I discovered the teenage daughter had some guy from the shooting galleries of Tompkins Square Park squatting in her walk-in closet. Yeah, seven years of babysitting, two summers au pairing, and three years of full-time nannying were more than enough. I'm still amazed that after my last day of my last job, in the building we're barreling toward, I managed to wait for Grace to get her shots so we could fly over the ocean—instead of running across it—to shack up with Ryan in the Hague.

In the lower Seventies the cab halts yet again and my gaze lands on a black woman pushing a towheaded child, who has the glazed, contented look children assume in strollers (on a good day). Suddenly the child's face lights up. I strain to see a blonde standing at the corner in a lavender dress, smiling broadly, shopping-bag-laden arms outstretched as the two approach. The mother rushes toward the stroller, grin in place—bypassing its passenger to hang her straining bags on the titanium handles—and with a few words to the pilot, she continues past unencumbered. The child erupts into a shocked wail, raising a tortured belly against the NASA-grade nylon straps restraining him—and our cab inches onward into the Sixties. I feel myself starting to slide down in my seat.

"Nan."

"Yeah, babe," I answer, keeping my eyes on my BlackBerry as I scroll to my lone client's latest missive. Which I start to answer in a tone designed to entice copious referrals. Which will, God willing, multiply into an actual consulting business.

"You look like we're driving by a house you got caught TPing."

"Uh-huh." I hit send and feel a firm grip on my bicep as Ryan lifts me from my near-horizontal slouch.

"You're thirty-three." He raises an eyebrow.

"Yup," I concur as the cab pulls to the curb and I slip the device into my handbag.

"You speak three languages."

"True." We both reach for our wallets, but he gets to his first, tugging out a twenty to pay our fare.

"So—"

"So she was a very scary lady." I press my lips together to refresh my gloss.

"But now you can be very scary." He touches his forehead against mine as he lifts to return his wallet to his back trouser pocket. "It could be a scary-down."

"I'd prefer it be a nothing-down." I pivot to face the caped door-man as he opens the cab door and, against every instinct, step out under the shade of the pale gray awning. Then, as another doorman pushes back against the brass-encased glass to the somber dimness of the Xes' lobby, I one-eighty to the departing cab like Grace entering a vet's office. *Oh, this? Here? That's—no. No, thanks! I'll just—*

But Ryan solidly encloses my hand, and after a few pleasantries with the staff, thankfully neither of whom I recognize, we're en route to the mahogany elevators.

"So far, so good," Ryan stage whispers as he pushes the up button, setting it aglow.

"I've thanked your parents for moving to Hong Kong?"

"In your wedding speech. Twice."

The door rolls open and I drop my head, hair falling in my face as I stare intently into the gleaming marble tile. A pair of black velvet slippers with embroidered jester monkeys emerges from the elevator, and I tighten my grip.

"Hello, *Mr.* Rallington," Ryan says pointedly as he guides me into the mahogany cab. The doors slide closed and he hits eleven. "I don't get the slippers thing."

"And that's why I love you." I look up into his brown eyes and he smiles, little lines crinkling in the corners.

"Hmm, our old stomping grounds," he murmurs, sliding his hand down my suit. I lean in for a deep kiss, flashing to when I would ride this very elevator, praying to run into him—H.H.—the Harvard Hottie who lived just two floors above my employers. We come up for air as the cab opens to the familiar vestibule. "You made it!" He raises my hand in victory and reaches into his trench for the keys.

But our repartee evaporates as the front door closes us inside the emptied home, vacant after years of subletting. Standing in the front hall, we find ourselves suddenly quiet. Ryan releases me to take off his coat and we hesitantly venture inside his parents' former apartment, footsteps amplified by the lack of orienting furnishings to absorb their sound.

I take a tissue from my bag and wipe at my smeared gloss, realizing that we've bamboozled ourselves. All conversations about this final walk-through, only weeks after our own, had focused on whether I'd have the balls to come to a building, a neighborhood I've flatly avoided when visiting the city for holidays. The discussion revolved around the probability of making it from point A to point B without seeing *her,* Mrs. X. Not point B itself, and what it would be like for Ryan to be the one to hand over the keys to his childhood home. Or for me to stand in an emptied apartment whose layout is identical to the Xes'.

"It's weird, right?" He crosses his arms over his folded trench and hunches into himself, looking a bit lost.

"Yeah," I murmur, rubbing his shoulder.

"I guess we should . . ."

"Walk through?"

He turns and leads the way. I follow as he stops in each room and gives a little nod. When we get to the end of the hall of bedrooms, I feel a bruise of sadness gaining definition in my chest.

"Grover's—"

"My—"

"—room," we speak at the same time. Ryan walks inside as the mid-April sun streaks through the shutters onto the exposed herringbone floor. He wanders over to the window and I step past him, drawn to the adjoining bathroom. Standing in the doorway, I feel the shudder of Grayer's sobs as we sat on the edge of the tub two floors below—the terror of not knowing what to do, how to help him breathe, the helplessness as his fever raged, the sweltering steam of the running shower amplifying the panicked fog of having this four-year-old's life left in my twenty-one-year-old hands.

"No way!"

I spin to see Ryan crouching under the shutters, the radiator box askew as he lifts what appears to be a dirty hairball to me. "Han Solo." He unfetters the figurine from its debris. "I hid him here when my brother was little and kept tryin to play with my cool shit. Crazy." He stands and dusts off his trousers, the particles billowing into the slatted sunshine. It takes me a minute to register that he's nodding to himself with progressive intensity. He grips the brown plastic and turns to me, his lips pursed, eyes sparkling. "I want this."

"We can't afford this, remember? We're building ours out of a bomb site a hundred blocks north."

"No. *This.* Family, children—a child."

I nod, tucking my hair behind my ear. "And we will."

"What are we waiting for?"

"Um, *four* working fuses, a kitchen. My business getting off the ground. Getting our feet planted in one country for more than a year—"

"I'm ready." He looks around the room, a revelatory smile spreading from ear to ear. "I'm ready, Nan. Let's not rent out two floors. We'll rent one and keep the other for kids—"

"Plural?" I ask, starting to see patchy blurs where he's standing in the dust-flecked light.

"A baby. I want to have a baby. With you. Now." He steps over, fervently taking both my hands, the Star Wars action figure wedged painfully between our skins.

"I'm . . ." I withdraw from his grip, the yuck of my tenure in this building flooding back as Han Solo somersaults to the floor. "I—*this* is totally changing our everything, being completely responsible for another person's life, their happiness, twenty-four seven until we're dead. It's not some nostalgic impulse purchase."

"Okay." He bends to retrieve the toy. "I'm giving you that because we're in this building. That's your freebie for the week."

"Thanks." I bite my lip.

"Nan, it's not like we haven't talked about this."

"But *this* was down the line. I don't know if I'm ready."

"How can you say that? You were an amazing nanny!"

"But that doesn't make me an amazing mother! Not the same thing." I slice my arms in front of me, my bag dropping to my wrist. "At *all.*"

"Hello!" The broker's voice echoingly trills down the hall accompanied by the jingle of keys. "Mr. Hutchinson, you better get going;

the buyers are going to be here shortly. Did the subletters leave everything spic-and-span?"

The final walk-through completed, we're soon squashed into the rear
of the law office's steel-paneled elevator in the lunch-hour crush,
where Ryan reaches for my hand and I muster a reassuring squeeze
back. The car glides to a stop on thirty-seven and we wriggle through
the branches of lofted takeout containers onto the landing. My heels
sinking into the plush green carpeting, I hold his arm as we make a
left into the law firm's hushed reception area. I try to soothe my face
into the image of the sane, elegant wife, the kind who accompanies
her husband to offices like these to sign thick documents of impor-
tance. Not the kind experiencing a Euripides-level impulse to reach
under her skirt, rip her reproductive organs out with her bare hands,
and throw them at the mahogany wall.

"Ryan!" A portly elder statesman rushes through the adjacent
double doors, one fat hand extended to shake, the other at the ready
to pat. "What an excellent start to the week! How are you? How's
your father?" he exclaims in a manner suggesting a cigar wedged in
the corner of his mouth. "I'm so sorry they couldn't fly back to be
here for this. Boy, they're selling at the perfect time. Word is the
bubble's about to blow."

"Well." Ryan steps out of his grasp. "I'm really sad they have to sell,
but Dad wants to open a branch in Seoul and seed money's seed
money."

"Anyone who can afford to capitalize on the Asian markets right
now can't go wrong. So we got all their power of attorney documents—
good time to embezzle something, huh?" He chuckles, leaning in
conspiratorially. "You want to embezzle something?"

"Gordon, this is my wife, Nan." I offer my fingers for a squeeze.

"You are lovely! Ryan senior didn't do you justice." My back is
duly patted. "I'm sorry we missed your wedding. God, that's gotta be,
what—"

"It'll be six years this coming June," I say.

"Oh, right, yes, it was the same weekend as Max's graduation from

Stanford. How about you—any little Hutchinsons yet? Your father must be dying for a little Ryan the Fourth."

We exchange a marital look that should make oxygen masks drop from the ceiling. "Not yet," I say, smiling my sane, elegant wife smile.

"Well, don't put it off. I tell all my clients now to plan for an in vitro offset in the prenup."

"Pardon?"

"In vitro offset. If she pisses away a hundred, hundred fifty thousand with no output, you can deduct it from the settlement."

"Oh," I say, trying to get my eyelids to relax. "Great. Shall we go in?" I follow along a low-ceilinged corridor lined with signed John Grisham posters as they discuss the last time Gordon and my father-in-law played golf. Was it in Hong Kong? Was Hong Kong still British then? Ha-ha-ha, I trill to some racist golf-ball-Asian-lady joke I thankfully didn't quite catch.

"And here we are." Gordon opens the door for us to a conference room, where our gaze is immediately drawn to the wall of glass overlooking Central Park all the way to our new neighborhood to the north.

"Oh my gosh! Nan!" A beautiful woman bounds up from the buyer's side of the table and rushes to hug me.

"Citrine," I say, startling, her face so out of context.

"Oh my gosh, this is amazing! Are you the sellers? That's crazy! Come meet my husband!" She takes both my hands and leads me around the large rectangle, past their lawyer and broker, to a dour man, easily in his midforties, sitting comfortably under his Savile Row suit and slicked-back hair. "Honey, this is Nan Saunders."

"Hutchinson, now," I say, gesturing to Ryan, who looks to be enduring another of Gordon's jokes.

"Right, of course, you're married! We went to Chapin together, honey." She puts her arm around my waist and I smell honeysuckle. "We've known each other since we were five! This is my husband, Clark."

"Another one." Clark stands and extends a meaty hand. "Seems like Citrine can't go a block without running into someone she knows. You ready to do this thing?"

"Clark," she admonishes as he checks his Patek Philippe. "Such a banker," she says to me. "Can you imagine? *Me,* the artist. Married to a banker." She releases me to lift the bouclé sleeves of her jacket, the interlocking C buttons glinting in the sunlight, her paint-stained fingers emerging to prove her point. I'm pivoted to face her large green eyes. "Wait, I thought you guys were in Stockholm?"

"No," I say, taking a tiny step back from the intensity of her gaze. The same tractor beams that made classmates hand over Barbies, bracelets, and boyfriends has grown no less potent with age. "I mean, we were. We moved back a month ago. We've been living wherever my husband's work with the UN takes us." I hear how that sounds. "I was getting my master's."

"Wow, this is so crazy—the broker told us the Hutchinsons were an older couple living abroad." She glances to her husband for a gesture of corroboration and he nods. "You guys need better PR."

"Oh," I say, laughing. "No, it's his parents' place. They're also doing the expat thing—they've been in Asia for a little over ten years now. Ryan's just handling the sale for them. Ryan?"

"Hi." Excusing himself from Gordon and their broker, he comes over, a hand extended in greeting. "Ryan Hutchinson."

Citrine touches her pointer finger to his chest. "You don't recognize me?"

He shakes his head for a moment before his eyes suddenly widen. "Citrine?! I didn't place you without a headband. Wanna fox-trot?" He steps in and strikes a leading pose.

"You guys were in Knickerbocker together?" I ask as Citrine laughs.

Clark shakes Ryan's hand. "Clark Cilbourne. What's Knickerbocker?"

"Seventh-grade dancing school," we all reply in unison.

"All the cool girls brought their dresses to school on Thursdays," I recall with a sigh. "Tatiana had a Laura Ashley floral with puffed sleeves that I just thought was the living end."

"You weren't in Knickerbocker," Ryan says, just re-realizing this, as he does every few years.

I shake my head remorsefully. "My dad didn't want me to go, because *he* had gone and remembered it as pure torture—"

"It was!" Ryan confirms.

"*But,*" I continue, "it was the last boat out of Taipei for meeting boys. Either you went to Knickerbocker and two-stepped with guys who didn't clear your shoulders, cementing bonds of friendship that would endure until mad adolescent passion ensued—or you didn't have sex until college. There was little middle ground."

Everyone laughs and Ryan surreptitiously squeezes my ass.

"Okay, let's get seated and get signing!" Gordon claps his hands with a hollow thud from the head of the table.

Over the next two hours, reams of paper are passed around and signed and signed and signed. As I'm not legally involved in the proceedings, there's nothing for me to do except be silently supportive while Ryan inks away decades of memories. Citrine is in the same support boat and we share smiles of solidarity across the table as her husband faces the far more daunting task of writing $6.5 million worth of checks and promissory notes—*$6.5 million.* In a building that allows for no more than 50 percent financing. I hope that these plural children we're apparently having are happy, well-adjusted people with all their fingers and toes—and a passion for investment banking.

At last the final document is ratified, notarized, and spat on and we are freed. Ryan checks his BlackBerry and walks over to the glass to make a call. I signal that I'll meet him out front and find myself making my way to the ladies' with Citrine, snaking into the labyrinthine bowels of the firm, past cubicles of exhausted, unshowered twenty-somethings stoking the fires of the windowed partners.

"It is *so* great to see you," she says, holding the heavy Formica door for me.

"You, too."

"I finished *Wonder Boys,*" she says.

"Oh?" I hedge, opening a stall door.

"You recommended it. At our tenth reunion."

"Oh my God," I acknowledge, recalling the cocktail party I cashed in all my frequent flier miles to come back for. "Right, yes, I was on a Chabon kick. How did you like it?"

"Loved it. Have you read *Straight Man*?" I hear her ask over the gray metal divider.

"Richard Russo? I've been meaning to . . . I should go buy it—"

"No—don't!" she cuts me off as she exits to the sinks, taking off her jacket and folding it over her arm to wash her hands, revealing a Rage Against the Machine T-shirt. She smiles to me as I join her at the mirror. "This is my going-to-a-midtown-law-office outfit— like?" I return her smile. "Anyway, I'm giving up my studio and its wall-to-wall paperbacks. Why don't you come out for dinner and I'll load you up?"

"That'd be great," I say, not quite believing the invitation.

"Someday they will make a soap that gets these stains out." She dries her indelibly multicolored fingers and opens her purse, extracting a business card, brick red on one side, Miró blue on the other, her name and gallery information in bright yellow ink. "How's Wednesday?"

"Oh, yes, that's perfect," I say, handing her my own Kinko's bulk print card with a logo designed by my grandmother.

"Terrific." She slips out the pen that was holding her bun in place, letting her famous strawberry blond locks cascade to her waist like a Garnier commercial. Gripping the Bic between her teeth, she twirls her hair back up and resecures it. "Call me if there's any problem. Otherwise I can meet you when you get off the L."

"L?"

"I'm in Williamsburg." She gestures to her jacket. "Do not judge an artist by her wifely buttons."

"Darling!" Grandma flings open the brushed-steel door to her new loft in a kimono and black satin flip-flops. "Where's Ryan?" she asks, giving me a quick kiss before retreating to resume preparation for tonight's dinner party, reuniting her with my friends, for whom she's always been a surrogate fairy grandmother. I lower my heavy tote of materials from the afternoon spent running my client's orientation training.

"Oh, Ryan had to stay at the office. He sends his regrets," I say,

privately relieved to put a few hours and drinks with old friends between Baby Timing Conversation and BTC the Sequel.

"Well, poop," Josh, my best friend from NYU, says, getting up from
the gray velvet couch in the vast loft's sitting area.

"Poop. Poop," his three-year-old, Pepper, gleefully repeats as she
gallops along behind him to give my knees a hug.

"I was looking forward to hanging with him," he says, kissing me
hello over three-month-old Wyatt, strapped to his chest in a snuggly.

"Where's Jen?" I counter, picking up Pepper and slinging her onto
my hip as we all mosey back to the couches.

"The market never sleeps." He replaces Wyatt's expectorated paci-
fier as he reseats himself.

"Well, then, we are just a coupla single gals out for a good time!" I
say, raising my free hand in a finger-horn rock salute.

"Things have been insane since they bought Bear Stearns. She had
to cut her maternity leave by a month."

"Can they do that?" I ask, leaning back to ballast as Pepper gig-
glingly arches to touch her dad's hair.

"Oh yeah." He angles forward into her reach. "It's all hands on
deck. Jen's just psyched not to be on the other end of it."

Grandma emerges from behind the cloisonné screen that delin-
eates her kitchen with a tray of her signature truffled deviled eggs just
as the doorbell rings. "Nan, could you?"

"On it." I carry Pepper to the door and let in Sarah, my best friend
from Chapin, who flings her arms around both of us in greeting.

"You smell like puke," Pepper informs her.

"Astute." Sarah kisses the top of Pepper's blond head. "There was a
big ceiling leak over our lockers so I wasn't able to change my
scrubs." She leans into my ear. "And it's not puke, it's intestines."

Grandma glides over to offer an egg and cheek kisses. "Throw
those in the machine next to the stove and I'll get you some of my
yoga clothes." Within minutes Sarah is freshly swaddled in lululemon
spandex and Donna Karan cashmere.

"God, have I missed this," I say, settling back into a comfy dining
chair with a glass of wine in hand. "International adventures are
highly overrated."

"No, darling," Grandma says, ladling steaming lamb stew onto one of her pink Limoges plates that survived the Big Purge. "That's exactly why you have adventures—to make a humdrum night at Grandma's missable. Does Pepper like lamb?"

"The *baaa* kind?" she asks, looking up from under the English farm table, where she's rediapering her stuffed hippo.

"That's a 'no, thank you.'" Josh reaches to the messenger bag at his feet and extracts a peanut butter and jelly sandwich. Grandma hands him a plate and he presentationally arranges the four squares. "Here we go, Pep. Your favorite."

Pepper climbs up onto the chair next to him and nods in approval.

"Peanut butter—bold move," Sarah comments, polishing off the last egg.

"Communication glitch." He pours himself a glass of wine. "With Jen's hours at the bank, *I'm* the one who does all the pediatrician appointments. I take notes and most of the major stuff gets passed along, but somehow I forgot to mention peanuts as the new Agent of Death. Anyway, Jen always has the midget on Saturdays so I can meet my deadlines, and one day I finish early, come by the playground, and discover she'd been feeding the little lady Skippy since she had teeth."

Pepper tilts her head up and bears her jelly coated pearly whites at us.

"Isn't it crazy?" Sarah says. "When we were kids *no one* had peanut allergies. Josh, you should write an article about this for the magazine. In the ER, toddlers routinely come in with obstructed airways. This isn't parental hypochondria—these kids are tachycardic."

"*You* wore flammable pajamas," Grandma says, touching me on the nose. "And lived. Cheers!" We all raise our glasses. Pepper lifts her sippy cup. "To adventures and reunions!"

"To adventures and reunions," we echo, clinking rims.

"Speaking of reunions," I say, setting down my glass. "Guess who I ran into at the closing?"

"Hmm, does the firm also do divorces? That widens the field . . ." Josh muses, dabbing a globule of jelly from Pepper's chin.

"No. *At* the Hutchinsons' closing. As in the buyer."

"No idea," Sarah says, savoringly slurping her stew.

"Citrine."

"SHUT. UP." Sarah drops her spoon on her plate and shoves me.

I turn to Josh to explain. "High school queen-honey-buzz-buzz." I twirl my spoon from my forehead like antennae.

"*She* bought the Hutchinsons' apartment?" Sarah gapes. "That's *insane*. I mean, I heard her stuff was selling, but is she, like, Damien Hirst and I missed it?"

"She married some dude in finance."

"Goddammit!" Sarah slaps the table, the silverware rattling. "Why can't I marry some dude in finance? Night after night, I'm like, dear God, please let me sew up some dude in finance. But no, I get Harry with the perforated ulcer and bed sores."

"Honey, you are trying to marry out of the *wrong* hospital," Josh says as he sips his wine.

"So, what was she like?" Sarah asks, ripping the end off the baguette. "Did she steal anything from you? Or punch you?"

"She wasn't the puncher. That was Pippa. She invited me to dinner."

"Shut up!" Sarah squeals. Her shut-ups are varied and tonal like an Asian language.

"I think I'm going to go. Maybe she's grown and changed. We've changed."

"No. There's no way one of those bitches has grown a soul."

"Bitch," Pepper repeats.

Sarah is aghast. "Sorry."

"She has a linguistic honing device," Josh says, shrugging. "As long as she doesn't tell her kindergarten interviewer to go *fuck*"—he mouths—"themselves, we're fine."

"Look," I continue, "you're working crazy hours. Josh here is parenting up a storm. I need to scare up some new friends."

" 'Scare' being the operative word." Sarah arches an eyebrow.

"Well, I for one, am thrilled you're making new friends on this side of the Atlantic. Anyone want more potatoes?" Grandma dabs at the corners of her mouth, careful not to disturb her rose lipstick. "They're on the stove."

"I'll get them." Sarah pushes her chair back. "So, Fran," she begins as she retreats behind the screen, "speaking of adventures—this place is *amazing,* but I bet a little shocking in your circles. Nan tried to take me through it, but I need to hear it from the horse's mouth." She returns with the skillet and slides a few new potatoes onto each of our plates.

"Neeeh," Grandma says, pawing the table with her knuckled hoof and snorting.

"Neeeh," Pepper repeats, and giggles.

"Well, darling, you reach a point where you realize all the charming things you've accumulated are just going to be someone's headache in the not-so-distant future. And you have that *someone* over for dinner and they stare at all your charming things like the headache is already building, so I decided to be preemptive. Instead of the usual *après moi le déluge,* I asked myself if there was anything I'd never done that I really wanted. And I realized I went from my parents' town house to Vassar to my husband's apartment. And I wanted to have my bohemian twenties. In my eighties! So I got the fantastic privilege of being able to give my things to people while I can still hear them say thank you. And here we are." She lifts out her arms and we look across the fifty-foot room—past the couches floating in the middle, her four-poster bed adrift ten feet beyond that, all the way back to her pottery wheel and easel set up by the far wall of windows. "I did a little work—a friend had the genius idea of sealing the concrete floors in high-gloss polyurethane—isn't it fabulous? But I didn't finish the powder room until yesterday. It took me over a year to track down the original wallpaper, but, Nan, you must check it out."

"Yes, ma'am!" I put down my hunk of bread and scurry over to slide the steel door aside, stunned to find I've let myself into a replica of the bathroom she had on Fifth Avenue, the same peach chintz wallpaper backdrop to the same framed French paper dolls, and above, the same chandelier. Bamboozled twice in one day, I swallow over a sparkling lump forming in my throat. Eyes wetting, I sit down on the toilet seat.

"Nan?" I hear her knock and roll back the door a crack as I reach for a wad of toilet paper. "You all right?"

"Ugh, just being silly. You kept the bathroom," I try to exclaim through the disintegrating tissue.

"Re-created." She steps in and slides the door shut behind her.

"Why?"

"Well," she begins tentatively, reaching to the mother-of-pearl box of peach Kleenex on the glass shelf behind my head. "When I tried on selling the old place, the only thing that held me back, the only unfulfilled vision—I mean, I'd hosted parties for you on the terrace, I'd let out every room to every conceivable type of artist—the only thing I hadn't yet seen was your daughter playing salon in her mother's favorite hideout." She points to where the peach fabric stiffly balloons beneath the porcelain sink.

At that, I drop my forehead into my palms and watch big tears splash onto my skirt.

"And . . ." She lifts my chin, brushing my dampening hair off my face with a gentle finger. "Whenever I feel lost I can come in here and reconnect with my roots."

"You feel lost?" I wipe my nose, glancing at where the marble meets the glazed concrete beneath the door. "Liar."

"That's where the exciting stuff happens, Nan! I'm scared of people who always know where they're going." She steps past me to check her lipstick. "They're not thinking enough."

"What if that little girl doesn't—"

"Honey, no pressure." She pulls a linen hand towel from the ring and hands it to me.

"No pressure? You spent a year building a room for my unborn child to play in—unborn *female* child."

"I'm not discriminating. Now come have some cake."

I nod, standing to give her a hug before she lets herself out. I toss some water onto my face, trying to dodge the red-eyed grown-up reflected back in a mirror I used to have to reach up on tiptoes to see into. Letting out a long breath, I reshape the towel and return to the party.

"Oh!" Sarah's expression softens in concern as I rejoin the table. "You okay?"

"Yes, totally. Just a lot going on."

"God, it's been so long since one of us bawled." Sarah rubs my shoulder. "I'm a little bummed you left for that."

"I didn't want to kick off a chain reaction," I say, taking a slice of plum cake and pouring myself some more wine.

"Appreciated." Josh caresses the little downy pate sleeping against his chest.

"Nan, I'm sorry my hours are so absurd I haven't been able to see you more." Sarah pats my hand. "Sorry to be driving you into the arms of Citrine Kittridge."

"Oh my God, no worries, it's totally not that." I shake my head, passing a smaller slice of cake along to Pepper. "It's just, we got back, like, a minute ago. We're living out of boxes, everything's chaotic and covered in asbestos dust, I've only drummed up one client, Grace just finally stopped peeing every time anyone turns on a power tool, and today Ryan springs some major paternal urge on me."

"Great," Josh cheers as Pepper digs in. "Go for it. Jen wanted to make VP before she'd even consider it, but the Almighty had other plans. Her equities career is great and it's the most fun I've ever had."

"Really? The stretch marks and the nipple chafing not killing you?" I tilt my head.

"Your episiotomy heal well?" Sarah chimes in.

"Dude." I shake my fork at him. "Ryan's logging crazy hours; I don't *have* a you and we can't afford for me to *be* a you, so I don't know exactly how this is supposed to work."

Grandma passes around the whipped cream. "Oh, dear, then I sprung a powder room on you—you're getting it from all sides."

Sarah leans in to pour herself some wine. "Well, I haven't had s-e-x this calendar year, so at this point, even knowing who the father of your children is going to be seems like a huge privilege."

"No, no, it is," I backtrack. "I just . . ."

"Just what?" Grandma nods encouragingly for me to continue.

"We've been moving around so much that we haven't really talked about this seriously, as in, 'Okay, we'll start in blank months.' I mean, I assumed with moving home, buying the house—in the back of my head I *knew* this was the next conversation. But to start it at 721 Park?

It's just really strange to all of a sudden be so far apart on anything, especially something so huge, and what's even weirder is I don't really know why we're so far apart."

"Maybe the nipple chafing?" Sarah says.

"I'm not going to lie to you . . ." Grandma says wryly, picking up the skillet to take it to the sink.

After Sarah and I get Josh, Wyatt, and a passed-out Pepper situated in a cab, I check my voice mail as we walk toward the Franklin Street station. "Hey, babe, I was really hoping to reach you. I have to catch the last shuttle to D.C.—grain riots. I'm so sorry. But I walked Grace and I'll call you when I get a break tomorrow, okay? Miss you already. Sweet dreams." Bummed that I forgot to turn my ringer back on after the training, I text Ryan that all is well, I am full of lamb Provençale, and he should have himself some sweet dreams, too. I arrive home to a box of Mallomars and a bale of deli flowers in a plaster bucket full of water. And I swoon.

Hours later Grace barks sharply, jerking me awake from a dead sleep as she flip-twists onto all fours.

"Grace," I grumblingly reprimand, squinting through the darkness to where she peers out the bedroom doorway, like our night is about to go Lifetime. I stretch to the microwave-serving-as-night-table—1:23 a.m.—fumbling for my cell. She resumes barking with a ferocity that lifts her front paws in little jumps. Ears ringing, I grab the phone and it glows to life, illuminating a text informing me that my husband is currently tucked in at the D.C. Radisson. I put my finger over the nine, primed to dial for help, when I hear—

ZZZZZZZ . . . ZZZ . . . ZZZZZZ.

"Grace!" I scream with exasperation, and momentarily stunned, she turns to me. "It's the doorbell," I explain, as if this should reassure us. I pull on yoga pants, tug Ryan's sweater over my slip, and feel my feet around for my Adidas.

Grace is squared protectively in the doorframe and, seeing me dressed and in motion, she scrambles for her throw rope and barrels to the stairs. "This is not a walk. We are not walking." She wags her tail with blind optimism. Holding my cell, I feel for the light switch. The bare bulb comes to life, illuminating the hall, the second-story landing, and the vestibule below.

ZZZZZZZZZZZ.

ZZZZZZZZZZZ.

"Crap," I mutter, nearly felled by my flopping laces as I descend the final two steps into the once grand, now puke green and linoleumed foyer. I pull back the crispy, yellowed lace covering the one of two narrow side windows framing the door. A glimpse of a long-ashed cigarette smoking in a man's fingers jerks me back to the wall. Grace pants around her frayed rope as she stares intently at the bottom of the door, waiting for it to be opened. Not a chance. I glance at the dead bolt to confirm it's bolted and, with a dully clattering heart, back up to the railing.

ZZZZZZZZZZ—*fitz!* The light two stories above goes out. Bringing us to a last pair of working fuses. Fabulous.

"Fuck," I hear from the front stoop. I stare at the door's peeling paint with an intensity rivaling Grace's. "Look, just open up," he speaks in a plaintive slur. "I left my wallet in the cab ... and I just ... I heard you ... I know you're—fuck." I hear a thump and then something sliding heavily down the other side of the door.

Grace drops her head to sniff the jamb. I take a tentative step and ever so slightly lift the curtain. The streetlamp illuminates splayed khaki pants ending in shiny loafers. I make out slender fingers drifting open, releasing their grip on a black iPhone. My well-attired assailant is now slipping into unconsciousness? Death?

"Hey." My voice surprises me and sets Grace barking. "*Stop.*" I put my hands around her muzzle to listen ... Nothing. "Hey!" I slap the door.

"Yeah?" he coughs. "You're home."

"Who are you looking for?" I step around where Grace sits, ears squarely perked.

"Um ..." I hear a scuffle; he's attempting to stand up. "I'm looking for a ... Nanny?"

My throat goes dry. I peer back out through the frayed lace covering the pane between us. "What?"

"Yeah, Nanny. Are you—"

"Stand in front of the glass. On your right." . . . Nothing. "Hey!"

"Yeah."

"Your other right."

Suddenly my view of the stoop is filled with a swerving face—a man—boy—somewhere in between. Beneath the mussed blond hair, atop the faintly freckled nose are two bloodshot blue eyes. They look out at me from the striking bone structure that unmistakably conjures his mother. I push my forehead into the cold glass, feeling at once a hundred years old and twenty-one. "Grayer?"

2

"You know me," he states flatly, taking a half step back from the window.

"Grayer," I repeat to the teenage incarnation of my last charge.

He swerves out of view, sending me fumbling for the locks. Grabbing a restraining hold of Grace's collar, I dart outside just in time to hook his belt loops as he tips over the stoop wall and retches onto the garbage cans. Bending my knees to counter his heaving weight in the frigid night air, I note that the heat is the one thing that fully functions in the house looming above us.

"Okay . . . done," he croaks, and I pull him upright, his body loose like a harlequin, emitting a thick aroma of liquor and nicotine. He rakes the sleeve of his peacoat across his face and stumbles back to lean against the closed door, his eyes focusing as Grace growls through the wood.

"You're taller than me," is all I can say, realizing this is actually happening.

"You have, like, a pit bull in there?"

"A golden retriever."

"I had one . . . I was allergic . . . as a kid . . . had to get rid of it." His eyes roll back.

"I think you should come inside." I gesture to the knob. He nods, momentarily righting himself, and I awkwardly maneuver around him to open the door. Grace grabs her rope and jumps up to greet us.

"Woo. Hey." Grayer pats her down, reaching a hand to the banister and swinging himself in a large arc to sit on the bottom step. I relock the door and turn to stare at him in the streetlight spilling through the transom's stained glass.

"Grayer," I falter, reaching far into my brain for the speech I'd once prepared for this very moment. "I'm so, *so*—"

"You a witch?" he asks, resting his head against the wall.

"What? No, I—"

"Cooking meth?"

"Okay, *I* didn't just show up at your house puking."

"It's just . . ." He waves his hand around the decrepit foyer, which Grace takes as an invitation to wag over and lick the remnants of his upheaval off his coat.

"I'm—we're, my husband and I are renovating." I cross my arms over Ryan's sweater. "How did you find me?"

"My mom's files. Some notes about the Hutchinsons and then, you know, Google."

I feel an unexpected burst of pride in this demonstration of his smarts—immediately extinguished as he fishes through his pockets to draw out a pack of American Spirits. "No." Grace backs up, head down. "Sorry, but no, you can't smoke inside."

"This is inside?" He cradles the pack between his hands. "This isn't, like, the confound-the-mutants antechamber and those doors open to a fat pad?"

"No, this is . . . it has a lot of potential."

"Right." His eyes drift close and the cigarettes slip to the step below. *"Grayer."*

"Yup."

"Why are you here?"

"To tell you to go fuck yourself." He inhales in two quick sniffs, eyes still closed.

My stomach twists. "Okay."

His eyes flutter open, seeking mine in the dim light. "Okay?"

"Yes. I mean, yes, I understand. I—"

"Okay?" He throws his hands out and jerks forward, his elbows landing on his knees. "Great! That's great! Because, you know, you talked a lot of shit to be someone I have to fucking *Google*. You wanted to give them *the desire to know me*, huh? But you walked out like the rest of them. So fuck. You." He drops his head and splays his fingers across the back of his neck.

"Grayer." I reach out to him, but he jerks away.

"What." His voice thickens. Oh my God, he's crying. I crouch to try to meet his gaze, but his long bangs hang thickly between us. "Fuck, I'm such a pussy." He burrows his palms into his eyes. "We got back from the country last night and he's moved out—for real, gone—and she dug it up for evidence and I just watched it and the thing is, the thing is . . . I don't even know who you are." He reaches for his coat pocket and wrestles something out, the force of its release slapping my cheek. I reel from the sting. "Christ—sorry. I didn't mean to—" He drops the VHS tape and it clatters to the chipped tile between us. Holding my face with one hand, I pick it up and tilt it in the shaft of colored light to make out the faded "Nanny" written on its label in her controlled script.

The nanny-cam video. She saw it—kept it . . .

"The things you said . . . and I don't know . . ." he murmurs, and I kneel down to reach my arms around his grown-up frame, pulling him against me. "I don't know you."

"I'm Nanny, Grove, I'm Nanny." And he slumps into me, passing out.

"Shit."

I inhale awake the next morning, my eyes opening to see Grayer Addison X standing in the middle of my living room—what will be my living room—what is now partial subflooring, partial parquet, dotted sparsely with inherited furniture recently liberated from storage. "Hey." I run my hand through my hair and unfold myself from Grandfather Hutchinson's wing chair. "How you feelin'?"

One hand resting on his hip, the other holding the loop of his peacoat tag, he pivots, eyeing me warily, and I realize that he was aiming to slip out. "I can't find my phone."

"Yes, your phone!" I stand, pain shooting through my stiff neck. "I, um . . ." I rub at the base of my skull and step over to the mantel. Grace jumps up and starts to figure eight between us. "I know. You need to pee." I pat her shimmying rear as I swipe the cell off the soot-stained marble. "It's here." I reach out to give it to him and he stretches to take it without moving a step closer. I stand awkwardly as he folds his coat over his arm to check his e-mail.

"Grayer, I'm really glad you found me," I begin my speech, acutely wrong in the light of day currently filtering through the *New York Times*–covered windows.

He nods with a vacant smile—the one he must use to dismiss his mother, his eyes at half-mast as he scrolls the phone.

"So, what I'm trying to say is that, well . . ." I trail off, feeling suddenly like I'm trying to get him to walk me to cafeteria brunch after a keg-fueled hookup.

"I should go." He lifts the arm holding his coat and the air passes over it, simultaneously reaching both of us with the aroma of his vomit.

"Let me get you a bag! To put that in. You don't want to carry it like that out on the street." I lilt past him, transforming into a Febreze commercial.

"Sure." He walks behind me, through the tool-laden workstation that will one day be my dining room, to the gutted kitchen, where I fumble in the remaining cabinet until I find the plastic bags.

"We've been moving everything around for the contractor to start. I guess technically they've started, but, man, are they taking forever to really get going. So . . . here we go!" I shake one out with a loud snap and he drops the coat in and takes a step back from me. "Do you want some coffee? Crap, the fuse is out. I could do it in the upstairs bathroom. Maybe some water?" I swipe Grace's bowl off the floor and pour in her breakfast.

"I'm good."

I put the bowl down and Grace descends upon it like this is any other day. "Okay, well . . . I feel like I should make you something or . . . something."

"I gotta go. Thanks." He turns, and I have to rush to catch up as he navigates to the front door. I study his broad back, searching for courage, struck that I don't know if what I want to say is, at this point, really for him or for me. He stops in the foyer and looks down at his loafers. "I was kinda . . . drunk last night, so whatever I said—"

"Don't give it another thought." I slice the air emphatically.

"Thanks for, uh, getting me onto the couch."

"Of course. You're a lot heavier than you used to be." I smile, but his face tightens.

"So, okay then . . ."

"Grayer, look, I've got to say this, so please, just—"

"I can't." He clenches his hand around the plastic straps of the bag and lifts his gaze right past me to the cracked ceiling. "My family's going through some shit right now and I lost it, that's all. I'll be fine. It's all . . . fine. Sorry I bothered you."

"But you didn't! You didn't bother me at all—"

"'Cause you're preparing your Fight Club recruits?"

Surprised, I laugh and he grins for a moment. That boy, I know. "You're really funny. You were always really funny."

"Can you—" He gestures his bag at the locks.

"Yes." I undo them and pull open the door. "You're free."

Grace traipses in from the kitchen, licking off her blond chops.

"Bye." He nestles his palm, the size of her whole head, between her ears. "Bye." He turns and offers his hand for me to shake as they have taught him to do. I shake it. This is wrong. I am doing this wrong, again.

"Don't be a stranger," I hear myself say.

"Okay." He steps out into the bright sun and tromps down the steps.

"Wait!"

He turns back, squinting up at me. "You said you lost your wallet; let me give you money for a cab."

"I'll walk." His shoulders lift as the sharp spring breeze whips across his oxford, pressing it against his frame.

"Please, Grayer, let me at least give you one of my husband's coats—"

But he continues down the street, bag twisted on a wrist, hands plunged into pockets, shoulders hunched in the cold, as I race for something—anything—to say that will get him to stay, buy me a few more minutes to fix this, knowing with sickening certainty that there's nothing that would make him turn around.

Staring at the quarter-sized patch of Pepto-Bismol–hued paint on day two of no Steve, I tilt my head and wait for the paint to bubble from the bathroom wall. As the heat gun box has promised it would. F'ing power-tool boxes with their confident primary colors and photos of fresh-faced folks with one hand on their denim-clad hips and the other lifting said tool like it's light as a toothbrush. No sweat, no blisters, no balloon of profanity attached to their pleasantly smiling mouths. As if the photographer stumbled upon them as they were deciding between eating an apple or just picking up this tool here and installing a shower. No hint of the aching arms, stiff back, fried fingers, or God knows how many layers of sickeningly pink paint laughing at the tepid tan I am currently giving it.

At the slightest sweating hint of chemical separation, I lay the gun on the nearby edge of the sink and set to scraping and sanding and scraping and sanding. I may not be able to find out where in that cesspool of a basement the backup circuit breaker is. I may not be able to get a single electrician to come north of Ninety-sixth Street for another damn week. I may not be able to get in touch with my goddamn contractor, whose opening act of gutting two bathrooms and one kitchen has been followed by resounding silence. And I may never be able to get Grayer to listen to an excruciatingly long overdue apology. But I'm . . . getting the . . . hideous pink paint . . . off this . . . @#%^★ molding. "Fuck!"

I drop the sanding block and stuff my bleeding knuckle into my mouth. Grace waddles over, head down in her assumption that all expletives issued from me are hers to amend. "Okay," I mutter around my curled fingers. "I'm okay." I reach over her attempted licking and turn on the sink. The water shoots out in three spastic brown blasts before eking into a steady trickle, under which I stick my stinging wound.

I take a deep breath and sit on the edge of the tub as the coolness dribbles over my fingers. "See that?" I nod at the six-inch stretch of bare wood on the window frame that the last five hours of labor has uncovered. "All me." Grace flops her head on my knees. "Thanks for being here." I drop down to kiss her furry snout, catching sight of my cell as it lights up by the toolbox.

..ailing red droplets in the paint curlings, I grab it, hoping it's Ryan returning my calls so I can tell him about Grayer, but instead I'm surprised to see a Swedish area code. "Hello?"

"Nan?" an older gentleman croaks on the other end of the line. "Nan Hutchinson?"

"Yes, this is Nan Hutchinson," I drop into a professional octave. "How can I help you?"

"Philip Traphagen, here."

"Yes?"

"My secretary got your name from the university. You were a consultant here at my firm's office in Stockholm . . . last fall, I believe."

"Yes! Yes. The Tipton Fund." A rapid succession of slides from my final graduate internship fly through my mind's eye: white man, white man, white man—distinguished only by the monogram colors on the cuffs of their custom shirts. Not a clue. "Of course. How can I help you, Mr. Traphagen?"

"Well, I'm on the board of my alma mater in Manhattan—that's where you are now, yes?"

"Yes, yes I am." I glance out the window at the Key Food bags that appear to be blooming off the backyard tree.

"It's a splendid preparatory institution, but we're in need of a consultant."

"I'm delighted you thought of me." I wipe my wet hand across my T-shirt and grip the phone, back straight, wallet open.

"Well, we were a bunch of cranky old coots and you brought some order to the place." I flash to the weeks of sessions it took to get formalized employee reviews to replace the Tipton tradition of promoting based on a "feeling about a guy." "And the school's in a bit of a crunch—their director of staff development, which in *my* time was the headmaster, but hell, I've only been on this board twenty years." He lets out a disgusted huff. "At any rate, this woman was due back from her maternity leave yesterday and sent a resignation note in her place. So they think the position needs to be filled, but I prevailed inasmuch as we won't make it full-time again. We've been burned, you understand."

I give a noncommittal hum of understanding.

"There were reservations about hiring another woman, but I told them you've already had kids so you're not flighty."

I inhale, my mouth momentarily stuck wide. "I don't actually—"

"And they need someone ASAP. I suggested my college roommate, former head of Choate, has his own consulting outfit now, but they want to go with a business consultant again, someone who speaks our language. Anyway the cap's three hundred."

"Three hundred?"

"An hour. Tops."

I elatedly wave my injured hand in the air. "Well"—I hold my voice steady—"as it's a school, I would be willing to consider it."

"Fantastic. Since she went on leave I've wasted God knows how many weekends on the phone with these people and their grievance committee. That faculty is a noisy, contentious crew. You know academics, like to hear themselves talk. The headmaster will be expecting to interview you this afternoon at the school."

I scramble through the tools for a pencil and step to a free stretch of Pepto wall to scribble. "Great, let me just open my agenda—"

"I'll have my secretary call you back with the details. Thanks so much."

"Of course."

"Our board has some very established members in the business world, not a bad set of contacts for you," he tosses out as an afterthought that makes me jump in little hops, sending Grace's head atilt.

"I look forward to meeting them." I steady my breath.

"Very well. Good-bye."

"Good-bye." Nan Hutchinson Consulting Client Number Two!

An hour later finds me still digging pink paint from under my nails as my cab alternately races and brakes on the West Side Highway in a cluster-fuck of rush-hour rushers.

"You want I take Fourteenth Street?"

I pull my BlackBerry from my bag to double-check the address. "It's at Sixteenth and Ninth."

"Meatpacking District. I take Fourteenth."

"Great." I gather up my tote, containing a hastily compiled, if generic, plan for breaking through faculty "noise." The cab pulls off the highway to inch along a Fourteenth Street I recognize from *Sex and the City* DVDs, but nonetheless blows my native mind. It looks like every major Madison Avenue flagship has unmoored and drifted south to settle on what I recall from my adolescence as a foul-smelling stretch of godforsaken blood-soaked cobblestone. Perhaps Intermix is now sharing storage with hanging cow carcasses. Perhaps fashion's finally won and Manhattan's abandoned eating altogether.

"Is here." The cabbie tilts his head and I fish for money as I scan out the window to the hulking white building with its grid of distinctive circular windows.

"No, this is Safe Harbor House," I say, referring to the shelter for runaway teens. I check my BlackBerry.

"Is street," he says with certainty as the passenger-side rear door flies open and a teenage student with a monogrammed Louis Vuitton backpack leans in.

"Sorry," she offers, but stays put.

I scooch over to get out, peering up to where the ghostly silhouette of the words "Safe Harbor" can be seen in the cement of the building's facade. I trade places with the girl and her friend in a whir of strong perfume and Marlboro Lights, dodging their tossed butts to arrive at brushed-steel double doors and, to my relief, a discreet glass sign quietly announcing THE JARNDYCE ACADEMY 1878 in the etched block font of a boutique hotel.

Intrigued, I let myself into a white gallerylike space and am greeted by a well-dressed receptionist seated at a white desk. "May I help you?"

"Yes, Nan Hutchinson. I'm here to see the headmaster."

"Just a moment, please. I'll let Gene know you're here." She picks up her phone.

Running a straightening hand through my hair, I take in the gleaming lacquered floor and circle of white resin tree stumps beneath what I believe is a Chihuly chandelier, trickling down in a million white glass twirled tubers from the double-height ceiling and illuminating the hourly rate Philip quoted. My eyes land at the back of the hall, where the spine of a staircase is incongruously shrouded in scaffolding.

"Ms. Hutchinson?" I turn to see a young woman approaching from a door on the right. "It's okay, Meredith, I've got it. Sorry to keep you waiting—"

"Not at all, I just walked in, actually."

"Oh, good. Gene asked me to meet you—he's coming to my homeroom next period and thought it'd be great for you to see the kids in action." She pulls her hand from the pocket of her trapeze sweater. "Ingrid Wells. History, Forensics Club, and eleventh-grade homeroom."

"Nan, the potential new director of staff development." We shake, her bangles making a silvery ping. "Am I crazy or didn't this building used to be a shelter for runaway teens?"

She nods. "And now it's for—"

"Runway teens," I fill in.

She laughs. "I'll take you through the back way." She gestures for me to follow her toward the scaffolded stairs. "It's off-limits to the students, but much faster. The building's just being finished."

"Didn't Jarndyce used to be in the East Fifties?"

"Yes, the middle and lower schools are still there. But a few years ago the board sold the air rights to that building in order to buy this place and gut it. The Jarndyce of the new millennium is . . ." She gestures to the chandelier as we pass under it. "Luxury education." I trail her through the arc of faux stumps and a plywood door at the base of the scaffolding, letting us into a drywalled stairwell. "This building was only supposed to house the high school," she explains as we ascend one flight. "But the parents protested at the thought of having to send their drivers to two separate locations for pickups and drop-offs, so the middle school will join us next year and this will be their floor." On the landing she opens the door and my eyes are immediately drawn to the antiqued mirror panels on the hallway ceiling. Yes, just what seventh graders need: reflective surfaces. "And they recently closed on another property in the neighborhood for the lower school—over by the highway."

"Wow." I step out behind her into the corridor of barn-planked flooring that runs the length of a city block, lined on either side by backlit boxwood hedges in narrow rectangular zinc planters. "And I was psyched to have a locker."

"Right? It's raised some hackles in the faculty. Some took early retirement last year. But, personally"—she leans in—"I love it. I live in Bed-Stuy and get to spend the day in a Domino spread. I don't know if it's done jack for the kids' self-esteem, but it's been great for mine." As I laugh she looks to me, her brunette topknot listing. "So, you're in the running to be the new Shari?"

"Shari?"

"Shari Oleson. Our ambassador to the board."

"Ambassador, I like that. I always think my job could use a little diplomatic immunity. Yes, I'm interviewing."

She withdraws her hands from the pockets of her twill sailor pants as we approach the next set of double doors, the hall turning to the left.

"And through here"—she pushes into them—"this becomes the science floor, where my homeroom is currently situated. Due to a backorder on some desks coming from Germany a few of the floors are still doing double duty."

"Gotcha."

We pass into the next section of hallway, where, interspersed between the black classroom doors, the walls are lined with life-sized holograms of famous scientists from Marie Curie to Stephen Hawking. "So, this is my temporary homeroom." She gestures to the door behind her, from which emits the clamor of contained chaos. "I'm just going to make sure no one is pile-driving anyone in there. Gene should be here any second, are you okay waiting?"

"Of course, thanks for the tour."

"Sure, good luck," she says before hustling inside, leaving me staring at Mathilde Krim, who's staring back at me while holding her microscope.

"Isn't it fantastic?" a man calls out as he approaches from the opposite end of the hall. "We're trying to up the Harry Potter factor. Gene DeSanto, headmaster. How's it going?" He strides over and pumps my hand.

"Nan Hutchinson, hello! There's a Harry Potter factor?"

"Well, Rowling set the bar high, you know, in terms of kids' expectations. Kids expect a lot of excitement these days."

Feeling my face doing what Ryan calls my Twitches of Disbelief, I pivot it back to the holograms. "I expected a stallion to save me from a shipwreck, but Chapin never seemed to care." He laughs as I recover my composure. "It's a pleasure to meet you, Gene. I'm delighted to be here, delighted by your school's consideration."

"You, too, you, too. Philip Traphagen raved about your work. Shari really left us in the lurch, you know." He's younger than I expected, forty-five, tops. And with a slight Long Island accent I wouldn't have thought to be well received in these parts. I'd have assumed they'd hold out for a little Yankee lockjaw, someone who says "yar."

"Yes, I'm sorry to hear that. But from what Philip shared I think my business training makes me a strong fit for Jarndyce."

"Yes, our board has a real interest in applying the efficiency of the for-profit sector to education."

"Oh, interesting. That sounds like exactly the vacuum that drove me from non-profit to business consulting in the first place. And while I do currently have another client, I am confident I can coordinate—"

"Great, because we just don't have the bandwidth to launch a full-scale search at this point in the year." He scratches at the back of his neck.

"So you're not meeting with other candidates?"

His cheeks redden. "Well, I mean, Philip was happy with you—and the trustees don't want to cut the position altogether. They definitely prefer a cushion between themselves and the faculty."

Three-hundred-dollar cushion, reporting for duty. "I'm delighted to step in, Gene." I put my palm on his arm reassuringly. "Perhaps you could tell me a bit more about what the role requires?"

"Absolutely. As you can see, our facility is on its way to being state of the art. *State of the art.*" His enthusiasm tips him slightly forward. "We had a team prospect across the country, going from MIT to Stanford, reporting back on the cutting edge of education technology. And we are implementing it all *right here.*" He points down between his Docksiders. "And, of course, with that come a few organizational tweaks. Shari had been interfacing between the board and the faculty to roll those changes out." He purses his lips, his expression souring. "You know, we both started on the same day and I thought she was just great, but jumping ship like this really blew my socks off. Apparently she's just really loving being home with the baby. Anyway . . . the point is we're pretty much done tweaking, but we'd want you to be on call for any staff development needs that may arise. And, of course, we'll keep you on retainer," he adds, as if this is customary. Wow. Who's bankrolling this place?

"I'm sure we can work something out. This seems like a truly exciting time to join your team. What was your capital campaign, if you don't mind my asking?"

"Not at all! Fifty million," he proudly declares, his chest lifting his navy blazer so that the crests on his brass buttons glint in the light. "Of course, things have gone a *hair* over budget." He clears his throat. "But under the direction of our new chair, Cliff Ashburn, we just invested our endowment with X Wealth Management, plus I'm ramping up our fund-raising this fall—we're on the short track to becoming the Harvard of prep schools."

"X Wealth Management?" Is the name a coincidence or, in addition to leaving his family, has he also left the bank? "Any connection to Mr. X?"

"You know him?" He cocks his chin to the side.

"I do—I did . . ." I pause. "I knew . . . their son." Which just sounds weird. "I was his nanny."

His head ticks back on its axis. "You were a nanny?"

"In college. Before my master's."

He balks as if I've revealed that a stint at the Hustler Club subsidized my BA. "Well . . ." he prevaricates, "it *is* an impressive family. Are you still in touch?"

Technically? "Grayer was just over at my house yesterday."

"Marvelous." That seals it. "Long-term investment in a child—that's what we believe in here at Jarndyce."

"So, where did they steal you away from?" I move us along.

"Assistant vice principal, PS 348, Nassau County." His voice drops to a monotone reserved for admitting embarrassing facts of public record. Like when celebrities on the red carpet are probed about their latest YouTube debacle.

"Oh, that's great!" I exclaim with untempered gusto, the answer only making his presence here more confusing. Private schools of this caliber are like the National League or American League. There are minors and majors and strict rules. New York City heads are scouted from the top positions at the private schools of Cleveland, Boston, or Philadelphia. They are not plucked from the strawberry patches of Long Island. It's one thing to eschew the ranks of the educational elite when choosing your consultant, it's quite another when choosing your headmaster. "That sounds like it must have been good preparation for—"

"The board brought me in to steer us through this transition," he says tightly. "The old head didn't share their vision." He clears his throat. "Shall we go in?" He reaches out for the doorknob, a LIVESTRONG bracelet peeking out from his cuff.

"Great!" I smile. So what Gene lacks in pedigree he makes up for in his ability to share a vision.

We enter Ingrid's homeroom, where the kids chat among themselves as they slouch on the rubberized floors beside empty stainless steel cases that will one day hold Bunsen burners and jarred specimens. Taking in the arrival of their headmaster, they straighten somewhat, their listless expressions perking. Across the room I spot Ingrid setting up a podium with the help of a diminutive student wearing a black straw porkpie hat. As Ingrid takes a seat, the girl lowers herself to the floor, resting her head against one of the chair's legs like a loyal spaniel. I follow the back of Gene's blazer as he wends over to the far wall, careful not to step on the professionally polished nails of girls lounging in black pleated miniskirts, their black over-the-knee socks flashing swaths of nubile thigh. Atop long-sleeved scallop-necked tees in a range of pastels, some have draped black cardigans or sweatshirts around their shoulders, an appliquéd crest visible in the folds. The boys sprawl among messenger bags and Apple devices in black flat-front chinos. Their white dress shirts peek out crisply from black blazers embroidered with matching crests, and the sherbet hues of their ties echo the shirts of their female classmates. Individually, a *Teen Vogue* spread; collectively, a little Pink Floyd.

Gene finds a spot for us to stand by an anatomy diagram, while Ingrid approaches the podium. He turns to me, his charisma recovered. "You know, the thing about it was, Nan, my predecessor just wasn't excited by the prospect of change. Even the new neighborhood. They sold his apartment and bought my family a condo in Chelsea."

"Oh, I love Chelsea," I cheer as if he'd asked me to move in, thankful to see kids lining up at the podium, bringing this sort-of interview to a pause so I can get my bearings. To review: Shari had a baby and left, hurting Gene's feelings and pissing off the board, even though she "pretty much" saw the "tweaks" through to completion, and now the board wants to pay me to be "on call" in case they need a "cushion"—*not* part of this principal's job description—for potential future organizational tweaks? Yup, no clearer than when I ventured under the Chihuly fifteen minutes ago.

"Agnès b. designed them for us," Gene whispers proudly in my ear.

"Sorry?"

"The uniforms."

"The seniors are here for announcements," Ingrid calls from her chair as a trio of kids snake up through those seated.

"Today's field hockey game against Dalton is at four. Please come cheer!"

"Drama Club tickets for *Caucasian Chalk Circle* go on sale today. Come by our table after school, buy a ticket and a vegan brownie!" The seniors don't stand directly behind the podium so much as lean on it for conferred support.

I take off my trench and fold it over my arm as the last senior steps forward wearing an elaborate feather headdress. "The Save Venice Club will be selling handmade masks in the senior homeroom all this week. Every dollar raised goes directly to Venice."

The town criers make their way out and Ingrid takes the floor, returning Gene's wave. "Hey, guys! And welcome, Headmaster DeSanto! So, as today is the third Tuesday of the month, we will be holding our final round of competition for junior class keynote speaker at

the convocation of our helipad the Friday of Memorial Day weekend. Chassie, come on up." The small girl stands from where she was
leaning against Ingrid's chair, hastily removes her hat, and makes her
way to hover behind the podium with a stack of note cards. She has
dirty blond hair, in both senses, and little fingers she tucks up under
her chin in nerves.

Ingrid cups her hands around her mouth as she reseats herself.
"Let's hear it for Chassie, guys!" There is a smattering of halfhearted
clapping.

With a quick glance of gratitude to Ingrid, Chassie clears her
throat and, rolling back her shoulders, begins to speak. "I believe that
the helipad is a perfect metaphor for departing Jarndyce. Next year
we will leave equipped to lift off and up, to see the world with vast
perspective," she says in a small voice, her chin just clearing the wood.
"But not without ambivalence. As much as we would like to see ourselves as Pynchon's Chums of Chance, climbing into our blimp and
touring through the very center of the world, we will still struggle to
leave that which has nurtured us." Chassie, her voice shrinking, continues on, from *Jason and the Argonauts* to Kubrick's *2001: A Space
Odyssey,* occasionally stealing sidelong glances at a nearby cluster of
boys, who snicker obnoxiously. "Ultimately, to honor the Jarndyce
education is to soar."

"Thank you, Chassie." Ingrid steps forward, clearly impressed as
she pats Chassie on the back of her cardigan. Everyone claps. Chassie, blushing furiously, moves to the side and all heads turn to an
oversized boy sitting in the middle of the cluster of boys, sporting
identical hairdos that look like an adolescent take on the middle-age
comb-over, or as if they've found their grandmothers' bob wigs and
thrown them on backward and slung to the side. The kid in the
middle looks a little nonplussed. "Go, DZ!" one of the comb-overs
shouts in encouragement and, recovering, the kid lumbers to his
feet. I think DZ is attempting a swagger, but his limbs are too long
and his body too thick. He should be playing football in a cornfield
somewhere, from the looks of him, really violent football, not over-
shadowing a forensic podium.

Ingrid continues enthusiastically, "And now Darwin's presentation!" *Darwin?* Oh my God. I lean forward, squinting to place the most psycho of the psycho kids from my nanny heyday who used to beat the crap out of his caregiver, Sima, while his mother stood idly by. The large forehead, the pug nose, the pronounced jaw—features that have yet to come together. Not like Grayer, I allow myself to think. Grayer turned out beautifully. At least externally.

"Wassup?" He raises a palm to his fans as he looks out at the room. "Yeah, so today I'll be speaking about, uh . . ." He grips the sides of the podium, leaning back, away from the task at hand. Note-card-less, his eyes dart around, looking for . . . "Yeah." His gaze fixes on the opposite wall. "I'll be speaking today in the spirit of our motto." He gestures to where "Nostrum Amicus, Nostrum Defero, Nostrum Universitas" arcs in red construction paper across a bulletin board, quite a lot of plural possessives for a motto. "What my opponent failed to mention is . . . who do we take with us as we launch off this pad into the great blue yonder of our futures? Our friends." A few whoops go up. "The friends we made here, in *our* community. And we go out together and serve *our* world." As his freeballing gathers momentum, an oil slick of confidence spills from his mouth, engulfing his face and transforming it into something far more attractive than it has any right to be. He showers the crowd with a cocky grin. And I know that if I were fifteen years old, my entire day would be taken up with trying to get him to notice me. And I would probably be very, very sorry once he did.

"This school was founded in 1878 by a group of men, business buddies, club members, who wanted to create a place where they could write the charter and mold their sons' young minds in their own image. And that tradition has been passed down from generation to generation, surviving both the coed revolution of the seventies and the affirmative action debacle of the eighties." A few heads in the audience tilt. "Then, in the nineties, we sought to expand our scholarship program, allowing people from outside our community in." His friends nod. "But that isn't the . . . helicopter our founding fathers envisioned. So I think we should take this opportunity to . . . celebrate our community and our friends and hope that the world out there looks and feels as good as Jarndyce."

"Okay!" Ingrid shoots over. "Thank you, Darwin. So, let's take our vote. Who thinks Chassie won?" The students look around uncertainly at each other. Clap for DZ and have a convocation speech that sounds like Leni Riefenstahl's version of the school brochure or—what? Be ostracized? Stuffed in a toilet? What are the kids doing to each other these days? They take a middle-of-the-road approach, clapping a mediocre endorsement, leaving plenty of room for cheering. "And who votes for Darwin?" Ingrid asks in the same tone. They seem to pause to remember their previous pitch of enthusiasm and replicate it exactly. Darwin's flushed face darkens and Chassie sinks into her black sweater. "Okay, then, I'm the deciding vote and, based on preparation, Chassie, you win," Ingrid pronounces, shaking her hand. "Congratulations! And good work, Darwin. Maybe next time a little more prep?" I begin to estimate how many tiles and lighting fixtures I could afford by lining up a string of other clients while collecting this retainer. Because while there's easily a student—or five—who would benefit from an airdrop in the Sudan, the faculty seems pretty on top of its game.

Chassie extends her hand to Darwin, but he storms off. She looks slapped. A bell chimes. Not the aggressive bleat of the traditional school bell, but a melodious Gregorian gong. From the steeple? Do they have their own hunchback? Is it the last headmaster?

"Digital," Gene leans in to whisper the answer as, in a whoosh, the students grab their Vuittons, Mulberrys, and monogrammed Goyards and flow past us out the door. Not one of them stops to talk to Chassie, who, hat in hand, finally shuffles out behind the stragglers after receiving a last encouraging arm squeeze from Ingrid.

"Ingrid." Gene makes his way upstream to her with me in tow.

"Yes?"

"A word?"

"Sure, Gene." She dismantles the "Save Venice" display.

"Sorry, Nan, can you give us a minute?"

"Of course!" I step a few feet away and stand awkwardly, deciding to busy myself with checking my BlackBerry.

"Yeah, I'm not really sure we made the right call here." Gene frowns. Really?

"Really?" Ingrid jostles the rolls of poster paper to settle into her arms.

"Yes. I think with some coaching Darwin could have gotten there, don't you?"

She smiles. "Gene, he farted his way through it. That boy didn't put a minute of research into this. And I've seen him prepared, it's not like he doesn't know how."

"There was a core idea there, though."

"Jarndyce had scholarship students the first year it opened. It was a key part of Ralston Jarndyce's vision and a not-so-small fact I love about this place."

"Of course, of course, but don't you think you could have developed his metaphor? Isn't that your role?"

"I do it with him every week in Forensics. But Chassie clearly did extensive preparation and that should be rewarded."

"You're not letting her obvious affection for you cloud your judgment?"

"She's been a little clingy this semester, but that's to be expected, given her home situation. I'm with her almost twenty hours a week, between one activity and another, so I'm a natural target for her ... transference. I take that responsibility seriously, Gene, but right now that's irrelevant. Did you see how Darwin blew past her ..." She shakes her head with concern.

Gene stiffens his lower lip and sucks through his teeth. "But *her* parents are not going to be on the roof, sitting beside me on the stage at the helipad convocation, Ingrid. Grant Zuckerman is going to be sitting on the stage."

"I know—I'm really surprised Darwin didn't take that into account." She darts her eyes to me.

"The entire school—every alumnus of stature will be there—all of New York watching, Ingrid. It needs to be a big success, symbolically launching the school above its competitors."

"I hear you. And Chassie's speech is going to wow them." She tips her head to upset her bangs from her eyes.

Gene looks at the carpet and continues carefully. "I'm really excited about where this school is going. The board of trustees is really excited." He crosses his arms. "It would be *unhelpful* if they got the impression the faculty is less than excited." And it strikes me that Philip may have gotten the noisy, contentious party backward.

"Okay . . ."

"Excellent, excellent," Gene says with a conclusive tone before stepping over to me. "Nan, I'm delighted to have you on our team. My assistant will be in touch about setting you up and we'll call you as we need."

"Thank you, Gene. I look forward to working with you."

"Now, unfortunately, I have to run to a meeting, can you find your way out?"

I nod. Let's hope so, or I may end up in your jujitsu cages or particle accelerator.

He turns to leave and pivots back. "So Darwin then, Ingrid?"

Dumping the poster paper in the garbage bin, she sucks in her lips. "I already told the kids what we're doing, Gene."

He stares for a minute, hedging. "Why don't you take a few hours to think it over and stop by my office after class." He nods at her. He nods at me. He leaves us with the Bunsen burner bases.

"And . . . that's Gene!" Ingrid says with false cheer as she stares at the door slow-closing on its high-tech hinges.

"So, what type of development was Shari offering the staff?"

"Oh, you know, buy-in workshops, role and responsibility sessions, that kind of thing. She could have saved a ton of time by just passing out faculty kneepads. When we got back from Christmas break they announced they wanted to make changes in health care to offset the design costs. *That* had everyone freaking out and bugging her on her maternity leave."

"Wow. But that's gone by the wayside?"

"Something about the revenue from the new investment plan."

"Gotcha." I drop my BlackBerry in my bag and glimpse the videocassette from Grayer that I tossed in at the last minute with hopes that the public library might have a VCR. "Ingrid, does the school have an AV room?"

"Are you kidding? Spielberg's jealous."

"Actually, I just need a VCR. We only have a DVD at home." And no hamster wheel with which to power it.

"I have a mixed media machine in my classroom you can use, if you want."

"That would be awesome," I say as, with a resurging jumble of curiosity and ambivalence, I pull out the tape.

Not fifteen minutes later I lean back against the desk, remote in hand in the darkened classroom, watching the grainy video of my tear-streaked twenty-one-year-old self ranting into a teddy bear on the night of my dismissal from the Xes'. I'm immediately struck that I look too young, too unworldly, to be speaking with so much conviction.

What must it have been for Grayer to see this girl, not five years older than he is now, messily pleading on his behalf?

Squinting at the complicated remote, I locate the volume and increase the scratchy voice from the flat-screen speakers. There in Grayer's bedroom, his toys squarely shelved as always, I pace on sun-burned legs while they are miles away in Nantucket. As the video cuts from my desperate, pointless entreaty for them to know and love him to three seconds of loud snow and then to my rant against Mr. X and his failings as a father—"Raising your child is hard work! Which you would know if you ever did it for more than five minutes at a time!"—I realize why his wife kept it—in case custody was ever at stake.

I stare into my own cried-out eyes, shocked by my certainty. God, was I certain. And righteous. Tilting forward, I shakily press pause as my twenty-one-year-old self glares out at me and unflinchingly brands me afresh with the stakes of parenting—the damage you can wreak when you willingly disregard the sacrifices required, resent the chaos that ensues, and shirk the responsibility for the heart with which you are entrusted.

Here's what I know: there's only one way to do this—running straight into it at a hundred miles an hour, arms and eyes wide open.

And I'm *not* there.

More alarmingly, I might never be.

3

As the first town cars pull into the fountained redbrick courtyard of Grayer's school, I glance at my cell. Seven fifty. Last night when I sat in the wingback chair, staring at the tape in my lap, I could hear Ryan's ringtone in my bag. Afraid to chance that my revelation would come pouring out, raw and ruinous, I hit ignore and soon found myself Googling Grayer right back, tracking down his Facebook affiliation to Haverhill Prep and jumping on the downtown train to Carnegie Hill before the sun was even up.

Chilled in my quilted jacket, despite the sun rising in the side street, I wrap my arms tighter around myself. A trio of girls passes close, surreptitiously flicking lit cigarettes from their hips to the butt-strewn gutter. Getting worried I've missed him, I stand on my toes, craning to see through the arriving throngs—their hair alternately wet or professionally blown out—knocking back a colorful assortment of energy drinks. And there . . .

"Grayer!" I call, and he turns, steadying his face against registering any expression.

He tugs out an earbud, holding it poised to return. "Yeah?"

"Hi." I step closer.

"Did I forget something?"

"No, no. I just wanted to talk to you. I feel really crappy about how we left things. Yesterday—" Two girls lope past, leaning into each other to giggle, presumably at me, the middle-aged stalker. "And a long time ago," I add. "Is it possible we could talk? Maybe go get a coffee?"

"I've got class." He lifts his hand back to his ear.

"Maybe I could walk you?" I catch him by the elbow.

He steps back from my grasp. "Look, just say whatever and I'll go, okay?"

"Okay." I tuck my hair behind my shoulder, piecing together twelve-year and twelve-hour-old thoughts. "I'm sorry. I'm so sorry I left. That I let myself—let myself get so scared off. That me being scared was bigger than saying good-bye, helping you understand, fighting for you. I didn't know how. I still don't know, but I should've done something—in person. It's not like they were going to kill me, right?"

He takes me in from behind his long blond bangs and clears his throat. "Okay."

"Okay, so I want to do something. Tell me how I can fix this, how I can help you."

He cracks a smile. "Okay, easy, Drama, it's not like I'm dying or anything."

"No, no, I'm not suggesting that. But you said things were shitty at home and if there's anything I can do. Anything at all . . ."

He nods in deep thrusts, one hand tucking into his blazer sleeves as he grips the strap of his inked-up messenger bag with the other. "I'm cool."

"Okay." I find I'm leaning forward on my sneakers. And that I don't feel even an inch better.

"So you're not going to, like, follow me now, are you?" He starts to walk, one loafer lining up behind the other, into the thinning flow of students, winding his headphone wire around his black iPod.

"No!" I force a laugh. "Not unless you want me to."

He shakes his head no and ducks into the courtyard.

I lean back against a parking meter and stare at a Red Bull can, half crushed beneath a Lincoln's idling wheel, not knowing what to do, or even how to walk away.

"Nanny?"

I raise my chin to see him jogging back to the iron gates.

"Yes?" I walk quickly toward him.

"There is . . . something."

"I'm on it!"

He leans away. "It's not for me. It's for my brother—"

"Brother?!"

"Stilton. He's seven and trying to get into this boarding school—

the only one that'll take him at eight—and then I'll apply to colleges nearby to keep an eye on him." His face takes on a seriousness that makes my heart tighten. "My dad's moved out and my mom's tranqued out of her mind, but I was able to pull some family strings and get an interview this week. There's supposed to be an adult there—"

"You got it."

He smiles, unmistakable relief in his eyes. "What's your number? I'll text you the details."

"Great!" I wait while he tugs out his phone and then punches it in.

"Cool." He puts out his hand. "Thanks, this is cool of you." And I don't throw my arms around him, I don't break down crying from the relief at this chance to right things, I just take his hand and shake it for the second time in as many days.

That evening, as soon as the two little arrows on my BlackBerry shoot off in opposite directions like exuberant dance partners, I wait to see if I got a message from Grayer or Ryan while I was on the train. Nothing. Hoping Ryan is still in meetings, I exhale when my call thankfully goes straight to voice mail again, because I know if we connect it'll be impossible not to download my turmoil on the baby crisis—and I don't want to add to the actual global crisis he's already triaging. Following Citrine's texted instructions, I veer off from the boutique-strewn main drag of Williamsburg and head west toward the East River and the industrial area that lines it.

"Hey, babe, it's me," I begin after the beep, being the wife he needs right now. "I know you're up to your neck in this grain shortage— can I say that? Can you be up to your neck in the lack of something? Anyway, you sounded exhausted. I'm sorry we keep missing each other. I'm on my way to dinner with Citrine, but hopefully we'll catch each other tomorrow." I pause for a second, debating telling him about Grayer in a voice mail. "And I feel really crappy about how we left things. Sorry. Love you, bye."

I make another left, and down a poorly paved, unlit street I find the graffiti-sprayed door Citrine described and ring her buzzer. A swaying huddle of the extravagantly tattooed and heavily pierced pass, heading to and possibly from a bar. Somebody's babies. Between Jarndyce's *Elle Decor* spread for sixth graders and waiting in Haverhill Prep's fog of Axe and apathy, I'm thinking if I even ever got to ready, I'd totally raise kids in the suburbs. In the fifties. The 1850s.

After a few moments the buzzer sounds, letting me into an equally graffitied stairwell. I climb the three flights of stairs and open the fire door to her floor.

"Down here," she chimes, holding out a candle at the far end of the dark corridor. "One by one the hall lights have burnt out and my landlord's a dick." She snuffs it and pulls me into a tight embrace—and again, honeysuckle.

"Hey! Thanks so much for having me out."

"Of course, come in!" I follow the trajectory of her extended arm into her studio. As she bolts the door I turn around to see her entryway is created by a raw wood structure that houses her kitchenette on one side, a bathroom on the other, and above it all, a sleeping loft. The rest of the room is open, ringed with windows and reeking of turpentine.

"Sorry about the smell—I was stretching canvases. I was supposed to help Clark oversee the move this morning, but he got so type A about the whole thing I had to get out of there. Want some wine?" she says over her shoulder as she turns into the kitchenette.

"Sure!" I walk around to take in the space, which is lined with layers of finished paintings resting against the walls and stacks of boxes filling with the contents of her half-emptied bookcases. A ping emits from my bag and I take out my BlackBerry to see a text. FRIDAY 4PM 721 PARK 9B THNX GRAYER.

The interview's at their apartment? She'll *be* there? He said she's tranqued. *How* tranqued?

"Here." A drink in each hand, Citrine crosses to me in brown suede high-heel over-the-knee boots atop brown leggings, a chunky brown sweater on top.

"You weren't stretching canvas in *that*?" I ask, turning off my BlackBerry and fears, past and present, for the evening. I rest my bag on the windowsill.

She laughs. "No, no, I always clean up for dinner." She hands me a delicate glass on a slender stem. "Cheers." She touches our rims, making a beautiful ping, and I'm surprised mine didn't shatter it's so fine. "It's a Château Lafite, just so you savor. Clark sent over a case when he realized I was offering prospective buyers Australian Shiraz. He's so supportive." She beams as I take a welcome sip. "Isn't that a great name, Clark? Clark," she repeats with exaggerated tongue movements. "Every time I say it I feel like Margot Kidder. Come, sit down." She plunks herself onto a kilim floor pillow, curling her long legs under her. "Sorry, I already sold my couch to some dude off craigslist."

I lower myself onto the one across from her in turn.

"You okay?" she asks.

"Totally." I try to mirror her graceful perch. "After we left Africa I swore I wouldn't sit on the floor again for at least five years, but this is on a pillow, so, all good! Oh, and no couscous. No floors or couscous."

"So Moroccan for dinner is out?" She smiles. "My God, you guys really have been everywhere."

"Not *everywhere*. And, at most, two years at a time. But it gets old. Making friends you know you'll be leaving. Never really fixing anything up. Always sleeping on rented mattresses. The most exciting thing we've done since we moved back was go and buy our own." My shoulders rise at the memory. "No one else has ever slept on it. Or made a baby or delivered a baby."

"Really?"

"In our third apartment—judging by the stains."

"Okay, killing my vision of foreign affairs."

"No, no, it was great. Really." I imbibe a large mouthful of the full-bodied wine. "Until one day it just wasn't. I woke up and said, 'I want to go home.' "

"Home—that's what *I'm* grappling with!" Her face animated, she sets her glass down on the floor and passes me a bowl of Marcona almonds from a wooden crate serving as a side table. "I've been here since I graduated from RISD. Even after the wedding last June I still come here to work every day."

"It's a fabulous space and no one has studios like this in Manhattan anymore."

"Thank you. Clark doesn't get it. When I graduated this was all I could afford. And over the years my work started to sell, but the neighborhood's gotten trendy and the rents have risen and it's still all I can afford."

"I know. Ryan and I were just gobsmacked by what's happened to New York City real estate since we left."

"Clark said you bought a house. A real house? With a basement and a roof and everything?"

I lean forward to scoop up some almonds and the hard pillows slips out, dropping me to the floor. "Yes, such as it is. We're on day three of an arbitrary work stoppage, but I'll bore you about that at dinner. You guys really bought a *great* apartment. It's a layout I have decorated and redecorated many times in my mind."

"The second bedroom's going to be my on-premise studio and I'm giving up my lease. Happy ending, right? It's so weird. Many fights." She peers into her wineglass. "Many, many fights."

"Why?" I ask softly.

"I mean, I moved in with him on the Upper East Side in his high-rise apartment with the forty-nine-inch TV and the black leather sofa, the whole standard-issue bachelor blech. But I come here every day and"—she catches herself—"I *love* him. I love him. Me prenup is *insane*. Nobody has a prenup like mine. He said, 'Babe, I want you to be protected.' Isn't that amazing? So I put up with the couch and the neighborhood and the people—who wouldn't know provocative art from dogs playing poker. I mean, when you think of our childhoods, don't you want to run to the ends of the earth?"

"Well, not so much my childhood as other people's."

"Oh, right, you were a West Sider."

"Yes, we had *perfect* parenting on the West Side. Nope." I shake my head. "I just meant I was a nanny in college. That literally put me on the first plane out of here."

"You were a nanny?" she asks, eyes widening.

"It beat waitressing." I shrug.

"Oh, gosh, sorry, no." She puts her hand to her sternum. "I know

I'm crazy lucky that I had an annuity in college. Truly. I've just never met a nanny. I mean since we were kids."

"At Brown I cleaned houses."

"You are hard-core." She makes a bowing gesture with her forearms. "It's a shame we didn't hang out more in Providence."

"I pretty much hid in a slice of chocolate cheesecake and then I transferred," I admit wryly.

"Funny. Anyway, we're agreed the Upper East Side is a little inbred. Clark's from Trenton, but you'd *never* know it." She pokes the air with her rainbow hand, two fingers pressed to her thumb as if holding a cigarette. "He put himself through college, got a job at Morgan Stanley, and worked his fucking ass off. Now he runs his own hedge fund. He amazes me."

"That's awesome. How'd you guys meet?" I ask, taking another sip.

"I was having a solo show on Bond Street—I was dating this bass guitar player at the time—and Clark walks in, he's a *serious* collector, buys two of my paintings off the bat, tells me I'm a great investment, and asks me out." She stretches up, her long fingers intertwining. "So, he wants to live on Park Avenue. I get it. I noodle around with paint all day—this is his dream? I'm happy to give it to him. More wine?"

"Please." I hold out my unbelievably light glass. Probably made by elves.

"So what were you doing while Ryan was working?" she asks.

"Business consulting—organizational development. Originally I majored in Child Development. But the first few programs I worked at out of school were epically dysfunctional. I mean, staff meetings like a page from *Who's Afraid of Virginia Woolf?* It didn't matter the country or the level of funding, the grown-ups consistently needed more help playing well with others. I became really interested in how to get organizations to run effectively—so the people *they're* trying to aid actually receive it."

"Wow, that's amazing—I never worked in an office. Some days I crave group dynamics so badly I want to pay people to hang out by my sink and talk to me about *Lost* while I make tea. So, Stockholm?"

"Ryan put in to transfer someplace I could also get my master's."

"Uppsala?"

"*Yes,*" I say, surprised. "I can't believe you've heard of it. It's only forty minutes outside the coldest place on earth."

"I had an exhibition there in '02." She tips forward onto her knees, legs still folded. "This is so great! I feel like it was total fate I ran into you. To be with someone who understands the whole Chapin thing, but gets that it doesn't define you. Or means you don't have to work." She empties her glass in one gulp as some guys on the street outside are shouting for Tanya in a way that would make me, were I Tanya, turn out my lamp and lie still on the floor. "And yet I get so sick of people in the art community who have no manners. I love my friends, but I'm thirty-three. I have nothing in common with the people who go to parties looking to steal something." She abruptly unfurls and lifts to standing on those boots in one motion, like Madonna doing yoga. After all these years she is still mesmerizing in a way very few people are, and if I were a man I would buy her art and send her cases of imported wine. "I'm starving. How do you feel about cheeseburgers?"

That night she brings me to DuMont Burger, site of the best onion rings I have ever had. They are the size of Krispy Kremes and we polish off two orders over a surprising amount of shared laughs. Then back to her apartment to load me up with a box of dog-eared paperbacks, and a call to Clark's limo to take us both home.

As the car pulls up to drop her in front of the Xes' building, I remember, with sudden nausea, that I have a date there not forty-eight hours from now. The driver pops out to open her door before the caped attendant can get there. "You okay?" she asks. "You went white."

"I used to work here. Ninth floor."

"The Xes?" she asks, a strawberry blond eyebrow arching. "The doorman says she's 'strict.'"

"Oh, good. I was afraid the intervening decade might have softened her. Still strict. Excellent."

"I'll give her your regards if we pass in the elevator." She kisses my cheek in a last whiff of honeysuckle and swings her feet to the side-walk.

"Only if you want a fish put through your mail slot."

She cracks up. "Please let's do this again soon. You *have* to come over and help me figure out what we're doing with this place. *Please.*"

"I would love that," I say, meaning it.

"It's a date! And let me know how you like *The Sixteen Pleasures.* Okay, wish me luck on my first night." With that, she hops out and he shuts her door. I watch as she disappears behind the brass-framed glass and a minute later the car cleaves from the curb to drive me north. I flip open my phone to check the latest text from Ryan: MTNG RUNNING N2 WEE HRS. NO WORRIES, CRAPPY. TALK TMRW. XO R

Slouching into the leather, I dial one of the few people I know are still thinking full throttle at this hour.

"Hello, bug." Mom answers the phone. "I love having you in my time zone."

"And yet we're still talking in the middle of the night."

"Eleven thirty is not the middle of the night and when did you get old? Hold on. It's Nan," she says to Dad. "Who else do I call bug?" She comes back to me. "When he has his left ear on the pillow I don't think he can hear a thing."

"So." I finger the black stitching on the armrest. "I have a poten-tially scary meeting on Friday."

"New client?"

"Yes," I say, only partially lying. New, old—same diff.

"Nan, that's great! I knew your business was going to take off."

"The thing is . . ." I crack the window to let in the night air as I try to isolate *what* the thing is in the general feeling of clammy that see-ing Mrs. X again induces. "The connection is through some nanny work I did and I might run into a few old faces—"

"I have just the thing! I'll send it to your iTunes account right now."

"iTunes? Don't tell me, you have a 'Say No to Say Yes' dance remix?"

She laughs. "Even better. One of my clients turned me on to it a few years ago and now I give it to anyone whose ex is screwing with their shelter vouchers. So we'll see you and Ryan for dinner Friday? I was thinking Chinese."

"Yes to Chinese and let's hope Ryan is back by then." I touch the gold lotus pendant he gave me last Valentine's where it rests warmly between my collarbones.

"You getting lonely over there? You want Dad and me to come for a sleepover?"

"Uh, no," I laugh. "But thanks."

"All you have to do is ask. See you Friday."

"Love you. Bye."

4

"Now I don't know exactly what you have in mind, but I pulled a few things and lay them on the bed." On Friday, having abandoned my mother's suggested podcast for empowering divorcees, I follow Grandma into the loft to see a fan of dry-cleaner bags basking in the noonday sun. "Your mother believes that in confrontational situations, holding the purity of your intention is enough. I say, hold it in Chanel!" She sweeps up a pale pink tweed jacket with the signature gold buttons, the empirical armor of the neighborhood, as Citrine identified. "Your new clients are like those people you worked for in college?"

"Yes," I affirm, feeling doubly bad about fibbing to her, but I just have to get through today and then tell everyone about it years from now when it's just this really great altruistic thing I did and not the stupid thing I'm about to do.

"Now, I didn't take out the skirt, because I think you should pair it with those crisp jeans you're wearing so it doesn't look like you're trying. Here." She hands me a large dark blue Jimmy Choo purse that picks up the flecks of blue in the tweed. "And . . ." She opens a shoe box with a pair of pristine navy Chanel ballet flats. "These you can keep. I have never worn them. I was having a farty moment. And this." She opens a red Cartier box on the bed and extracts a string of pearls. "Your grandfather gave me these on our twentieth wedding anniversary. Your father traded them once for a bag of pot, but we got them back. There. Pair that with the fresh-out-of-the-package T-shirt." I hold up the one I was instructed to buy at the American Apparel on the corner. "And you are good to go." She snakes the cool pearls into my palm.

"Grandma, I can't thank you enough, this is fabulous."

"I'm glad you called." She takes my shoulders. "I know you know how to make potable water in the desert and build a hut out of twigs, but this is a different jungle and Manhattan is not for the unshelled slug."

"Can I quote you on that?"

"If I don't use it as the title for my *memwah*," she says, swanning the air with her kimono sleeve.

I kiss her and go into the bathroom to don my shell.

And then all at once a combination of trains and one-foot-in-front-of-the-other puts me back under the gray awning and the doorman is swinging open the door. "Hi. Nan Hutchinson. I'm here to see Grayer X," I say, willing his mother to be tranqued as promised. And in Tahiti.

"He's expecting you." He points the way. "Elevator on your left." And spotlit urn to my right—yes, I know.

I round the corner and get in, pressing nine. And then eleven—Citrine could shoot me up with whiskey and a Valium. We can all be tranqued! God, that's what my tenure here was missing—unilateral sedation.

But when the door opens I obediently exit and let it slide shut behind me. Taking a deep breath, I reach out and press for the bell.

"Cooooooomiiiiiiiing!" I hear a kid's voice Doppler to the door, past it, and back again. It swings open and a boy with black hair and deep green eyes stands rib-height before me, leaning into the knob in an impressive arc before releasing it to spring himself upright. "I'm Stilton. You must be Nan-neh!" He makes a little Flamenco flourish on the second syllable.

"It's Nan, if you don't mind, and I am charmed to make your acquaintance." I hold out my hand and he shakes it.

"Nan. Thanks for coming." He stares up at me, beaming. "Grayer said you would be perfect and you are."

I blush.

"I didn't say perfect." Grayer rounds the doorway from the kitchen, his oxford unbuttoned, his Haverhill tie loose as he passes with a silver tea service balanced on a tray. "Hey."

"Hi."

I watch as he rounds out into the living room and returns a moment later, sans tray. "You can put your bag in the coat closet." Grayer needlessly points to the door, behind which his folded stroller used to sit.

"So where is your mo—" I'm interrupted by the lobby buzzer ringing in the kitchen, sending both boys spinning into each other.

"I study the Food Network and I love to watch French," Stilton rat-a-tats. "I mean, ugh." He pounds his forehead with his palm.

"Stil." Grayer grasps him firmly by the shoulders. "Take off your shoes and do a lap."

"Now?" Stilton asks, incredulous.

"One lap. It'll clear your head."

"Your guest is here, Mr. Grayer," I hear a woman with a South American accent call from the kitchen.

"Thanks, Rosa!"

With a grave nod, Stilton pulls his feet from his loafers, swings back both elbows, and sets off in socked-foot, speed-skater circle on the polished marble of the foyer. I step aside as he corners the velvet-draped table, so unchanged that I half expect to see my own handprints on the glass.

"This looks exactly like I remembered it." I turn to Grayer, who has buttoned his collar and is now focused on knotting his crested tie.

"Uh-huh." Grayer tosses Stilton his loafers as he rounds back to us, cheeks flushed, face relaxed. I smile at Grayer, my mouth opening to compliment him on his brothering skills. "Please?" Frustration evident, he holds his hand out for my bag and drops it in the coat closet. "Get ready," he instructs me as he swings his jacket off the bench with his pointer finger and flips it on in one move. "You cool, Stil?" He runs a smoothing hand over Stilton's bangs.

"Cool." Stilton nods, still catching his breath.

"We are cool, calm, collected, and smart," Grayer murmurs, eyes locked with his brother's as Stilton repeats him.

The bell rings and, following a motion from Grayer, Stilton steps forward and opens the door without flourish. "Hello, I'm Stilton X, thank you for coming."

"Hello, I'm Chester Dobson." The man in his midforties takes a card out of the pocket of his corduroy blazer and hands it to Stilton. "Thank you for having me." He leans down to shake Stilton's hand, the light from the chandelier illuminating his bald patch.

"This is my brother, Grayer."

"Hello." Grayer steps forward. "Thank you again for making the exception in your application schedule, Mr. Dobson. I know this is last minute, but my grandfather always spoke highly of his time at your institution." Grayer shakes his hand in turn and gives him solid eye contact. Good, this is going great.

"That's wonderful to hear." Chester fluffs. "He seems to have been an exceptional man, head boy and then, forty years later, head of the trustees. I'm sorry I never got to meet him."

Stilton clears his throat. "I really want to go to your school. It would have made my grandfather really proud." He delivers his line with intense conviction. He turns to me. "And this is my mom." I startle, automatically looking behind me—to no one. "Mom?"

"Y-yes, yes," I stammer. "I am his mother." My voice rises with each syllable. "Their mother." Trying to steady myself, I shake Chester's hand, emanating maternal warmth from the soles of my ballet flats, wondering if this is the beginning of the story of how I lost my accreditation.

"You look so young to have two such strapping boys."

I laugh demurely, channeling our absent host. "Start the Botox early and then you'll have no wrinkles to erase." I try to relax my forehead into something remotely approaching paralyzed. "Please, won't you come in and sit down?"

Grayer leads the way for them as I follow behind, indulging in a full non-Botoxed facial reaction. OH MY GOD!!! Now she's going to come home and find me *playing* her?! Is there a *worse* way to revisit this woman? How much time do we have? They must have accounted for that. Probably gave her a spa day. I pause on the threshold. And *really?* I'm about to be interviewed in this *same* living room, where, other than the tea service on the coffee table, not a *single* thing has changed?! Not one throw pillow.

Feeling the chain in the lining of Grandma's Chanel grounding me, I round the side table and paste my placid back on. "So, Chester, how can we help you today?" Joining Grayer and Stilton, I take a seat across from him on the velvet couch I don't think I was once allowed to rest my tush on.

"Are we waiting for Mr. X?" Chester asks.

"Sadly," Grayer jumps in, "our father is closing a deal today and couldn't be here. I certainly hope that won't count against Stilton." He places a hand on his brother's shoulder and Stilton's loafer ceases tapping.

"No, of course not," Chester says in a way that comes out sounding like yes, of course. "Well." Chester lifts his brown leather briefcase to the thick glass and clicks it open. "I'm sure you understand why schools are putting such an emphasis on the home visit these days." Not a clue.

"Of course. Tea?" I say.

He dips his head in agreement and I lean forward to busy myself with pouring, placing a shortbread biscuit on the thin saucer as he continues. "I mean, what happened over at Cleveland-Ashcroft last year is any school's worst nightmare."

I look questioningly at Grayer, who is sitting straight, knees together, hand still clamped on Stilton's rigid shoulder. "Three students died. You remember, Mom."

"Oh, of course." I hand over the teacup. "Was that Cleveland-Ashcroft?"

"Well, that's excellent," Chester says, popping his biscuit in his mouth in one bite. "That's every school's hope, of course, that you won't remember, that the name of the school isn't permanently tarnished."

"I'm sure. And exactly what happened again?" I ask, handing a filled cup and saucer to Stilton, which he passes along to Grayer, who places it back on the glass next to the service.

Chester swallows. "Two killed themselves after college acceptances came in—hadn't gotten in where they'd hoped—and one, drugs."

"Ah, right," I say, nodding my head. "Such a tragedy for the families." He doesn't nod back. "And the school, of course," I add, earning the nod.

"So you see why we want to make sure that every student has a stable and supportive home environment. Especially a school like ours, which follows the example of our sister school in England, taking them at eight. It is the British norm, you know."

"So I've read." I put my arm around Stilton and he leans stiffly against me. I look around, realizing I was wrong about the unupdated design: what once was brown is now beige, what once was beige is now cream, what once was lattice is now damask. Even the contentious eight-thousand-dollar draperies, while still the same mushroom-hued silk, have a slightly different ruffle. Subtle changes, but time-consuming, I'm sure.

"So tell me about Stilton's childhood," Chester entreats, reaching across to help himself to a second cookie as he withdraws his notepad and pen from his briefcase with the other hand.

"Well." I pause, as if trying to pick from the seven years of fantastic memories I have to choose from. "He was such a good baby." Chester writes nothing down. Too generic? "Well, I, um . . ." Three sets of eyes. The sound of the grandfather clock ticking. A trickle of sweat down my side. "Well, you know how it is with two boys." I give an awkward laugh. "I wouldn't say it was until Stilton was . . . four. Yes, four"—I finally say something with conviction—"when Grayer was older and busy at school that Stilton really came into his own. He was a delight." No writing on the pad. "He loved to dance," I offer. "With jazz hands. And wassailing. Every year at Christmas we'd go from floor to floor and wassail for the neighbors." The pen starts to move. "We did fashion shows. You know, to figure out what we've outgrown. Oh, and he wouldn't go anywhere without his father's business card. It eventually got so frayed I clipped it to him in a bus pass holder. And if he had a nightmare the only song that would soothe him was 'Ninety-nine Bottles of Beer on the Wall.'" I let the memories come as the pen scratches furiously across the page. Stilton looks up at me, entranced by this version of himself. "And that's when he developed his distaste of Teletubbies," I wrap up, and see that Grayer's face has gone slack.

"Excellent. Marvelous, marvelous," Chester chirps, capturing my last thoughts and returning the cap to his pen. "Can I have the tour now?"

"Of course," I say, wishing my face actually was paralyzed so it wouldn't keep looking horrified. "Stil, why don't you lead the way, bug?"

Stilton stands as Chester collects his briefcase. "Please follow me, Mr. Dobson."

They go ahead and I tug Grayer back. *"Your mother?"* I whisper.

"Relax," he hisses, taking long steps to catch up to his brother. I scurry behind them, arriving at what was once one of the guest bedrooms. Every surface is now covered in cutouts from *The Economist* and Stilton is showing Chester his scale model of the Supreme Court.

"This is a lovely room, Stilton," Chester says. It *is?* For a law student, not a seven-year-old. Chester crouches to examine a tiny gavel. "Are you sure you want to leave it?" I see a funny flicker across Stilton's eyes. He looks to Grayer, who mouths something over Chester's shoulder. "I want adventure. I'm ready," Stilton says firmly.

Chester laughs. I remind myself to join him. We all laugh.

We then walk out through the shared bathroom to Grayer's room and it's only the mission at hand that stops me from studying every inch. A decorator's vision of a teenage boy's habitat, circa Yale when they still had butlers, it's immaculate, despite the distinct aroma of discarded boy gear I'd venture was hastily shoved under the bed. We come out at the other end of the hall and turn to go past Mrs. X's room to her office. I am confused when, instead of her doorway, there's only a large Chinese armoire in that corner. Of course they did construction when Stilton arrived to increase her precious privacy.

"Okay, well, Mrs. X, this has been a delight," Chester thanks me as we return to the entrance hall. "I will file my report and make my recommendations to the committee. Again, all of our applications were in some months ago—"

"I'm sure my family will take your making an exception into account when calculating their annual donation," Grayer says pointedly, shaking his hand.

"Excellent, excellent." Chester clicks his heels and Stilton clicks his in turn.

"I really want to go to your school. It's all I talk about," Stilton repeats fervently.

"I'll file my report today, but, of course, the final decision isn't up to me." Chester takes his coat from Grayer, and with a smile and a wave, we shut the door. At the sound of the elevator closing I slump to the marble.

"YOUR MOTHER??!! *Are you out of your minds?!*"

"You did great!" Stilton, reanimating, squats down to throw his arms around me. "You were awesome. Wasn't she awesome, Grayer? Did I do it right? I think he really liked me. He really, really liked my room—"

"It was good, Stil. You were awesome." Grayer tugs at his tie, his shoulders, his everything dropping.

"So." I peer up at him, extending my hands. "What happens when you get in and parents' weekend rolls around?"

"*I'm* parents' weekend," Grayer emphatically cuts off my line of questioning. "And we need your help with one more thing, then you can go."

"Forgery?" I gamble, climbing back up along the wall. "Want to break into your trusts early? Ooh, where else can I go today as Mrs. X?"

"Believe me," Grayer mutters, walking past as I pointlessly wipe my jeans from the dustless floor you could still eat off. "You don't want to go anywhere right now as Mrs. X."

"What does that mean?" I call after him as I follow the boys back to the bedroom hallway.

"Yeah, you might want to lose the jacket," Grayer says, shrugging off his to the carpet beside the massive Chinese armoire. "I could do this myself on wood, but the rug creates bitchin' resistance." I still don't get it. Not even when Grayer leans into the cabinet with his whole weight and begins to push. "Are you going to help, or what?"

I step to the other side, crouching to slip my fingers under the black lacquered base.

"Okay, fine, yeah, let's lift," he concedes. "On three."

We raise it and I stagger backward a few feet, dropping it at Grayer's grunt. I stretch up to see the unaltered doorway to their mother's bedroom. "She's *here? You blocked her in?*"

"Insurance," Grayer says blithely, as if he's Ocean's fourteenth.

"Grayer?" I hear her voice from the other side of the door. It opens.

And there she is.

In a long men's undershirt, her unwashed hair matted, her bare face, well preserved for her late fifties, creased. "Whatwasthatnoise?"

"It must've been upstairs." Grayer tosses his bangs from his eyes. "The renovation on eleven."

She nods, her gaze unfocused.

"Mom," Grayer continues, his expression flat. "This is the new tutor."

I stand before her frozen, breath held. She offers her small hand. "Nice to meesshou," she slurs. "Please pardonmyappearance." She pulls down the hem of the shirt, revealing more of her bony sternum. "Okay." She shuts the door.

Grayer glances at Stilton, whose gaze is trained on him. As it has been since I arrived. And with her standing there only a second ago to complete the tableau, I place it as the same vigilant attentiveness I've seen in this hallway, in this apartment. Only Grayer is now the object, not the viewer. "Ready to tackle homework?"

"Yup."

"You did good, little man." Grayer reaches out to tousle his hair, setting Stilton grinning from ear to ear. "Eggs and soldiers for dinner?"

"Awesome!" Stilton jogs down the hall.

"Stil?"

He pivots to us, his heels arcing on the oatmeal Berber, and Grayer swipes his eyes in my direction.

"Thank you, Nan-eh!"

"I think Chester Dobson totally loved you—good luck!" I smile and wave.

"Be there in a sec," Grayer calls as Stilton continues on. When I turn back to Grayer, he's already strutting away from me toward the front of the apartment. I follow, trying to narrow down the question. "What happened to your mother?"

"Percocet, Darvocet, Vicodin. I'm guessing she hoarded the leftovers from every sports injury we ever had—probably suspected there'd come a day when he'd've had enough of her bullshit. Listen, I have to check on Stilton. Sometimes, after dealing with Mom he'll just ... and we've gotta keep him moving, keep his grades up. I'll meet you in the kitchen. If you take the back elevator you can go out the side of the building, in case Chester's still in the lobby."

"Now I'm the help again? Grayer, can you stand still for one minute and talk me through this?"

"No." Grayer touches his tented fingertips to the thin glass still protecting the velvet-draped table, fixing me with an intensity that takes me aback. "This *has* to work, you understand?" And I do. I may not have gotten the particulars, but like the ASPCA ads that show the puppy and the dynamite and the burlap sack and tell you to use your imagination, the particulars are irrelevant.

He leaves to tend to his brother and I reluctantly exit the foyer to the kitchen, where I find Rosa folding the mountain of laundry boys generate. "Hello, I'm Nan," I introduce myself.

She drops a balled pair of socks and scuttles around the island. "You new tutor?"

"Sure," I say, because in for a penny ...

"Get paid up front."

"Pardon?"

"Up front," she repeats furtively, grasping her tote from the breakfast banquette and extracting a folded piece of newsprint. With a quick check of the door she unfurls it to a half-page picture of a man hunched over, getting into a limo with Carter Nelson, the forty-something onetime Oscar-winning actress. I read the caption. Oh my God.

I grab it from her and lift it to study. "Oh my God."

Riveted, I peer at the photo of the couple leaving Da Silvano, Mr. X mostly obscured by Carter protectively holding the collar of her peacoat shut with her gloved hand, her thick auburn hair falling like a barrier around her startled face. "Are you sure he didn't win a date with her at a charity auction? Or pay someone to Photoshop this? How could he get—"

"He packed up and left last week while she was in country visiting friends with the boys." She pulls another folded piece of newspaper out of her purse and smoothes it on the granite counter. "Last Saturday." It's Page Six. The caption reads, "A new Mrs. X?"

"Carter Nelson?" Following in the footsteps of Jane Fonda and Ellen Barkin?

"They came back Sunday and Mrs. X go crazy. Pulling out boxes all over. Her office a mess. And then quiet."

"Quiet?"

"The phone no ring. No visitors. Mrs. X usually holds lunches two, three times a week. Now nothing."

Grayer rounds the corner and Rosa swipes the papers up as I reflexively step in front of her, my face beating in shame like we've been caught snorting a line. But he walks right past us and opens the back door, leaning out to press for the service elevator, dangling Grandma's warrior purse from his other hand. With a quick look to Rosa, I take my bag from him, sliding past into the dim little vestibule with the garbage bins. I turn around and the door clicks closed.

"Grayer?!"

He swings it back open. "Oh, yeah, thanks." He starts to reshut it before suddenly pausing to step into the wedge of light. The corners of his mouth lift as he peers down at his loafers. " 'Ninety-nine Bottles of Beer on the Wall'?" he asks.

"Yes," I answer.

He shuts the door.

Utterly drained by this twisted jaunt down memory lane, I am fingering keys inside my bag as I trudge up the brownstone steps, deciding which of the frozen Annie's I'll heat up in my night table and how many *Daily Shows* I'll watch on my laptop, when my front door whips open. A pang of fear is replaced by joy at the sight of my husband standing on the saddle, his tie askew and the collar of his T-shirt peeking from beneath his unbuttoned oxford.

"Hey!" He grins, jogging down to relieve me of the straining Key Food bag in exchange for a kiss.

"Hi," I murmur as we're lip to lip. He gathers me in a bear hug and Grace scuttles onto the stoop to circle us with a wagging tail. Nuzzling into Ryan's neck, I reach down and pat in her general direction.

"The colonel got food poisoning, so the agenda was cleared for the night," he reports into my hair. "I don't have to be back in D.C. until ten a.m."

"Sad for the colonel. Happy for me." Pushing our fight completely from my mind, I slip my hand in the crook of his arm and we follow Grace into the vestibule, discovering it aglow with Botanica candles in a rainbow of colors. "Oooooh."

"Oh, that? That's nothing. *That's* the appetizer." He positions me in the center of the space and then steps to the wall by the door, where, with a sweeping flourish, he flicks the light switch. The bulb two stories above us burns to life, illuminating the stairs for the first time in a week.

My palm flies to my heart.

"And!" He steps forward and turns me to face the living room. Wiggling his eyebrows, he swipes his hand inside the entrance and the lamp on the mantel emits a yellow glow.

My other palm slaps atop the first. "Upstairs works, too?" I ask breathlessly.

He nods, bursting with pride.

"Mr. Hutchinson," I gasp. "Take off your pants."

"It's official," I say to the candlelit bedroom ceiling as Ryan traces his finger in lazy circles on my stomach. "You, plus this place, equals adventure. *You* are the essential ingredient, without which I feel like I'm being filmed by the Maysles brothers."

"I don't know, I think you'd look pretty cute with a skirt on your head." He rolls on his side in the mess we've made of the sheets.

"If that was all I was wearing." I nuzzle my face into the warmth of his chest.

"Yeah, your point being?" He wraps his arms around me and, rolling himself on his back, pulls me on top of him. "So, how was your day, dear?"

"This, A plus. The restored electricity, A plus plus. The rest of it . . . kinda weird," I demur, not ready to package what I can't even add up for myself. "How about we order in?" I sit up.

"Great. I vote Spanish. What do you mean your day was weird?" He lifts onto his elbows and I bend to kiss him on the forehead before climbing off.

"Remember Grayer X? The, um, you know, the boy I nannied for my senior year?" I pull on his sweater.

He gives me a wry flat-faced head tilt. "Uh, yes, I think I recall."

"Right, so," I continue, letting my hair drop between us as I pull up a pair of his pajama pants. "He kind of stopped by the other night and apparently is having a tough time. And I felt bad and he asked me to help him with this thing, so I did. And that was my day! Do you want the sweet plantains?"

"Whoa." He sits up fully. "Back up. Grayer X came *here*?" He points at the floor.

"Yes."

"How did he—"

"He found that nanny-cam video I left for his parents and he watched it and then he Googled me. He's still a smart kid."

"Wow. How old is he now?"

"Sixteen. And he has a seven-year-old brother."

I realize I'm holding my breath for a verdict as I watch Ryan flip his legs to the side of the mattress and pull on his soccer pants. "And he came here?"

"Yes."

He stands. "To ask you for help."

"I think he came here to see who I was. That family, and I'm using the word loosely here, has been about as toxic as I feared."

"What help did he ask for, exactly?"

"A boarding school interview for his little brother. It was no big deal, just a little stint at their apartment, providing some support while the school did their home visit."

"You went to *their apartment*? In the building I practically had to put a gun to your head to get you to walk back inside?"

"Yes, but—"

"To help *that* woman. The scary one."

"I wasn't helping her. I was helping Grayer."

"Is that . . ." He runs his hand back and forth through his hair. "Is that a good idea?"

"A good idea," I repeat, folding my arms in the doorway.

He reaches his hand across his bare chest to roll his shoulder. "Nan . . ."

I stare at him, my heart pounding defensively as I jump from ice floe to ice floe in the current of my uncertainty. "Look, he's a child. And I was just helping them with this one thing so I can get closure and that's the end of it."

He drops his shoulder and shrugs. "Okay, good. Well, I'm happy for you."

"He showed up and the pain he was in—I just felt like I owed him. I've always felt like I've owed him, you know that." He nods. "I just wanted to connect with him, have him forgive me, I guess."

"And did he?"

I purse my lips. "It didn't come up." We stare at each other in the flickering light. Grace thumps her tail from where she lays nearby.

Ryan goes over to a box and pulls out a clean T-shirt and socks, patting her on the head on his way. "It's only"—his head clears the shirt—"I thought we were working on getting more comfortable with the baby thing and I'm thinking, given the look on your face when we were in my old room, hanging out with your former employers, especially this one, isn't going to help with that."

An almost delicious wave of anger rolls over me, giving me the chance to leap to solid ground from my confusion. "More comfortable isn't enough, Ryan."

"What does that even mean?"

"Do you want me to order or not?" I flip on the overhead.

"Nan."

"Sorry, but I'm starving." I pivot to stride down the landing, Grace scampering to her feet to gallop behind me. Ryan pads after us.

"I can't even bring this up, then," he states more than asks from the top step.

"You're not even *here* right now, Ryan." I jog away from him down the two flights. "Feel free to bring it up and then fly back to the colonel."

"Work is hectic, but it's not always going to be like this."

"This Jarndyce gig has the potential to introduce me to a lot of clients. My work is going to be hectic, too, you know." On the last flight I stomp the squeaky step and hop the rest two at a time to the tile floor. All of a sudden there's a loud crack and I spin to see the highest three steps caving with Grace teetering on top. Ryan bounds down to the second-floor landing as I scramble back up to reach out, but neither of us can get there in time. The chunk of steps implodes while Grace does a slow, sickening scamper-fall into the chasm, her hindquarters dangling into the closet beneath.

"Grace!" I scream, climbing up the crumbling pyramid of wood as Ryan dives onto his chest on the landing above to stretch down to her.

"Hey there, girl," he says softly. "It's okay. She's okay."

I balance on the closest secure plank as she grips her front legs on the remaining step in a cloud of dust, panting calmly, like this is just where she lives now.

"She's a tough cookie." Ryan lets out a sigh. "Like her mother."

I twist my mouth to one side and look up at him. "We're going to figure this out, right?"

"For starters, want to grab the ladder and rescue me so I can rescue our dog?"

I smile sadly at them both. "Sorry."

"Me, too. And I'm not saying this will be easy. I just . . . love you, and both our jobs have had us looking out for other people for a long time. I'd like to actually look out for our own, wouldn't you?"

I nod in agreement, letting the relief at this armistice override how little connection I feel to any desire to fulfill its terms. And worse, for the first time in our relationship, with this nod, lie to him. "I'll get the ladder."

5

Citrine touches my wrist as I wrap up the story of my Jarndyce interview, which, despite the breathtakingly beautiful retainer check for ten thousand dollars that arrived by messenger, has yet to materialize into a billable hour. "I can't imagine being back in school—I mean, it's not as weird as going back to Chapin, but still, didn't you feel old?" She walks on.

"Oh no, yes." I continue as I follow her down the uneven pavement. "And at the same time freakishly not. Like, I could immediately peg who the cool kids were and I felt a little nervous around them. Maybe some part of our psyches freezes on the worst day of seventh grade and never recovers."

She laughs knowingly, even though, if memory serves, her seventh grade worst was measured in degrees of Catherine Oxenberg–esque perfection. "I see the girls in my new-old neighborhood now," she says, her ankle wobbling a bit as we go over a spot where a nearby oak has transformed the surrounding sidewalk into a skateboard run. "And it's insane—they're so . . . chic. We were . . ."

"I don't want to say dirty."

"Certainly the hair."

"Remember you and Tatiana and Alex had a contest to see who could go longest without shampoo?"

She grins. "And you wore your dad's blazers to school."

"Oversized everything, scrunchie buns and practical shoes—it was a great time to come of age."

She drops her canvas FEED tote to the sidewalk, steadying it between her black sneakers as she tugs her hair out of a makeshift knot to cascade down her back, pre-Raphaelite against the black sheen of her down vest. She places the rubber band between her teeth. "So when do you start?"

"Apparently I have. I'm on call for . . . I guess we'll see for what. I mean, the students were a little much, but this teacher was *great*. If I can advocate for her and her colleagues, or at the minimum help them navigate these 'tweaks,' I'll be thrilled. And in the interim that'll be me having my tubes tied."

"God, if only."

"Right?" Realizing it's started to drizzle, I glance up at the silver haze drifting through the dark gaps between buildings from the low clouds above. I look back to see Citrine pulling her refreshed bun taut, her face suddenly drained of all its luminescence.

"You okay?"

She nods, her gaze moving past me to the warehouse behind us, an indoor architectural salvage yard she's been dying to take me to. She lifts her bag onto her shoulder, the sparkle returning to her tone. "We're doing this. I'm so excited. Did you start *Brideshead*?"

"Yes." I did. A page is a start.

"Spectacular, isn't it? The themes inspired a series of lithographs I made in '04 on religious versus sexual passion. And they had a lintel here last time that was quintessential Waugh. It must've been ripped from some palazzo on Fifth. Shame." She leans into the glass door, ringing the brass bell above the frame, and I step behind her into the musty, dimly lit warehouse. We stand for a moment like two stars on an action movie poster, taking in the floor of peeling carved wood and the range of sherbet-colored porcelain.

"Incredible," I murmur, dropping my head back to admire the Tiffany-era stained-glass panels hanging from a ceiling covered with what looks to be every type of industrial lamp and sign used east of the Hudson in the prior two centuries.

"I get all my mixed media materials here. I love this place." She unsnaps her vest, her yoga clothes still damp beneath. "All the history." She starts coughing.

"Careful there," I say, patting her back. "I think the history has spores."

"But don't you love it?" she asks, recovering her voice.

"Add one working toilet and a microwave and this is pretty much my house."

"You're so lucky." She picks her bag up and we start walking the narrow aisles. "Clark's architect keeps dragging us around these stainless steel showrooms and I'm just, like, there's no heartbeat. I don't want my home looking like a stranger picked out everything down to the food in the refrigerator. But this!" She steps over to an ornate wood mantel resting against a thick stack. "This has *soul*." She extends a black-legginged leg as if she was leaning and pretends to hold a cocktail.

I point at the errant rusted nail jutting dangerously close to her vest.

"You don't like it."

"No, I do! Sorry, it's just, currently, while I'm missing three stairs and a contractor, I'm kind of dreaming about someone picking out everything down to the food in the refrigerator. In fact, coming home to a fresh carton of milk and some working doorknobs would be my idea of Christmas."

"You're just running low on inspiration." She takes my hand. "Come on, they have the *most* fascinating things downstairs."

An hour later we've snaked our way through the mildew-saturated catacombs displaying the remnants of New York's prewar fixings, with Citrine's sheer delight at every last piece of cracked tile, chipped knob, and tarnished letter serving as our torch.

"Oh my God, these are *fantastic*," I hear yet again as I sift through a bin of dusty mortis sets. "Nan, look." I turn to the far end of the aisle, where Citrine, loaded up with collected finds under both arms, carefully displays a metal plaque with her outstretched fingers. "It's from the factory next to my studio! Well, now it's a demolition pit, but it used to be a glove factory. I'm totally getting it. How are you doing down there?" She shuffles toward me, careful not to drop anything.

"Good." I continue to dig in the dusty crate of metal parts. "Just looking for a mortis set for our bedroom door."

"A what?"

"In order to keep the original glass knob, which does not currently catch closed, I was told I needed to find an original 'mortis set.' At which point I devoted too much time on Wikipedia learning the history of mortis sets. I have forever lost this along with the part of my brain now completely filled by stair pitch gradations and bathtub flanges and their varying requirements."

She smiles. "I'm one conversation about kitchen triangle configurations away from blowing my brains out. Wow. Is that a . . ." She steps around me and wanders out into the aisle. I look down at the three seemingly identical brass boxes on the cement floor and—eeny-meeny-miny-moing—choose one. "Nan?"

"Coming!" Dusting off my coat, I follow the sound of her voice to discover Citrine sitting inside a massive alabaster bathtub.

I peer at the orange sticker on its side. Eighteen thousand. "Wow."

She lolls her head to me along its rolled rim. "Come sit." Pulling her sneakers up and clutching her treasure like a kid keeping her toys from floating away in the bubbles, she makes room for me to climb in at the other end.

Lowering my bag between my legs, I sink back into the perfectly calibrated curve. "This is nice."

"Isn't it?"

I nod, resting my head on the cool stone to gaze up at the network of pipes snaking overhead.

"You know," she says, "it reminds me of Tatiana—her mother had a tub like this in their Lake Cuomo house. In her bathroom. Did you ever see it?"

"Never invited." I smile at the idea.

"Oh."

"Do you two still see each other?"

"No. I mean, I run into her, but when she turned twenty-one she got a trust from her father and then she married a trust and neither of them has to do a day of work. You wouldn't recognize her. She had her boobs done. She gets Botox. It's gross. And it's not like she's doing anything interesting. She just goes to the gym all day. That's where I see her. Yoga class. She's got a staff of, like, seven taking care of her two-year-old."

"Tatiana had children?" I screech, unable to temper my shock.

"I know!" She laughs. "Scary, isn't it? Nan, everyone's getting so blah. I'm so psyched I found you. We have to get the boys together and hang out." She knocks my ankle with the toe of her Puma.

"We should."

"Don't get too excited."

"Sorry." I fiddle with the hardware in my hand. "Ryan and I— we're just having kind of a weird patch of ... weird, so." I nod.

"Renovations are stressful. All the millions of little decisions—"

"It's not really ... he wants to start a family, like, yesterday. And I don't know ..." My voice faintly echoes back to me as the motion sensor lights clank off in the adjacent aisle. "Being back here—I'm suddenly confronting the enormity of that kind of commitment. And just how much you can fuck someone up if you half-ass it." Her head nods slowly up and down, her expression blank. "It's just, Ryan and I've done so much together, been the only two English-speaking, non-blowfish-eating people on so many adventures that the fact that I'm afraid to talk to him about *this* is just really kind of alarming, you know?"

"I'm pregnant." She stares at me.

"W-wow," I stutter. "Citrine, that's ..." But she's so still, her face so masked, that I can't read which direction I'm supposed to go— congratulations or I'll be by your side at Planned Parenthood.

"A surprise," she finishes for me dryly.

"How are you feeling?"

"Shocked. Sick."

"What does Clark say?"

"I haven't told him yet. I haven't told anyone."

"Thank you." I reach out to touch her hand, as I'm out of neutral questions and her voice is only getting flatter. "For telling me."

"Of course I'm going to keep it."

"Of course."

"I mean, I was always irregular so I thought the nausea was just bad hangovers. By the time I figured this out—I'm already three months. I have a group show in Stuttgart in September and two pieces due to the Japanese. I have to keep working."

"You will."

"I'm not Tatiana." She stares out at the other unmoored basins. "I can't lounge around shoe departments all day."

"You don't have to."

"You think?"

I look down the stretch of alabaster at her, sprawled across from me in all this dust, holding her potential art in her lap with her paint-spattered fingers, her hair a tousled mess. She's beautiful.

And she's in it.

"I really do, Citrine. No one's in charge of you but you. It can be however you want it to be." As I hear myself say this, I see through a sliver of open door, behind which I could just jump in and do it, this mother thing.

"Yeah . . . yeah. I need a drink."

"Me, too."

"How about chessy pasta for two and you drink for both of us."

"Deal. I'm treating myself to this mortis set." I hoist it over my head.

She smiles. "And I'm treating myself to this tub."

Heavily buzzed from drinking a three-course dinner's worth of Pinot Noir for two, I sit on my spectacularly new sanded steps and flip through the mail, blessing Steve for finally showing up and getting something done in a timely manner. One cannot be heavily buzzed on the only stretch of her home that is not a deathtrap, glazing over a J.Crew catalog and thinking of maybe sleeping right here until morning—and be a mother. One cannot.

Perhaps someone who charged an eighteen-thousand-dollar bathtub that came from the presidential suite at the Plaza with her husband's American Express Black card—she can. Someone who has her career established and already read multiple oeuvres—she can do it.

But this one, debating using her coat as a blanket and shoes for a pillow—cannot.

"Eighteen thousand. For a bathtub," I say to a disinterested Grace, racked out along the length of the doorjamb.

An envelope flitters out from the stack of catalogs and I have to steady myself with the edge of the stair before reaching down to focus in on it, the familiar scrawl making me instantly, sweatily sober. I swipe it up and tear into the heavy paper.

> Dear Nan,
>   Please join me at my apartment at three o'clock Thursday, May 1st, for tea as a thank-you for your help.
>
>   Best,
>   Mrs. X

Well . . .

Fuck.

Me.

6

Thursday afternoon, on the lookout for Steve's minivan, I lift a flap of the yellowed *Times* off the living room window and stare at the cars splashing past on the puddle-strewn street. Steve left for Home Depot four hours ago and at this point I'm desperate to gauge whether he's even coming back today, or whether he passed a derelict property just as the enthusiasm not evidenced since we interviewed him finally resurfaced, compelling him to leap out and renovate it with our lumber.

Here's what I don't want: a fiercely barking Grace adding that certain je ne sais quoi to the message I've been harnessing my mojo to leave. I look down at her, lying on the floor, strategically dead center to track me as I pace in my sweat pants and Grandma's Chanel jacket. She lifts her head to return my questioning gaze and I project our tacit Beckett routine: Let's renovate. We can't. Why not? We're waiting for Steve. Oh.

Mojo harnessed, I release the newspaper and stride purposefully to seize my phone from the mantel, where I've strategically placed it beside an empowering picture of Ryan and me learning to surf. Idon'twanttogoIdon'twanttogoIdon'twanttogo. But I owe it to myself to find out what thanking me for my help looks like. I square my shoulders and hit the little green phone icon on my cell.

Ringing. Oh God, instantly sweating rivers. It's picking up! I open my drying mouth—it's her! It's her on a machine! Oh, thank you, Jesus!! I am flooded with sweat. I shrug off the jacket as I'm greeted with an electronic beep.

"Mrs. X, hello! This is"—*beep!*—"Sorry, this is"—*beep*—"Crap! I, this is"—*beep*—"This is Verizon calling"—*beep*—"Never mind." I jam my finger into the scroll ball and the phone clicks over. "Hello?!" Shitshitshit!

"Ms. Hutchinson?"

"Yes?"

"This is Janelle in Gene DeSanto's office."

"Mm-hm?"

"Can you be here at nine p.m.? There's some kind of situation and the board is coming in."

"Yes, of course. Wait, nine p.m.?" I repeat back to her, grabbing a pen from the mantel.

"Yep. Thank you. Good-bye." I click off, scrawling *Jarndyce 9pm* on the wall.

Okay, just climb right back up—call right back, do it, now, GO! I hit call. I'll just say it was a joke. I'll say I was breaking the ice by crank calling—ringing!

"X residence."

"Grayer?" I startle.

"Who's speaking?"

"It's Nan, Nan Hutchinson, hi!"

"Hey."

"Oh my God, I'm so glad you answered! If you were here I'd kiss you."

"O-kay."

"So, is your mom there?" Pleasenopleasenopleaseno.

"She's napping."

I toss my pen-clenching fist overhead. "Too bad. Could you give her a message for me when she, um, wakes up?"

"What," he challenges more than asks.

I dig my toe into the gouge between the subfloor and parquet. "Just that I'm delighted to RSVP to her tea."

"What tea?"

"She invited me to tea."

"Why?" he scoffs.

"Um, to thank me, she said." I pull my foot back before I invite a splinter. "Why, do you think it's for something else?"

Silence.

"Grayer?"

"Look, I don't know. You don't have to come. You don't have to be friends with her or anything. I mean, I'm sure you're busy."

"No, it's—did you hear back from Chester?"

"He's in. Look, I've gotta go."

"Of course. That's so great for Stilton. Please tell him I said congratulations and, um, good to talk to you."

"Yup. You, too, Verizon." He hangs up.

"You're going to have to wait for intermission to be seated." That evening I'm greeted by one of the students sitting behind an incongruously pedestrian folding table in the white stump circle. Finally called to service, I secure my dripping umbrella and glance down to see the banner taped to the table for *The Caucasian Chalk Circle*. "Our credit card machine broke, but we're accepting checks."

"Credit cards? How much are the tickets?" I ask, unbuttoning my suit blazer and checking to see how soaked my patent leather pumps are beneath the darkened hem of my trousers.

"A thousand." She takes in my expression. "It's a benefit."

"For?"

"The school." She picks her thick braid off her shoulder as if it were a small pet that'd been napping there and sticks the end in her mouth. "To send the Drama Club to Venice next year to work with a real commedia dell'arte troupe."

"The Save Venice Club can't sport them the cash?" I ask.

She just looks at me blankly.

"Actually, I'm here for a meeting. What's the quickest way to Mr. DeSanto's office?"

"Oh, they just finished that yesterday," another girl informs me, pointing to the newly unveiled formal staircase wrapping up the wall behind them. "Up those stairs and make a left."

"Thank you." I take them two at a time as I did at Chapin, remembering how, on the descent, I'd hold on to the banister and fly over the last four steps of every flight to land with a delicious thud, softened by my Doc Martens. Best to do after three o'clock when the building emptied and I could gain momentum all the way down from the library. This is how we entertained ourselves without holograms.

Disoriented by entering the second floor from the opposite end of the corridor, I take a few moments to get my bearings and find the plaque indicating the entrance to the Headmaster's Suite. I push the door open and look up at the paneled walls, which display enough crests and framed photos of bygone—really bygone, as in bloomers—prep school memories to do a Ralph Lauren stylist proud. While a jarring break from the aesthetic just outside, I must admit it a strategic choice for the sanctum where parents pull the trigger on committing to forty thousand after-tax dollars a year in tuition—a tad more subliminally suggestive of the Ivy League they're gunning for than lacquer and Lucite.

"Your name?" A secretary behind a Chippendale desk calls to me above the Mozart softly tinkling from hidden speakers. I am surprised that instead of the Gibson-girl pouf suggested by her surroundings, she sports a Rihanna wedge. "Your name, please?"

"Hi, yes, it's Nan Hutchinson."

She runs her long, zebra-printed fingernail down a typed list and checks me off. "The board's meeting in Mr. DeSanto's office." She points me past the tufted couches to doors bracketing an impressive stone fireplace. "It's the one on the left. You can go ahead in."

I thank her and let myself into the headmaster's office, which is nearly as large as his conviction. Clicking the door shut behind me, I spot Gene leaning back against the front rim of a scrolled antique desk, facing what I presume is the board—judging from their bespoke attire and intense expressions of engagement—occupying the three silk settees that ring the Aubusson rug. The men look poised to leap from their seats and ring the Stock Exchange bell and the female half of the crowd is nothing like the line of sweet-faced matrons who filed into Chapin's headmistress's office for tea. No one is wearing a headband or low pumps or even pearls. And not one person looks happy.

Behind Gene's desk two men and one woman, in notably unbespoke boxy suits, cluster around a Dell laptop displacing Gene's iMac.

"Nan, Nan, good, you're here," Gene welcomes me. "Now we can start."

I beam a professional smile and commence inching carefully over crossed and tapping glossy shoes in the alley of space between the couches and a three-foot-wide leather replica of a tortoise serving as a coffee table.

"And *why* is she here, again?" a large man, under whose weight the nearest silk sofa is listing slightly, asks. I recognize him from C-SPAN as Congressman Grant Zuckerman, Darwin's father.

"She's the new Shari," a woman sitting beside him hisses as I arrive at Gene's side.

"I just don't see why we have to bring more people into this," Grant continues to bark. "We don't have any other admin staff here. My team can manage it." He waves his hand at the boxy suits behind Gene and me.

"Grant, Philip vouched for her. I'm sure she's signed something," says a blond woman with a Princess Diana haircut and deep voice, whose oxblood trench dress matches the velvet damask wallpaper. "Now let's get this bullshit finished so I can catch my daughter's curtain call."

"Sheila, none of us want to be here," another woman admonishes from across the room. I recognize her as a panelist on some Bravo show, but can't remember if her empire is chattel, clothing, or cuisine.

"Yes, I'm Nan Hutchinson. The new, uh, Shari. Pleasure to meet everyone!" I boost my voice to direct all heads my way. "And it sounds like we have our work cut out for us tonight, so if one person could volunteer to give me a two-minute overview and a time check for how long we're going this evening, I'm happy to get us moving."

"Jesus Christ," Grant mutters. Everyone stares daggers at me.

"Okay, well, maybe one of you?" I gesture to the suits futzing with the laptop to see if I should step around the desk.

"No!" several trustees shout at once.

"Not yet," Sheila adds. "It may not be necessary."

"Yeah, thanks, Nan, um, maybe you could just go over there?" Gene motions to the nearby wall.

Face beating, I nod heartily. "Totally!" I take a few steps back and try to lean against the damask wallpaper as if I came here tonight with the express purpose of doing so.

"If I may?"

"Please, Cliff?" Gene encourages.

I turn and realize the man sitting in the crook of the U is Cliff Ashburn, Metropolis Bank CEO and *Wall Street Journal* centerfold, whose graying temples frame an average face that has been powerfully pheromone-enhanced by mind-boggling success. He takes a moment to remove his glasses, polish them on the end of his tie, check against the light, and return them to this nose, all while everyone waits, rapt. Someday I will be so confident in my ability to hold focus I'll lead a meeting slouched in a corner. "To recap," Cliff says calmly to his clasped hands, "exactly how many people are aware of this incident?"

"Darwin was the intended recipient of the e-mail," Grant answers. "He then, understandably, stupidly, forwarded it to three friends—"

"My son, Jamie," a blockbuster thriller author says, shooting her hand up, her eyes on the carpet's weaving ribbons.

"My son," a man echoes.

"And the Boyer kid," Grant finishes.

"Thankfully, the Boyer kid was here getting ready for his eight o'clock curtain," someone fills in. "And hasn't seen it."

"We already seized his computer," the woman behind the desk informs the group.

"We've seized *all* their computers. And their iPhones."

"How did this come to light again? I'm confused," the Bravo panelist asks, nervously tugging at the Hermès Kelly watch fob that dangles off an olive leather strap, matching the purse resting against her slim ankles.

Grant shifts his girth. "My son, Darwin, had the good sense, after his error in judgment, to send it to me out of fear and concern for the girl and for the school. I grabbed my laptop, raced to the airport, and set this triage in motion."

"Excellent." Cliff nods. "Fast thinking—quick response time—

we're ahead and on top. Has anyone contacted the girl's mother?" he inquires as his cell rings in the breast pocket of his thin gray blazer. He slips it out to silence it without a glance.

"She's been starring in an Albee play in the West End," a woman answers. "My husband's trying to transfer the production to Broadway."

"Okay, so then if the gravity of the situation can be impressed upon Darwin and your two sons." He looks at each of the three parents in turn, eliciting reflexive swallows and nods of commitment. "As board president, I'm comfortable saying we've contained this."

"Can it be contained?" Bravo questions, the fear in her voice palpable.

"If everyone does their part," Sheila replies, smoothing her dress. "At the network we constantly sit on information in order to maintain the access to and cooperation from people we need. Quid pro quo."

"*Really?*" Broadway Transfer is intrigued.

"It was tough for Anderson Cooper to accept, but I brought him around."

"Okay, next steps," Cliff states. "Obviously, these are children, and children require supervision." His assesing gaze lands on Grant.

"I think what we need to be asking is how the hell this happened on Gene's watch." Grant, his face reddening, narrows his eyes at the headmaster in turn. "Gene?"

"Yes, of course." Gene snaps to, propelled to take a little step forward. "I sincerely apologize—"

"Don't apologize—I want these kids fucking policed." Grant lumbers to stand, taking the ball and running with it right off the field. "We're entrusting them to *you,* Gene. You mold their academic lives, their social lives, and, starting now, their fucking cyber lives. You cannot continue to blow off that responsibility."

"Cliff?" Sheila swivels to him for his thoughts, as do we all. He nods approval.

"Get the faculty in here." Emboldened, Grant drops to a steely timbre. "I want everyone in the screening room in sixty minutes."

While the board maintains its encampment, I am at last called to duty and join Gene in pulling up seats alongside his receptionist at her desk in order to activate the snow chain. I apologetically rouse teacher after teacher—priced out of the Drama Club's benefit performance—from their comfortable couches in the outer boroughs at nine thirty on a Thursday. Then, when I reach the end of my assigned list I make fake calls, rousing my voice mail, just to avoid having to talk to the grumbling board, whose newly focused ire is crystallizing on the other side of the mantel.

By ten thirty every bucket-sized stadium seat in the screening room is filled. From where I stand with the board members against the velvet-curtained walls, I can see pajama legs peeking out from under the raincoat hems of the seated faculty. "If this is their way of telling us health care's back on the table, I am going to take a shit in Gene's office," someone mutters. I twist to see Gene at the top of the room, distinctly not coming over to introduce me to Cliff as he said he would once we were in here.

Based on what I've overheard on the en masse trek from his suite, what's about to commence falls directly under my new job description, and as much as it sucks for my introduction to the faculty to fall on the heels of their being dragged here in their pajamas, I take a steadying breath and approach Cliff and Sheila. They confer at the far end of the platform in front of the full-sized movie screen, heads bowed. "Hey! I know you have your hands full here, but I just wanted to formally say hello."

"Hi," Cliff says, shaking my outstretched hand and looking back to Sheila.

"Nan, we're about to begin," she says, brushing me off, the telltale smoker's lines around her mouth crimping.

"Yes, no, I know. It's just that since I'm officially here as the staff developer I thought perhaps I could be—"

"What you can do is go back and stand by the wall. Tonight's far too important for a road test."

"What Sheila means is that we have it covered. Why don't you continue as an observer tonight," Cliff suggests with a commercial charm that makes the role sound like a first-class seat to Dubai. He smiles a dismissive smile and gestures for Sheila to begin.

"All right, all right." Sheila claps her hands and I retake my place on the sidelines as instructed. "I'm sorry to have dragged you away from *Law & Order,* or whatever it was you were doing, but unfortunately, this is a situation requiring *immediate* attention. A situation that would not have come to pass in the first place if everyone here was doing their jobs properly." She pauses, pivoting left to right, allowing her withering gaze to spray the room. The other board members glower in agreement. "The health and well-being of our student body should be your *number one* priority and yet you have *failed.*" And I can see how a faculty/board cushion might be helpful. "Are we clear?"

Tired heads nod.

"Okay. This clip was sent to Darwin Zuckerman in the eleventh grade and he, in turn, erroneously forwarded it to three friends. We have contained the flow of information. Thankfully, out of concern for the school, the boy's next act was to forward it to his father. And here we are. With his permission we are projecting Congressman Zuckerman's desktop directly to the screen. Go ahead." She nods to someone in the projector room and the screen fills with Grant's inbox. The arrow moves and clicks on an e-mail attachment from Darwin.

The QuickTime file begins to play.

The camera wobbles as two hands fill the screen, straightening the lens, setting up the shot. The auteur steps back and I recognize Chassie, in a pink peignoir with marabou trim that's much too big for her, climbing up on a satin bedspread under a large four-quadrant Warhol portrait of a woman who was one of my favorite actresses in the eighties. Chassie turns around, her inherent awkwardness not helped by fairly blatant inebriation. "Hi, Darwin," she slurs in a seductive voice from a kneeling position. "I'm sorry about the helipad thing. I'm glad Ms. Wells ended up picking your speech, really. I really am. You'll do a much better job. And you're wrong—the win totally still counts. It does. It's just, it's just . . . Ms. Wells. She's a bitch." I scan the darkened audience for Ingrid as Chassie pauses, rearranging herself so her stringy hair falls over her shoulder. "How are you? Do you miss me? I bet you miss me."

I put my hands up over my face because I can't bear to see what's coming next that's gotten a member of Congress and his PR bomb squad on a plane.

"Do you miss this?" I spread my fingers to see Chassie drop the peignoir on one side, exposing her breast. Please let it end here. "How about this?" Another awkward breast-reveal and then her knees seem to go out from under her on the satin bedspread. "Whoops!" She rights herself and starts fondling her nipples, desperate to be seductive, and I take a moment to thank God that the most embarrassing thing we could do in high school was drop off a bag of Red Hots with a guy's doorman.

She leans across what must be her mother's mirrored vanity table, ringed with old headshots and magazine covers, picks something off the crocheted doily, and holds it up. The unmistakable blue bottle of Fruition. "You like that old picture of my mom in the front hall, right? That ad?" She runs the gold cap under her chin and across her breasts. As if doing an Estée Lauder spot in *Barely Legal*. And then, with a final sodden smile, she leans back, spreads her legs—and makes it disappear.

Disappear.

With a swirl of the animated arrow, the clip ends and the screen reverts back to Darwin's e-mail as the lights come up, the message fading in the breathless nauseated hush.

I peer around the room. All the teachers have some part of their hands over their faces.

Sheila crosses back to the center of the platform. "You get the gist. We showed you this so you could all have the accurate information firsthand and not go around playing a game of telephone like sixth graders. And also so you understand the gravity of what's at stake when you *don't* take your responsibilities seriously."

Unclasping his hands from behind his back, Cliff steps forward to join her, a congenial smile on his face. "Good evening, everyone. My colleague, Mr. Toomey, has come in to give you a lesson tonight on monitoring your students. How to review their MySpace pages, how to see their Facebook profiles, how to follow them into chat rooms and read their blogs."

"To make sure nothing like this can ever again threaten the school," Sheila adds. "Are we paying attention?"

"What about Chassie?" All heads turn. It's Ingrid. She stands in the top row, bewildered. "Is she okay? I mean has someone spoken to her? Notified her? What about our psychologist? Has Mildred reached out to her?" She points to an older woman whose expression makes it clear she doesn't want to go near this with a ten-foot disinfected barge pole. "Okay, then what about her mother?" Ingrid tries.

"She's doing a play in the West End," Sheila offers as if it's an explanation.

Ingrid lifts an eyebrow. "Well, does Chassie know this is being circulated? Clearly that was not her intention. She needs to know. And she needs support. Counseling. This is not a productive or safe way to communicate. And she's not the only student here who's confused on this point. This"—she flicks her palm at the screen—"is about something much more endemic in Jarndyce culture." She looks to her colleagues below, but they busy themselves with picking at hems and buttons. I lift my brows and strain to catch her eye in silent support. "If we say we want to modernize the school, when are we going to address these attitudes?"

"Point taken." Cliff nods before widening his gaze to encompass the room. "Any other quick questions before the training? I know it's late and the other board members and I have been here all evening."

"So, then . . . what will be done?" Ingrid tries again. "At least in terms of Chassie?"

Cliff looks encouragingly up at her. "What's your name?"

"Ingrid Wells, the aforementioned bitch." She leans onto one hip with a self-deprecating smile that quickly turns serious. "I know these kids."

"You teach them—not the same thing," Grant admonishes, heaving himself off the far wall.

"I coach Chassie and Darwin in Forensics, I'm a faculty advisor to the eleventh-grade homeroom, and I have them both for U.S. history."

"History," Grant repeats for the benefit of the other parents, as if she's just said "clowning."

"I think they need help," Ingrid continues, and I realize her hands are trembling as she shoves them in her coat pockets.

"They?" Grant growls, his face once again tinging sanguine. "Who is *they*? Just because my son was the focus of this stupid girl's debasement doesn't implicate him in this in any way."

"I'm not saying implicate, I'm saying reach out to—"

"My son was the victim here, let's keep that clear," Grant bellows, "and if I could toss that Chassie girl out on her ear, I would. You can't shirk your real responsibilities to these kids by sitting around a hug circle all day, *Ms. Wells*. And you want health care," he adds derisively. IamonlyobservingIamonlyobservingIamonlyobserving—

"Okay, shall we begin?" Mr. Toomey hustles onto the stage on Cliff's cue and, with relief, the board members turn to file out. "Let's start with a few Internet basics."

Biting the inside of her cheek, Ingrid slowly sits down. As Toomey speaks, my eyes wander back to the screen and for the first time I make out Darwin's concerned e-mail to his father.

Dad, how fucking cool is this? Are you coming home this week?–D

"What do you mean, *made it disappear?*" Ryan asks from the other end of the line sometime after one a.m.

"I mean stuck it where the sun don't shine."

"Ouch."

"I love you." I lay my pen atop a sloping pile of notes on the mattress, my makeshift workstation.

"You love me?"

"I do."

"Why?"

"Because you get the ouch factor." I lean back on the propped pillows serving as my desk chair.

"Well, I hope I run into Grant Zuckerman in the Capitol building after this breaks. I'd like to see that smug shit taken down a peg."

"I give it twenty-four hours." I glance to the web of hairline cracks in the ceiling. "Kids pleasuring themselves with Fruition. Talk about Estée Lauder rebranding. It has Fox ticker tape written all over it." I replay the video in my mind's eye with my digital scrim blocking the image in stripes. "Poor Chassie. In her mom's clothes, on her mom's bed. It was a child psychologist's thesis paper."

"So, what's next?"

"I think when the board's had a night to sleep on it they're going to want to run some kind of workshops on 'sexting'—that's what the kids are calling it—and I'm going to be ready with a proposal on how to train the teachers. So, wait, when *are* you coming home?" I pull over my Filofax, Mrs. X's note sliding from its pages to the duvet.

"Well, I didn't want to say anything until it's definite, but there's talk of sending some of us to the grain dispersement centers for a few days—maybe longer. It doesn't help that warlords are skimming off what little there is."

"*They're sending you to stand up to warlords?* Hope you bring that letter opener your parents gave you for Christmas. Oh, and your briefcase might slow a bullet. Don't they have people with plastic shields they can send?"

"Yes. But those people might need me to tell them why they're there."

"This sucks." I slap the Filofax, my wedding band hitting the binder clasp. "At least when we were in the middle of nowhere we were in the middle of nowhere together."

"But now you have your friends around you, that's what you wanted, right?"

"I guess."

"You guess?"

"No, I mean I do. Josh and Sarah are superbusy. But Citrine's turning out to be a pleasant surprise—"

"And there's always the Xes."

"Ryan."

"Any word from them?"

"Actually." I slide my gold band back and forth over my knuckle. "She has invited me over for a thank-you tea."

"You're fucking me."

"I wish."

"Me, too. When's the tea?"

"Thursday." I take a breath. "And I'm nervous as hell."

"That's crazy." I can hear the smile in his voice. "I'm proud of you."

"Thanks, man." I smile back.

"No, I mean getting your closure. That's pretty damn cool."

"And go you, directing the people fighting the warlords. So, you're gone for a few more days?"

"Yeah, looks that way . . ."

"God, I miss you."

"You, too. So any more thoughts on the baby front?"

I inhale. "I've had my hands full."

"I know. Just thought I'd check in."

I stare out at the wall of wardrobe boxes in the periphery of the bed lamp. "I can't find the contractor, Ryan. The stairs got fixed, but he's not returning my calls."

"I'll keep an eye out. Maybe he's on safari with the electrician."

"And how would this work, exactly, with a baby?"

"Nan," he says sternly, "I would never have taken this position if we had a baby."

"So you're quitting your job?"

"Nan?"

"Yes?"

Silence. "Nothing. Get some sleep. You'll need your strength when the story breaks and they want you on *Larry King*. I love you. I'll be home soon."

7

One week later, the story hasn't broken and he isn't home.

I walk out my front door with Grace straining on her leash. The rest of her day must be such a letdown compared with the raw excitement that my departure from REM signals. Not that I made it anywhere near that restorative vicinity last night. Instead, I got into bed, where, while Grace snored, I fitfully ran all the possible scenarios that might take place at 721 Park hours from now. Scenarios where I scream at her. Scenarios where she screams at me. Scenarios where we scream at each other. And a particularly satisfying version where I graze her with a flying porcelain Pekingese. What could Mrs. X thanking me even mean? Sincerely, as in, *Thank you for full-on parenting my child while I went shopping?* Or sarcastic, as in, *Thank you for giving me the worst childcare story on the block, insolent college student who didn't know her place, and then coming back twelve years later to aid and abet my children barricading me in my bedroom?*

I'd laid perfectly still with my eyes closed, waiting for the sky to brighten, and then, during that painful protracted whole minute it took me to get not-naked and downstairs, grab a baggie *and* her leash, Grace broke into a demanding yodel, accompanied by one Torvill and Dean–worthy spin.

As she relieves herself between two parked Hondas in front of the house, I look down at a card on the sidewalk and recognize my name inked beneath the smut of shoeprints. I bend down to gingerly lift the mint green postcard by my fingernails, twisting it to read that as of yesterday, April thirtieth, I have a package waiting for me at the post office.

I dart into the bodega on the corner to grab a *New York Post.* I hate giving Murdoch any of my hard-earned cash, but they so are the ones to break the Fruition story. If it's going to break at all, which, as of today, crosses my own invented deadline. Tomorrow I'm back to the adjective-light *Times*—much as I'll miss the smattering of Page Six references to Carter Nelson and Mr. X on a red carpet tour— *Turandot* at the Met, *Sleeping Beauty* at City Ballet, and an indie film premiere. "What hedge-fund titan kept Lever House open an hour past closing for a rendezvous with his actress girlfriend?" I cannot imagine Mr. X *ever* made time to step out with his wife five nights a week. Maybe this is how he woos. That or Carter Nelson inspires him in a way no woman has. Or maybe he's finally at an age where he can manage his empire without putting in the punishing hours. Hopefully, he's found a few to spend with his boys.

Mulling this over, I tie Grace to a parking meter and head into the post office. At the window I hand in the card and use the wait to scan the pages for any mention of Jarndyce. Still nothing. Amazing. They really made this disappear. They stuck it where the sun don't shine. Which perhaps is also where my retainer is headed f I don't hear from them soon about my sexting proposal. The woman returns from the back with a small brown paper box—roughed up at the corners and plastered in a quilt of stamps. "Someone loves you in Africa," she says, handing over a form for me to sign.

"*Sit.* Alice, *Alice,* sit. Good—Josie, *no.* Sit. Girls! Josie, sit. *Sit.* Alice, *Alice . . .*"

Holding the box under one arm, I tilt my weight to my other sneaker as I wait for my heart rate to calm and my parents' four-month-old springer spaniels to get the memo on the other side of their front door.

"Dad," I moan from the hall, looking down appreciatively at Grace's graying temples as she pants patiently. "We just jogged here from the East Harlem post office, can we do the training class once we're inside, lying on your kitchen floor?"

"They almost have it, Pixie." I hear him through the heavy wood. "*Alice, Josie . . .* and we are sitting! Good girls!" Chirping barks erupt into the hallway. "*No!*" And are instantly silenced. The door cracks open, and two little black noses wedge themselves out, sending Grace backing up behind me.

"You're all rosy cheeks!" Dad pulls me into a hug over a whir of black-and-white fur.

"I told you, I jogged here from my hood." I inhale his familiar scent of PG tips. "I need a really big glass of water and a consult."

"So do we," he says from where he's directing his brood back inside behind me. "Have you had breakfast?" he asks as he walks to the kitchen.

"Honestly, I haven't even brushed my teeth." I place the box on the Hungarian wood chest that's served as an entry table since I was crawling. The girls crisscrossing at her paws, Grace trots past me as I slip off my sneakers. I watch the three of them make their way down the well-worn Persian runner, past the living room toward the bedrooms, in search of the lady of the house. "Dad, why aren't you at school?" I call out, unpeeling Ryan's Carhartt from where I tied it around my waist and hanging it on the coat closet knob.

"Building brouhaha," he answers as I meet him in the kitchen. I gulp down the water he hands me and refill my glass from the fridge door. "And we're having parent-teacher conferences this morning anyway."

"I see." I grab a bagel from the Zabar's bag on the counter and the butter from the refrigerator and slide them onto the non-*Times*-strewn section of the table. "So, I got an unnerving present from Ryan," I say as I remove Mom's files to free up a chair where I can flop.

"Is he all right?" He turns in concern.

"Oh no, he's safe. It's not—no one sent me his head." I pause, my thoughts swirling. "I kinda need to consult the parent with the ovaries. She in her office?"

"Yes. *We* got an unnerving letter from the co-op board," Dad says, his jaw muscles constricting as he lifts a stack of graded papers into his cracking leather briefcase. "It's sent your mother into a state."

"What'd it say?" I ask, mouth full of bagel.

"I'll let her fill you in." He glances up at the clock. "I've got to get going. Girls?" Dad calls entreatingly into the hall. "Girls?"

"Calm and assertive, Dad."

He squares his shoulders and drops his voice. "Come."

"Totally bought it," I whisper. He grins, his mustache lifting as the scratching scramble can be heard barreling toward him. I watch through the doorway as he bends to lift them to eye level one at a time. "Be good. I'll be home at four thirty." He turns to me. "It helps them to know the schedule."

"You're such a good dad."

"And they've got the barking thing down. They really do."

"Impressive." I lift my glass to him.

"Jim, wait!" Mom calls from the office that was once my bedroom on the far side of the apartment. "Call me on your break and hopefully I'll have gotten this resolved." Her voice gets louder. "You have your cell?" She appears in the doorway with Grace, her hand over the phone.

He pats the pocket of his tweed blazer, kisses her, and gives me a wave. I wave back as Grace slurpingly stations herself at the girls' water bowl.

"Nan, I'm so glad you're here! I'm on hold with these *assholes*," Mom hisses before darting her finger up to return to her caller. "I understand that, but we've been tenants of this building for thirty-eight years." She pulls her glasses up into her gray hair. "Tenants who have *always* had dogs. These dogs are *not* perpetually barking. I promise you. I have witnesses." She crosses her arm over her white cotton turtleneck and rests her hand in the crook of her other elbow, her cameo rings crunching together. "The next-door neighbors love these puppies . . . Uh-huh. Well, then let's talk about what's really going on here. Tim Schwartz and that wife of his want our apartment for their nursery and they are using the co-op board and this flimsy excuse to get it . . . I see. Well, I would like to speak to him directly." She sticks her hand in the pocket of her green wool trousers. "I would like him to tell me to my face that he is evicting us because a woman who has an entire floor of this building can't find an inch to put her children. Yes, yes, he can call me at home." She clicks the phone off and claps it down on the butcher-block cart. "Dammit. Girls!" Mom bends to swipe a pig-face oven mitt that's fallen to become an instant chew toy. She stands back up and returns it to its hook by the stove. "Hi!" she says with false cheer.

"Oh my God, what's going on?"

"Well, the Schwartzes upstairs have found out that we're one of only three renters left in the building. Because she's just done in vitro, *again*, and is having triplets on top of her twins—not that I've ever seen her so much as push a stroller—and has her eye set on *our* home. So, your father goes down to walk the girls this morning and her law-yer—at six a.m., mind you—her lawyer is waiting in the lobby to personally hand him this notice on behalf of the co-op board. So that's not suspicious! This notice that states we're in violation of our rental contract because of shareholder complaints about barking. No warn-ing, nothing. Remember when everyone this side of the park had a big dog or three? Now it's hairless cats and hamster-poos. Our pup-pies' learning curve has given that Schwartz woman her edge. In this market. There's no way we can afford to buy. We were about to retire!"

"Did you call your lawyer?"

"I've called three." Of course. "Unless they're on retainer, most don't return calls until after the sun rises." She drops her forearms to the butcher block.

"I'm so sorry!" I walk to her, my shins screaming in protest.

"I don't even know how we'd afford to rent in the city now. Your father will need to keep teaching. He'd have to commute in from whatever we could get in the suburbs. Maybe we could rent out there? I suppose we could always stay with you if we have to, Lord knows you two have the space ..." She drums her fingers, her eyes glazing over as she rolls through her options. One toilet and a bed-room door that doesn't close and my parents. I won't just not have the baby, I'll not have the sex.

"Oh, I'm sure it won't come to that," I say as I look over to see Grace wedge herself between the wall and the table, guarded by chair feet and out of puppy range.

"You have four floors, right?"

"Including the basement. But just one working bathroom and everything is in shambles and we'll have tenants—"

"We could be your tenants," she calculates. I panic.

"But we'll need the space for kids!"

"Oh, Nan," she cries, her tense features breaking into a huge smile. "That's the first time you've said that!" She puts a hand on each of my shoulders. "Kids! Are you pregnant?"

"No, no, no, just—"

"Starting?"

"Well—"

She pulls me into a hug. "That's just the most wonderful news I've heard all morning. Make that all year."

I slump with her arms still around my frame. "It's not feeling wonderful."

"What do you mean?" She pulls back to study me, hands on my biceps.

"I mean I feel the opposite of seeing babies in strollers and wanting to stick them in my pocket or whatever women with ticking clocks say."

"And Ryan?"

"Oh, Ryan's vision is crystal." I step around her and out to the hallway to bring in the box. "Exhibit A." I withdraw its contents, a colorful knit glove with a different animal puppet on each finger.

"Ohhhh," Mom croons, taking it from me to slide her hand inside. "It's wonderful!" She wiggles the animals at herself.

"It came with a note that said, 'I'm just asking for you to try it on.'"

"He's so great." She slides her hand out and lays the toy on the counter, where we both stare at it with opposing expressions. Glancing at my face, she picks up the glove and gives it to me. "So, you're not ready, that's all."

"Is it?"

"Sure." She grabs a mug and fills it with coffee from the carafe.

"Can you tell *him* that?" I slide down the refrigerator to the cool linoleum and pull the puppies onto my lap. "I need a note from my mom saying I'm not ready to be a mom."

"You can tell him, Nan."

"I tried." I lay them out on their backs, head to tail, between my outstretched legs.

"Do you want eggs?" She squints down at me. "I could go for McDonald's."

"I live a block from every fast-food outlet in America. I came here for Zabar's."

"You know how a crisis makes me crave a Sausage McMuffin."

"So, that's it?" I rub their pink bellies.

"Scoot over."

I lean to one hip, careful not to disturb the puppies, as Mom wedges open the refrigerator door behind me to pull out eggs and sausage. "I just wait to be ready?"

"Yes. Do you want some?"

"No. And what if I don't get to ready?"

She bends to retrieve a fry pan from the nearby cupboard, pausing to consider this. "Then," she says, her voice sadly resigned, "I guess you won't have children."

"So we're all just waiting for me to have a feeling or not? That's horrible."

"That's a revolution, Nan. That's *your* right that I fought for. What do you want me to say?" She looks down and I can see there's so much she's not saying, trying not to say, that I weigh her inquiry carefully.

"I guess . . ." I look down at the girls' pink ears flopping open, their eyes slit as they grow drowsy. "That I should get over this paralyzing conviction that a good mother is one hundred percent ready. And that when the baby comes out it'll all just magically be okay."

"No, you don't." She shakes her head, the flame bursting blue under the old Le Creuset skillet.

"I do. I want to hear it's all going to be okay."

"Well, of course it's going to be okay. It just might not include children."

I look up at her, trying to suppress my sadness at her resignation, trying to access the feeling of gratitude at the empowerment she is aiming for, when a grinding sound comes through the ceiling, startling the puppies and Grace to barking on their feet.

"Shush! *That* is Carey Schwartz's new SUV for toddlers, which she lets them drive around at all hours. And our two seconds of barking a day is the violation! Why she needs three more up there I'll never understand." She cracks an egg into the pan and it sizzles as I wave Grace over to hush her. "Just don't wait too long, Nan. Don't wait so long to be ready that you have scientifically induced sextuplets. What would you do then?"

8

Worried that my backfiring conversation with Mom had established a bad precedent for the day, I'm pleasantly surprised when the lunch with my client, a software company, goes smoothly. Buoyed, I announce myself with conviction to 721's doorman at precisely three o'clock. He looks dubious. "Is she in the city?" he asks.

"She should be. She's expecting me."

Less than convinced, he does a little spin to the brass console, lifting the receiver. "I thought she was in Europe. Usually she's in, she out, ladies coming and going, deliveries, but—Hello? Mrs. X? You have a visitor. Okay!" He pivots back to me, smiling. "Go right on up."

I get out on nine and ring the doorbell, praying, despite the hour, that a sock-footed Stilton will appear and skate circles around us for the entire encounter. Unless she really is going to thank-me thank-me. Then I'd like him to do a quick oil painting of the event.

Silence.

Silence.

Then a small voice. "Coming!" Finally she opens the door and stands there looking even more fragile than she did two weeks ago. She's swimming in ecru silk wide-legged trousers and a long silk jacket open above a matching shell top, the toast colors doing nothing to brighten her colorless face. "Please, come in. It was so good of you to travel all this way. I just don't have the energy to be out and about right now. Grayer tells me you're living in Harlem."

"Yes, we bought a derelict house the city reclaimed and are fixing it up," I say, following the direction of her outstretched arm toward the living room, somehow sure that Grayer omitted the fact that he'd actually been there. "It's going to be beautiful when we're done."

"Pioneer spirit, how lovely," she says, touching where her collarbones approach beneath her throat. "I never had that. Please, sit." She gestures to the couch opposite where she settles herself. "Tea?" she asks, leaning forward to pour from the same service used to woo Chester Dobson.

"Thank you."

"I apologize there are no sandwiches or scones. We've run out of everything and Rosa just up and quit on me, I've no idea why." She gives a mirthless laugh.

"So what're the boys eating?" I ask jocularly.

She looks at me blankly as she hands me my cup. "Pizza? Grayer hasn't asked me for money so I'm assuming their father is giving them cash. Grayer doesn't come into his trust until next year. Milk?"

"Thank you." I cut jocular from my repertoire as the conversation switches tracks, and take the silver-rimmed pitcher from her. "Grayer told me about Mr. X. I'm so sorry."

She sits back, crossing her veined hands in her lap. "*Grayer* told you?" she asks. I hesitate for a moment, unsure what I'm admitting to.

"Yes," I finally say.

She raises a seed-pearl comb from her dark blond hair, no longer the near-black it once was, and readjusts it. "So you don't read the *Post*?"

"No." I don't cop to this week's habit.

"It's all so tacky." She brushes imagined crumbs from her pristine lap. "So, so *tacky*. And to think of the lengths I have gone to . . ." She looks into the empty fireplace before regaining her bearings. "It's just tacky."

I smile softly, awkwardly, genuinely commiserating, whether she's referring to his behavior or the coverage. It *is* tacky. "What do you imagine Elizabeth would've made of all this?" I venture, mentioning her daunting mother-in-law.

"Oh, she's still alive." She leans forward. "When her sister died she sold the house in Boston and moved into her family mansion in Greenwich. Forty minutes away. And no call of support from her. I guess we know which side she's chosen." She flares her diminutive nostrils and purses her bare lips before reclining and recrossing her hands. "So." She pauses. "I asked you here to thank you." Okay, yes,

yes, you did, we're on the same plane of reality. "With Stilton's acceptance letter came a phone call. *Apparently* I made a very charming impression on his evaluation."

"I'm so sorry," I rush.

"Don't be." She raises her cup and saucer from the table. "It's something they've learned from their father, I expect. Deceit."

My face stings. "I think they were trying to spare you any additional stress, under the circumstances."

She looks at me for a moment, weighing accepting my gracious spin. I take a tight breath. She smiles. "That's very kind."

"They're wonderful boys and I'm thrilled to hear Stilton was accepted," I say earnestly, despite the fact we seem to be dancing closer to the moment where she hurls scalding Earl Grey in my face.

"You remember Grayer, of course." I lean back slightly at this acknowledgment that we met before two weeks ago, my hands still ready to grab Grandma's Choo as a shield. "But Stilton . . ." She smiles to herself. "He's my happy surprise."

"He's wonderful. And Grayer's great with him."

"I had a few miscarriages after Grayer started at St. Bernard's." She sniffs.

"I'm so sorry," I say, thrown by the deepening intimacy. "I can't imagine. That must have been awful."

"It was . . . painful. Finally they said my eggs were just too old." She gives a little laugh on "old" the way some people whisper disease names. "We found a marvelous egg donor, just marvelous." Her pallid eyes light up for the first time since my arrival. "PhD, proficient in the violin, adorable girl. So we tried that way for a couple of years, but by then they said my uterus had 'timed out.'" Again the little trill on what I'm taking as code for menopause. "But we were so *attached* to the donor, such an *enchanting* girl, so we found a surrogate to carry the baby. Of course, by then, with the demands on Mr. X, leaving the bank and starting his fund, we decided it was easier to use a sperm donor. Et voilà. My darling boy. He is *such* a love, isn't he?"

I pause to add that up. "He really is. I saw his room. His passion for the Supreme Court is really something." I laugh. She smiles blankly.

"Grayer seems to have been a wonderful influence on him. I remember what a good time we had together," I say, testing the cloudy waters.

"Hm." She makes the sound with her lips closed, a small smile playing around them. She nods to herself for a moment, eyes on the Audubons.

"We had so much fun together—"

"Right," her voice comes back firmly. "You babysat him a few times," she states.

"I, uh—" My breath catches and we stare at each other. And then suddenly her face softens. "But you were his favorite. I do remember that."

The front doorbell rings.

"This has been lovely." She brushes imaginary crumbs from her lap. "I'm so glad we had this time together. Would you mind getting that for me? I don't have the strength to get up."

"Not at all." I stand. So . . . we acknowledged that I worked here—kind of. And that Grayer and I were close—relatively. And that's as far as we are going—probably. I cross back to the entrance and open the heavy front door to two Chanel-clad ladies in their midfifties. If Lewis Carroll and Tom Wolfe collaborated this would be their Tweedledee and Dum. Identical blond blow-outs, identical bouclé suits, one robin's egg, the other pink, identical black Kelly bags, identical black flats, similar patrician good looks probably preserved by the same tasteful dermatologist.

"Bunny? Saz? Come in," Mrs. X calls weakly as if the oxygen had suddenly gone thin.

The two ladies skirt past me to rush in and kiss her pale cheek. "Honey, how are you doing?" they both intone with almost southern verve as they sit on the couch facing her. "Are you *all* alone?" One leans in pityingly.

"I'm hanging in." Mrs. X smiles bravely.

"We are *so sorry* we haven't been to see you sooner—"

"Any sooner—"

"We have been up to our *eyeballs* with the benefit—"

"Our eyeballs—"

"With the new *program format*—"

"The 'eco' considerations—"

"An *organic* menu—"

"But you have been on our minds—"

"In our *prayers*—"

"In our hearts."

Mrs. X nods, letting their weightless words hang in the air for a moment like Chinese lanterns. I stand awkwardly in the doorway, uncertain if I'm supposed to excuse myself, uncertain if I got what I came for, or if that's even available to me. "Yes," she says, "when the e-mails abruptly stopped—well, we know how stressful the final weeks of planning are. It was so considerate of you to spare me this year with everything I have going on. Girls, I want you to meet a dear, dear friend of mine, Nan Hutchinson." *What?!*

Mrs. X extends her arm up to me. She pulses her fingers into her palm and I realize she wants me to take her hand. Oh, sweet Jesus. But I do. This random stranger who babysat her kid a few times takes her hand and she presses it against her cool face. "Dear Nan. She's Dorothy Hutchinson's daughter-in-law." The Tweedles murmur appreciatively as I struggle to keep my shock from reading. "When Dorothy couldn't come herself she sent Nan." She fixes me with an unprecedented smile of affectionate gratitude that I'm disturbed to feel some antiquated part of me, however tiny, desperately drink in. "Who has insisted on being here every day to look after me. Nan, this is Barbara and Susan."

I blink down at them.

"Nan?" Mrs. X prompts.

"Yes, hello." I free myself from her cheek to shake their freckled hands.

"How *is* Dorothy?" Susan inquires.

"Good!" This one I can answer. "She's made a life for herself in Hong Kong, still doing her photography."

"Well, give her our best. New York just has not felt the same without her!"

"So." Barbara opens her purse and sets a small paperweight-sized scale on the coffee table. "What do you have?"

104

"Nan, darling," Mrs. X asks, "would you be a dear and get that envelope I left on the bed?"

I find myself nodding and then exiting to turn down the twisting hallway to her now pewter-toned bedroom, where I see, atop her unmade bed, a bulging manila envelope. The curtains are open to the flat light of the city outside, but the room smells like sweat and confinement. My curiosity mounting, I walk quickly back with the envelope.

"It's just these few odds and ends," Mrs. X says, extending her arm once more to take it from me. She spills its contents onto the cloudy glass between them, gold bracelets, necklaces, and rings clinking into the Limoges boxes and gardening books that accessorize the table.

Barbara pulls out a black Smythson notebook and starts weighing each piece before putting it back in the envelope. "This is good," Barbara affirms. "My guy on Forty-seventh will give you a great price."

"It's not that I need the money," Mrs. X asserts. Again that nervous laugh on "money." "It's just I want to liquidate everything that wasn't itemized on our insurance before this place is inventoried."

"Smart," Barbara says. "How's your prenup?"

Mrs. X pauses, her pale eyes rounding to make her look more doll-like. "Generous." A faint smile. "What with *two* boys to look after." She traps the tip of her tongue between her teeth as Stilton's cash value is laid bare.

"I just got three thousand for my great-grandfather's old war medals," Susan interjects. "I took myself to Golden Door." Mrs. X whips her head over. "Before the benefit planning took over," she amends. "Eyeballs. We are up to our *eyeballs*."

"I don't understand," I finally say as Barbara squints at the tiny lever bouncing into place under the weight of a large Dior cocktail ring.

"Gold is at record highs. There's a global shortage," she says, recording the ring's weight. "I went with my son-in-law to pick out my daughter's engagement stone and the guy behind the counter offered me cash money on the spot for the necklace I had on. I went home and cleared out all the old junk I never wear anymore and the next day I got that fur coat Randal wouldn't buy me. Okay, done." She slips the bulging envelope, notebook, and scale into her purse. "I like to preweigh. They're *Jews.*" She mouths the last word as they stand. "I should be down there early next week and then I'll drop the money off with your doorman."

"Can't you stay for a cup of tea?" Mrs. X asks, her tone reminiscent of entreaties to her husband from years ago. "*Please?* Or we could meet for supper later? At Swifty's?" But they move toward the hall, seemingly eager to distance themselves from the specter of their own marital follies writ large. "Forgive me if I don't get up," Mrs. X calls after them, her voice spinning into a breathy wheeze. "It's only my doctor said I'm not to move around too much." The Tweedles freeze at the threshold. Pause. And pivot, their Ferragamo bows moving in unison.

"Are you okay, honey?" Susan asks, coming no closer.

"Oh, yes, it's just that, oh—" Mrs. X huffs to herself. "I promised myself I wouldn't tell anyone until it was over. I didn't want to worry you."

At that they fly back to their seats on one straight Bill Irwin–esque vector, their knees bending as they approach. "Honey, you can worry us—"

"We are here for you—"

"*Anything—*"

"Anything at all." They both lean in, eyes widening like dogs awaiting scraps.

"It's going to be *fine,*" Mrs. X says definitively. "But they found a lump." She drops her gaze to her lap and suddenly this ghost of a woman makes awful sense. My face goes hot, then numb, because I have wanted her to suffer . . . but not like this, not physically, not literally. In a vacuum, in a way that couldn't affect Grayer. Which, of course, is ridiculous.

The Tweedles leap into a cacophony of Appropriate Responses. Mrs. X holds her palm up. "I'm just waiting on a plan of action. They haven't determined the protocol yet . . . I'm just tired, that's all." She gives a weary smile and, whatever may or may not have passed between us, I feel horrible. For Grayer. For Stilton. For her—sick, scared, and so obviously alone.

"Oh, *honey*," Susan says with gravitas before pulling a small croco-dile diary out of her bag. "Now let me make some calls. Leaf Burman went through this last year and she knows some fantastic people. She had this man who would come over and just hold her feet for an hour a day. She said he could see the tumors in his mind."

Mrs. X's eyes widen at the thought. "I just want to rest. And maybe a few people to cheer me up."

"Done."

"And, of course, while I'm obviously not up to holding my previ-ous position as committee chair, I would still like to help in any way I can."

"Of course, *of course*—"

"Yes—"

"Absolutely—"

"Only—"

"It's just—"

"Small thing—"

"Silly, really—"

"But . . . Carter Nelson went to Spence." That can't be good.

"Yes?" Mrs. X asks, head tilting.

"So they already approached her about being the honorary chair-person this year. Because of the writers' strike and the pending SAG strike, she had time," Barbara rushes to add. "You know we haven't had any star power in recent years and we thought it would help sell more tables. Tables have been selling a little . . . slowly." She releases the last word seemingly against her will. "Perhaps fifty thousand a table was ambitious."

Devastation passes over Mrs. X's face like a fast-moving cloud and then a smile breaks as she sits back into the trio of throw pillows. "Of course. Whatever is best for the benefit. I have loved steering it all these years, but obviously, my *health* prevents me this year," she says, staring levelly at the two women who have misplaced her number for almost a month. "Well, no matter. Just tell me where it would be most helpful for me to sit. I'm obviously not up to hosting a table of my own this year."

The Tweedles look at each other, momentarily aghast before Barbara recovers. "Of *course*. Of *course* you'll want to be there. And you can sit at my table, honey."

"*And,*" Susan adds, "Stilton should perform in the show."

"We already have a lower-school student from Haverhill Prep," Barbara protests.

"*Ye-es.*" Susan shoots Barbara a look. "But we can make an exception."

"Well, that is so kind." Mrs. X smoothes her lap.

"Isn't it!" Barbara smiles broadly, angrily. "Now you *really* have a reason to be there," she can't help adding in her ire. "Saz, let's go."

I show the Tweedles out with promises to call my mother-in-law and pass on their love. Upon returning to the living room, I look down to where Mrs. X sits dwarfed by her own furniture, the spoils of a war fought within these walls, and I feel sadder for her than I ever imagined possible. "I'm *so* sorry. Is there anything I can do for you before I go?" I ask. "Or at all? Any errands you need run?" Any movie stars you want shot?

She rearranges the panels of her jacket over her legs. "Thank you. That is so kind. But I'm really fine."

"Are you sure? Why don't I run over to Food Emporium and just stock up on some basics?"

"Grayer does the shopping. We're fine. Truly."

"Can I ask?" I rest my hands on the back of the facing couch. "Does Grayer know?"

She startles. "No . . . no, he doesn't." She stares across the room and out the window.

"Because I think he thinks, they think, you have been, uh, under the weather for other reasons."

She turns back to me. "Yes, he has been completely withdrawn since his father left. Cold, really. So hurtful." She nods to herself. "Yes, I should tell him." She stands. "He should appreciate what I'm going through." She strides to the front door.

"Right, yes, I meant . . ." Regretting I brought it up, I swipe my bag and hurry after her. "Could I be of any help with that? Perhaps we could get him a doctor to talk to in case he has questions, or a therapist? Someone to support—"

"Oh, he should hear it from me. He should know his mother is sick. Potentially terminally sick." She takes the knob and opens it. "But maybe you could help . . ."

"Yes, I'd really like to be there for him." While he's appreciating this.

"How nice. I was thinking 'The Rime of the Ancient Mariner.' " She ushers me out to the vestibule.

"Sorry?"

"For Stilton's performance at the benefit. It's Bunny's favorite poem. Could you help him memorize it? Since you're helping your in-laws with the renovation of their place."

"Oh, it's not—it's sold—that's the new—"

"I thought Grayer ran into you in the elevator."

"Right! Yes. Well, they sold it," I scramble. "To a friend of mine. From Chapin. That's why I was here. Visiting her. And Grayer and I ran into each other in the elevator. And he recognized me. And yes."

"Lovely. Well, Stilton thinks you're 'perfect,' whatever that means. So perhaps you'll pass that perfection off onto his recitation? I don't have the strength at the moment."

"I'd be delighted. When do you think you'll talk to Grayer and Stilton?"

"Oh, not Stilton, oh no. He adores me."

"Right."

"Maybe I can even get you a spot to stand backstage. All ten Manhattan private schools uniting for one evening every year to raise funds and bring our community together across academic divides. It's our Palio."

"But the Sienese aren't coming together," I surprise her by getting her reference. "They're competing, sometimes to the death."

"Exactly." She reaches past me to hit the button for the elevator. "It will be marvelous. Good-bye." I open my mouth to return the phrase, but, as seems to be the new family custom, she's already closing the door.

9

"So she did *not* thank you."

"Affirmative," I answer into my cell before biting off a piece of pizza crust.

"That sucks," Ryan summarizes through a yawn.

"Are you falling asleep on me?"

"I've been in a windowless room for two days. This is my half-hour break to shower, shave, nap, and, this is a direct instruction from the colonel, have a brain wave. I don't think I'm even going to get dinner."

"You just had pizza. It's midnight in December and we are about to kiss for the very first time," I remind him.

"Right, sorry." He inhales and I know he's pulling himself up against his pillows in an effort to wake up for our attempt at a long-distance date. After playing through a "quick trip" to Africa or a rendezvous in between, we decided the best, and comparably priced, gift we could give each other was a roof membrane. "So we're on the steps of the Met," he repeats from a billion miles away.

"Yes." Sitting on a metal chair beside a burbling copper water installation, I look straight up in the sliver between the midtown high-rises and see a stamp of cloudless sky. Not wanting to return from my lunch break with my software client with pizza grease spotting my skirt, I readjust the paper bag shielding my lap. "In their proximity."

"And I believe we were discussing this exact same woman and how much she sucks."

"You are correct."

"And then . . . you planted one on me."

"Ry, that is so not what happened!" I pop the last piece of crust in my mouth. "You kissed *me*! You know you kissed me. When are you going to admit it?"

"Come on, you were sweating me. It was all you," he says his familiar line. "I was the Hottie."

"I never should have told you."

"You didn't, your grandmother did. Ugh. This is ridiculous. Come get in bed with me, woman."

"And leave all the mad passionate nothing that is my construction-filled, perpetually dog-walking life in your absence?" *Beep.* "Shit." I pull the phone away. "That's Jarndyce. Can you hold on a sec?"

"Babe, I have to be up in seventeen minutes and rested enough to find a solution for the starving families leaving their—" *Beep* —"by the side of the road."

"Leaving their what?"

Beep.

"Dead children. It's fucking brutal."

"Oh my God, Ryan, that's—" *Beep.*

"Are you going to get it or are we ignoring—" *Beep.*

"No. Yes. Shit—it went to voice mail. Sorry, I'm back. But you should really go to sleep. Thanks for the date."

"My pleasure." His warmth tinges with concern. "I know you're managing a lot, Nan."

"Yeah." I take a long swig of Poland Spring. "But nothing that comes within a million miles of what you're dealing with."

"If only it were a competition. You going to be okay till I can get back?"

"Totally. Just please focus on your own stuff. Seriously, don't worry about me."

"I fucking love you."

"And I love you. Sweet dreams, Hottie." I hang up and hold the phone, staring through my sunglasses at a pair of tourists stopping to unfold a subway map. They are thin with a lot of hair and colorful sneakers—round-eyed and young. He tugs her arm and she drops against him, head back for a deep kiss. Grinning, they come up for air and I feel a sharp pang.

Then my attention is pulled to a sobbing child being speedily strolled by a woman who looks to be on her last nerve as she steers with her elbows while trying to get a straw in a soy-milk box.

Right.

I look down at the message light pulsing on my BlackBerry.

"Nan, Gene DeSanto, Friday—lunch period. Need you here a-sap. DEFCON four. Call my secretary, Janelle, back or just, uh— get here."

As soon as I can wrap up the software client's training I splurge on another cab ride to find out if Chassie's "sext" has finally shown up on YouTube. I stride into Gene's parlor just as he's ushering Sheila and Cliff into his office, his face ashen at whatever has necessitated the president and vice president of the board to drop work in the middle of the day. "You really didn't need to—"

"Please, Gene," Cliff scoffs as Gene guides Sheila by the elbow around the brass andirons.

"And with the benefit next Saturday," she adds. "We need this re-solved and buried."

"Can I help you?" Janelle asks, not looking up from the newspaper splayed across her leather blotter as I pass.

Gene spins to catch sight of me, one hand on the doorknob. "Oh, Nan, apologies. Can you sit tight?"

I stop short—"Of course"—and take a seat in a wing chair, decid-ing the transportation expense meter has officially started. I reach into my bag and pull out my new copy of "The Rime of the Ancient Mariner." Staring at the tight paragraphs of prose, I'm grateful, given his mother's situation, for the opportunity to support Grayer, if only as dramatic coach to the family.

Coleridge is just freething his speech from the bonds of thirst— which should come trippingly off Stilton's tongue—when Gene's door reopens. "See, Gene," Cliff says as he helps Sheila on with a white knit coat that matches her underlying dress. "This is not a cri-sis. It's just one individual reacting to information they shouldn't have had in the first place." The three share a nod of agreement before Sheila and Cliff walk out together.

Gene, the color having returned to his face, takes a deep breath and turns to me. "Can you hold one more sec?"

"Sure." I pause, my pencil skirt now hovering an inch above the chair. He leans his torso into his office and has a whispered conference with someone.

"Yes, yes, okay, excellent," he ends audibly before straightening. "Okay, then. Nan, come in." I stand and follow into his office. "You know my second in command?"

"I don't believe I do."

"Nan, this is Tim Hess, he's just gotten back from an educational conference in Beijing."

I turn to the tired-looking man seated on the couch by the door and grasp his hand as he half rises. "Nice to meet you."

"Espresso?"

"Thank you." I take a seat on the center sofa as Tim gets up to pour me a cup and refresh his own from a tiny steaming carafe on the sideboard.

"Thanks for coming down, Nan. And for your patience with us. We've had to do a little regrouping." The two share a smile. "But we now have a solution that the board feels great about. And we feel great about. And that is just—great," Gene informs me as he takes his seat behind the desk.

I nod, waiting to hear what the "this" is as I sip from the delicate demitasse, eager finally to pass my "road test" and start submitting sizable invoices against that retainer, so I can hire a new contractor who can show up and actually work, so I can sit on/eat off/soak in something not covered in volcanic volumes of toxic dust. Tim takes a seat, resting an argyle-socked ankle on his knee, fingers in a splayed prayer position.

"Thing is, there's a player on the team who, well, who ..." Suddenly Gene's mouth twists, his boyish cheer dissipating.

"Might not be on message," Tim intones, dropping his head to pinch the top of his nose.

I slide the cup and its saucer onto the leather top of the tortoise table somewhere near its rump, take my yellow pad from my bag, and twist open my pen.

"Someone . . ." Gene waves his hands over a model Parthenon decorating the corner of his desk. "In need of some guidance."

"Green around the ears," Tim adds, pushing his bifocals into his thick blond hair.

"And the board feels that were this situation to come to the parents' attention, they'd be reassured that we already brought you in to address it. We're addressing it. So Tim here just had the brain wave that you could . . . professionally develop Ingrid. The way Shari did with Calvin and some of the others."

I try not to seem stunned. "Your voice mail indicated this was a crisis. Has Ingrid been an issue for some time," I fish, "or is this a recent problem?"

"Ingrid's incendiary, plain and simple," Tim directs the comment to Gene as he stretches his fingers to their full extent in front of him.

"I'm striving to practice what I preach here, Nan. Jarndyce is about taking potential to its fullest. You can appreciate that," Gene reasons. "The students gave Ingrid rave reviews on her three-sixties. We'd like to make this work. We'd want you on this full-time. So, what do you think?"

"Well," Full-time? How could Ingrid possibly require full-time development? "I should mention that I have another client I'm working with at the moment, so I would need to—"

"The board's prepared to double your rate if you can put that project off."

"That's a generous offer, Gene." Screw Steve. Hello, Ty Pennington.

"Excellent!" He rounds his desk with an arm extended to me as Tim stands. "Positivity, Nan. *Can do,* as my dad used to say." He pats me on the back, simultaneously steering me toward the door. "It's in the Jarndyce DNA."

Moments later I spot Ingrid's office door just as she emerges, arms laden with books. "So they called in the cavalry, huh?"

"If by cavalry you mean me." I smile. "Do you have a few minutes to talk before the next bell?"

She glances up at the Nelson Ball Clock in the hallway. "If we can talk while I set up. I'm glad they called you. When Gene shunted me out of his office this morning I didn't exactly get the impression action was about to be taken."

I follow her across the corridor into her classroom, where she slides her texts on the long Danish midcentury table in front of the desk clusters. "So you know why I'm here?"

"I was the one who brought it to their attention."

"You were?" I rest my bag on the end of the table.

"Yeah, I told them *this* they can't ignore." She opens her notebook.

"Well, I have to say, Ingrid, I'm really impressed that you asked for support—that you identified this as an opportunity for growth."

"I can't do it myself. The school has to step in." She looks up from her neatly written notes.

"Effective escalation training is one of my—"

"Escalation? Why would we want to escalate their behavior?"

What? "Not the students. You. Wait." I squint, confused.

"Me?" Students pour through the door, volleying loud conversation as they slump into their chairs. *"Me?!"* she repeats.

"You thought this was about working with the kids? I'm so sorry, no, I'm supposed to be providing professional development for you."

She stares at me, struggling for words. "Is that how Gene described it?"

"It is actually. He—"

"Wow," she says quietly.

I twist my head, following her shifted gaze to Darwin, who strides in with his fingers pounding into his Sidekick. Actual human side-kicks wrestle around him, their testosterone scrum breaking apart over a cluster of seats in the rear. "I'm sorry for the confusion. I know you have to get started. I'll just sit in on this class and we'll get this all straightened out afterwards, okay?" I say, turning back to see she's gone the color of milk. "Ingrid?"

She drops her eyes to her fingertips, resting on her notes.

"This has nothing to do with your teaching, it's strictly school politics, I promise you."

"Class is starting," she calls out through me. "Everyone sit, now."

Great start, Nan. Really, you got a master's in this? Totally paying off. I sweep up my bag and get out of her way, sitting on the low bookshelves near the door. Chassie slips in right before the gong and slides into the desk beside me, cloying perfume invading my nostrils. I find myself dropping my eyes, the way one does when passing a celebrity or ranting schizophrenic. She's wearing lipstick now, in addition to the potent scent, and her stringy hair is aggressively flipped to one side.

Ingrid clears her throat and takes in the restless collection of students, ease evaporating. As she begins addressing the class she is stilted, tentative.

Scared.

Oh, God, I broke her.

Darwin snickers pointedly from behind his open laptop.

"Darwin, what are you writing?" Ingrid narrows her eyes at him.

"Same as everyone else." He flicks his wrist at the rest of the students' laptops—his jaw locked, his eyes flaring. *"Notes."*

"Notes about this lesson?" She steps out from behind the long table, her arms folding protectively in front of her.

"No-o," he says slowly.

"Then what? Why aren't you working on this lesson?"

Everyone looks from her to him and he seems to savor his time in responding, his voice taut. "I'm not working on the lesson . . . 'cause . . . you haven't started teaching it, *Miss* Wells."

A scattering of smirks break out, with varying degrees of sheepishness. But a handful of students roll their eyes at him and turn to their teacher, awaiting, along with me, for her to serve him a triumphant blow. Instead, she seems to shrink into herself as she shakingly takes up the electric stylus from the table and approaches the flat-screen board. As she starts writing, Darwin purses his lips, his nostrils flaring. "Well," he spits. "I guess that's that."

Ingrid clanks her stylus down and walks directly over—to me. "Can I see you outside?"

"Of course!" I quickly follow into the empty hall and wait for her to close the door. "Ingrid, I'm so sorry for the confusion. I'll leave you to teach and we can totally talk about this after school."

"After school I have a staff meeting to attend, Forensics Club to lead, sixty-two papers to grade, three tests to write, and a field trip to plan. Today . . . today is just not the . . ." She fidgets with the fraying cuff of her fitted oxford. "Today is shit. So with all due respect, can you just come another day or whatever because I really just . . . can't."

Before I get a word out, she's opened the door to the din of voices and closed it abruptly behind her, leaving me flanked by the daguerreotypes of historical figures in American finance lining the walls. My bag buzzes. My BlackBerry. I feel around my wallet and keys to grab it.

"The new Shari!" I swivel to see a bespeckled man strolling toward me, open leather satchel in his arms.

"Yes, hi, it's Nan."

"I'm Jeff, medieval lit."

"Jeff." I regroup as I see that I have two texts waiting. "How are you?"

"Better than Ingrid. Pretty f'ed up, don't you think?"

"Forgive me, what exactly are we talking about?" I ask as I open my messages to see they're from Grayer: CALL ME and WHERE R U

"The website. That's why you're here, right? They called the Hall of Justice back into action."

"For what? Jeff, what has *happened*?"

"Ah," he says with resignation. "Step into my office."

Still holding my BlackBerry, I lean over Jeff's shoulder as he boots up his computer and clicks onto the Web and then onto a social networking site, typing in "Ingrid Wells." The screen fills with a picture of Ingrid's face Photoshopped onto the body of a centerfold, implanted, shaved, and spread. My stomach drops as my eyes dart down a stream of vile accusations—statements that would make Rush Limbaugh crave sensitivity training. Fifty percent porn, fifty percent character assassination, cloaked in racist epithets, it's the last things you would want anyone to think about you, ever.

"Who *did* this?" I ask.

Jeff scrolls down the page to where the "Founding Member of the Ingrid Wells Sucks Big Black Cock Club" identifies himself. Oh.

"I found it this morning while doing my job of 'policing the cyber life' of our students. In a sick way you kind of have to admire the kid, he gets building a following."

Beneath Darwin's name is a list of boys who've pledged their allegiance, and at the bottom, as of ten minutes ago, Chassie.

"I don't understand, Gene said Ingrid's very popular."

"She was—is. But Darwin's suddenly taking her on and he has a lot of sway round these parts."

"This page was created right after the—Estée Lauder incident," I say, using Gene's preferred lexicon. I look to the date the "club" was founded. "And you told Ingrid . . ."

"Immediately. She was calm. She told Gene. He lost his shit."

"Which is why I'm here," I say through my fingers.

"You saw Ingrid that night. That's her thing—she wants the administration to address the issue at its source." He rolls his eyes. "Force them to hold up a mirror. Not gonna happen."

"Thanks, Jeff." I pull up my bag and make my way directly back to the *Little Foxes* film set that is Gene's office, where Janelle has me wait. I use the opportunity to call Grayer's number, only to get his voice mail. SORRY, I text him. BEEN N MTNGS, U OK?

WHATEVER, I get back a minute later.

GRAYER! DO U NEED ME OR NOT? No little red light. GRAYER? I text again.

But nothing. Between his come-here-go-away routine and sitting outside the principal's office, I'm starting to feel like a junior myself.

The minute his door opens, I stand as Gene strolls out with Tim, all smiles.

"Gene."

"Nan! How'd it go with Ingrid?"

"Great!" We both turn to see Ingrid in the doorway, her jacket and bag clutched to her chest. Tim makes a beeline to what I presume is his office on the other side of the fireplace.

"Gene." I turn back to him. "I really wish you'd told me about the website."

"And I wish you'd told me *I* was the problem," Ingrid says, her

mouth trembling. Oh God, please don't cry. There'll be no coming
back from this if you cry.

He scratches at the back of his neck. "Come on in, ladies."

I wait for Ingrid to pass and then follow her inside, where Gene
perches on the corner of his desk like he's about to expound on the
Poetics. "Have a seat."

"I'll stand." Ingrid clutches her jacket to her chest, looking unfortunately like a petulant teen. *Keep it together. Keep it together.*

"It's been a challenging day," I intervene. "Maybe Ingrid and I can
get coffee and catch our breath and we can all discuss this situation
later this afternoon?"

"I don't want coffee and I don't want professional development. I
want to know what the plan is. Gene, what're you doing about Darwin? You can't just ignore him like you did with Chassie. Because, I
don't even care for me. I can take it. But it's a cry for help, for boundaries. *Boundaries*, Gene—*this* is why we don't reward kids for doing
crap work. He needs a talking-to. His parents need a talking-to. His
parents need to be talking *to him*." Tears start to roll down her cheeks.
"He's making it . . . impossible . . . to teach him. Is that what you
want?" She rakes her sweater sleeve across her eyes.

Gene leans so far back he's almost parallel with his desk, as if her
tears might jump across the room and burn his khakis. "Ingrid, listen
to yourself. *I. I. I.* This is not all about *you,* okay? The board is very
concerned about what you may have done to incite such—"

"Fuck the board." She drops her head back. "I'm talking about our
responsibility."

"You see what I'm up against?" Gene says to me.

"Great!" Ingrid looks accusingly at me. "Great, no, that's just—
great. Thanks for the support." She swings a fist up in mock cheer.
"I'm gonna go get ready for my next class and then I guess I'll see
you all Monday for another great day of can-do." And with that she
leaves.

"Fucking impossible," Gene mutters.

My hand vibrates. ST VINCENTS CANCER CENTER 16TH N 9TH.

119

10

"I'm looking for a Mrs. X?" I ask between huffs as I lean over the treatment center welcome desk and attempt to catch my breath after the half-block sprint from Jarndyce.

"One moment, I'll check the list." The guard in the suit and tie smiles pleasantly as he runs his finger down the stack of printouts in front of him. "Do you know which doctor she's seeing?"

"I—I don't. She has breast cancer ..."

He smiles encouragingly.

"Her son, Grayer—sixteen? Tall, blond? He texted me about ten minutes ago that he was here." I bite my lower lip.

"He's meeting Dr. Rosen in the library." Another guard, having ended his phone call, stands to point me past the interior sliding glass doors. "Around the corner and down the hall."

"Thank you! Thank you so much!" I scurry inside and down the bright skylit hall, glancing in each door I pass. Reception. Lab. They're in the library? I jerk to a stop as I arrive at a set of double doors that open onto a tranquil room lined with bookcases. But the armchairs, the tables—are empty. I lean back out and strain to look down the hall—the heart-wrenching sight of two gaunt patients in wheel-chairs, a bald woman doing a crossword, but no sign of the Xes. I step back inside and over to one of the tables, where, in a low pool of lamplight, medical books are sundered around a notebook covered in jerking scrawl.

Sniff.

I whip around. In the corner, one of the club chairs has been turned to face the wall. Over the high backrest I see a hooded sweat-shirt pulled over a bent head. I glance back at the notebook and then down under the table at the collapsed messenger bag inked with its familiar graffiti. "Grayer?"

He clears his throat but makes no move to turn to me.

"I'm so sorry. I was stuck in a meeting. I came as soon as I—"

The sweatshirt hood nods haltingly up and down.

"Where's your mom? Is she okay?"

"Home and no."

"Grayer, I'm so sorry." I pull up a chair and sit behind him, dropping my bag between my feet. "What exactly do you know?"

"What the fuck do *you* know?" His voice is hoarse. Angry.

I exhale. "Well, I know that your mom has breast cancer, but that she's working with doctors to get the care she needs."

His shoulders lift in a short, blunt laugh. "The care she needs," he repeats.

"That's funny?" I ask gently.

"Hilarious."

"Okay . . ."

He clears his throat again. "Just go."

"You texted me. I don't want to just go. You're upset. Understandably. This is *huge* information to try to make sense of, Grayer. You shouldn't have to do this alone. I can . . . I can . . ."

"Yeah?" He angles his head to me, revealing only the profile of his nose.

"I can find out who her doctors are and we can make an appointment with them. And I'll go with you and we can get every question you have answered—"

"Like, is she going to die?" He turns away again.

I peer at the back of his head. "Yes, like that."

"'Cause it doesn't say there." His pointer finger, protruding from the sleeve pulled to his knuckles, jabs toward the pulled periodicals. "And it's not online. And my friend's dad, who's a surgeon here, canceled on me. And she, she won't tell me who her doctors are, so good luck with that, because she doesn't want to *upset* me more—" His voice breaks, his hand clamping in front of his face. "I can't do this to Stilton—tell him—without having all the information. He won't be able to take it. He still needs her, depends on her. I can't . . ."

I reach my palm out to his shoulder and he drops forward at my touch, his hood grazing his knees as his shoulder lifts and falls, his covered head sinking into his splayed fingers. "You shouldn't be alone with this. Let me help you."

He takes a long breath in, pulling himself together. "I have to get home to my brother."

"I'll go with you."

"Thanks, but no." He tugs forward and away from me to stand. "I've got it under control."

"You sure?" I ask his broad back.

He wipes at his nose with his sleeve. "I just said so, didn't I?" Hood still obscuring his face, he crosses to the table to gather up his things.

"Well." I stand, unsure of my next move, unsure what he'd even accept from me. "I'm glad you texted."

"Right," he spits, dropping the notebook in his bag and jerking the zipper closed. "So you could not come."

"Hey. I'm here." My voice hardens. "You may not remember what here looks like, but it's this—a grown-up, standing in front of you and offering to help you figure out what you need next, even when she can't see your goddamned face."

He twists; the eyes finally meeting mine are round, shocked. I hold my breath, ashamed I'm calling him on his shit in St. Vincent's Comprehensive Cancer Center.

He lifts off his hood, sheepishly revealing the splotches on his cheeks.

I nod softly in acknowledgment of the gesture.

He slings his backpack onto one shoulder. "You can buy me a Red Bull."

"What?"

"Since you're here. I used the last of my cash on the cab down."

"Okay . . ."

"I mean, that's what I need next."

"Okay." I pick up my bag.

"Okay." He walks with me out into the hall and to the sliding glass doors.

"But I'm buying you coffee." I wave thanks to the guard as we pass. "Red Bull will put you in an early grave."

We step out into the brisk air and he breaks into a grin as we approach the coffee cart on the corner. "Nice." He cracks up as I realize what I've said.

"Oh God, I meant—"

"Really, you *gotta* loosen up." He shakes his head, still grinning as he orders, and I pass him a dollar.

"Thanks," I say sarcastically.

"Yeah, thanks," he says so quietly I think I may have imagined it. Before I can respond, his hood is flipped up and, coffee in hand, he jogs away down the subway stairs.

That evening I exit the train into the sprawling Columbia-Presbyterian medical complex and spot the green neon shamrock from two desolate blocks away. When I push open the bar door, Sarah is tucked into the first red Naugahyde booth, already halfway through a pint and a cheeseburger. She looks up with a smile that matches those of the 1973 soccer champions in the faded photo above her shoulder. "I'm *so* glad you called."

"I can't believe you're free. I thought you might have a hot Friday night date."

She shakes her head. "From eight to twelve. Then I have to go back."

"You're kidding." I slide into the booth, riding the ridge between the two permanent butt indentations.

"I was going to sleep. But this is better." She pushes up the sleeve of the waffle Henley that buffers her from her scrubs.

"I can't believe you can drink and go back to work."

"I can have *one* beer." She holds up a grease-tipped finger. "At eight o'clock, which will be fully metabolized by midnight, when I will have a double espresso."

I shake my head, in awe of her stamina. "What you guys do to your bodies in the pursuit of healing others—"

"The irony is not lost on me. So what's up?" She takes a hearty bite as I knit my fingers on the tabletop.

"What can you tell me about breast cancer?"

She slumps forward dramatically across her plate.

"Please?"

"Nothing." She straightens up, mustard on her scrubs. "I can tell you nothing about cancer from eight to midnight. Let me tell you about Brad and Angelina going for a bi-gendered quorum or about the geriatric specialist with the nice hands and infinite patience who texted me 'had a *nice* time Friday.' What does that mean? Nice, like bridge with your nana? Or nice, like, *niiiice.* I can't respond until I know what he means."

"You can decipher five words?"

"You have a lot of time to nurture your inner life while administering an enema."

"So, breast cancer," I steer her back.

"Yee-eee-ees," she concedes in multiple syllables, addressing the fireproof tiles, dropping her shoulders, giving in to me. "Wait." She flags the waitress over. "I changed my mind. Can I get some cheese fries? You want anything?"

"Burger and a glass of whatever she's having, please."

The waitress nods her sprayed gumball-red hair and takes away the oily menus.

Sarah sips her beer. "You know you can look all this up on the Internets."

"Not alone in that house. At the bottom of every site, if you scroll down, it says, 'Nan Hutchinson, the air you are breathing will give you and your dog polyps and black lung.'"

"Who is it?" Sarah asks.

"Grayer's mom."

"Yeesh." She winces. "That poor kid."

"I know. And he has the task of telling his seven-year-old brother. That's why I'd love some information."

The waitress drops a Velveeta-drenched plate of skinny fries with a clatter. "Shoot," Sarah prompts, digging in.

"Okay, so, I'm getting this all in oblique half references, mind you, but it sounds like she's having a lumpectomy and then a round of chemo."

"Okay, lumpectomy is a good sign. They didn't need to do anything radical. So we can assume the lymph nodes are unaffected. Then it's all about rate of recurrence. The sooner it comes back the worse the prognosis. And then there's metastasis. Breast goes brain."

"I think that's what he must have read at the library."

"Grayer?"

I nod.

"And keep him offline. There are ten million sites that are just designed to terrify. If he wants some virtual support send him the link for standup2cancer.org." She draws the 2 in the air with her greasy finger.

"Thank you. I think virtual support would be . . . about all the support he's getting. I just . . ." I take a deep breath, the image returning of his hunched figure descending into the subway. "When he was little he had horrible nightmares and I could soothe him. Now he's afraid of something crazy real and I don't know how to help."

She reaches across and squeezes my hand, leaving a smear of ketchup on my wrist. "*This* is helping. I see it every day—the people who get the flowers and cards, even if their family is far away—you can feel the love coming at them from all sides. Being there any way you can helps. Grayer will feel this, I promise."

"Thank you. Okay—moving on." I wipe at the Heinz stripe with a napkin.

"How's Ryan? Have you had a *bébé* yet?"

"My husband is single-handedly solving the world grain shortage from an undisclosed location with spotty cell service and monitored e-mail. But my dog hasn't fallen through anything this week, so that's a plus. Oh, and an overzealous electrician magically showed up—mine is not to question—and now I have disturbing gouges running up every wall, including dangerously close to my brand-new steps."

"So the tap-dance studio you were planning to open on the top floor may have to be put on hold?"

"Did I tell you my parents may get evicted?"

"Shut. Up."

"But that's okay, because they'll just move in with me! And Mom can run the tap-dance studio, while I'm working for a paycheck to hand over to our nanny and my husband is halfway around the world having a nicer day just knowing his child exists." I take a clump of fries, succumbing to their gooey power.

"Okay," Sarah says, wiping off her fingers before pulling out her red ponytail elastic and slipping it on her wrist like a Kabbalah string. "First of all, at least you have a husband. I have a text message and chlamydia, but not from the same guy. You own your own home. I'm going to be in my little cement-bricked cell until I'm done with my residency."

"Chlamydia?"

"Yeah, it's not a big deal. I mean I work in the birthplace of anti-biotics. It's just gross. I mean, it'd been fourteen months since I'd had sex and *this* has not incentivised me to make more time for a personal life."

"Sarah, I'm so sorry."

"Yeah." She takes another bite of her burger as the jukebox flips from "Angel of Harlem" to "One." I rack my brain for anything else from my boring life I can offer on the same scale of intimacy that won't just further underscore how married I am. "Citrine's pregnant."

"You're still hanging out with her?" she asks incredulously.

"She's nice. And she reads a lot."

"Nan, she used to throw lit matches at us."

"That was Alex."

"Guilt by association. They were mean bitches then. They're mean bitches now. What?" She takes in my scrunched face.

"I don't know . . . it's just . . ."

"Yes?"

"If their childhoods were anything like Grayer's, I get why those girls were so angry. They didn't have the things we had. Like bedtime stories and . . . attention. I feel sorry for them."

"Well, I don't." She wads her napkin and throws it on the leftover slice of iceberg lettuce sitting on her plate. "I feel sorry for the preg-nant mother in the auto accident whose leg I saw amputated this morning. I feel sorry for the guy whose AIDS test came back positive. I don't feel sorry for the spoiled-brat brigade."

"Sarah."

"What?"

"You're punchy."

She smiles. "Sorry. Sorry. I'm sorry. I am suffering from too much perspective. Right now anything short of code blue feels like a day at the beach wrapped in cotton candy dipped in kittens. I promise after my residency is over I'll be drowning in sympathy for Citrine and Tatiana. Who knows? I might even be their dermatologist."

"Or ob-gyn."

"Or cardiologist. If they have hearts."

"But you could be in Omaha by then," I say, feeling a pang at the thought of losing this proximity again.

"I might," she concedes. "But I'll be back. After my fellowship." She drains her beer. "It's New York. Everyone comes back. Look at you."

11

As the elevator rises Monday afternoon I shiver, drenched from the downpour lashing the sidewalk as the deluge of April soaks into May. I secure my umbrella and play through, if being home with his mom is just too sad for Stilton, maybe Citrine might let us hole up in her place. Or I could take him for frozen hot chocolate. Is Serendipity still serving that crack? There's always one of the five billion Dunkin' Donuts. At the very least I should have had something sugary and comforting delivered over the weekend, instead of just willing Grayer's discussion with Stilton about his mother's health to go bearably from forty blocks away.

The elevator stops as I pull the deli daffodils from the tote just used to transport Grandma's armor back to its rightful owner, feeling a modest degree of accomplishment that I am now comfortable wearing my own clothes to this apartment. So there's that. The door rolls open and . . . nowhere to go.

The entire vestibule floor is lined with open umbrellas in a patchwork of Burberry tartans and Aquascutum earth tones. I take a few shuffling paces in, upending the domes onto their tops, dripping water onto the marble. I trip as I try to steady myself on the slick stone.

"Nan-neh!" Stilton slip-slides into sock-footed view—good sign. "Happy Cinco de Mayo. We had tacos at school."

"Hola! How are you?"

" 'Day after day, day after day'." He drops his voice and his chin and his head. " 'We stuck, nor breath nor motion;/As idle as a painted ship/Upon a painted ocean.' You're making a ruckus."

"Sorry," I apologize, trying to clear the knee-height designer debris from my path. "Whose are all these?"

"The ladies'. Can I take your coat? The closet's full. I'll put it in Rosa's old room—Mom says I have to stop calling it that," he catches himself, his palm flying to his forehead.

"That's okay. Thank you, sir." I pass off the daffodils and bend to add my umbrella to the others.

"Rosa's gone. She's a deeply selfish woman with no sense of loyalty," he sums up her tenure, just as Grayer also once parroted his mother when describing my predecessor. "What're these?" he asks.

"Flowers."

"Oh." He peers down the heart-paper funnel. "I'll put these in there, too." He holds out a hand and I unbutton my raincoat, hearing a wave of laughter from inside the apartment.

"Is Grayer home?" Folding the wet side in, I pass it to him and he drapes it over his arm.

"Not yet."

"So . . . how are you guys doing?" I ask, stepping out of my Kermit green rubber boots and placing them out of the way to dry. I slip my work flats out of the tote, knowing full well what Mrs. X would make of catching me barefoot in her home.

"Nan? Is that you?" she calls from the living room, her voice more diminished than it was on the phone. "You got my message—so good of you to come."

Stilton slip-slides away into the kitchen and I round the vestibule corner and see, through the open gallery archway to the living room, women in their midfifties sitting on every tasseled cushion, perched on every wrapped arm. Even the extra dining chairs decoratively astride the mantel are filled. And what women. A glance places them as having grown up a stone's throw from this room; or, like their hostess, having impeccably absorbed the native mores. Delicate, lined faces sit in contrast to solid hands, strengthened and weathered from years of dressage, tennis, and gardening. And even if their faces and hands were obscured, I would know them from the day's uniform: sixteen pairs of wellies, sixteen pairs of riding pants, sixteen Anne Fontaine blouses, sixteen ponytails—expensive, impeccable, and a tad boring in their restrictiveness. Is there a blue-blood bat signal that goes up? A dollar-sign silhouette projected against the cloudy sky?

And on every flat surface sits a get-well bouquet, one more elaborate and out of season than the next. Thank you, Stilton, for hiding the deli flowers that were for your heretofore neglected mother.

Mrs. X extends her French cotton–encased arm. "This is our dear, dear family friend, Nan Hutchinson, Dorothy's daughter-in-law," she says, addressing the assembled. "She has been a godsend helping Stilton with his performance. I hate not doing it myself, but—"

"You don't have the strength," the nearest ponytail chimes in, fussing with the thick brown and cream H blanket draped over Mrs. X's legs. "And not another word about going for chemo alone. I will be by your side for every treatment." The sentiment is echoed around the room.

"Oh, no, I won't hear of bothering you." Mrs. X seems flustered by the outpouring of affection. "Nan is here and I—I can manage."

"Now, I respect you not wanting us to speak ill of the boys' father," one of the women says as she leans over to a side table and picks up a dried citrus rind that has escaped the confines of its potpourri bowl. "And I know his fund's been very good to us all. But, I'm sorry, he's being an asshole."

"Buying Carter Nelson that emerald necklace at Christie's was just tasteless."

"Have you called John Vassallo yet? He'll get you thirty percent above the prenup, guaranteed."

Mrs. X looks at her concerned friends, who momentarily have the rapacious air of spectators at a cage match. "I've been so . . . tired. But no, no, you're right. I should call someone." She hasn't unleashed the hounds? What's she waiting for? His money to ripen?

"Well, it was a pleasure to meet you all," I say, giving an encompassing wave. "I'm just going to start with Stilton." I back out and cross to the kitchen, where Stilton is standing at the counter, double-fisting from a cookie platter. From the all-you-can-eat cookie buffet. Every peach granite surface is covered in cellophane-wrapped, doily-covered foil platters of biscuits, crumpets, muffins, and scones, both chocolate-dipped and naked. Scratch the Dunkin' Donuts delivery.

"Take it easy, there, kid, I don't want you crashing before the fourth stanza." I drop my tote on the counter.

"Grayer makes me cookies on Saturdays," he says through a full mouth, spraying crumbs as he points to the jar by the sink. "From a mix. Now we have real cookies and people over and Mom wears clothes."

"I'm glad things are going . . . well." I look down at him as he swallows. "And you're doing okay?"

" 'Water, water, everywhere.' " He spins away, canting. I walk quickly behind him through the dining room, where it's impossible not to get a mental flash of Ms. Chicago and her place cards. " 'And all the boards did shrink;/Water, water, everywhere;/Nor any drop to drink.' "

"So how does this benefit roll out exactly?" I ask as we arrive in his room.

Stilton takes off his school tie and carefully wheels it up into a coil. "Each school sends three kids to perform, lower, middle, upper. It's supposed to be based on grades and good behavior and stuff, but last year everyone knows Liesle Greenborough only got in because her mom hosts that talk show. She forgot the lyrics three times and then just stood there and giggled while the song finished. It takes a real pro to do Gilbert and Sullivan. You can't send in just anyone. That's what everyone said." He places his tie wheel on his desk and hands me his copy of the poem.

I sit down on his Gordon tartan bedspread and look at the picture of Ruth Bader Ginsburg pinned to his bulletin board. "So, the Supreme Court?"

"They take care of the Constitution. I'm more into the Food Network, but Grayer thought the court thing sounded better." He swivels his bedside lamp so I can see the picture of Padma Lakshmi taped to the brass shade. "My parents were gonna take me for dinner at Perilla last year for my birthday so I could meet Harold Dieterle."

"Wow, that's so cool. I love *Top Chef*—I watched it online in Sweden."

He shrugs. "Zagat hadn't rated it yet and they didn't want to go downtown." He pulls out from under his desk an old bathroom stool hand-painted with his name buoyed by balloons and hops atop, holding his arms out like Socrates. " 'He prayeth best, who loveth best/All things both great and small;/For the dear God who loveth us,/He made and loveth all.' Should I be praying for my mom?" he asks without pause.

"Oh."

He looks at me with sudden intensity.

"Well, praying for people is never bad," I say carefully.

"Because when the ladies leave, they've been telling me to pray for her."

"What does Grayer say?" I ask.

"He says Mom can take care of herself and praying isn't going to make Dad come back."

That's why you want to know—the departure, not the disease. "I see . . . Well, it's always a good thing to send people we care about happy thoughts."

"I asked my dad to come."

"Oh?"

"To the benefit. Grayer said it's really gonna help. I called Gillian and she said she'll do her best."

"Who's Gillian?"

"Dad's assistant. She only wears black. She's scared of swans."

"Well, that's great! I'm sure he'll be there." Given that his girlfriend is chairing it.

"Mom says he's a very disappointing person. 'It is an ancient mariner/And he stoppeth one of three.' " And we're off. Seven straight stanzas without stopping. Then, raising his arm, Stilton twirls his hand at the wrist and bows.

I leap off the bed, applauding and whooping. "That was amazing! Can't we cut it there? Do you have to do the whole thing?"

"Mom says all of Part One. I have a week. And *Throwdown* is in reruns."

So I sit back down and we plod forward, Stilton alternately lying on the floor or bouncing and slapping at his cheeks as he tries to remember. He is alarmingly determined, seemingly holding himself

to a standard of perfection as a solution to the situation as he understands it.

The unmelodic bleat of the back doorbell sounds and Stilton leaps
from his stool and flies into the hall, shouting, *"I've got it, Mom! Don't
get up!"* as he passes through the dining room. I follow, eager to snag
a buttery palmier to fuel me through the remaining thirteen stanzas.

I arrive to find Stilton trying to tug a cellophane-wrapped tray of
tea sandwiches from a man's hands in the doorway.

"Stilton, heel!" Stilton releases his grip. "Sorry, can I help you?"

"Yeah. *This* is a gift. But the three sandwich platters I dropped off
this morning weren't. Her credit card was declined," the man says
with a thick Brooklyn accent, his baseball jacket dripping from the
rain. "And my instructions were not to leave without payment."

"Stilton, why don't you go work on the mariner's arrival and I'll
be right there." I take the tray from him and slide it on the last free
bit of granite real estate. "How much?" I ask after Stilton's cleared the
doorway, figuring I'll pass a note to Mrs. X.

"Including today, three thousand."

"For tea sandwiches?" I lower my voice. "There has to be a billing
mix-up. Sir, she's having a party right now, but she can call you
when her guests leave. She's not well. I'm sure your boss will understand."

"My boss is paying twice as much for eggs, bread, milk, and gas as
he was a year ago. I am freezing and soaking because we no longer
use the van for local deliveries. So I'm sure my *boss* will not give a
shit." He pushes his finger into the buzzer, sending an ear-grating
squawk through the apartment.

"Nan? *Nan?*" I hear her approaching call.

"Sir. *Please.*"

Mrs. X rounds the corner and he releases the bell. "*What* seems to
be the problem?" She crosses her arms, her pale hands disappearing
against the white fabric.

"Your cards were declined," he says loudly. "I need cash."

She rushes toward him, her voice hushed. "Well, I don't have any
in the house. And I'd appreciate if you were mindful of the fact that I
have guests in the other room."

"You gotta give me something." He moves his finger threateningly to the buzzer.

"Wait." She spins, wide-eyed, the bevy of trays catching her attention. "All right. Since your beautiful store seems to be everyone's first choice for gifts, moving forward, your boss can pocket each as a credit against my debt."

He thinks for a moment. "What if the gifts stop?"

"They won't." She summons her full Mrs. X–ness and steps closer so that he has no choice but to back out into the landing. "I am very sick. My friends are very concerned."

"Lady, I can't leave empty-handed."

She purses her lips, turning to open a nearby cabinet door and pulling out six thick crystal tumblers. "Nan, there's a drawer of paper bags next to the sink."

I find them and hand her one, which she fills with the glasses, her face flushing furiously. "These are Fabergé and cost five hundred each. Tell him he can hold these as collateral. I will be seeing my husband this Saturday. I will be in on Sunday morning with the cash. Your employer is not to pawn these, understand?" She shoves the bag into his chest and slams the door before he can answer.

I reach for a palmier and place it into my mouth, so as to have something to do while she runs a shaking hand over her hair and takes a bracing breath. "This is funny to you, isn't it?"

"Not at all," I mumble truthfully through a dry mouth of cookie.

She fingers her collar. "I just need to see my husband so we can get this straightened out."

I swallow, guessing the fire sale of gold didn't go far. "Of course."

"He's been extremely busy."

"Yes. Or perhaps that lawyer your friend mentioned could do it for you?"

"No, I'm not calling a lawyer. It's not just your possessions they itemize, but every decision you've made. I'm not handing over the life we built for scrutiny."

"No, of course," I say, having no idea what I'm validating. We both pivot to where the doorknob is turning again. "What now?"

It swings open with Grayer attached, head tucked. The sweet aroma hits me before he's even set foot in the kitchen.

"Oh, Grayer," his mother mutters with annoyance. He gives a cursory wave, eyes on the floor. "*Why* can't you use the front door?" Fingers again working a Sidekick, Darwin strolls in behind him. "Darwin!" She perks up, her game face returning. "Hello! How's your mother?"

"Recovering from the Palm Beach Easter festivities. Such a treat to see you, Mrs. X. You're looking lovely as always." He is all charm. Charm and bloodshot eyes.

She blushes and fluffs herself at his attention. "How your mother can leave such a delightful son to live all the way down there I'll never understand."

"It's Dad's congressional district—gotta press the local flesh, right?" He sounds like a politician himself.

"Of course," she demurs. "Well, if you ever get lonely rattling around that big old apartment all by yourself, we're happy to have you anytime, you know that. Come in and say hello to my friends?" she coquettishly entreats over her shoulder as she returns to the living room.

The moment she's out of sight, Grayer leans back against the refrigerator, dropping his head to his chest. "You're such a fucking kiss-ass."

"Fuck you, douche." Darwin peels back cellophane; he cups one hand to his damp blazer and uses the other to plunder cookies.

Grayer lifts his head, focusing in on me. "You're here."

"You're high."

He smiles, eyes slit.

"Well, now that we've got that sorted." Darwin heads for the living room and a round of coos go up to greet him.

"You two are still friends?" I ask.

"Looks that way." Grayer steps forward, gripping the granite to stare down at the platters.

"You know he's started this shitty site against a really good teacher?"

"Yeah. But how do you?"

"It's on the web. The world can know about it."

"If anyone cared." He picks up a cookie and snaps it in two before returning both halves to the tray. "Can we not talk about this? I'm sure Stilton's waiting for you."

"Actually I was hoping to grab you. He seems pretty tuned in that something's wrong, Grayer. Maybe it would be better for him to just know?"

He looks over at me. "Not until my dad calls and tells me what the plan is. You just work on that poem and make sure Stilton is ready to charm his fucking socks off." And with that he leaves.

12

The next morning, realizing I'm mumbling the wretched "Rime of the Ancient Mariner" under my breath, I spot Ingrid approaching under cover of her striped umbrella and wave from the dry security of my own. "Hey!"

She straddles a large puddle to join me in the doorway of La Perla. "Hi."

"Sorry, I could've sworn this was a diner last time I was over here, but that was an embarrassingly long time ago and I think, actually, a few blocks south."

"It's fine!" Her tone is cheerful, her eyes are not.

"There's the Little Pie Company a few stores down, but it's probably early for that."

"It's fine," she repeats as she jumps back across the puddle, and we scurry through the rain and into the bakery, where the warm, sweet air saturates our damp clothes.

She turns to me as we shed our wet coats and hang them on the under-counter hooks. "I'm really mortified by what a mess I was in Gene's office on Friday. I just wanted to tell you in person I don't strive for that."

"Trust me, Ingrid, we've all been there." I take in the black suit she's chosen in exchange for her usual trapeze sweaters and corduroys. I'm sure, with this choice of armor, she was aiming for professional, but the effect is severe. Given how caustic she appeared, I would have advised going for sweet and disarming—a baby bunny costume, perhaps. "I just want to reiterate I'm really sorry for any role I played in the confusion."

"Thanks." She smiles back, again from a distance, as she climbs on her stool and clasps her hands on the Formica. I glance over the menu in the challenged search of an item that won't leave me in a sugar coma for this afternoon's rehearsal with Stilton. "How'd it go yesterday?"

"Good. Weird. In U.S. history they're presenting their midterm research projects, so I can just sit in the back and listen. In homeroom the kids were really quiet . . . I think. I can't tell what's my own paranoia." She fidgets with the edge of her menu. "I had to have my fiancé disconnect our Internet on Friday night so I couldn't keep checking which students were joining the club."

"It's still up?" I ask, shocked.

"I talked to a lawyer friend this weekend, showed him the site. He said it's fully actionable. But Gene's still fact-finding," she says acidly. "Testing the waters, taking temperatures. Yesterday he threw around just about every cute metaphor to mask inaction you can think of."

"Well, I guess it's complicated."

"It shouldn't be," she levels back.

"Of course, you're right." I blush. "Completely right. In my day they'd have been expelled so fast they'd already be enrolled at one of those schools that advertise in the back of *The New Yorker.*"

"It's *insane.* We're teaching these kids that the rules don't apply to them, that exception is their birthright. That's *exactly* who I want ten years from now running my bank, editing my news, deciding on my health care for real." She pauses and looks down at her menu, tucking a swoop of bangs over one ear. "Sorry, sorry."

"Ingrid." I lower her menu. "You're in a shitty, shitty situation. I've been in shitty, shitty situations. Situations that seemed—that probably were—impossible to navigate without getting scraped up, at *best.* I just . . . don't want you to have to do this alone. I know you're required to train with me now, but let's try to see this as an opportunity. I have Gene's ear and I really want this to work out for you. And for the students you teach."

An electronic rendition of "Ride of the Valkyries" pipes up from her coat.

"Sorry, that's the school." She roots around in the folds and withdraws her cell from the coat pocket. "Hello?" She listens for a moment. "It's Jeff. Four more sites posted last night." Her eyes go wide. "Targeting four other teachers," she says to me. "And he's one of them."

By the end of the day, the waiting room outside Gene's office is getting a workout that would do its decorator proud, with students slouched on every tufted surface. Deprived of their phones, they resort to telegraphing with jerks of brows and slants of eyes, a silent symphony of expression as fourteen faces await their turn, all guilty of founding membership to inflamatory, frequently grammatically incorrect, and—as Ingrid wants to force them to confront—litigable pages on social networking sites.

I step between their long legs to Janelle, whose patience is wearing thin, both with me and the crisis that has kept her besieged well after hours. "Hi again! Any chance you can get me a quick five minutes with Gene between trials so I can advise the teachers and they can head home?"

Her face is impassive. "If they stop sending kids in here, we can all go home."

"I'm sorry, I know you must be so ready to get out of here, too."

"My sister is watching my daughter. She has to leave for work in an hour. It takes me that long to get back to the Bronx and another twenty minutes to walk to her apartment from the train. So, yes. You could say I was ready."

"That's asinine!" Grant booms from behind Tim's office door, jerking everyone's attention to where he's commandeering a meeting of flustered parents and trustees.

"I'm so sorry." I turn back to Janelle. "Maybe I could have one of the teachers man your desk?"

"Gene won't go for that." She picks up her red cell with a faded Chiquita banana sticker on it and checks the time again, sighing. "Look, your best bet is to wait and grab him next time he breaks."

"Thanks." I drum my fingers on my hips, gauging how long I can leave the teachers festering in the library before they return to catastrophizing what is, to their credit, a catastrophe.

The door to Gene's office opens and he emerges, resting his hands on his braided leather belt, having discarded his blazer hours ago. Tim comes out behind him, looking pained. "Okay." Tim clears his throat. "Here's what's happening. Next up the Homos Love Phelps's Tight Sphincter Club followed by Mrs. Twill Teabags Nazis."

But as the kids start to stand, Cliff Ashburn returns from the hall, slipping his BlackBerry back in his pocket. He crosses through their mess of long legs to rap on Tim's office door. Grant opens it, but Cliff is already walking away past the mantel. "Why doesn't everyone come into Gene's office," he says loudly enough to carry, "and they can resume dealing with the kids after we've left." The students stare as their parents shuffle, like livestock in a shoot, from Tim's office into Gene's. Last one to slip in, I shut the door.

"We have some questions." A woman outfitted in an array of patterned Tory Burch, from T-tipped toe to T-topped head, steps forward.

Gene looks to Cliff and Cliff holds out a palm for him to answer. "Absolutely, shoot." Gene takes his place in front of his desk, rubbing his hands together.

"How will this incident be addressed on our children's transcripts?" she asks.

"Well, let's see . . . cited as a suspension for an ethics violation, I guess."

"What ethic has been violated?" Another woman steps forward. "My child is *not* applying to colleges next year with a suspension on his applications."

"That's not what fifty thousand a year in tuition and donations adds up to, Gene," a father states, loosening his tie.

"I can't only take down the web pages," Gene says plaintively. "They'll just continue to proliferate and we'll all be back here in a week—"

"What about the *school's* ethics violation?" Grant demands.

"What about my child's privacy?" T-patterned woman continues with growing outrage. "What about *their* right to express themselves? What about the fact that your staff read what's considered someone's *diary*?"

"It's inappropriate. It's outrageous." A mother holds her hand to the elaborately beaded glass and wire necklace tied at her throat.

"Well . . ." Gene sucks in his lips. "We did tell them that they were accountable for the students' virtual lives . . ."

"A metaphor!" Grant scoffs. "We didn't mean *literally*. We meant they should have a handle on things."

"I think"—I step forward from where I've been leaning against the door—"that intention might have been obscured by Mr. Two-mey's step-by-step technical instruction. The teachers were definitely under the impression that this was their mandate." I strive for the tone of a well-rested stewardess.

Cliff clears his throat. "Well, the faculty are off the sites as of now. Off-limits. There, done." He tugs at the points of his French cuffs, posing the question: If a kid pulls down his pants in the virtual woods and no one's there to see it . . . can he still get into Harvard?

Sheila crosses her arms. "The larger crisis at hand is what we plan to do about the spin."

"The spin?" Gene squints as he scratches at the five o'clock shadow peeking out around his chin.

"Yes. These kids have friends, siblings, and half siblings at other schools. You just need one kid to tell their parent and word will spread. As we just decided, we're not going into the benefit this Saturday with fifteen students suspended. It makes our student body seem—uncouth. We have to be proactive about putting this story into the community or it will bite our reputation in the ass."

Everyone looks wildly at one another. Not the ass!

Although, as I well know, having attended one of these schools myself—albeit at a time when the tuition was such that my class-mates' parents included a librarian, an artist, two nurses, and one dance teacher—these parents see the aforementioned fifty thousand as an investment in the brand their children will be wearing for life, trotted out at every job interview and cocktail party; it will buy them entrée into colleges, clubs, and gated communities. For the reputation of the school to suffer, it would be as if they walked out of Bergdorf's with their ten-thousand-dollar bags dangling off their elbows, only to find them being sold on the street for twenty bucks.

"First thing tomorrow morning Gene and I will sit down with the Alumni Relations Department. And to that end I'd like to propose that perhaps we've misread the situation altogether." Sheila sits down on the couch, exchanging a glance with Cliff as she talks, picking off a stray piece of dust from the calf of her black cigarette pants. "I think, as we identified Friday, this is the work of one teacher. One teacher who was teaching too experimentally and the lines of appropriate discussion got blurred. Our children were . . . confused."

"Sorry?" I ask. "I think now I'm confused."

"Yes, Ingrid Wells should explain herself," Cliff echoes, breezing past my query.

"In the school paper," Sheila says slowly, decisively. "We'll do a special edition that comes out tomorrow. Parents will read it. Discuss it with their friends who have children at the other schools. By Saturday night, it will have framed the conversation in the community."

Gene looks to me and I shake my head no. He fumbles. "I see where you're coming from, Sheila . . . Ingrid is . . . I don't know that she'll be amenable to—"

"This is our name. We risk impacting our capital campaign," Cliff states simply.

"Our *helipad*." Necklace Mother shakes her head in horror at the prospect.

"Or our headmaster's apartment," Grant says, bringing it home. "That would be a shame."

"I have to *what*?" Ingrid asks me for the third time in as many minutes.

I look out at the drawn faces of the teachers, sitting in the illogically mood-lit periphery of the student library on a smattering of cowhide beanbags. Knees forced to their chins, they stare at me from the shadows, their eyes glowing like mice. I crouch so as not to be towering. "Write a letter for the student newspaper explaining how the lines of appropriate discussion were blurred in your classroom— they're bringing in the editors as we speak—so they can print a special edition for tomorrow to circulate before the benefit."

While Ingrid parses this out, an older woman with a steel gray man's haircut sighs heavily and attempts to cross her loafers, only sinking further in a shoosh of Styrofoam beads.

A man my father's age thuds his mug down on the floor and lumbers to stand, the bag beneath him concave from his girth. "The board chose to sell the air rights to our beautiful—"

"Historic!" pipes Man Haircut.

"Yes, historic midtown building so we could work here at this— this South Beach spectacle. Fine, that's their goddamn decision. They were banging day in and day out, gassing us with paint fumes so they can have their precious convocation on the roof with the Shakespeare garden and—"

"Helipad." Jeff smirks.

"Yes, right. The helicopter pad so our students need not be bothered with debasing themselves in limos out to their country estates. The teachers' lounge has been requisitioned as a meditation room for the students, spring break is a mandatory College Recommendation Letter Conference, and then the health-care cuts. My wife is on medication and I'm on a teacher's salary with a mortgage and two kids in college. The board wants to call it corporatizing? Well, we call it unconscionable." The teacher, who is increasingly bringing to mind Jason Robards, pulls his freckled hands from his tweed blazer's pockets. "Now to have them indulge this humiliation, to *validate* it, well, I just . . . we *have* to put our foot down." Everyone erupts into applause.

"Thank you, Mr.—"

"Calvin. History. My family, back to my great-grandfather, has a Jarndyce education and they didn't need a helicopter pad to get it."

"Mr. Calvin, I appreciate your candidness."

He stares at me evenly, mincing his lips beneath his gray mustache, holding his colleagues' attention, and I turn back to Ingrid. "So, what do you think?"

"I just can't follow what you're—This is *my* fault?" She stares at me from across the dim space. "I have to—"

"Stay employed." My hands find my hips. "So you can live to teach another day at another school where you will go, when you're ready, on your own terms." I fight the urge to throw my coat around her and carry her to some progressive charter where the parents are humble and the ceilings unreflective.

Man Haircut slaps her palms on her knees. "You know they can choose not to renew *any* of our contracts and replace us with kids Ingrid's age at a fraction of the cost."

"Not without cause," Ingrid corrects her. "They have to make a case."

"And I don't see that," I say, although I'm starting to. "You *are* the history of this school."

"They're not interested in *history*," Mr. Calvin retorts. "If they want Ingrid to apologize for this disgrace, well, then . . ." His voice quiets and he looks down at his faded loafers. "The lines are clear. That's it. I'm taking a stand." He crosses his arms and hope breaks on Ingrid's face.

"Great!" I encourage him. "You have power in numbers. If you all band together, you have sway over this situation."

"Precisely." He reknots his tie and bends to swipe his coat from the floor. "As of tomorrow morning, I'm resigning from the Grievance Committee."

Clamoring in agreement, the other teachers climb to their feet. Jeff is the last to join them, unable to meet Ingrid's eyes as she seeks him out.

I spin to Mr. Calvin. "Disbanding the committee is only going to give them more power."

"*More* power?" he asks sarcastically.

"Look, the sites are coming down." Jeff shrugs sheepishly in Ingrid's direction. Mr. Calvin waves his hand and the crowd passes through the library door.

Alone, Ingrid looks to me from her beanbag. "What are you thinking?" I ask.

She nods her head, her lips pressed flat. "I'm thinking that my fiancé lost his job and we just got a notice that as of June first our rent's going up. So . . ." Her head sinks into her hands in a sign of capitulation. "Is Darwin writing a letter about his role in this?"

"Yes."

"I know I could defuse this bullshit if I could *just* discuss it with him," she says intently.

"I guess now you can, only ... with the Manhattan private school community as an audience."

"I don't know if I feel comfortable publishing this, Mr. DeSanto." Chloe, the seventeen-year-old editor in chief of *The Jarndyce Times* drops Ingrid's letter on his desk and taps her Roger Vivier buckled flats as only someone who took an after-school nap, ate a warm chef-prepared dinner, and then got in a town car can.

Gene, Tim, Janelle, Ingrid, and I look in bleary-eyed misery at her and her trio of Scoop-clad, if scoopless, editors.

"Why, Chloe?" Gene asks, his stubbled chin resting on his fists, which are resting on his blotter.

"Because why does *she* get a voice? She has a voice! She gets to express herself all day long. All the teachers do! This is our paper. Plus." She juts out one black-legginged hip. "I don't think she's really sorry."

Ingrid lets out a stifled sigh that seems to satisfy Darwin, sprawled on the couch opposite, to no end.

"Look, Chloe," Gene tries again. "It's been a long night and this needs to be published first thing. I think Ms. Wells has done what we've asked her to do. She's taken responsibility for setting a tone in her classroom that could have been misconstrued as inviting virtual free-form feedback. Perhaps if you and your editors read it again."

Chloe weighs this option. Janelle's eyes close, her head falling forward.

"Maybe if we heard it," one of the editors suggests. "She should read it out loud to us."

"I would consider that." Chloe crosses her arms.

Ingrid shoots up, grabs the red pen from Chloe's hand, swipes the letter from Gene's desk, and crosses it with a huge *X*. She flips the piece of paper over and scrawls as she speaks: "Dear ... students ... I'm ... sorry ... It's ... all ... my ... fault." She hands the paper to Chloe. "Okay?" She spins to Darwin. "Enough?"

He brightens into a grin. She stares down at him, her cried-out eyes pushing through his mask of smugness, which, to my surprise, fades, as does the grin. And suddenly he looks as miserable as she.

"Chloe," Gene sighs.

"Okay, fine." Chloe shrugs. "Whatever. I have an obligation to express my editorial opinion. Which I've done. We can go with the first version."

"Hallelujah," Janelle mutters.

13

"Nan-neh!" That Saturday evening Stilton opens his front door in a dark suit, his hair slicked back, coiffed like he's about to carry wedding bands down an aisle. "Nan-neh!" His eyes widen. "What happened?!"

"My bedroom ceiling collapsed." I look down at my cell. "But I'm not late. We're not late. I have a plan." I clap my hands, little powdery puffs of plaster dispersing into the air. "Are you ready?"

"But you look like a ghost."

I turn to the vestibule mirror and see why my fellow straphangers were staring: I didn't fully shake out all the dust from my hair and my face is still patched with chalk and my dress . . .

"Hop, hop!" I press for the elevator and Stilton gets in beside me.

"It starts in twenty minutes." He bounces onto his toes. "My mom left hours ago to go to the hair place. Why are we going up?"

"Five minutes and I will be clean and changed." We get out on eleven and, coming to my prebenefit rescue, Citrine opens her front door and I hesitate to step into her embrace. "Op, be careful, I'm *filthy*," I say as she squeezes me.

"No, I'm filthy and you just try to get close to me over my boobs, just try it," she says, stepping back into her drop-cloth-draped entrance hall. In the week since our last lunch date, she's filled out beneath her husband's trashed oxford and her cheeks look fuller. She cups her cleavage. "It's like carrying around a bra full of produce in a camp dare. I keep wanting to put them down, only I'm stuck. Fuck breast-feeding, man! Fuck it. I just want my body back. Oops, sorry." She notices Stilton. I try to focus on her words, but am distracted by men in matching white jumpsuits scurrying past in all directions, carrying equipment and materials like manic insects facing a frost. I want to reach out and throw myself around a passing ankle and beg one of them to come home with me.

Stilton steps around me and holds out his hand. "Nice to meet you."

"Citrine, this is Stilton, master poem reciter. He lives on nine."

"We're late," he updates her.

"Come, let me show you the progress and then we'll find you a dress."

"We're late," he repeats.

"Five minutes!" she calls over her shoulder.

We follow her past the team with blowtorches blistering the pale yellow paint off the foyer walls, into the living room, where another pair of men are removing the sledgehammered remains of the dividing wall to the dining room. "We're not supposed to have any workmen on Saturdays, but we've found as long as they stick to quiet pursuits we get away with it." The French doors Ryan wants Steve to replicate lie on the floor, panes shattered.

"I wanted an open flow." She swings her arms up and down like Martha Graham. "Less stuffy and farty."

"Sure," I say, standing in the now Versailles-sized space, open veins running through walls where every bit of wiring has been ripped out.

Stilton looks around, jaw dropped. "It's our house, but like we all died and aliens came and made it different."

"Yes." I nod.

"Let me show you the kitchen." She holds her left hand out and when she takes mine, something scrapes me and I pull back. She laughs, blushing as she looks at her fingers. "Oh gosh, sorry, I'm not used to this thing and it's a weapon." She is staring—we're both staring—at an easily six-carat diamond ring with matching chunky eternity band. "I dug it out of my jewelry box—I just figured since I'm starting to show, I should try to look married. I was getting these horrible stares at the gym. Oh, guess who I've started taking prenatal yoga with?"

I shrug. "Hester Prynne?"

"Tatiana. She's having her second. We're going crib shopping together tomorrow. How crazy is that? I've been really surprised—I forgot how funny she is. She got all worked up about throwing me a shower."

"Well, please tell her I'd love to help. I really took on baking in Sweden."

"Oh. Cool." She pushes through the swinging door from the dining room into what was once my favorite room here. I loved the old refectory table, the piles of newspapers, the dog beds. Now it's just four raw walls with a few capped-off pipes protruding from them. And a red placemat-sized patch on one, as if the days-old space had a birthmark. "Puttanesca," she says, acknowledging the stain. "I got so angry at Clark I threw a takeout container at him last week. The pasta missed, but I got him with the salad. He got balsamic in his eye." She leans back on her hip with a half smile. "What's the worst thing you've ever thrown at Ryan?"

Sarcasm?

"I hit Clark in the head with a corkscrew last year." She laughs. "That was bad. I thought he'd need stitches."

"You're kidding. What were you fighting over?"

"Oh, who can remember, right? You know when you just want to smash their face in?" Smiling fully, she pinches my waist as Stilton walks around, his head torquing left and right, a confused expression as he tries to reconcile the raw space with his kitchen. "Anyway, I'm turning the corner. Now that I got my bathtub I may give Clark his *Battlestar Galactica* design. I mean, it's not like I cook. We'll hire our chef now, and then he and Clark can finish it together. You need an outfit!" She abruptly changes course.

"Yes, she does," Stilton agrees. "Because we're late."

"We are not. You're so great to do this. If the electrician hadn't been mucking about in the attic, the bedroom ceiling wouldn't suddenly have rained plaster on me and my entire wardrobe."

"Not at all. I'm so fat. I can't get into anything I bought for this season and it's all just sitting there with the tags on." She leads us through three layers of meticulously taped plastic, carefully unsticking the blue strips from the wall. "I have them triple-tape this wing in every morning. So far, so good. I hate dust. We could just stay at a hotel, but I think contractors go faster if you're on-site." We duck

under the flap opening into the once floral-covered walls of the
Hutchinsons' bedroom, with the beautiful view of the landscaped
roofs of Park Avenue.

"Who would imagine this high up you see trees?" I sigh enviously.

"I know! We've left it for now, so I have a refuge. We just threw up
a quick coat of paint and some curtains, but after they finish the public spaces this'll be gutted." The walls have been frescoed the palest
lavender, with matching heavy silk drapes. These were not hastily
grabbed at an Uppsala Christmas fair. "Okay, so let me pull some
things." She opens the door to the room that was Dorothy's office,
now filled with rolling garment racks, and wheels one in. There is
indeed a white tag dangling from every sleeve.

"Okay, this shindig you're going to is all of New York society under
one roof, united by the prestige of private education. Elegant and in-
tellectual." She rifles the rack while I try to keep from slipping off her
silvery bedspread in the once-black crepe shift I was going to wear. "I
mean, it's not like when you're at a benefit for something frivolous,
like the ballet or the Costume Institute, and you can wear some cou-
ture confection. Or something so god-awful, like Darfur or rape or
AIDS and you need to distract with something really upbeat and
bright—this is more like the New York Public Library, you know?" I
don't. "This is spring-weight cashmere. This is"—she whips a dress off
the rack and toreadors it in front of her. "Carolina Herrera!"

"It's great. Put it on," Stilton instructs.

"Oh, Citrine, I can't. It's too beautiful," I say of the chocolate knit
and satin dress. "What if someone bumps into me with a drink?"

"Oh, who cares? My hips are going to move in the next few
months. *Move.* My feet are going to go up a size. My pelvis is going
to go out a size. Permanently. I will never be the same size or shape
again." She takes in a stilted breath and glances to the ceiling for a
moment. "I will have to get rid of everything. So grab it while it's still
au courant."

Leaving Stilton to bounce his butt anxiously on the bedspread, I
duck into the bathroom. "Use any of the washcloths in the basket by
the sink—they're all clean," she calls after me. I quickly wipe myself
down, unpin and shake my hair out over the bathtub, and try the

frock, spinning to admire it in the mirrored cabinet doors. It is the single most stunning thing I have ever put on, apologies to my wedding dress. The cap sleeves hit at the perfect spot, making me look as if my passing acquaintance with lifting heavy things is a lifelong gym habit. The drape of the skirt is feminine and sharp all at the same time. "Wow, Citrine, I love it." I come out.

"It's perfect—it's yours!" She claps.

Stilton claps. "Let's go."

"Thank you so much. Can I just leave this here and grab it from you next week?" I hand off the trashed dress. "It's embarrassing—I mean, I have clothes. Just nothing currently not Ghost of Christmas Past–ish."

"Have you tried triple-taping where the work is done?" She places the dress on the floor.

"That would mean taping myself out of my only working toilet."

"Nan-neh!"

"Yes! On it!" I step back into the bathroom and retwist my hair.

"How did you learn to do that?" she asks, leaning in the door-frame.

"My grandmother."

"That's nice. I never knew mine. One drank herself to death. The other had a stroke. Did I ever tell you my grandfather made my mom drop out of college to look after her? I mean, he could've hired someone. I think he never wanted my mom to go to school in the first place. He wasn't a real women's libber."

"What happened?" I ask, weaving the last pin against my scalp.

"Oh, well, thank God she died, as my mother puts it." She sticks the corner of a finger in her mouth and bites off a jagged paint-stained cuticle as I reach into my bag for my mini Trish McEvoy makeup palette to repair the damage. "She finally got to move down to the city and meet my dad. But by this point, she was already in her late thirties. I think when I came along she was a little burnt out on caregiving, you know? And when I was only ten Dad was already seventy and she was doing it all over again."

"You have an older sister." I suddenly remember a girl with the same Titian hair waving to Citrine across the cafeteria.

"Three. Half. The oldest two graduated from Chapin before we even started. I'm closer in age to their children."

"Weird," I say as I regloss my lips.

"Yeah. That's why I kind of stayed out of the whole scene. The Kittridge name—that's their thing."

"I'm sorry."

"Nah, its okay. I have a new name now." She smiles and looks down at her rings again. "You think by the time the baby comes I'll be used to all of this?"

"All of what?"

"Being married, living here, wearing jewelry . . ."

"If not . . ." I turn to her, snapping my clutch shut, noting how the well of confidence in *others'* ability to juggle motherhood is always overflowing. "Put the rings on a string around the baby, put the baby in a bjorn, keep painting."

"Yeah." Her face hesitantly brightens. "That's the plan."

"You're killing me!"

"Okay, let's go!"

14

Minutes later I give Stilton my hand to hold as he hops from the cab on the corner of Park and Fiftieth, his clammy fingers pulsing mine in the cadence of Coleridge. We quickly cross the street and hustle down the block because the entrance to the Waldorf Astoria is barricaded behind layers of town cars, from which emerge some bizarre parody of a 1950s nuclear family. Fathers and sons don matching ties, mothers and daughters don matching outfits, all custom-made, I assume. Unless this season's Gucci includes peek-a-boo blouses for eight-year-olds.

We shimmy our way in through the glitzy throng, a markedly different crowd than the old guard assembled in Mrs. X's living room. These are the women who have gleefully disseminated their husbands' wealth all over town in the pursuit of forever looking like spoiled coeds; more Real Housewife than real deal. I make a note to update Citrine before her progeny mandates her attendance. As we jog up the carpeted stairs of the grand lobby and over to the check-in table, they all eye one another's attempts at pint-sized *Vogue*. "Hi, this is Stilton X, he'll be performing tonight." I squeeze his thin shoulders through the wool of his blazer as we await his name tag.

"School?" the student volunteer asks.

"Haverhill Preparatory." He nods officially.

"Elevator up to the ballroom. Follow the kids to their area and there's a door at the back marked 'performers.'"

"Excuse me, but I am expecting a tie." Stilton steps away from me, his hands gripping the edge of the table, puckering the cloth. "Gillian, my dad's secretary, said she would messenger it."

"Here?" the girl asks, looking halfheartedly at the open cartons of gift bags lining the floor behind her chair.

"I thought it would be in our lobby, but it wasn't, so it also makes sense she sent it here. So we can match."

"Is there maybe anywhere else in the hotel where it could have been delivered?" I offer.

"You can try the concierge, I guess."

And we do. The concierge, the reception desk, the manager's office, the mail room, even the gift shop.

I check the oversized grandfather clock, confirming it's not yet seven. "Brooks Brothers is still open. Pick any color you want and I'll hop in a cab and get it while you warm up."

"But I don't know what color *he's* wearing." His arms crossed over his narrow chest, he leans his head back against a column.

"Navy?" I guess. With a puppy-on-a-stake motif? "Why don't I run over and grab a blue one."

He wrings his hands, looking down anxiously at the carpet's fleur-de-lis.

"Or!" I reach. "You could be the badass who went rogue! Very John Varvatos. Bond at the racetrack. Obama on the trail."

"We have to match, Nan," he sighs.

"Okay . . . so." I glance back over the tops of the potted palms at the clock. "I will intercept him when he arrives and get him to lose his tie, too."

His face lights up. "We'll Obama together!"

"Yes! But let's get you backstage, okay?"

He throws both hands in the air and flicks his thin wrists. "Lead the way."

We squeeze into the elevator for the top floor with two all-boy families and a mother wearing what I assume is a Marc Jacobs mini-dress, given its Mia-Farrow-meets-Mrs.-Roper vibe, with her grade schooler, who might actually be wearing a size zero of the same dress. The elevator slows and the doors open to a flash of lightning and a clap of thunder. BOOM! We all instinctively back up, children trying to squeeze behind their parents. Then, looking left and right, like members of Mystery, Inc., we inch out onto the landing to find other families, appearing equally terrified, emerging from the elevators on either side of us. The hallway is thick with hip-high—for adults, shoulder-high for kids—fog. A person in a silver unitard comes rolling past, bent back like a hoop.

"What the fuck?" the dad behind me asks.

"They got Cirque du Soleil," his wife answers through clenched teeth. "It's Canadian."

Another blinding clap of thunder and the little girl beside me bursts into tears. "Darling," her mother says, aggressively tugging her along into the haze, "it's a *circus*. It's *fun*."

We follow them past the bar tables and into the room designated for children. At the weddings I've attended here, this is usually where cocktail hour is set up. Instead, the mass of Seventh on Sixth on Park on children is huddled together on the carpet, seemingly under attack from a cadre of mimes.

Spotting three young girls dressed in Mandarin costumes, singing arpeggios in the corner, I steer Stilton over by the shoulders. "I have to ask," I say as we approach.

"We're Ping, Pang, and Pong. We're doing the lamentation aria from act two of *Turandot*," one answers.

"I almost guessed that. Can you direct us backstage?"

She points us down the wall to a door with a "performers" notice taped to it.

"Where are the high school students?" I ask Stilton.

"They used to rent out suites downstairs during the party, but three years ago the police got called and now, unless they're performing, they just stay home."

We push through the marked door into what is really just a screened-off section of the kitchen. From the other side we can hear and smell dinner being plated above shouted instructions. As the door swings shut behind us, I catch a rocking motion out of the corner of my eye and realize a metal chair has been pulled into the corner of the otherwise deserted area, and on it a couple is doing something on the spectrum of making out to making a baby.

"Darwin!" Stilton calls in greeting before I can spin us back out.

Darwin looks over, his cheeks flushed, and I recognize Chassie as she hops off him to pivot to the wall and secure the open trousers of her red pantsuit.

"Hey, Stil-man." Darwin holds out his hand and Stilton rushes across the red Formica tiles to slap it. "Your dad's making a grand appearance, right?"

Stilton lifts on the balls of his feet. "We're going to both not wear ties. It'll be cool. Hi." He waves at Chassie.

"Hey," she says softly, flipping her newly platinum hair over her shoulder as she leans back against the wall.

"Well, nice to meet you, but we got to practice," Stilton tells them.

"Us, too," Chassie says, nodding her head in deep drops. "We're doing a Clinton-Romney debate." Her words come out slowly.

"Oh, great. Is Ingrid here?" I point at the door behind me.

Chassie's face sets. "We voted her *off* Forensics."

Seeing my eyebrows raise, Darwin tugs his Sidekick from his blazer pocket and scrolls his e-mail. "Whatever. She brought it on herself, back-talking my dad." He taps on his keyboard while Chassie peers over his shoulder. "Who thinks the site is hilarious, by the way. That shit got blown way out of proportion."

"Is *that* why you posted it, to impress your father?"

Chassie suddenly slips forward, a hand landing hard on Darwin's shoulder to steady herself. He grabs her waist.

"Are you okay, Chassie?" I ask.

"Totally. Yeah." Her hand still gripping his blazer, she bends down under her chair. "My mom texted to take a Xanax for my nerves. It's just hitting me fast 'cause I didn't eat dinner. Guess I better hydrate!" She motions cheers to Darwin with a highball glass of dark liquid. He reaches under his chair for a sweating glass of his own.

I turn to Stilton. "Let's go warm up." Somewhere G-rated. And inform Gene about the booze cruise setting sail back here. We push back through the filling children's room, where a pyramid of muscular men in gold unitards with a bronze intestinish pattern is on deck trying to entertain the corralled kids, but they're so . . . close and so . . . muscular. The children seem to be inching back on their sitz bones.

In search of Gene, we cross the hall into the filling ballroom, which has been transformed into the big top. The tablecloths are black, the chairs are black, the candles are black. And above it all, acrobats dangle from jewel-toned banners of fabric, spinning above our heads to music at once spastic and eerie. Seemingly oblivious, parents peek at the place cards, rearranging names, avoiding the man in whiteface who's honking a bicycle horn and squirting people with his bouton-niere. "It's French," I hear a woman hiss to her splashed husband as he dabs himself off with a cocktail napkin.

Yet, despite the circus theme, there is nary an unpaid adult in the child's room, nor are children welcome in the ballroom. In fact, Stil-ton and I are both garnering some not so subtly disapproving looks.

I crane my head, but there's no sign of Gene. So Stilton and I wend our way to the most unobtrusive corner, where parents peruse the items up for bid. As Stilton begins his tongue twisters, I scout for some other Jarndyce authority figure and notice a strange sequence repeating itself. As is typical of a silent auction, the women barely restrain themselves from elbowing one another out of the way to scribble down bids and contact information, high on the thrill of acquiring luxury items below market value frosted with a creamy tax deduction icing. But as the husbands make their way in from the bar and are pointed to the items in contention, the wives, avoiding their friends' eyes, surreptitiously cross their bids out, their plumped lips curdled in a tight line. I nudge in and see names scratched out below a cruise to Japan, dinner with the soon-to-be ex-president, a Fred Leighton necklace. The only item still holding is a meeting with War-ren Buffett.

"Mom!" Stilton suddenly cries, slaloming through the round tables over to the turbaned figure entering the room under one of the four archways. She winces at the contact and he drops his arms to carefully take her hand, prepared to be her date. She smiles feebly down at him, extending a small wave in my direction. I return it and leave the silent-auction dance of contemplation and resistance to greet her properly, the Host Committee on my heels.

"Darling!" Bunny and Saz get to her first in the wide doorway, extending a sapphire committee brooch and pinning it to the lapel of the golden raw silk caftan Mrs. X has paired with the turban.

"You are *so* brave."

"So brave."

"To venture out."

"*Such* a good mother."

"Stilton, you are lucky."

"*So* lucky."

The ladies cluck and fuss, bringing a blush to Mrs. X's un-made-up cheek. But just then the air behind her turns white.

"Carter!" a chorus of voices call out on the landing and, through the open doors, I see that a phalanx of press are now positioned in the fog flow. Carter Nelson makes her way down the line with an en-trancing smile, hands dangling beside the emerald peplum of her New Look–esque evening dress, which complements the storied seven-figure Christie's acquisition strung around her neck. She is absolutely stunning. In person her skin is even more luminous, her red hair shinier, green eyes more captivating. I sense the female en-ergy around me pinch.

A man slides up beside her and slips his arms around her waist. The camera flashes spark double-time.

Mr. X.

Holy. Shit.

Twenty pounds lighter. A thousand follicles thicker. A jowl down. Wow. A decade shaved off his sixty-plus years, the paparazzi shots did not do the makeover justice.

"Daddy! Daddy! Take off your tie!" Stilton rushes away from his mother and into frame, and I'm as surprised as Stilton looks when Mr. X heaves him to his hip, wincing only slightly. "This is my eight-year-old son, Stilton," Mr. X addresses the cameras. Stilton leans in and whispers something in his ear. "Sorry, seven." He clamps his hand over Stilton's, which is attempting to loosen the green knot at his father's neck. "He'll be performing tonight." Mr. X returns his other arm around Carter's waist, an impressive family picture forming around the virile husband with a grip on a boy two-thirds his size. At my elbow, Mrs. X's blush evaporates faster than the dry ice. "I'm here tonight to support my son and support the schools by bidding big."

He drops Stilton and follows Carter into the room, right past his wife. Mrs. X stands there for a moment, her face tight as the commit-tee hustles in on Carter's heels, Stilton trailing her peplum and mumbling about Obama. I'm hedging whether or not to follow when suddenly Mrs. X winces. The ladies freeze, staring at one another, brooches facing inward. Then, tacitly, they diverge, half following Carter, half coming back to Mrs. X to escort her to her table, bring her water, a cracker, a damp towel.

Just then, Sheila makes her own grand arrival, looking regal, a golden hair clip pinned behind one ear. I excuse myself and weave over to her on the edge of the parquet dance floor. "Sheila?"

Her eyes focused over my shoulder, she leans forward to air-kiss beside my cheek and then pivots away. I touch her arm. "Sorry, but do you have a quick moment?"

"Of course," she says emphatically to those around us, and follows me a few feet from her welcoming cluster. "Yes?"

"I'm sorry to bother you, but I can't find Gene, and two Jarndyce students—Darwin and Chassie—are drinking backstage. I thought someone should know. Chassie said she'd taken a Xanax and seems tipsy."

"And this will affect their performance," she surmises, her face darkening with concern.

"Well, that, and—"

"Or is it just a little something to take the edge off? Stage fright and whatnot. They're speaking clearly? Do you think they can perform?"

"I think maybe someone from Jarndyce should go back and check on them and, at the very least, cut them off."

"Cliff!" I turn to see him arriving, a stately blonde, presumably his wife, in tow. And Ingrid—appearing mildly stunned—on his arm. Sheila looks back to me, her body already angled to his group. "Let's not make a fuss tonight. With everyone here. Gene can deal with this on Monday." She brushes away in a perfumed breeze to where Cliff is displaying Ingrid to a circle of parents. I bite my lower lip, gauging what to do next, as Ingrid walks over in a vintage cocktail dress, shaking her head in disbelief.

"Oh my God," she says, voice low, "Cliff and his wife invited me to Park Avenue Spring for dinner."

"Did you have a food taster?"

"Right? It was so awkward. Over ginger soufflé he tells me I just need to show my solidarity with their 'vision' tonight and we can quote 'move forward.'"

"Forward is good," I say, smiling. I touch her arm, relieved for her. "Ingrid, I was just backstage and—"

"Sorry to interrupt." Cliff appears at Ingrid's side. "But I want to introduce you to some of our biggest donors."

"Sorry!" She twists back over her taken elbow as he leads her off.

"Have you seen Gene?" I ask.

"By the bar!" she calls, sending me to inch my way into where the crowd is concentrated, pressed closely enough to unwrinkle one another's Fortuni.

"So I'm confused," the woman ahead of me addresses her companion. "They did or didn't fire her?"

I peer over a ruched shoulder and see her friend is holding a clipping of Ingrid's letter to the editor in her cocktail ring–laden fingers. "She just came in on Cliff Ashburn's arm, so they must have it under control."

"We tried to get rid of one at Buckley, but after three years they have automatic contract renewal. The burden's on the school to build a case against them. It's disgraceful—they have us over a barrel."

"And it was just kids being kids, I'm sure. You know how it is with the help. They don't have our sophisticated sense of humor. I'm sure this boy was just being clever and she got the wrong impression. At brunch the other day my husband made some joke about wetbacks and my housekeeper, who's Puerto Rican, mind you, got so offended. I mean, *come on,* we voted for Obama."

"You're so right."

"And what was she doing on his Web page anyway? That's the real question. It's appalling. *Our* teachers would never violate a student's trust like that."

"It's the neighborhood." Her friend lowers her voice, tilting her head to reveal her cascading canary diamond earrings. "Can you imagine sending your children to the Meatpacking District for school?"

"It's because they let in media parents."

"And children with low math skills."

"It's tacky."

"It's gauche."

"I feel sorry for the kids."

"Two white wine spritzers."

"Ladies and gentlemen," Bunny booms into the microphone on-stage before stepping back to adjust the volume. "Please take your seats. Your appetizers have arrived and tonight's performances are about to begin. And after each child entertains us, we'll be bidding on an item to benefit that child's school."

The room darkens further as parents scuttle to take their seats and pick at their limp greens. "We will begin with Suzie Goldfarb-Wang from The Brearley School, doing her interpretative dance of the periodic table of the elements." Before the room has even quieted, she is flying across the stage in a white leotard with black lettering. I find a good standing-room spot among the faculty as Goldfarb-Wang unfurls herself from the pose of uranium to wild applause.

"Okay," the auctioneer announces, "Brearley has donated an original signed Kandinsky lithograph. Who would like to start the bidding at fifty thousand?"

A woman sticks her hand up. Her husband cups it back down to the tablecloth.

The room goes quiet. The twirling fabric crawlers freeze. They're still stuck up there? I can see, across the room, cascades of sweat dripping onto the tables and guests. Some people are shielding themselves with their programs.

"Fifty thousand?"

The wives shift in their seats, playing with their jewelry to restrain themselves from bidding.

Bunny rushes onstage and takes the mike from the auctioneer. "Sorry, that is a typo. Twenty thousand."

"Apologies for that, folks," the auctioneer says as bids go up and the room relaxes, except for a gentleman at the back who levitates out of his seat. Presumably the donor. Bunny takes the paper from the auctioneer's hand and runs a pencil through a few items as three collegiate third graders prepare to reenact the chain of British succession. Which they do with two wigs, three hats, one fake finger (Boleyn), and a wide ruff collar. It is a feat. Then we wait through a limp bid for an hour of Tucker Carlson's time and then Stilton takes the stage. I cross my fingers and look into the crowd to make sure the Xes are paying attention. I spot Carter's hair, which catches the halo of Stilton's spotlight, but the seat beside her is empty. As is the seat between Bunny and Saz.

Shit.

My eyes fly to Stilton as he inhales a deep breath, his chest bellowing, a hand in his pocket, and he's off. " 'It is an ancient Mariner/And he stoppeth one of three.' " At an almost chipmunkesque gallop. Not that anyone notices as they continue their whispered conversations, heads bobbed in pairs. I surreptitiously hustle my way to the double doors and out into the emptied hallway. I rush down to the restrooms and stick my head in the ladies'. "Mrs X!" I call . . . Nothing. I let the door close, stymied, my pulse speeding. Suddenly I pick up voices from the ajar cloakroom door across the hall.

"I told you it's just an accounting oversight," I hear Mr. X as I approach.

"You've been saying that for over a year," she retorts. "Only now you're gone. And Gillian flatly avoids my calls. It's not as if I'm calling to beg you to come home. I simply want what I'm entitled to. I mean, Jesus, you're spending millions on her—that necklace alone." I twirl my hand at the door crack, willing them to wrap this up without prompting.

"Oh, for fuck's sake. Here. Here's . . . three, four, five . . . here's a thousand and I'll have the rest wired into your accounts tomorrow."

"I honestly . . . how could you do this to me, making me corner you."

"How could you show up here looking like Gloria Swanson? A little over-dramatic, don't you think? You look like your mother." Oh my God—they're in for the long haul.

"Go back to your *actress.*" She hisses the last word with a sixteenth-century disdain. And I fling open the door to the cloakroom. They blink at me, stunned by the light like chickens in a coop.

"Your son is performing right now," I say, my heart pounding on his behalf. Scowling, Mr. X pushes past me, his wife brushing my other shoulder, torquing me like a turbine.

"Mr. X," I hear myself say, stopping him. He spins around as she continues on. "Fathers and sons are wearing matching ties tonight. Since Stilton doesn't have his, we were hoping you might take yours off." He looks as if I've suggested he remove his pants. "Just . . ." I smile entreatingly, motioning to loosen my make-believe tie. He storms off.

I just slip in the door to the ballroom as Stilton declaims, " 'A sadder and a wiser man/He rose the morrow morn.' " I clap wildly as the lights come up and Stilton takes his bow, his smile withering as he spots his parents weaving between the tables back toward their seats.

"Haverhill has donated a walk-on role on *Gossip Girl,* opening bid fifteen thousand dollars." Once again the eyeballs swivel, napkins twist, smiles quiver from being held too long.

"Eighteen thousand!" Mr. X barks as he pulls out his chair. A smattering of applause surrounds his table. Mrs. X's face is inscrutable.

"I guess his fund steered clear of this subprime mess," a man at the table in front of me whispers to his wife.

No other paddles rise.

"And . . . *sold* to the gentleman at table two."

"My son will love that," Mr. X shouts up to the auctioneer, and Stilton looks confused. "My other son," he adds.

"Dude!" someone cheers from the doors down the wall from me. All heads turn, even the acrobats. "That's really . . . just totally . . ." Jacket on, hood up, Grayer jogs through the tables toward his father. "We could go together—" He trips over someone's satin-sheathed toe, lunges forward, and grabs the edge of a nearby table. "I'm—" And sends a glass of Cabernet tumbling onto a trio of evening dresses. "Sorry. Shit." Then he grabs a napkin from someone else, knocking over his ice water and dropping the linen on the floor before backing away. "Dad." Grayer spins as Mr. X stands to grasp him by the shoulders. Oh God, he's—

"Drunk," Mr. X growls as I step forward into earshot. Mrs. X stands. Carter stands.

"No! I'm just . . . really . . . it's awesome that you would get me this. That's, just, I didn't see that coming, so thank you." Grayer bobs his head. Mr. X releases him and looks as if it's taking everything he has not to wipe his sullied hands on his silk pocket square. Grayer's loopy grin drains away, he backs up a few feet, and then, bumping into a seated blonde, tucks into himself to run out the double doors.

Mr. X pivots to his wife's table in the pin-drop silence of the room, his muscles harnessed into a tight smile. *"Clearly,"* he says, his voice raised, "I've underestimated how the stress of my wife's illness is affecting the children. I think maybe it's best if the boys come stay with us. Lord knows we have the room and can provide a stable environment while she convalesces."

Mrs. X gives an equally tight smile and somehow shrinks further into her caftan, a steadying hand on her neighbor's chair as she reseats herself. "That's very kind. Very kind. I'm just exhausted from the treatment." Her voice fades as her turban comes level with her dining companions.

And suddenly everyone is talking at once. Stilton—oh God—who has witnessed this all from his lone position on the looming stage, takes an uncertain bow and races into the wings. I follow, running out of the ballroom and through the children's room, pushing the door into the performers' space just as Stilton arrives from the stage side, nearly crashing into his immobile brother, who stands with Darwin over Chassie's convulsing body. "Oh my God."

The door bumps against my back. "Anything I can do to help?" Ingrid asks gently.

I move aside and she gasps, stepping inside to drop to her knees at Chassie's side. "What happened?" She whips her phone from the pocket of her dress.

"I don't know. I don't know," Darwin's voice is high and terrified. "One minute she was fine."

"Grayer?" I turn to him.

"I—I just got here." He pulls Stilton into him and pushes his hand up into his own hair, his hood falling back as I watch him wipe at his nostrils.

"She had some of her mother's Xanax and she was drinking," I tell her.

"This is more than that. Is she epileptic?" Ingrid dials 911.

"No." Darwin's voice rises hysterically. He lunges for Ingrid's phone and turns it off. "No. You can't call anyone. We'll get in trouble. Fix her."

"Darwin, give me the phone," she says firmly. But he just stares at her, paralyzed as Chassie's shaking body goes limp. "If this is coke," Ingrid continues with the same controlled tone, "her airways are shutting down. If we don't call 911 she will die."

"I'll call." I fumble for my cell, but Darwin hands the phone to her, his head slowly nodding. Ingrid places the call as Chassie's lips tinge blue. "Fuck, fuck, fuck." Darwin paces. "I'm so fucked. *Fuck!* Why did she have to be so stupid?"

Ingrid lifts Chassie's head into her lap and listens to her breathing.

"How do you know all this?" I ask as I tug a jacket off a nearby chair and drape it over Chassie's legs.

"My brother died when we were in college."

I look at Stilton's terrified face. "Grayer, take Stilton home." Grayer can't lift his eyes from Chassie. *"Grayer."* He focuses on me. "Can you get him home? Are you sober enough to do that?"

"Yeah, yes," he stummers.

I take a twenty from my clutch and push it into his hand. "Go, get a cab."

He nods and pulls Stilton out the door. "Everything is going to be fine here, Stilton," I call after him. "Chassie is going to be fine!"

"I'm going with them." Darwin backs away.

"No." Ingrid freezes him with the firmness of her tone. "You're staying to help your girlfriend."

"She's not my—"

"Darwin! When the EMT gets here they're going to need vital information only you can provide."

"No, no, you don't understand. He'll *kill* me." He continues his manic pacing until, on the other side of the screen, we can hear pandemonium as the stretcher arrives. "Fuck. *Fuck.*" Suddenly Darwin lunges for his backpack, whips out a small baggie, pulls it open, downs the powder, and throws himself to the red linoleum just as the screens fall to the floor and the EMTs blow in. Stunned, Ingrid and I stand back and let them tend to the children, plural.

The sky is still dark when I shudder awake in the vinyl hospital chair at the end of Chassie's bed. Chassie's chest continues to rise and fall as she sleeps, the oxygen line snaking from her nostrils. "Hey." I stretch, looking over to where Ingrid is staring out the window into the rooms across Lenox Hill's courtyard, her hands braced on her lower back. "Any news?"

"Not yet." She turns to me, the circles under her eyes matching the inky purple of her cocktail dress. "Thank you for staying."

"Of course."

"I still can't believe Sheila shrugged you off," she says quickly, clearly having been turning it over in her mind since I fell asleep.

I nod, no longer sure what to say. "Did Gene reach her mother?"

"He talked to the housekeeper. He said it would be easier for him to keep trying from home with the time change." She rolls her eyes. "I should check my cell again. I'll duck outside?"

"Sure."

A nurse sticks her head in the doorway. "You brought the boy in, too?" she asks me. I point to Ingrid.

"Yes. I'm his teacher." Ingrid steps forward. "His parents haven't arrived yet, they're flying in from Florida."

"Well, he's up if you want to see him." She tilts her head at Darwin's room across the hall.

Ingrid glances at me and hurries past the nurse. I follow her in, hanging back as she comes around his bed. He lolls his head to her. He doesn't look small, or even childlike, but wrung out. His face, from his lips to his neck, is stained black from hours of vomiting charcoal. His eyes are bloodshot. His hair is damp and matted to his forehead. Ingrid takes a paper towel from the nightstand, dribbles some ice water on it from the Styrofoam cup of melting chips, and applies it to his forehead.

"You stayed?" he croaks, his voice barely audible.

"I did." She brushes his bangs to the side.

"Stubborn," he manages.

"*Ms.* Stubborn," she corrects him, patting the cold towel across his brow.

"My, uh . . . letter to the newspaper was kind of . . . harsh."

She holds the towel and peers at him, letting the silence sit, perhaps waiting to see if he'll address the website. "If your intention was to hurt me, you succeeded," she says simply. "I'm not trying to make you or any other student think like me, Darwin. I'm just introducing a range of viewpoints, something, hopefully, you and your classmates'll always have exposure to." To my surprise, he nods as he lets his eyes drift closed. "We don't have to discuss this right now," she says. "I'm just glad we're talking. Glad you're okay." She smiles while tearing up from what seems like a mixture of relief and exhaustion.

The sound of high heels hurriedly clicking on the linoleum approaches from the nursing station around the corner. I turn to the doorway to see Grant Zuckerman and a very tan woman with puffy eyes in a floral trench on his arm. A woman I recognize from long ago, despite tauter tear-streaked skin and fuller flight-chapped lips. "I'm his mother," she declares as Ingrid and I take a step back, and she drops her purse on the blanket to take her son's hand. "Where's the doctor?"

"Mr. and Mrs. Zuckerman?" The resident hustles in with the nurse in tow. He lifts Darwin's chart from the foot of the bed. "Let's just take a look here . . . Yes, your son is fine."

"*Fine?*" his mother questions.

"His toxicology levels were dangerously high when he was brought in. But we pumped him full of charcoal, so he'll be pretty sick for a few days, but he sustained no lasting damage."

She stares at the doctor so hard he looks back to the chart, lifting the top page as if something new will reveal itself. "Oh, oh," she splutters, shaking her head. "He's going to." Dropping Darwin's hand, she spins to her husband. "I am dragged all the way up here from Palm Beach in the middle of the night for this *bullshit*? He is paying me back. Every cent. We are docking the charter fare from his allowance."

Stricken, Darwin goes to talk, but can only cough, black spittle spuming from his mouth. Ingrid grips the wet towel with both hands. "He's had a really rough night—"

"*Christ*." Grant lasers in on her, Darwin watching intently with sunken eyes. "So you could've just let him sleep it off?"

"Your son was on the floor when the EMTs arrived." Ingrid's unable to contain her incredulity.

"And now he's fine!" his mother spits. "Aren't you, Darwin?"

Darwin nods in one deep thrust, his gaze dropping to the stiff sheet. The monitors hum.

"You *disgust* me," Grant announces to the bed, his expression unguardedly overwhelmed. "No sense of protocol, no sense, period."

"He needed help," Ingrid tries. "He *needs* help. Let me get you some coffee and you can have a moment alone with him and when you calm down I'm sure you'll—"

"Fuck this," Grant declares predominantly to himself. "I'm not going to be lectured by you. Tinsley, let's get back to the airport."

"What about discharging him?" the doctor asks.

"She can do it." He jerks his head at Ingrid before taking his wife's elbow and she grabs her purse as they walk hastily out, the nurse hurrying after them to sign the forms.

Exhaling a shaky breath, Ingrid lifts the towel toward Darwin's forehead.

"Don't," he croaks. "Fucking. Touch me."

I am too bleary-eyed when I slam the cab door and jog up my stoop, counting the minutes until I can text sweet dreams to my husband, am in bed, and this day can be put down. Too focused, as I stick my key in the lock, on getting Grace, in our bedroom and hours past her evening walk, to blessed relief. Too confused, as I swipe the light switch inside and gear up to mount the staircase, to make sense of the undeniable fact that there no longer is one.

15

Later that morning I find myself riding up in the Xes' elevator, my head pounding in exhaustion, still wearing what I pulled on to walk Grace. In concession to the standards of their zip code, I raise my arm overhead and sniff my sweatshirt to check if the spackling of deodorant is working. After waiting until six a.m. for Steve to bring a ladder tall and sturdy enough to support the descent of a two-hundred-pound man and a sixty-pound dog, and then restraining myself from beating him with it, I woke on my air mattress on the living room floor at seven and had to pee in a bucket.

At least we didn't have to resort to the fire department, who would have condemned our sorry asses right onto the street. Us being me and Grace. Ryan was, I believe, enjoying the turndown service at the Lilongwe Hilton. Yes, while he was sleeping soundly in a down surround, daybreak found me achieving some level of nineteenth-century hygiene with a bowl, a kitchen towel, and a half-empty bottle of Joy.

By eight Mrs. X had called to request my assistance and here I am, tired, punchy, and deliciously underdressed. Yup, this is me. Giving a shit. About impressing. You. Saz answers the door in ironed jeans, an IZOD shirt, and ballet flats. "Nan, good morning."

"Hey, Saz."

"Nan!" Mrs. X calls from the dining room. "In here!" I follow to where Mrs. X sits in an oversized terry-lined silk bathrobe, surrounded by takeout bags from Payard, her unturbaned hair twisted up with a clip. "Nan, thank you so much for coming. It was actually Saz's idea. I'm just in no state today to help them pack. Last night took too much out of me."

"Happy to help," I lie, without bothering to add the usual exclamation point. "How are they?"

"Well, Grayer can't wait to get out of here, I'm sure, after that little display—honestly, I'm going to be on the phone all day cleaning this up—I just hope my voice holds out."

"Honey, don't overtax yourself." Saz reseats herself beside Mrs. X. "Despite your husband's best attempts to drop the blame at your feet, everyone knows Grayer wouldn't have ..." Her eyes go to the drapes as she searches for the words. "Acted out like that if his father wasn't leaving you in the lurch. Croissant?" She offers me the bag.

"Thanks." I wriggle out a brioche because it won't make crumbs and I'm not sitting down. "It seemed like everyone really enjoyed themselves last night."

"It was a disaster." Saz snorts, pressing her fingertips to the flakes on her plate. "We barely covered our expenses. I'm supposed to be at Bunny's right now for a postmortem, but I can't face it." She smiles at Mrs. X.

"Well, I'm going to head in and help them pack."

"Grayer spoke with someone on Carter's staff and they're expected by noon."

"Great, I'll get them downstairs."

"Oh ..." She looks fretful.

"Yes?" I ask warily, having engaged with this look many times before.

"Well, if you could just see them there." Mrs. X pulls her robe closer around her and ties the sash. "Get them settled. I doubt someone like Carter, who's never had children, knows the first thing about getting the boys settled."

The taxi makes its way down Park Avenue toward Tribeca in halting church traffic increments as I try to maneuver Stilton's duffel to allow some circulation in my thighs.

"Thanks for helping us pack and stuff," Stilton says from beside me on the backseat, listlessly fussing with the bag's toggle.

"Of course." I smile and nod, still trying to gather the moxie to check in with his brother about the concoction of substances he ingested last night. Every approach I compose has me fast-forwarding to his "What, *now* you care? Fuck off" go-to response.

"Oh, man, my lacrosse stick!" Stilton wails, his hand smacking his forehead.

"In the trunk with the rest of your stuff," Grayer calls from the front seat. "And whatever we didn't get today, we'll send for. Cool?"

Stilton knits his eyebrows and stares out over the pile of his earthly possessions at the passing buildings, their windows glowing in the late morning sun. I free my arm from under the giant red nylon potato pinning me and wrap it around him. "But who's going to pack it?" Stilton leans forward, grabbing the base of the opening in the plastic partition with both hands. "Mom can't."

"I'll do it." Grayer shrugs matter-of-factly.

"But where will *I* be when you pack?" Stilton continues. "Are you going to leave me with her? And who's going to take care of Mom? Huh, Grayer? Who's doing that? Rosa's gone—"

"Stil." Grayer drops his head to his chest.

"Grayer," Stilton mimics.

"Stil!" Grayer whips around, sending him slumping back next to me. "Dad wants us to *live with him*. He's *taking* us." His eyes dart across Stilton's face, willing him to get it. "We're not getting left with her—you don't have to go to boarding school. This is a good fucking thing! And the bonus is an Oscar-winning superstar who'll get you new shit *and* make Dad happy. So just, be cool to her, understand?"

Stilton nods solemnly, absorbing the gravity of the stakes.

Grayer spins back around. The taxi is silent, save the cabbie talking in Swahili, the light in his Bluetooth earpiece glowing. I run through three thousand things to say, warnings about tempered expectations, apologies for leaving him to such desperation, reassurances that someday they'll be shot of depending on such narcissistic nut jobs for their survival. And meanwhile, um, easy on the drugs.

"Nan?" Stilton turns his face up to me.

"Yes?"

"Does Carter have any pets?"

"I have no idea, Stil. Why?"

He pushes his pursed lips to one side with his finger. "Maybe it'd be nice if I talk to her about animals."

Staggering under the weight of Stilton's duffel and a tote of the boys' combined sports equipment, I list toward the brushed-steel elevator keypad. "What floor?" Grayer asks from beneath his own multitude of suitcases.

I press the bag between my torso and the wall and winkle the ripped piece of yellow pad out of my sweatshirt pocket. "Eleven," I read, squinting in the ambient lighting. "Your dad's been here for how long?"

"Full-time for the last month. Anyone's guess before that."

"Have you been here?"

"Since Dad moved out he's brought us to his skybox at Yankee Stadium for a Red Sox game. That's the sum total of our logged bonding and there were, like, thirty other people there the whole time."

"They had a sundae bar with Ciao Bella," Stilton adds as the elevator opens onto a stark white vestibule with only a Lucite . . . thing.

"But now," Grayer cheers as he lumbers out, a suitcase straining off each arm and a garment bag hanging around his neck, "we'll be living somewhere he'll actually want to come home to, so that'll change." Grayer smoothes Stilton's hair and then nervously pats down his own blond bangs.

"Ready?" I ask, suddenly also nervous for how well I want this to go for them and the fact that the closest I've come to this level of celebrity is a tea ceremony with Desmond Tutu. And there were, like, thirty other people there the whole time.

They both nod. I tug out my ponytail and quickly shake my hair, wishing my Over It could have held off till after this visit. "I can't believe I'm meeting Carter Nelson in yoga pants."

"I'm sure she does yoga," Stilton asserts.

I push the glowing button and hear a sonorous chime.

Carter herself opens the door, rubbing her hands over her well-documented face. "Hi, guys," she says, pulling out a smile beneath her tired eyes.

"Hey, hi." Grayer smiles, blushing. He looks at her and then at the floor, awkward—sweet. How could she not eat them with a spoon?

"I love your art here." Stilton gestures grandly to the Lucite chunk. "It's cool because it's see-through and also . . ." We all watch his mind race. "And also because it's interesting to look at."

"Oh." She seems confused. "It's an umbrella stand, but . . . thank you. Come on in." As she doesn't offer to take our bags or instruct us to leave them, we shuffle like pack mules into the moss-colored entrance hall. I can't help but think as she struggles to open a pair of massive limed oak double doors opposite, her shoulder blades poking through the thin cotton of her dark green T-shirt, that Mr. X likes his women tiny.

The doors give into a sweeping fish tank of a room ringed with fourteen feet of floor-to-ceiling glass. One side looks across the Hudson to the shoreline of New Jersey. The other faces directly into an identical building, twelve stories open like a doll's house, every tiny detail of each sun-bathed apartment visible, with only the narrow street between us. Stilton unburdens himself from the sagging backpacks he's carrying, one in front, one in back, and runs over to the glass to lean his forehead against the pane. "Is that the West Side Highway?" he asks, pointing down. Is that someone applying mascara? I'm tempted to point across.

Carter comes up behind him and plants her thin legs astride his, wraps an arm in front of him, and tilts his head up with her other hand. "Yes," she says warmly, her signature thick red hair falling in her face. "And no skin against the glass. I only have someone come in once a week so let's not cover the view with fingerprints." She releases Stilton, who seems unsure if he was cuddled or admonished, his eyes darting to Grayer's as she turns to me. "It's just I hate having anyone in the apartment." Yes, he likes 'em tiny *and* charming. "And definitely not while I'm home. You're the nanny?"

"No, just a—family friend." They're a family? I'm its friend? "With the boys. I'm a friend of Grayer—and Stilton." I'm not sure why I'm clarifying, except for the not so far-fetched possibility that George Clooney or Cate Blanchett could walk in and she'd introduce me erroneously as Mrs. X's friend, and then I would be in their minds forever linked with that woman.

"This is really nice," Grayer says, waving Stilton over to him in the sparsely furnished room. "The way you've . . . done the place," he adds carefully, having learned from Stilton's failing to discern art from utility. "It's very chill."

"Oh, thanks. I can't take a lot of visual information in my nest. So, your room is the last down the hall. I hope you don't mind sharing—*containing the chaos*," she sings. "Take a right at the fork." The fork?

I walk them down the full length of the building, past multiple doors and finally a horse-sized mural of a bent antique fork, to the last room on the right. White floors, olive-tinted cement walls, two white twin beds, a stainless steel desk, floor-to-ceiling glass—it feels like I'm dropping them off to be experimented on. Stilton beelines to the nearest bed and releases his backpacks with an "Oof." He immediately reaches shoulder-deep into one, pulls out a scrap of paper, and presses it to the stainless steel sconce. Padma Lakshmi. We all watch as she slowly unsticks and swishes to the floor.

"I'll go uptown tomorrow," Grayer rushes, unstrapping himself from his suitcases. "And get whatever you want. We will make this place feel like home."

"Yes! Totally," I add with forced certainty, because Stilton looks like he's just waiting for the cue to tilt from happy ending to despair.

Grayer takes the duffel bag and tote from me and lowers them to Stilton's bed. He reaches in and pulls out a fist of stuffed animals, which he places carefully along the white duvet where the mattress meets the wall. "We'll just get your little guys set up here . . ."

Stilton turns toward the beckoning windows, fingertips extended. Fine. If they can get through this and the worst that happens is he rebels with finger-pad sweat, this will have been a raging success. "Look," he entreats.

We extend our gaze to the twin glass building across the street, where a girl who appears to be about Stilton's age sits on the floor of her own white room, drawing. Having noticed Stilton, she crawls a few paces across the sheepskin rug to the window and holds her paper to the glass—"HI."

"Hi," Stilton mouths back, waving.

"Hey." We whip our heads around. Carter grips the doorframe with both hands and leans into the room. "I'm making tea. What would you like?" she addresses me.

"Oh, I—Mint? Grayer?"

"I'm great." He smiles again, shrugging. "We're great, thanks. The room is awesome."

"Good. Oh, ignore her." Carter tips her chin up toward our little artistic friend in the tie-dye sweater. "I think she's a fan."

"Oh." We nod, as in this neighborhood it is quite possible for this girl to be the world's youngest celebrity blogger. Grimacing to herself, Carter retreats.

"Okay, guys, I'll be right back," I say as Grayer continues to populate the barren space with the colorful contents of Stilton's bag.

"We're cool, Nan." He looks at me over his shoulder, shaking his bangs out of his eyes.

"Cool!" I give him a thumbs-up.

"I mean, you can have your tea and head out."

"Sure. So I'll just, maybe, give you a call later, make sure you're settled in."

"If you want."

Stilton turns back from the window to watch me.

"Of course I want."

Grayer stands, a stack of folded shirts in hand. " 'Cause we're all set. I mean, I've got this covered."

"Okay . . ."

"Seriously."

"Right, of course, no, you seem all set. Can I talk to you in the hall for one second?" He slumps out behind me and I lower my voice. "I just need to know I said this, so indulge me here—after spending the night sitting up in a chair while they pumped your friend full of charcoal." He looks flatly at me and I barrel on. "The whole drunk-high thing is a great way to check out from the bullshit you're dealing with, but not so good for your brain, heart, or future, the things I care about—that Stilton cares about—okay?"

"Okay," he says quietly, probably to shut me up. But way better than the go-fuck-yourself I was anticipating.

"Okay." I turn back into the room, where Stilton is holding his own paper up to the glass.

"She has a newt," he says. "Named Twinkle."

"Excellent. So that's great!" I walk to the window and bend to hug Stilton. And then turn to Grayer, who once again extends his hand. I shake it. "Call me, either of you, any time for any reason, okay?"

"Yup." He seems to register me afresh. "She's cool, Nan. And my dad'll be home soon. Go back to whatever it is you do."

"I'm a consultant, actually. I, um, help people work better to-gether," I offer, as he has never asked.

"Oh." He smiles, tipping his head, his hair flopping to the side. "Yeah, I can see it. That's a job?"

"Yes. Sort of, I'm getting it off the ground now. Trying to—"

"I should really get Stilton settled."

"Right. Okay, so, bye, guys!" I smile broadly and back out of the room.

"In here," Carter calls as I make my way up the fifty-foot hallway, seriously playing through if she'd notice if I quietly moved in with Grace. I follow her voice into . . . one of the most bizarre domestic spaces I've ever entered, including a yurt and an Icelandic model home. The yards of stone countertops and wood cabinets mean it must be a kitchen, but there are no discernible appliances of any kind, not even a sink.

"Researching a role?" I ask, pointing at the small mountain of pink and gray newsprint covering the island that sits in the middle.

"Yes, I'll be playing Carter for the rest of my life." She peers into a cabinet of metal canisters and extracts one marked "Ginger" and one marked "Mint."

"Sorry, I didn't mean to imply—"

"No, I'm sorry." She smiles. "I'm tired."

"Late night?"

"Well, it was a little more drama than I signed on for when they asked me to be honorary chair. I don't like scenes. And I just came off the fourth He-Man movie." She opens the canisters and extracts a tea bag from each. "Three months in Guatemala. Everyone got sick."

"They're doing a *fourth*?"

"I know. We're so middle-aged. But they're huge in Asia and sometimes running in front of a green screen makes a nice break from the death, death, crazy, ill, war, and sterile that are my usual stock and trade." Carter stares at the antique Asian kettle on the counter as the first wisp of steam finds its way from the opening.

"Is that a . . . ?" I point at the magical stone beneath it.

"I hate appliances." She hugs herself. "I tried, I really tried. I thought, maybe I just hate cheap appliances, so when I moved in here I did the whole thing chef-grade." She waves her swanlike arm at the wall. "Twelve-burner stove. Aga. The whole bit. But, you know? I just hate them. Ripped them all out." The steam finally bursts from the kettle with a trainlike whistle. Carter reaches down and flips open a panel just under the counter and twists a knob to the left. She picks up the hammered metal handle, using the hem of her T-shirt as a buffer, and pours the water into two mugs. She walks over to the wall and pops out a flush metal lever to open a hidden fridge. "Milk?"

"Please."

She pours it from a glass bottle. "I get it delivered every morning from a farm upstate. No hormones. It's great." She swivels the handle of the mug to me.

"And the stove?"

"Hidden under this granite." She raps it with her small knuckles. "Which conducts brilliantly. It'll crack eventually and need to be replaced, but I travel so much I get a good six months out of it at a time."

"And a sink?" I ask, fascinated.

She walks over to the window and lifts the section of counter by its edge, which pops up like an old-fashioned throne toilet lid to reveal the stainless steel basin. "That way I can just toss things in there and I don't have to see them. At least that's the idea, but the thought of it is so gross I usually get up in the middle of the night and do the dishes." She leans back against the—stove? sink? counter?—and dunks her tea bag in and out of her mug while I wait for biscuits to rise from the floor. "So, I wanted to ask you what their schedule is."

"Grayer's really the one to ask, but . . ." I think for a moment as I blow on the vapor wisping off my tea. "I'm guessing they'll need a car to school. It's on Ninety-second, off Madison. I know Grayer starts at eight thirty, not sure if it's the same for the lower school. So coming from here, they should maybe be picked up by seven thirty just to be on the safe side. I'd ask Grayer how long it takes them to get going in the morning. My guess is if they're up by six thirty they're fine. I don't know about getting home. Maybe Grayer can wait for Stilton at school or vice versa and they can take the subway down together. Do you have an extra set of keys or an alarm system? Maybe if you just leave a note with your doorman—"

Carter's eyes well.

"Oh God, is it something I said?" I clank my mug onto the granite, hot water splashing over.

"No, sorry." She dabs her eyes with the cuffs of her sleeves. "I'm just so tired, and this is my month off to sleep and I don't want kids."

I glance behind me at the doorway and drop my voice. "Should I bring them back—"

"No, they're fine. He's really excited they're here. And me, too. It's just, I mean, I've decided not to have any of my own, so it's just intense to have kids around right now. You know there'll be no polar bears or penguins by 2050? I will not raise someone to believe there's a future when I know full well there isn't," she declares. "Do they have any allergies?"

"N-not that I know of," I stutter. "Is their father going to be around?"

"I think he's in Zermatt tonight—back tomorrow." She opens a cabinet under the counter and tosses her tea bag inside. "God, he's so great, isn't he?" For the first time since we arrived, her energy lifts to the charisma that makes her leap off a screen. "I never saw myself getting remarried—" My tea goes down the wrong way. "You okay?" I cough, holding up the hand of fineness. "It's just so refreshing to be with someone who has nothing to do with entertainment. Who can talk about global realities. A grown-up." She looks into the yellow liquid and takes a sip. "He's not pissing his money away on Maybachs and souped-up Ducatis. I mean, he gives so much to charity. And he's scary smart—I'm so into him—sorry." She whips her head up from the tea. "I forgot you're her best friend." *No!* No, I am not.

"I'm really not. But, congratulations."

"Don't tell anyone. I'm not wearing the ring till I do Letterman."

"Of course." Just how I rolled out my engagement. And as fun as this is. "Look, here's my cell. You know, in case." I pull out my wallet and hand her my card.

"So anything else? My assistant could take them to *Spring Awakening*. Would that be fun?" Yeah—maybe not the optimal week to introduce the seven-year-old to musical incest. "I tried on doing a proper Sunday dinner . . ."

"Oh, that would be great!"

"But then I thought . . . lamb . . . I don't feel up to surrounding myself with pagan fertility symbolism right now."

"Sure. Right . . . um, maybe once you recover from Guatemala," I begin carefully, placing both hands on some hidden something to steady myself from dropping to my knees and begging. "It's just the boys could *really* use some TLC right now. Especially Grayer. He's been through so much—I think he's been parenting Stilton for a while, if not from the beginning. He could really use some of his own."

Her nose and brow accordion in on each other. "Isn't he a little old for that? I mean, you get to a certain age and it's, like, come on, kids, sink or swim."

"You know, I should probably get going!" I bid her farewell and go back to stick another business card to Stilton's lamp, right under a freshly taped-within-an-inch-of-her-nose Padma.

I wave to them as the elevator door closes, shouting up the shaft at the ceiling: "And the bike path on the Hudson! It's really pretty! Get her to rent you bikes! And Battery Park—check out the ferries! *Go see* Wicked*!*"

I step out to the lobby, struggling not to go back upstairs, trusting that I have to leave them with people actually legally involved in their lives, and walk toward the C train, trying, *trying* to stifle a Miss Clavel alarm that has just hit a deafening volume.

179

16

"This is totally unnecessary, Ingrid," I say as I tug the thin plum-colored ribbon. It falls away from the diminutive cardboard box as she waits with bashful anticipation, her legs tucked under her desk chair.

"Oh, it's just something little." She drops her wrist, her bracelets clanking against the brushed steel. "I saw it in one of the shops on Atlantic and thought of you."

"That's so nice, I'm now consulting your very consciousness," I joke, lifting off the top and reaching in for what I realize is a brass cheerleader's cone for a charm bracelet. "Oh, Ingrid, I *love* it."

"I thought it was less cheesy than pom-poms. Plus, metal pom-pom charms kind of look like . . . something else. It's for your key chain or junk drawer, or whatever."

"*Definitely* key chain." I reach in my bag for my keys and clip the charm to the metal loop, holding it up so we can both admire how awesome it looks. "I *love* this. It may be one of the coolest gifts I've ever received. Thank you."

"Well, you didn't have to stay with me at the hospital all night."

"Oh my God, there was no way I was leaving you to face that by yourself. But you were grace under fire, seriously."

"Well . . ." Her eyebrows lift as she picks at a stray thread on the hem of her red cotton dress. "It wasn't *my* father."

"Amen. Speaking of, should we?" I stand, lifting my bag from her desk.

With a glance to the clock, she unfolds herself from her chair, slipping her bare feet back into her stretched-out flats. "Let me just grab my papers for next period and I'm right behind you."

Janelle reaches out and proffers a large cardboard delivery tray from Pastis as we approach her desk outside Gene's office. "Can you guys grab that?" As I take it from her, his door opens and a pale Darwin emerges, looking like he's been living on that charcoal diet. The door shuts behind him.

"Hey." Ingrid walks over, her arms crossing as she hunches against the air-conditioning driving from the vents artfully obscured by the crown molding. "How are you feeling?"

"Okay. Thanks." He purses his lips and looks to the left of her.

Janelle's intercom emits a buzz and she waves at us before readjusting her knit poncho. "You two can go on in."

"Later," Darwin murmurs, but Ingrid reaches out to his forearm as he goes to pass. He looks down at the point of contact and then at her. "I want you to know it's my opinion that, despite the code of conduct, I believe you should stay here and get support. I'm gonna fight Gene on this. I'm not participating in any effort that leads to your or Chassie's expulsion."

He blinks, his face wavering between guarded and stricken. "Well . . . your prerogative."

"It is." She affirms. "See you in class." She squeezes before releasing him to reach for the doorknob. Waiting for Darwin to lumber past, I follow her inside, tray first, where I'm surprised to see that, in addition to the Zuckermans dominating the central couch and a hovering Gene and Tim—Sheila is in attendance. Sitting catty-corner to Grant, she wears a pinched expression above a short-sleeved white organza blouse and perches cross-legged beside a man I don't recognize. Khaki suit, brown wing tips, manila file resting on his lap. General air of boredom and annoyance. Another Jarndyce dad? Are they overseeing the expulsion?

"Oh, fantastic! I'm starving!" Suddenly a woman I immediately place as Chassie's mother scuttles in from behind us, her disarrayed blond hair billowing Calèche, before the door clicks closed. She lunges for the tray, grabbing the cup marked "latte" and throwing my balance off. "Was that Darwin I just passed in the hall? Wow, he's grown. NFL material, eh?" Patricia Warner smiles at the Zuckermans. "Gene, you should know, it's hard to find the ladies' room. You might want to stick something on the door that's a little more lady-in-a-skirt. I don't really think of seahorses as female-identified." After a half beat of surveying the options in front of my chest, she plucks up a wax paper bag and drops onto the other end of the couch from Sheila, reaching into the butter-seeped paper and emerging with the ripped-off claw of a croissant. "I got home last night from the airport and there's not a single piece of food in the house, just six sticks of butter in the freezer and some very old Skinny Cows." She rolls her eyes. "Teenage girls." She pops the whole thing in her mouth to Tinsley Zuckerman's ill-concealed horror. I realize I am also watching Patricia Warner chew and, after sliding the tray onto the turtle table, settle myself on the remaining empty couch, gallantly taking the end closest to Grant. It's hard to reconcile this blousy blonde with the whippet-thin star I worshipped in the eighties—my bedroom walls traced her journey from finding sunken treasure to befriending misunderstood robots to seducing married men.

"You must be Ms. Wells." Patricia turns full wattage to Ingrid.

"Yes, hello." Ingrid steps forward and puts out her hand. Patricia takes it and pulls her down into a hug, her fingers extending the last bit of croissant past Ingrid's back. "Thank you so, so much. You were there when I couldn't be."

"Of course." Ingrid's neck turns the crimson of her dress as she straightens, and I notice Grant's redden in turn.

"I brought you something." Patricia rummages in her shell pink Hervé Chapelier tote to extract a program from her show. "Here. It's signed by all of us, even Albee."

"Oh, thank you." Ingrid takes it and seats herself beside me, holding the slightly crushed gift atop her class materials.

"I'm just so glad Chass and Darwin were surrounded by the love of the school community when it happened, am I right?" She glances to the Zuckermans. "Did they send over any jam?" she asks, a crumb wedging in the coral lipstick feathering at the corner of her mouth.

Gene bends to rifle the cardboard unsuccessfully. "I'm sorry, Patricia. As soon as the table arrives from Denmark for the private dining room I'll be able to host you all properly."

"No matter." She licks away the crumb. "Maybe you could teach my daughter the basics of a grocery list." She adjusts the folds of her loose peach sweater, which drapes down long in the front. "I mean, she has the housekeeper at her disposal." Yes, as soon as we get through the drugs and alcohol we can take on everything else she puts in her body, right down to your skin care.

"How is she feeling?" Gene asks.

"Oh, Chass's *fine*." Patricia tosses her buttery fingers. "She's sleeping it off. Good for her. She won't make the same mistake twice." She laughs. "That's what you should be prepping for college—how to make a grocery list and don't mix your drugs."

Tinsley sniffs. "We've tried to keep Darwin a bit more sheltered than that."

"Chass's my best friend," Patricia rejoinders. "She can't see pictures of me in the dining room with Mickey Rourke or Robbie Downey or her father, for Christ's sake, and think I didn't live the go-go eighties. I don't lie to her. Ever."

"Okay, so let's get down to business." Gene walks back to rest one hip on his desk and clasp his hands over his raised knee, putting the bad mother–off on pause. "We're glad you could all make time to come in while you're in the city."

Mrs. Zuckerman rearranges the pleats of her floral skirt. "I wanted to fly home yesterday—my youngest's Bar Mitzvah is in less than two weeks—but Grant insisted we stay."

"Since Chass's still in the hospital, there's nothing much for me to do except finish going through my mail and check on the plants. Tonight I fly back. God bless her, I didn't have to miss one performance. Jeremy Irons said yesterday's matinee was transcendent." She smiles, pleased. "And my assistant set up everything for you, Gene, to fly over to see the show."

"That's so kind, Ms. Warner," Gene says, a bit awkward.

"Patricia, please. And not at all. I'm just sorry I didn't think of it sooner. I've arranged a lovely suite at the Dorchester for you and your wife July Fourth weekend and a little dinner in your honor that Sunday night."

"Well, thank you," he says, now clearly delighted. But the smile drains from his face when his eye catches Grant's. "Anyway, we want to review the events of Saturday night and how you ended up being dragged here in the first place."

"I just want to say," Ingrid jumps in bravely. "I know the student conduct code is explicit on this point, but I think both Chassie and Darwin need our support more than we need them expelled."

Grant shifts abruptly forward, his arms raising as if he might fly across the turtle and take Ingrid's throat. His wife puts a steadying hand on his arm to lower them back to his lap. "Well, now, let's not—no." Gene jumps in. "The point is, Patricia, Grant, Tinsley, we wanted to let you know that we are taking this situation extremely seriously."

"So we're going to help them, work with them," Ingrid affirms with relief.

"If I may." The man in the wing tips leans forward.

"This is Mr. Macmillan, our legal counsel." We all nod as Gene makes the introduction. I can't help but savor the warning these parents are about to get. I reach over and grab myself a croissant.

"Gene, why don't you begin with your prepared remarks," Macmillan prompts.

Gene takes a sip of water and launches in a tone both loud and formal enough for a commencement speech. "In light of the incident on Saturday evening—"

Macmillan clears his throat.

"*Your handling* of the incident, Ingrid," Gene corrects himself. *What?* "One in a number of mishandlings over the last month."

"Mishandlings? What have I mishandled?" Ingrid twists to Gene. I look to Sheila, but she has transitioned from pinched to unreadable.

"You were alarmist." Grant slams his hands on the turtle. "You jeopardized the reputation of the children's families and the school—"

"*I* jeopardized your reputation?" Ingrid strains for control.

"There were press at the event and the hotel has a physician on call. It's not the kind of reckless thinking that we value at Jarndyce," Macmillan intercedes.

"Therefore," Gene concludes, "you leave the school no choice but to terminate your contract—effective immediately."

"Ms. Wells." Macmillan extends a form. "If you'll kindly sign this document."

She takes it with a shaking hand and, stunned speachless, I lean in to scan over her shoulder what amounts to a fully binding nondisclosure.

Ingrid lays the document on the turtle. I look around the circle of impassive faces for a reflection of sanity, ending with Patricia. But she merely looks to the floor, sinking into herself, the folds of her sweater swallowing her like she did the devoured croissant. "You can't make me sign anything."

"That depends on what kind of options you want to give yourself," Tim retorts evenly.

"Ingrid." Gene stands upright. "I want to be able to write you a recommendation—" Sheila barely perceptibly shakes her head and, pained, he changes tack. "Just sign the thing so we can give you a severance check."

"Severance check." Grant snorts derisively.

"Please." Gene implores.

"She's entitled to have a lawyer review that," I say to Macmillan.

He flattens his eyes at me, just another of his long days of having to explain things to morons. "The only way she gets the benefits Gene just outlined for her is if that document leaves this room signed."

"So, if I don't?"

"You'll be hard-pressed to find a school that will hire you," Sheila answers.

"Wait." Ingrid swipes the air with her hand. "What are you going to tell the students? When do I talk to them—"

"Well, actually, we need to follow the board's new protocol for terminations." Gene stares at the carpet as if it were a Teleprompter. "In keeping with the transfer of other best practices from the financial industry, in which our board members are leaders, there is now a guard in the waiting area who will escort you to your desk. You can take your jacket and your, uh . . ."

"Bag." Shelia jogs his memory.

"Right, your bag. And all your personal things will be sent to you. So can you sign? We don't need to drag this out any longer, do we?" His eyes plead.

Ingrid numbly takes the pen from the lawyer's outstretched hand, stares at it—and drops it atop the papers. Standing, she walks past all of us, turns, mouth open, eyes darting around the room.

And with a bellowing of the door she's gone.

"Now what?" Gene looks to Macmillan.

"Don't sweat it. As long as there's a Jarndyce, that girl isn't teaching."

I pull my tongue from where it has stuck to the bridge of my mouth, a wave of frigid heat passing through me to the tight welts of the couch as I scream silently at my clasped hands.

"Ms. Warner, Mr. and Mrs. Zuckerman, the point is you can see we're taking action." Tim looks to Patricia, not bothering to dote on the Zuckermans. There's no need, the Zuckermans couldn't look more reassured. The Zuckermans look, in fact, loathsomely soothed. "We were even thinking of maybe revamping our drug and alcohol education to something more therapeutically focused."

"Hm." Patricia mulls this over, sweeping a crumb off her lap as she stands and gathers up her tote. "Just do me a favor, will you?"

Tim nods, prompting her to continue.

"Don't suck all the fun out of it."

I watch Gene's thick hands fumble with the key as we stand outside Shari's old office, a few doors down from his own, which I heretofore did not even know existed.

I have apparently passed my road test.

The flat smile I have been clinging to while Patricia, the Zuckermans, Sheila, and Macmillan exchanged niceties and said their good-byes is cracking, and I steal this unobserved moment to squint my eyes shut.

"Dammit." The key slips through Gene's grasp and clanks to the planked floor. He bends with a hand on his knee to swipe it up, his eyes fleeting across mine. "These are, uh—these are the tough days. Tough decisions." He turns back to the door. "But that's what the students count on us for." He slides the key in and turns the knob. Ambient light flutters to life around us, illuminating the sky-colored bookshelves that line the walls on either side of the room. Nestled amid the titles that made up the core curriculum of my graduate degree, judiciously placed Asian antiques cause my tightly hunched shoulders to involuntarily drop.

"This was Shari's office?" I step in behind him.

"Yes, she wanted something Zen. She called it her nest in the jungle." He chuckles.

"Right." I hurry across the cream flokati to the round window, pressing my forehead into the glass to peer down at the sidewalk. I see a hand wave down an approaching cab. It stops and a red-clad arm grabs at the handle, opening the door, and in a blur, she crumples inside.

I know that cab ride.

"Gene, I'm not comfortable with what's just transpired." I turn to where he stands against the closed door, looking utterly drained, his shoulders flanked by large black-and-white photographs of clouds. He scratches at the base of his head, his face twisting as the gesture turns into a massage of what is clearly a very stiff neck. "Gene?"

"Yeah." His arm drops slackly.

"Ingrid has, in every instance I have interacted with her, had the students' absolute best interests at heart."

"Well . . ."

"Firing her was fulfilling Grant Zuckerman's agenda, and you and I both know it. His son embarrassed him and he needed someone to punish."

"Nan," he says sharply, crossing the rug to open a lower cabinet door and crouching to peer inside. "You've been with us for what, a month now?"

"Just about."

"And I've been here twenty-four." He pulls out a half-emptied bottle of Scotch—Shari's? Gene's?—and reaches back in the cabinet to produce a paper cup. "All you know is what you saw, and that was one tiny piece of Ingrid's career at Jarndyce. Which, by the way, I need you to write up." He untwists the bottle top and, gripping it between his thumb and forefinger, pours a shot into the cup.

"Write up?"

"For our records." He knocks the drink back.

"If you're asking me to libel—"

"I'm asking you to record the facts of the work you did with Ingrid and the facts of how she made decisions during the incidents you witnessed. Not your opinion of them. Look, Nan, today was a bad day. I'm with you. But these are few and far between here. Let Ingrid go teach—"

"*Where,* Gene? You guys made it clear she had eliminated any chances of that."

"Oh . . ." He drops into a white leather chair, the bottle in his lap. "The Midwest or Seattle, maybe—I always thought Seattle'd be a nice place to live—and she'll find a more rural school that's the right fit for her. A public school somewhere that doesn't need our recommendation."

"What school's not going to want to know where she's been working for the past three years?"

"She could go abroad. Maybe Canada or Norway or somewhere. Look, she'll be happier not working for us. We'll be happier without her. It's just a matter of sorting everyone out and getting our values aligned in this organization. You have to admit it wasn't a fit."

"I'd like to think it was the Zuckermans who aren't."

"Christ, Nan, you're not going to pull a Shari on me, are you?" He stands. "I need an answer right now."

"You mean quit?"

"Yes."

"Gene, Shari wanted to stay with her baby. I'm just trying to understand—"

"Because we're going to really be ramping it up here." He strides to return the liquor to its hiding spot. "So now that we've gotten this business out of the way, why don't you spend the next week getting settled in here and up to speed with Shari's materials, and then let's regroup and start tackling our summer staffing plans. Okay?"

"Gene."

"Nan, tell me where else are you going to get an office like this? A retainer like this? Get yourself organized . . . make it your own so you can be up and running." He claps his hands and then, as if he'd almost forgotten, lays the key on the seat of the chair before pulling the door closed behind him.

Finally alone, I sit heavily in the white mesh desk chair and rub my hands over my eyes. I should tell him to go fuck himself. Find the village Gene was talking about on an ice shelf somewhere that won't care about Ingrid's tainted record and hook her up. Fuck.

I exhale, seeing, over the neat stacks of files spread about the Lucite desk, a picture of a bride being held by her husband in an orchard at peak bloom. I roll the chair closer and spot a white mug hand-painted with her name, its rim lipstick-smudged, sitting beside a browned flower arrangement. I pluck up its card with a picture of a stork. "Shari, happy shower! From the board."

Ah, the board. One minute they're taking you to Park Avenue Spring, the next they're banishing you to Norway.

Still holding the card, I walk over to the cabinets lining the bottom half of the bookcases and pull open their doors, spotting a jumble of heels and a shopping bag containing makeup. I take the bag back to the desk and look down at the phone; at its base is a little typed list of emergency numbers—an ob, Mt. Sinai, a woman's name, and then Scott's cell and Scott home. I pick up the phone and dial the home number. A charismatic man's voice informs me the Olsens are out and I should leave a message.

"Hello! Hi, this is Nan Hutchinson and I'm calling from Jarndyce, where I am, um, filling your old position. I see that you've left your personal belongings here and I'd be happy to send them to you. You can call me at your old office number or on my cell." I leave the number. "Thanks." I begin to put the personal things in the bag, pausing to open a file still propped up between the vase and the wall. I stare down at it, the mug still in my hand—it seems to be a spreadsheet . . . with all the teachers' names, including a few I don't recognize, down one side. Along the top are acronyms I've never heard of—TASV, ER, IBI, KL, IS-AM. IS-AM???

And I decide to help myself to that unoffered drink.

"So they're all settled with the dad, then," Josh affirms from where he kicks the soccer ball to Pepper across the patchy grass of Marcus Garvey Park Wednesday evening.

"What?" I ask, brain fried from trying to make sense of Shari's staff files for the last three days.

"The X boys?"

"Right. Yes, yes." I pause to think. "It's a relative term." I hurl a muddy tennis ball in the opposite direction and Grace races to catch it, silhouetted against the setting sun slanting through the tree line.

"More settled than the last time you were fired from his care." Josh jogs past me to catch his daughter's returned kick, his hands steadying Wyatt in the snuggly against his chest.

"I guess. I keep thinking I need to get them out of there."

Josh goes to kick, but pauses as we both watch Pepper squat down to have a conversation with something at ground level. "So stealing kids now. You that freaked about pregnancy?"

"No," I scoff as Grace returns to drop the ball at my sneakers. "I mean, I am freaked about pregnancy. That and raising a child when *there's no future.*"

"Sell that juicy nugget to TMZ and renovate your entire block."

"Renovate. Who paired *that* smooth-sounding word with what we're doing? I would like to co-opt eviscerate. We are eviscerating. And I will never undertake eviscerating another thing. No, I mean, I'm just starting to have this looping fantasy where I rescue them, rename them Hutchinson, and make all the men in my life happy."

"So Ryan's on board with this kidnapping adoption?"

I hold the ball in my hand. "It's a bit much to propose over the BlackBerry, to which his current location has restricted all our communication. You know, I worked out this morning this is the longest we've ever been apart—including when I had to take the bus up to

Cambridge senior year to see him. It sucks." I pull a knot of felt from its muddy surface. "Oh, it's absurd, I know. I just—I still feel like I'm supposed to fix Grayer. And there are moments—*moments*—where it seems possible. The thing is I'm so worried about screwing up my own kids, maybe I could just start out with half screwed and focus my efforts on the unscrewing, which, if I were fully in charge, I'm sure I could at least make some headway on." Grace looks at me expectantly, eyes sparkling, the corners of her mouth turned up as she pants, poised to tear off at my tiniest muscle twitch. "Besides, look how my dog loves this. I can't trek a baby out here every night. Grace'll become one of those forlorn animals in the ads for canine Prozac. I couldn't take it." I hurl the ball for her.

"If I can conduct a mini World Cup with a BabyBjörn, you can throw a measly tennis ball."

"Yeah, what's up over there?" I nod at Pepper, who is now singing her heart out to the grass.

"Pepper has very important business. You have no idea the amount of inanimate objects in this city that require entertaining. *And* we might be putting her out to work with a tin can, so it does a father good to see her practice with such gusto." He fidgets with Wyatt's hat.

"What's up, Joshy?" I step over to him.

"Jen was let go last week."

"You're kidding." My face goes slack. "Is it the baby—they can't do that."

"They eliminated her whole department. Replaced it with Bear Stearns' people. Hiring's frozen in her sector and, ugh . . . we're not going to get by on my journalistic prowess."

"Shit, why didn't you tell me?"

"Taking time for the dust to settle. We haven't even told our parents yet."

"So what're you thinking?"

"Well, we'll hold out as long as we can, but we're starting to have the ubiquitous Escape From New York talk for real."

"I'd totally offer you to have a floor of our place—"

"But it's under evisceration."

"But my pail to piss in is yours." He smiles and I put my hand on his arm. "Oh, man, I'm so sorry! Is there anything I can do?"

"You're a good friend." He shrugs me off with a dismissive tone that lets me know, as he has done over the years when discussing girlfriends and family, that he is through sharing.

"Well, can I at least offer you and your lovely children a humble Golden Krust beef patty, local *spécialité*?"

"And Wyatt here will take a Red Stripe, thank you, kind lady." He bows his head, happy to change topics. "Pepper," he calls, walking over to her, "how about a little Jamaican?"

"That's it, babe." I wriggle the soggy ball from Grace's muzzle and drop it in the pocket of Ryan's Carhartt. "Ready for dinner?"

At the d-word, Grace takes off toward the exit and then doubles back to keep pace with me and Josh and a still-crooning Pepper, darting back and forth as if I might renege. As we arrive at the street, I bend to clip on her leash, returning us to owner-pet status from the two lady companions enjoying sporting activity we were mere moments ago.

"You'd come visit us in Buffalo, right?" Josh turns to me, serious once again.

"Say the word and me and my stolen sons are there."

"And you're joking?"

"About the sons part, totally. No, they're fine where they are. I *want* them to be blissfully, finally fine right where they are." I put my arm around his shoulders, take Pepper's hand, and we all cross over toward Malcolm X Boulevard.

The next afternoon I find myself sprinting from Jarndyce to hurl myself in a cab, willing the traffic to part faster, move faster. In Carter's elevator I irrationally pound the buttons to make it close faster, rise faster. Catching my breath, I pull my phone out of my pocket to see if Stilton has called again since his last panicked, sob-strangled message.

The unlocked door opens and I stride into the smoky apartment, an activated detector bleating assaultingly overhead. "Stilton?"

Carter enters the foyer from the living room, a canvas jacket over her jeans, hands over her ears. "We can't find the circuit breaker!"

"Nan!" An anguished cry comes from the back of the apartment.

"Stilton?" I race toward his voice, Carter on my heels.

"Can't you help find the breaker first?" she asks. "Any second the sprinklers will go! He won't leave the bathroom anyway—"

"Because I told him not to," I call over my shoulder. "If he keeps his hand submerged, it'll manage the pain till we can get him to the hospital."

"Hospital?"

I stop in front of the doorway to a Carrara bathroom where Stilton sits on the toilet under a bower of decorative forsythia, his hand in the full sink, his face swollen, red and tear-soaked. At the sight of us he lifts it from the water and immediately cries out. Carter recoils. He doubles over, pulling his burn into his chest.

"Stilton," I say loud enough to be heard over the smoke siren and his screams. "Put your hand back in the sink!"

But he can't move from the agony.

"I can't take this!" Carter shouts.

"Stil, ssh." I reach down and gently guide him by the elbow, lifting his arm over the lip of the sink and submerging his hand in the cold water.

"Jesus," Carter mutters behind me. The alarm suddenly stops, leaving in its absence only a high-pitched whine in my ears and Stilton's whimpering.

"Got it!" Grayer yells from down the hall.

"Thank fucking God." Carter's fingers circle her temples.

"And I found the Percocet, Darvocet, and Vicodin." A panicked Grayer rounds the hallway corner holding three bottles. He sees me and stops short. "Nan, you don't need to be here."

"M-mom's voice m-mail wasn't picking up," Stilton stutters through his pain.

With a quick glance at Carter, Grayer shimmies past her into the bathroom to place the pills on the sink. "Carter has it under control, Stil."

She sits hard on the bathtub rim.

"And Dad's on his way." Grayer puts a hand on Stilton's back.

"He is?" I say, surprised. "Well, that's great. I'll stay until he gets here and then you guys can go to the emergency room."

"I mean, I left a message with Gillian," Grayer adds. "So I'm sure he'll be here as soon as he gets it."

"Okay ..." I say, trying to figure out how to escalate Stilton's aid without puncturing Grayer's belief in the change Carter is capable of effecting in his father.

"How bad is it?" I offer Carter the floor.

"You heard the screams," she says, declining it.

"Here." I turn to Stilton, with Grayer leaning over my shoulder. "Let's have a look." I gingerly pivot his wrist so I can assess his palm, which is covered in prune-sized blisters where it hasn't burned through to the meat. I wince. "What happened?"

"I was making macaroni and cheese for Carter because she said she was going to have a hard day and I wanted to surprise her when she got home. I turned the button to make the stove work and then I couldn't find the stove and then I touched the counter while I was looking—"

"It's an utter disaster in there. The damn thing's cracked after only a month."

"I'm so sorry," Grayer says nervously. "He won't do it again, Carter. I should have been watching him. I nodded off doing homework and I shouldn't have—I'm sorry."

"Right." I spin to her *Vanity Fair* face. "Do you have a plastic bowl we can use to keep Stilton's hand cold and wet on the way to the emergency room?"

"No."

"No?"

Arms crossed over her jacket, she backs out of the bathroom. "No." She tosses her small hands up, stamp-sized post-Letterman engagement ring glistening. "I don't allow plastic ... anything and ... those are *my* painkillers ... and I was about to handle this.

My homeopath will be here in, like, five minutes." She walks away down the hall.

Grayer crouches to search Stilton's face. "Stil, can you hang in there, just a little longer until Dad gets here? Please?"

"It hurts." Stilton looks at him as if he's not quite believing he's being asked to wait. "I want Mom."

Grayer's nostrils flare. "She's not coming."

Stilton's eyes widen.

"But Dad will," Grayer repeats with conviction. "I just don't get why you would . . ."

"What?" Stilton asks, wiping his nose on his other sleeve.

"Isn't it cool getting to see Dad in the morning at breakfast?" Stilton nods. "When they get married we'll move to a new place with real rooms for us. In Hollywood. Don't you want to meet Padma for real?" Increasingly pale and sweaty, Stilton is rapt. "So just . . . please . . . hang in there a few more minutes. And don't ever do anything like this without checking with me first. Ever."

I look down into the sink, where a shred of skin has come loose and is floating to the top. I search out Carter into the smokier end of the apartment, finding her in the olive foyer, typing on her Black-Berry.

"*Is* he coming?"

"He's *working,*" she says defensively. "I told Gillian this is silly, he shouldn't bother himself."

"Okay, let's take him."

"You don't want to go to the hospital."

"No. I don't want to go to the hospital. I went last week, so I feel like I've filled my annual quota. But Stilton needs Silvadene," I say steadily, holding myself back from adding *and antibiotics and maybe a skin graft.* "And a doctor to decide how much painkiller for his height and weight."

"No, you can't." She starts shaking her head. "I lead a very quiet life here. *Please.*"

"Nan, he's fine," Grayer yells down the hall. "Let's wait for the homeolady! Carter says she's really good! And then Dad will take us to the hospital! You can totally go!"

"This'll be in the magazines," she mutters to herself, hands fluttering in the air. "They'll say I'm an unfit stepmother—a child abuser." She turns to face me. "I never wanted this."

Suddenly we hear a strange cracking sound, like twigs snapping underfoot, and then footsteps pounding down the hall toward us. We turn to see Stilton, his Converses slapping against the pickled hardwood, his arm submerged in the forsythia vase to his elbow. "It's cold and wet. Let's go."

I press for the elevator, which springs open at my touch. Stilton darts in.

"Grayer?" One hand on the electronic eye, I call down the corridor, "Are you coming?"

Silence.

"Grayer?"

Nothing. I turn to Stilton, who's holding the vase up in the crook of his other arm, his face contorted in sweaty pain.

"Carter, I'm sorry. But he needs to go to the hospital right now."

I look back at her as I step in with him. Unable to meet my eyes, she tosses her hand, inhaling deeply through her nose. The door starts to shut. "Wait." I thrust my arm out, catching the cold metal. "Do you have Stilton's insurance card?"

"What?" she asks the floor.

"His insurance card." She doesn't look up. "Then please have Grayer text me his ID number. One of his parents must have it." God willing. "Thanks."

"You know you're ruining this for me," she says quietly.

"What?" I keep my hand on the electronic eye.

"New York. It may be ruined."

Shaking my head, I let the door slide shut.

Having finally gotten Stilton settled in bed with his hand submerged in a newly purchased, deeply offensive, water-filled Tupperware bowl, and with no fucking idea *where* Grayer even is, I make my way home from the subway, contemplating selling *this* nugget to TMZ. Ruined New York, she should be happy I didn't ruin her face.

I round the corner to my block and spot a town car parked behind our overflowing Dumpster, as our neighbors, some of whom stretch out their windows to get a better look, the metal in their curlers glinting in the glow of the streetlamps. I wonder if they know something I don't—that this is, say, Fat Cy's car. Fat Cy, who formerly owned the seized property and ran a very profitable business in it, thank you very much, before the City of New York stuck their motherfucking noses where they don't motherfucking belong and now he would like to take back what is rightfully his—at gunpoint.

So I'm profoundly relieved when Citrine emerges in a pale pink trench coat proffering three giant Eli's bags. "Surprise! I brought dinner!" she says, holding up the straining white and orange plastic.

"Oh my gosh."

"You said you were camping. I thought, slumber party! I couldn't bear the thought of you roughing it."

"Oh my gosh," I say again stupidly, looking at her holding out armfuls of plaster dust-free food, in her pristine cotton coat, and want nothing more than to get back in the car with her and slumber-party with the accessible toilets of 721. "You're so sweet! But know I'm living in a pit of despair. As you are a pregnant person, I honestly have to give you a full disclaimer that there is stuff going on in that house that may give us all flipper babies. I mean, once we're actually constructing *anything* I'm going all sustainable nontoxic, but right now we're all lead paint chips, all the time."

Citrine laughs and puts a hand on my shoulder. "I love you. You're so considerate. I promise not to lick the walls. Now lead the way."

I take the heavy bags from her as her car maneuvers out onto the street, and she follows me up the stoop. "Okay, brace yourself. We're kind of rocking the *Little House* thing right now, so let's put on our bonnets and get ready to kick it old school, like, *old* old school." I reluctantly swing the door open into the darkness and place the bags on the floor, where Grace commences inspecting them. "Grace, no." She sits and, panting, tilts her head as if I've just told her that I'm taking away her family's food stamps and bulldozing their shanty. "She knows it's dinnertime and thinks I'm having it hand-delivered for her from Eli's. It's an honest mistake for a retriever."

"Oh my God, she's so cute." Citrine grips her coat closed in the shadows.

"Wait here, where one day a fabulous vintage chandelier will hang." I grab the bare bulb's five-extension-corded wire and follow it back along the floor toward the kitchen. "Someone had knocked out the original walls decades ago and put up multiple plywood partitions—we think it was an SRO at some point. So we just tore them down and now we'll re-create the original floor plan." I'm careful to step over lumber and saws and buckets of nails, grateful for the little slivers of street light filtering in through the grimy back windows. "Those windows look out on a garden! Currently the site of New York's next West Nile outbreak, but charming in a *Dark Crystal* sort of way. They've started the rewiring, so my contractor rigged up the light from the generator, so just hold on and I will find, the uh . . ." I feel my way back to the switch. "He didn't attach it to the water heater, or any appliances, but he did leave me with one working bulb, so yeah." I find the lever and it hums on. "Ta-dah!" The bulb trumpets to life, casting its unsparing eye on the front third of the space. "So, this is it! Casa Hutch. Hutch-on-a-Crutch, we call it." I walk over to join her and we look up at the open landing that was once and will one day be my second floor. "Sorry, yes, there were stairs, but they collapsed, and in the next week or so, they're going to come give us a brand-new set, which'll be really exciting. So . . . what do you think?"

She cannot even fake it. And she is trying. Every ounce of her debutante training is straining to pull up the corners of her mouth like an Olympic lifter. But the weight of my war-zone abode is too much for her. "Oh, I see the—potential."

I swing back to the ripped open walls, the girl at the party wearing the secondhand dress, and start manically pointing out its stunning features. "The moldings! And the plasterwork! And the—the bay windows!"

"No, no, it's great, Nan, it's great. So much . . . character."

I follow her stricken gaze to the kerosene stove and the sleeping bag and the pee bucket and the ceiling-high pile of drywall and I burst into tears.

"Oh, God, I'm an asshole." She rushes to embrace me.

"No, I'm the asshole. I live here," I spit out in huffs. "I had the whole *world* to choose from and I picked this place." I sink to the floor, sliding on the sawdust.

"Nan, it's gonna be great."

"It's a shithole." I push Grace away as she tries to lick at my damp cheeks. "I'm so sorry. This is so not what you came here for. You don't have to stand on ceremony. You seriously can go."

"I'm not going anywhere. We have an Italian picnic!"

We find the broom and declare what was the entry hall a debris-free zone. I drag over the air mattress and put the sleeping bag on top and we lay out our picnic under our friend, the naked bulb.

"I had a plan," I say, taking a much-needed swig from the half-bottle-I-wish-was-a-magnum of Shiraz she brought, trying to pace myself for as few trips to the bucket as possible. "We would live upstairs in the lovely bedroom overlooking the wild garden while we updated the kitchen, rocking Trader Joe's and a microwave for a few weeks while we went stoveless. I mean, we lived in Africa. In huts. But everyone was in huts. I wasn't leaving my hut to get on a subway with people who had showered and ironed. I had no idea we'd need a new boiler, new roof, new *stairs*—that a facade could separate from a building, that a basement could be toxic. And it was so weird when the contractor told me. I was just like, *toxic?* My basement can't commit? You know, like, the word has been so overused I'd forgotten the original meaning, which is *will kill you*. And we had the house inspected before we bought it. By, it turns out, either the most incompetent engineer ever, or a psychopathic optimist."

"Wow." She laughs, gamely biting into a cold pizzette, her legginged legs tucked to one side.

"Wow is right. A bank's inspector would've caught these things, but the foreclosure price was so cheap we didn't need a mortgage. Of course, now we've had to take out a loan to cover the construction. So we have massive debt. And a gigantic pile of tinder in an up-and-coming neighborhood."

She rests her slice back in the foil container. "Do you mind if I lie down?" she asks. "I'm realizing how out of shape I am. I'm only halfway there and my lumbar is giving out." She slides onto her side. "Do you have anything I can use to rest my top leg on?"

I cast my eyes around the perimeter of wood and power tools. "Grace?" Following my strategic patting, she shuffles around on the mattress and recircles with a humph next to Citrine, allowing her to rest her top leg on Grace's golden back. "Oh, that feels great."

"Your shower invitation was really enchanting," I say, smiling as I picture the little foldout elephants. "It's on the mantel, over there in the dark. I'm really looking forward to it."

"Promise you won't leave my side the entire time? I'm dreading being in a room full of those women. Tatiana called Pippa and then Pippa wanted to host it and then she invited some other Chapies and the whole thing got out of hand."

"Well, my offer to help still stands. Oh, I forgot to ask, have you finished *Lucky Jim*?" I ask.

"Oh God, sorry, I think I kind of jumped ship on our little book club. I can't remember the last thing I read that wasn't a decorating magazine. I haven't even cracked the spine on *What to Expect*. I'm just slammed with all of this." I watch her feel around at the small of her back, grimacing. I reach my hand out and rub in circles, the way I used to with my sleepless charges.

"I really fucked up," she murmurs. I don't reply, letting the quiet sit between us as invitation. After a few moments she shifts her weight and I pull my hand away. "See, Clark and the architect—they have this vision. This shared vision. That I don't entirely get. I mean, I've seen the drawings. I'm not an idiot. I went to art school, for Christ's sake. I know who Frank Lloyd Wright is. I just don't get what Mission is mixed with an 'eighties vibe.' That makes no sense. I can't picture it. I can't picture what I'm agreeing to. Not that he needs me to agree. Because this architect, he's the best. He did the Dubai Ritz. He's cutting-edge. What if I just have an opinion about the fucking couch even though I'm not Kelly Fucking Wearstler? Vicente Wolf did his place in the Hamptons, I'm not kidding, and I'm not allowed to buy so much as a coaster for it. I thought this would be different. But he's not paying any attention to me. He hates my body right now. He can't even look at me. I don't know . . . I'm just . . ." She slips her clip to the floor, her hair tumbling down to the sleeping bag, as she closes her eyes.

"I'm sorry." I move the empty containers off her side of the air mattress in case she falls asleep. "I'm sure as soon as the baby comes you'll get all his focus," I say quietly, despite never having seen any supporting evidence in my years up-close and personal in that hood.

She tucks her hands up under her chin. "I hooked up with the faux paint guy."

My breath catches. She stares into the darkness.

"Don't tell anyone, okay? I mean, just once. And I didn't fuck him. I just . . . loved the way he looked at me. Pregnant and all. It was so fucking hot. I mean, I feel awful about it, but God, was it hot. So I can't go home. If I see Clark, I'll blurt it, I know I will. See, I blurted it to you. I can't be around anyone I know right now. It's too dangerous."

"Sure. Sure. No problem."

"You're the best," she murmurs, amazingly drifting off midrevelation.

Stone-cold awake from this alternate reality embodied in the sleeping, cheating pregnant woman to my left, I sit motionless so as not to arouse Grace from her gig as leg rest—wanting a moment unobserved to take this in. I peer up at the straw fedora Ryan got at that outdoor market in Cuba, hanging in shadow on a nail behind the front door, waiting for summer, waiting for walls, caked in plaster.

And I miss him. And I could never.

In the morning I'm awoken by the crinkling of a paper bag being placed by my head. "Citrine?" I inhale.

She's hunkering over me in her pink coat, the sun just rising in the open front door behind her.

"Grace?" I startle, before catching her out of the corner of my eye, sitting at attention where her leash dangles off the mantel.

"Sorry. Go back to sleep. I have to leave." She stands, the May breeze ruffling the detritus of our picnic.

I push up to my elbows. "You okay? Did you tell Clark?"

"What? *No.*"

"Sorry, I just thought since you were in a hurry—"

"There's a muffin in the bag." She slaps at the dust on her leggings. "I texted Lennox to buy it for you on his way to get me."

"Wow, thanks, you have really delivered on the food front." I sit up, scraping my fingers through my hair.

"Thanks for last night, it was, uh, fun."

"It was. Thanks for the picnic, really. And for breakfast!"

"Sure. So we're good?"

"Yes?"

"Great!" She hustles to the door and steps out backward onto the stoop, her hand on the tarnished knob. "You really shouldn't stay here, Nan. It's kind of beyond. Go to your parents' or something. Okay, see you!"

"See you," I say to the closed door, the space returned to its stuffy dimness. I rest my forehead on my knees and twist to see Grace as I blink awake. She lifts her ears and takes a step to me. "Okay, okay, you're next."

There's a pounding at the door. I climb up and, pulling my sweater down over my underwear, crack it back open. "What'd ya forget?"

"Mrs. Hutchinson?" A heavily cologned man looks me over, a cell phone at his ear. I dart my naked lower half behind the door. Grace runs over with a bark, trying to wedge her snout into the gap.

"Yes?"

"Yeah, I'm here for the remediation."

"Remediation?"

He holds a finger up and hacks a smoker's laugh into his cell. "That's what I told him! He's a total fucking douche bag." He looks at me. "You going to let me in or what?"

"Sorry, I don't know anything about a remediation."

"Wait, Ronny. Hold up." He puts his hand over his cell. "Your contractor, Steve, hired me? For the mold? I told him I gotta move it to today. I got another gig out in Queens so I can't start Monday. I got a truck full of my guys, we gotta get in here now. They're on the clock." He jerks a fat thumb at a quartet of Mexican men unloading a truck behind the Dumpster.

"Steve told me he was cleaning the basement himself." I grip Grace's straining collar.

"Nah, he's not qualified. You are talking about something highly dangerous here. I am a certified mold remediation professional." I look back to the air mattress, where the message light pulses on my phone. "You know they can't do any drywall on the foundation without remediation. So, you going to let me in? Or am I coming back next month and you're paying my guys for losing a day of work."

"No! Just give me a moment to—" But he's already returned to hilarious Ronny. I close the door, whip on my jeans, shove my feet into yesterday's heels, and return to the stoop. "Okay."

"Let's go!" He calls down to his crew and follows me inside, practically tripping over my campsite. "Jesus fucking Christ, you're *sleeping* here?"

"For a few days," I cry defensively as I flip the mattress against the wall, sleeping bag and all, and hustle over to the mantel for Grace's leash. Holding open my bag, I drop in my cell and wallet. "I have to call Steve. How many hours do you need us out?"

"Hours?" He emits another hearty laugh as the house fills with guys and equipment, Citrine's muffin crushed to a pancake in the stampede. "Try a week. We have to seal, clean in stages, dry the walls, run tests."

"A week?"

We all turn as the air mattress lets out a sad hiss. A guy with the assaulting ladder shrugs.

"This is going to take a week?" I call, trailing the boss into the kitchen, where plastic tarps are already being taped up to seal off, not just the basement, but everything leading to the basement.

"Listen, you want insta-cancer for you and your pup here, that's your death wish. But you're going to have to sign a release. This shit's Agent Orange."

"And then it won't be?!"

"Seven days, totally safe. You can eat off these walls."

I stare up at him, incredulous.

"Hey, you gonna brush your teeth before you go?" He leans down in the interest of preserving my dignity. "I would. *Garlic.*"

My cell starts ringing.

I swipe my toothbrush, deodorant, and the bag of Grace's remaining food from the sink. I hit answer on my phone, maneuvering us toward the door, just as a radio is plugged into the generator and the pounding of early nineties club music waves after me like a tsunami. "Hello?"

"Is this Nan Hutchinson?"

"Yes. Hold a minute, please." I grab my trench, laptop, and keys and get us down the stoop into the blinding sunlight, where my next priority is gum. Grace squats. "Yes?"

"This is Carter Nelson's assistant. You need to come collect your friend's kids, like, *now.*"

17

"Oh, you can't bring a dog in here."

"Bite me."

"Pardon?" The waif-thin man with an asymmetrical hairdo twists his face into a no-you-didn't.

"Sorry," I sigh, double wrapping my hand around Grace's leash as she strains to sniff Carter's Lucite umbrella stand. "Didn't mean to say that out loud. Look, I have my dog because you said I needed to come immediately, otherwise I would've dropped her at my parents'—which doesn't concern you. Can I just please see the boys now?"

"Oh, they're at school." He clutches his binder to his chest and leans his back against Carter's closed front door.

"*What?*"

"I mean, I assume." He glances at his iPhone. "I really don't know anything about it. I just got your card from Carter before she left for the airport and she said to call you because you're the mother's best friend—"

"I'm not. We're not. We're not even friends."

He stares at me.

"At all."

"Oo-kay," he continues. "She said call you to come collect them since we're shutting this location down."

"Location? Down? Because I took Stilton to the hospital?"

"Not in my purview."

"Do the boys know?"

"Carter doesn't do good-byes."

I look at him, my breath caught. "So they're at school right now with no idea that what they think of as their bedroom is currently being '*shut down,*' " I repeat, disbelieving.

"I swear." He points a finger at Grace and her snout follows to sniff it. "If that dog scratches the floors and it affects the resale, my ass is toast."

I look from Grace to him as he cautiously leans his meager weight farther into the door, opening it a sliver. "What's your name?"

"JJ."

"JJ, this morning I peed in a bucket—no, correction—*last night* I peed in a bucket. I have not seen an actual bathroom in over twenty-four hours. And that was in the St.Vincent's ER, not exactly an image to cradle on lonely nights. I'm hanging by a thin thread, JJ. A thread that will snap if I am now required to carry my sixty-pound dog down that long-ass hallway to the boys' room."

"Brain wave!" He twirls his finger into the air. "Wait here."

We do. He opens the door till it's flush with the foyer wall, and I lean my head in to watch the conveyor belt of movers circling in and out of the green corridor with heaps of bubble wrap. A second later, JJ emerges at the hallway's end, wending around the movers to return with two pairs of balled-up tube socks. "For its feet. Gen-ius!" he singsongs, tossing them to me.

"JJ?" I call out as I sweatily stuff the last of Grayer's clothes into the final suitcase, marveling that we got all this down here without a moving truck in the first place.

"Mm-hm." He appears in the doorway of what was the boys' room, a black Sharpie between his teeth, a roll of packing tape braceleting each wrist. Grace attempts to head over to say hello, lifting her paws like she's walking over chewed gum, socks flapping.

"Can you just give me a breakdown of what happened here?" I ask, wiping my hair out of my eyes with the back of my hand. "The breakdown of the breakdown?"

He drops the pen into his palm. "*Shut*down and it's private."

"JJ, nothing you say could possibly compare to the bizarre I've

witnessed here already, trust me. This is not for public consumption.
I'm not even really going to listen. I just need to be prepared when I
pick these kids up. So a seven-year-old doesn't think it's because he
burned his hand." I tug at the stubborn zipper. "For example, where
is the lovely couple moving *to*?"

"Oh, there's no couple. Hello, she's leaving him."

"She *is*?" I sit heavily on the suitcase. "This is unprecedented."

"He's sha-dy."

"He is," I concur, stretching out my cramped fingers before resuming tugging at the zipper under my calves. "Monogamy's not his
strong suit."

"No, honey. That wasn't even it." He brings his hands to his lips
and mimes locking them with a key. "I have to get back to work. You
know your way out?"

"Sure," I answer, trying to surmise what could have done it—she
finally noticed that's not his natural hair/jaw/waistline? "Would you
mind asking one of the movers to help me take all this down and into
a cab?" I stand and haul the suitcase to the floor with both hands on
the handle.

He shakes his head; not a hair moves.

"Otherwise I have to go back and forth with my dog, and her nails,
and I really don't know how long those socks will last."

He purses his subtly glossed lips at me.

"Thread snapping, JJ."

"Give me five."

"Just keep the meter running, I'll be back in *one* minute to unload."
I reach for the door handle before the cab has even come to a stop
at 721.

"With *the dog*?" the driver shrieks, looking back as if I've suggested
he sit tight with a starving panther.

"There's an extra five in it for you." I close the door on a panting
Grace and run into the Xes' lobby. "Hi! Can you please buzz up to
Mrs. X and let her know I'm dropping off her sons' things and the

boys'll be back after school? You have carts, right?" I ask, recalling they do as I scurry past the doorman to the service elevator to retrieve one.

"Miss?" He waves me back.

"Yes?"

"She not home." He shakes his head.

"Okay, well, then . . . I'll leave everything down here till she gets back. I just need a hand to unload the—"

"She at the hospital for her treatment. And I'm not supposed to accept any deliveries."

"This isn't a delivery, it's her sons' belongings. Stilton and Grayer?"

"Sorry, miss, no deliveries until she back from hospital."

I reach for my BlackBerry to check my schedule. "And what time will that be?"

"Oh, I don't know the time. She at the clinic. Hopkins—"

"Johns Hopkins? She's in *Maryland*?"

He shrugs.

"Mom?" I call as I knock on my parents' door, inciting a flurry of barking. I step out of my punishing, really-made-to-slip-off-under-your-desk heels and lean back against the brass cart, piled high with the boys' bags, which aren't getting any lighter. Grace curls up at my blistering feet, shot from a morning of adventure, happy to crash at the slightest whiff of familiar.

"No! Shush! Shush!" I hear Mom hiss before I see her through the wedged door. "Nan, hi. What's with all the stuff?" We both look down as the girls push themselves out into the hall, breaking into a mad chase of each other with pit stops to bark at an uninterested Grace.

"I need to stay here for the week. But first I need to drop this stuff off while I figure out what to do with the X boys. And I need a shower. Not necessarily in that order."

"No! Girls!" She reaches out to grasp one squirming pup up under each arm as they pass and drops her cheek to the doorframe. "Nan, we're on barking probation with the board. The girls will never keep it together with Grace here."

"Even with her locked in your office?"

"They're going to evict us!" she says wildly.

"Okay!"

"Go to Grandma's."

"But she's allergic, how can we—"

"Evict, Nan! As in *homeless!*"

"Fine!"

"Darling!" Grandma cheers through a surgical mask as she whips open her door to greet me and my pile and my dog. "Come in!"

I slump into her hug, my arms numb and useless after getting everything *back* in a cab and round-tripping it down to a block south of where I started. "Shower, water, food," I murmur, spinning around to heave the pile of stuff inside with Grace plodding behind me.

"Of course, I've already got the radiant heat fired up."

As I sit on the warmed stone floor of the shower room with sunlight pouring through the wall of milk glass—drinking in the delicious aromas of verbena and lavender and other such delicacies not possible with a bottle of Joy and a mixing bowl—clarity strikes. "Grandma?" I call out through the steam into the loft. "Gram?"

"Yes?" I hear her on the other side of the glass, hopefully making me a latte and cinnamon toast.

"Could you manage having Grace here for just a few hours while I run an errand?"

"I already have her set up on a blanket under the sink in the powder room. If I keep the door closed, I'm fine for a few. Go handle your business."

"Step one." I urge myself to stand. "Get out of this shower."

The rain that hit the Metro-North train in sheets has calmed to a light drizzle as I make the trek from the station to the Greenwich address of Mr. X's office. I look at my watch. Almost two. I hasten my step. I have exactly one hour to ascertain where Mr. X intends to take the boys tonight before they head home to find themselves locked out.

But even through my dueling exhaustion and latte-fueled rush, I'm impressed by the thick bloom of spring bursting from every manicured tree box. I inhale the sweet air with each quickening breath, turning the corner where the shops of downtown trickle off, and I catch my first glimpse of the lilac-dotted lawns that stretch into the parceled acres of estates a few roads yonder.

A Lexus SUV splashes by on the curving street and I catch sight of a boxy black glass office building at the corner, the three stories sitting incongruously beside a willow-bordered pond with two circling swans. Perhaps Mr. X and his colleagues stroll out on the footbridge for cigar breaks to chat billions and ash on Odette's head.

I weave through the dripping black and silver sports cars peppering the small parking lot and up to the glass-doored entrance, where an etched bronze plaque informs me that X Wealth Management can be found in suite 200. I make my way inside the black marble lobby, past the potted ficus and up the open stone staircase, where mahogany doors greet me at the second-floor landing. I take a moment to unbutton my trench and shake out my damp hair before pulling on the handle, stepping from the early nineties into that ubiquitous dark-wood-Persian-carpet-brass-sconce-hunting-painting aesthetic that must have rendered visits to *actual* men's clubs rife with the unshakable sense that one is either about to have assets moved or a will read.

The formidable octagonal waiting room is quiet. Taking off my coat, I step up to the reception desk, which is empty, its computer screen dark and leather blotter clear.

I fold my coat in on its wet outer shell and, laying it over my bag, pull at Grandma's chiffon blouse where it has dampened itself to my bra. One of the four doors opens and a shred of filtered daylight wedges across me as an exhausted-looking woman, arms laden with files, murmuring "Fuckfuckfuck," scurries to the door opposite before I can say a word. Another door opens and a pudgy-faced, twentysomething emerges, tieless, rumpled, coffee-stained, an unlit cigarette dangling from his lips—supporting my theory about the footbridge—only to storm past.

"Excuse me?"

He whips around, squinting in the ambient light. "Yes?"

"I'm here to see Mr. X."

Jerking his thumb to the left of the reception desk at the only set of double doors, he opens one opposite and I see into the quiet bullpen, where only a handful of the cubicles appear occupied. So Mr. X—whether they need it or not some guys just gotta piss all over square footage.

I take a deep breath, and, hearing Mr. X's grumbles on the other side of the doors, lift my hand and knock.

"Yeah," he affirms as if expecting me.

I press down on the handle and step into a palatial room, appointed in leathers and gnarled woods right up to a wall of windows that look out over the pond. Standing squarely in the middle of this serene view, head bent down, monogrammed sleeves rolled up, Mr. X flips through a yellow pad, his other hand bearing his weight atop a stack of files on the imposing desk. He waves me in with the other without looking over, continuing to grunt yes and no into his earpiece.

Seizing an opening I clear my throat. "Hi. I'm sorry to surprise you like this, but—"

"What the?" He looks up. "Hold on." I do. "Not you. What?" he growls, I'm now clear, at me.

"As I said, please disregard the implied drama of my just showing up here, but, given the ticking clock of your children's—"

"You a reporter?" He clicks a button on his earpiece and flips his pad over before bringing his free hand to rest on his crocodile belt.

"No, I'm—"

"Who let you in here?"

"I was waved in by one of your guys. He was chewing a cigarette?" I add stupidly.

He shakes his head at my attempt to help us sort this out.

"Mr. X, I'm Nan Hutchinson."

"Uh-huh."

"I used to take care of Grayer." Blank. "When he was four. I went to Nantucket with you? It would have been about twelve years ago ..." You were diddling that darling Chicago girl?

He cracks a half smile of disbelief that I'm taking his time with this. "My wife sent you? I wired her what she wanted. Tell her to go fuck herself."

"No one sent me. I'm the one who moved the boys down to Tribeca and I was asked by Carter's assistant to pick them up this morning."

He sighs heavily, dropping his gaze to the houndstooth chair behind him. "Jesus, you brought my kids here?"

"No, no, they're in school for"—I check my cell—"another hour. I tried calling Gillian's number, but there's no answer."

"Gillian's gone."

"Oh." I'm momentarily paused. "So, where do you want to take them?"

"To their mother, Jesus. Take them to the apartment."

"She's at Johns Hopkins, so that's not really—"

"Then drop them off. Grayer can handle it." He waves his hand dismissively and flips his pad back over, finger moving up to his ear-piece, situation dispatched.

"No." My turn to shake my head. "I don't think he can."

"Excuse me?"

"I'm here because I've become friends with your sons over the last few weeks. Grayer reached out to me when you left, actually. And these boys have been shuttled around, physically and metaphorically." I try to slow down, knowing this has to come out in order. "They're confronting a potentially dying mother and have nowhere *to be,* somewhere to exhale where one parent isn't constantly one foot out the door or scheming to keep the other's foot in. They don't need or care about anything fancy. Four walls and a television will do so long as *you're* taking care of them."

"Can't do it. I'm crashing here." He tosses his hand behind me at the crumpled throw on one of the Chesterfield sofas, the mohair pillow at the far end still imprinted from his head.

"Okay, I'll bring them up. You'll have to get them on the train for school and—"

"No, absolutely not," he says forcefully.

I stare him down.

"Got it." He slaps his desk. "Take 'em to the corporate hotel in Murray Hill. The business has a suite."

"Great." I exhale. "And what time will you be there?"

"*I'm* not leaving this building for the foreseeable future—major deal in play. Bring them to the hotel. The keys are in my secretary's desk. Come, I'll grab 'em for you." He pulls both hands away from the desktop and winces, his hands instinctively flying to his lower back.

"*I*"—I find myself crossing my hands over my heart, pleading— "am not taking them. *You*"—I point at him—"need to do this. Because *you* are their *father.* It's what a father *does.* He *takes care* of his *children.* He *doesn't* assign them to strangers to live in a *corporate hotel.*"

He reaches across his desk and grabs a small amber-colored prescription bottle, taps two white pills into his palm, and knocks them back, chasing them with a swig from his coffee cup. "But you're not a stranger."

"But I'm not a parent."

"FUCK! JAN!" he bellows, throwing his hands out violently, his body abruptly seizing in pain. *"Fuck."*

And I remember who I am trying to take on and shift a step back. "Nan," I correct, crossing my clammy arms over my clammy chest. He takes an angry step out from around his desk and I use the framed snapshot atop it of toddler Grayer to keep me from kicking off my heels and running back to Metro-North.

"Nan," he repeats, his voice dropping to a conspiratorial timbre as I feel him place both hands on my shoulders with an undue amount of weight. "Nannannan," he murmurs, walking me backward and turning me to the sofa in front of the fireplace. He sits me down atop the throw, lowers himself gingerly beside me, and turns to give me a conspiratorial smile. Dear God, is the man attempting to seduce me? I go to stand, but he holds me back with an entreating expression I didn't know his face capable of.

"Nan." He rests his elbows on his knees. "I am asking you to just give me a week. One week. It sounds like my boys trust you. They feel safe with you. If you could just take them until next Friday, let me get this deal closed. I will *personally* come and relieve you. I've got . . . an agent, a broker, someone looking into places for the three of us. Somewhere near their schools so we can spend more time to-gether. I want them with me—*of course* I want them with me. I'm not a monster. I couldn't stay with their mother anymore. It just wasn't good. Sorry, I know you're her friend—"

"Not. Not her friend."

"But I'm thinking you're the only person I want my children with in this crisis. And next Friday I will pick them up and get us settled and you will be relieved. Can you do that for me? I'll give you a grand in cash for incidentals. It's a huge suite—Jacuzzi baths, the whole nine. Can you do this, for Grayer and Stilton?"

And in that moment, I know what I'm worth. Because I care for these kids, I do, right down to my toes. But I've just learned, appar-ently, for plumbing I'm a whore.

18

Four nights later I use the time it takes for Grace to inspect every piss-soaked asphalt crack and cigarette butt of her charming new block to scroll my BlackBerry's to-do list for this week of mold-induced babysitting: (1) Get shower gift for Citrine. Who may or may not still be married, as there's no word from her. (2) Write up report of Ingrid "incidents," trying to straddle the task of writing an impartial indictment, and get it to Gene. (3) Nail down Mr. X's Friday plans and psych boys up accordingly. (4) Nail down Steve re: plumbing, electricity, stairs, doors, walls, floors, ceilings, and air. Psych self up accordingly. (5) Nail down Ryan to confirm we are, in fact, still psyched to be, to quote his proposal, "sharing this life adventure together." (6) Nail down definition of together.

I stare at the six-point font, wishing for certainty around navigating even one item. Why can't everything be as easy as walking into H&M and putting a week's worth of clothes on a credit card? As we come around the poorly lit redbrick corner of Thirty-eighth Street, Grace immediately starts to drool at the lingering aroma of falafel and the BlackBerry rings, perhaps calling with suggestions. "Hey," I say.

"*You're going to Citrine's shower tomorrow?* Shut. Up," Sarah greets me, picking right up from my two-days-old voice mail. "Who the hell has a baby shower in the middle of a Tuesday?"

"Maybe it's a cultural thing? Is she . . . anything?" I query as a man with closely cropped graying hair approaches from Fifth Avenue, lifting the lapels of his pin-striped blazer against the breeze.

"Take pictures, take notes, take souvenirs, I want to feel like I was there, high in the colon of 10021." As she talks I watch, waiting to see if the guy'll go into the building next door, which Grayer astutely ascertained, from the twenty-four-hour traffic of sheepish-looking men, is a "convenient East Side location."

"I'm thinking she has her artist friends—it should be a groovy crowd," I conjecture. "They'll probably give press-on baby bottle tattoos and handmade onesies from recycled drop cloths." Sure enough, the guy ducks in just as Grace strains to vacuum the shuttered gate of the shawarma establishment. "Grace, no." I tug her leash. "What're you doing tomorrow night? Want to join us for tacos? Come experience me in all my foster-parent glory?"

"Aw, can't. I'm babysitting for Josh so they can pack."

"You're kidding." I halt, hand to heart.

"Nope. Sucks."

"God, I feel so bad—I've been so up my own ass with the production of *Annie* I'm staging over here."

"Don't worry, he understands. Amazingly, they found someone to sublet their place while it's on the market. They're going to live with his parents in Poughkeepsie."

"Oh my God, *how?* It's tiny and overrun with dachshunds."

"I don't think he has a choice. Oh shit, hospital's paging me. Dinner Friday? You feel like schlepping up here?"

"You're on. You can help me through my postpartum depression."

"Remember, I want evidence of this so-called groovy crowd."

Hanging up, I tug Grace into the corporate hotel's lobby and, from under the gold-toned Buena Vida Corporate Residences sign, the night doorman gives me a welcoming nod. It is kind of delightful. How much more could it put us in the hole to hire him to sit on our front stoop at night and say "Evening"? I press twelve in the beige-tinted mirrored elevator and get out on the immaculate, if charmless, hallway to walk down to our temporary home.

"Stilton." Clearly having not budged an inch from the impossibly stiff maroon couch, he swings his head around as I open the suite door. "Come on, man," I moan as I step into the cramped popcorn-ceilinged living room and drop my keys on the counter of the open kitchenette lining the wall. "I said brush teeth, like, twenty minutes ago." I unhook the leash.

"But I think I know which briefcase has the million!"

"And how can I argue with that?" I glance at the clock on the microwave as Grace vaults up beside him. "Okay, I'll bring you your toothbrush and then we'll change bandages, cool?"

Eyes riveted to the screen, he nods. I drop my trench on the round glass dining table and walk over to knock on their bedroom door.

"Yeah?"

"Can I come through?"

"Yup."

I push the knob to find Grayer lounging on the queen-sized bed reading *East of Eden* with a highlighter in hand, as he did for most of the weekend. "Enjoying it?" I ask, crossing to their bathroom.

"It's okay." He grabs a pen from the paisley spread to scribble a note in the margin.

"You work hard," I say as I open the chipped medicine cabinet.

"Yeah, well, grades are important to Dad." He leans forward, shifting the lumpy pillows behind him and scooching back to straighten up.

"It's still commendable." I pick up Stilton's Spider-Man toothbrush from the swirled faux marble vanity and squirt it with paste.

"Deal!" Stilton cries in the other room.

Grayer drops the book between his raised knees as I cross back, pausing to swipe the Duane Reade bag serving as Stilton's burn kit from the dresser. "Thanks."

"Sure. You have enough light over there?" I reach my hand toward the wall switch.

"It's fine." He gestures to the room, which, even in the yellow pool of the bedside lamp, has all the charm of a roadside motel. "Just till Friday, right?"

"Right," I affirm as I pass through the doorway.

"Did Dad say *where* we're going to live?" he calls after me. "Because a friend at school said Julian Schnabel did a building downtown and that'd be pretty badass. I should call Gillian tomorrow and tell her to look into it." I exhale, turning back with a forced smile, unable to tell him yet another fixture in his life has disappeared.

WHOOF!

"Crap, hold on." I jog to where Grace has leapt from the couch to the floor. "Grace!"

WHOOF!

"Stil." I hand him his toothbrush and, dropping the bag on the coffee table, clasp her muzzle closed.

"Mwov." Mouth full of toothbrush Stilton flaps me out of the way and strains his neck to see the screen around us.

Whf! She barks into my hand.

"No." I try my deep, commanding voice as our lovely neighbor pounds on the thin wall, the McOil painting of horses shaking over our heads. Grace stares up at me, her eyes at high alert. "Gracie, it's the el-e-va-tor." I roll out the syllables phonetically for the hundredth time since we got here, as if her issue is being ESL.

"Gracie, come!" Grayer calls from his bed. I release her and watch as she bounds eagerly into their room and onto the spread beside him. He ruffles her head and it sinks down between her paws, her eyes closing. He nods at me and returns to Steinbeck.

"Thank you," I sigh, going over to shut his door as the intercom starts buzzing. I stride to the counter to pick it up. "Hello? . . . Yes, I'm so sorry. She's never been around an elevator before. I promise I will find a bark collar for her first thing . . . Thank you. Good night."

The doorbell rings. Jesus. "Sorry!" I call as I unlock the door. "She's never lived with elevators." But I'm guessing the woman wearing a patent leather trench, over seemingly nothing, doesn't care.

"I'm looking for Bob Smith," she says, eyeing me through four layers of shadow. "But a three-way'll cost extra."

"Who is it?" Stilton yells.

She backs up. "Hey, what is this?"

"That Dad?" Grayer calls eagerly from his room, the collective commotion eliciting more barks.

"No! No, it's just someone who's at the *wrong* apartment," I call for everyone's benefit, shutting the door to a crack. "Sorry, can I—"

"Citibank?" she asks, tugging her cell from her trench pocket, revealing the black lace of a garter belt.

"Sorry?"

"Isn't this the Citibank floor?"

"I really don't know. This is X Wealth Management's apartment."

"I gotta make a call." She hits a number and brings it to her ear, suddenly pointing above my head. "Oh, hey, the pony apartment!" I follow her finger to the framed galloping horses on the walls behind me. "I've been in this one before. Big tippers. Okay, good night." She waves as she turns her attention to her phone. "Yeah, give me the room number again?"

I shut the door. And lock it.

Stilton expectorates his toothpaste into his water glass and looks over at me from the couch, intrigued. "No elevators?"

"Nope." Resisting the urge to blue-light the entire apartment, I try to refocus on the good, picking up one of the plates Grayer left in the working sink, building to the euphoria of putting it in the working dishwasher. "We always lived in walk-ups. Even in Sweden our building only had four floors. And now we live in a house. Apparently she thinks elevators just want to break down the door and dominate our pack."

His attention split between the television and me, Stilton shrugs to acknowledge the possibility.

"And the next time you'd like me to move out of the way a 'please' gets me going."

"Sorry."

"No prob."

I start the washer, taking comfort in its diligent whir, and sit down next to him on the hard foam, glancing at the stampeding stallions, and hoping that the Buena Vida steam-cleans. I lift the Duane Reade bag from the coffee table onto my lap and pull out the supplies. Mesmerized by the show, Stilton holds out his hand and I carefully snip through the layers of gauze, peeling the bandage back, along with flakes of dead skin. Thankfully, Howie continues to commandeer his attention, because it's a queasy operation.

That done, I squeeze a little Silvadene on the thin membrane of new pink skin and buff it in with a sterile Q-tip, blowing to quell any sting before wrapping him back up. "You are officially mummified,"

I pronounce as the lady contestant agonizes between departing with hundreds of thousands of dollars or going for the big payday. She gambles.

"Thanks," he breathes, slumping back against me. I lift my arm onto the couch back and he rests his head on my chest, his frame warm, the connection natural. Easy. And I can't help thinking . . . what's so wrong with this—me and these two kids. I seem to sort of, kind of be doing a decent job at this. Why *can't* I find myself wanting to maybe pick up here, where I can wrap a hand and make a joke, offer to switch on a light, and we all get through another night in one piece? Glancing through the open door to my room across from theirs, I see Ingrid's report resting on the bedspread, not writing itself. But for these few minutes I will just sit, gently holding Stilton's healing hand, and watch someone risk what they never had.

The following morning I glance at Citrine's shower gift, glance at the roll of wrapping paper, glance at my closing paragraph to Ingrid's report, and then glance up at the microwave clock, the same sweaty orbit my eyeballs have been making for the last half hour. The intercom buzzes—shit—and I lift to reach across the Formica for it. "Hello?"

"Messenger," the doorman unceremoniously announces.

"Thanks, send him up."

As I throw myself back on the chair for a last speedy once-over, my elbow topples the tall stack of Shari's files still awaiting my review. I bend to gather them from where they've sprawled on the flecked carpet and swipe up what looks to be a memo from the office of Cliff Ashburn dated this time last year. The subject line reads, "How to Build a Case, Phase II: New additions to the grounds for dismissal of recalcitrant faculty. *Teaching Against School Values*: political insensitivity to climate in the classroom—needs only to be brought up by one student. *Identified Boundary Issues*: any mention of personal life—again needs only to be brought up by one student." My eyes dart down the page—"*Academic Error, Failure to Meet Community Standards*"—and then the memo concludes, "And lastly, *Inappropriate*

Self-assigned Mentoring: defined as a teacher extending any extra support to a student." TASV, IBI, IS–AM . . . the acronyms. I dig through my papers for the first chart I found in Shari's office and scroll my finger down, catching Mr. Calvin's name as the one with the most boxes checked.

Hearing a ping my attention is pulled to my IM box. **Hey sexy. I love you–Ry436.**

The doorbell rings—I toss the mess of files on the table and dart the three steps to open it. "Hi. I'm sorry, I just need a minute."

The guy sighs exasperatedly and shifts his bag to his other shoulder. "I have to charge you for waiting."

"Yes, yes, I know." I flip the dead bolt to hold the door open and stare at the blinking print icon, unsure now, with this new information, what to do.

"Nan?"

I love you, too! Where are you?

Only have few minutes–iChat?

Yes, yes, iChat! Yes! I shift the settings as I hear the messenger's dispatcher on speaker from the hallway.

"Lady?" he calls through the door.

"One more sec, sorry!"

I smooth my hair and readjust my laptop. "Hello?" I say into the static on the screen.

"Hello?" the messenger calls back.

"Sorry, not you!"

"Not me?"

I whip my head over and there he is, the image wavering but discernible. I reach out and touch the screen, his face is unshaven and sweat stains mar his shirt. "Babe," I say.

"Who's that?"

"A messenger. Are you okay? You look exhausted. Are they keeping you safe?"

"I'm actually reaching you from the only prison camp with Wi-Fi."

"Don't even joke—" The doorbell rings. "Shit. Hold on one sec," I beseech the screen. "Okay, coming!" I leap up and open the door.

Fuck it. "You know what, I'm sorry. This was a mistake. There's no package. Go ahead and charge me." I return to the table. "I'm back, I'm back. Are you coming home?" There's a long pause where he looks at me blankly, his hazel eyes tired. "Ryan?"

"What?" he squints into the monitor.

"Can you hear me?"

He shakes his head no. *"What's happening with Steve?"* he shouts.

"I can hear you," I say, louder.

"What's happening with the house?" he shouts again.

"I can hear you—you don't have to shout! I don't know!"

"Because I've been thinking." He drops his voice back, ruffling his hair with his hands. "I can't deal with this anymore."

"*You* can't?" Every cell in my body shifts course. "When you left me I believe we still had water and light!"

"What!" Back to screaming.

"When you left me! Left me!"

He leans into the screen, swiveling his head to the side to hear better.

"Is this working? Can you call me? Are you coming home?" He shakes his head no. No, he can't call? No, this isn't working? No, he's not coming home? *"Ryan!"* I shout into the laptop.

The screen goes black.

An hour later, I rest Shari's box of shoes, wedding photos, and other sundry items on the elevator floor and shift Citrine's hastily wrapped shower gift to one hip to pull out my BlackBerry for the fortieth time since I left Buena Vida. But neither has Ryan texted nor has Steve returned my emboldened four-alarm message. I need my husband in the same room with me and I need livable—like, by Western, first world, at-peace standards—in three days.

Nothing.

The car trembles to a stop on a small travertine-floored landing, containing two identical shiny wood doors set into opposing cream-papered walls. I press the bell beside the one with the sound of women's chatter behind it and a gray blonde in her fifties answers, wiping her hands on her uniform's black apron. "Come in," she invites warmly with a soft brogue, her eyes only slightly widening at the large cardboard box I'm towing. "I think you're the last. The ladies are through there." She points a weathered hand toward the living room, where I recognize former classmates of mine nibbling crudités.

"Do you mind if I just . . . ?" I gesture to a niche by the door and, with her nod, bend to tuck the battered box out of the way.

"Drink?" She picks up a silver tray from the present-free corner of the glossy art deco sideboard behind her.

"Thank you." I take a spritzer and add my gift to the mountainous pile, suddenly self-conscious of its multicolored-bunnies-wearing-party-hats wrapping. All the other boxes are monochromatic, gleaming and glamorous—Bonpoint, Bonpoint, Bonpoint, Jacadi—not a diaper cake among them. Or even anything from Babies "R" Us. Am I the only one who looked at her registry? Was I not supposed to? Is this not how baby showers work here? Are they *all* on Tuesdays?

I tighten my smile and head into the lemon yellow room, its high-gloss walls reflecting the noon sun.

"Naaaan!" our hostess greets me, leaning slightly down in her four-inch Manolos to touch a dewy cheek to mine. "Citrine said you were coming."

"Pippa, wow, I haven't seen you since—"

"Ninth grade." She nods her head, the square diamonds in her ears glinting. "Deerfield was the best thing I ever did." She runs a hand through her blond hair, which once was brown. "Make yourself comfortable—oop." Another guest comes in behind me and she excuses herself to greet her. Taking a gulp of spritzer and a canapé from an untouched tray, I weave past the clusters of wrap-dressed women, noting that, as in high school, the sole cosmetic enhancement allowed seems to be a subtle patina of Elizabeth Arden Eight Hour Cream on the lips, making my little swipe of eyeliner and dab of blush suddenly feel clownish by comparison. I have never figured out why this subset so frowns on makeup. I mean, of course they have nannies if they're expected to look rested without undereye concealer.

Sitting in the middle of a long green couch, Citrine holds court behind an antique coffee table. "Nan." She reaches out an arm to me, the spot she insisted I fill by her side occupied. "So sorry I haven't returned your e-mails. You know how it is. I've been crazed." The women bookending her nod in agreement, their very un-RISD blow-outs bobbing.

"Of course," I say, accepting her excuses, suddenly wanting to re-wind to the moment she got out of that Lincoln with those Eli's bags. Wishing I'd hustled her right back into her car—"Oh, I'm just here checking on the progress—no need to go inside! Let's take this picnic to my room at the Mercer!" Or maybe it wasn't so much the squalor as the fact that I know about her dalliance.

"I know I'm not really pregnant enough yet to be seated when I should be circulating, but let's pretend."

"Sure," I say, giving her slightly swollen hand a squeeze.

"But after Memorial Day half the crowd scatters to Maine, half to the Hamptons, and then someone's always in Europe, so we decided to do it early when *everyone* can be here to celebrate. And, of course, on a weekday when they're free." She rubs her burgeoning belly through her fitted cream top and gives a full smile. But her eyes don't meet mine.

"Well, I'm thrilled to be here." And really, screw your entire con-struction team, I'm great with whatever.

"Brunch is served," the Irish woman announces, pushing back the French doors to the dining room. Cries of "Oooh" go up from the thirty or so women, thirty or so diamond-decked hands flexing, palms out, in excitement. Some are Chapin alumnae, others are pri-vate school vets I recognize but have never met. And no one looks like she is about to whip out the baby-bottle tattoos.

"Naaan!!!" Suddenly I feel a hand on my waist, spinning me into Alex's embrace. "Nan!" she cries, enveloping me in perfume and soft hair. "Where's Toots?"

"Hi!" I pull back, able to admire her vintage equestrian buckle-print shirt dress. "You look fabulous."

"Is Toots coming?" Langly asks, squinting with a hungover air against the gleaming citrus walls.

"Toots—Sarah—had to work." I avoid explaining that Citrine and

Sarah aren't friends, that I, myself, am only here because of a real estate fluke.

"Work!" Alex turns to Langly. "Remember work?"

Langly's eyes widen.

"What're you two up to now? So, you're not still with—where was it—Ogilvy?" I try to remember which advertising firm she was skyrocketing through as we shuffle past the wall of nineteenth-century zebra lithographs into the stream for the buffet.

"Oh, Jesus," Alex says, fingering the Cartier Love necklace at her clavicle. "No, as soon as Roger and I started dating he begged me to quit. He said being director made me a grumpy bitch." She laughs. "No, Astin is a full-time job." She reaches down for a plate and fork. "Citrine's just finally getting it—she canceled her next show, thank God. Now she can relax and focus on the"—baby, say *baby*—"renovation. But my little monster just started kindergarten this year, thank God, giving Mommy a little free time to herself."

"Me—and my sha-dow," a woman sings knowingly with a smile to Alex as she passes with her plate en route to the living room.

"You have a five-year-old?" I am agog at how fast the time has passed.

"I always wanted to be a young mommy," she says smugly, reaching for a quartered carrot muffin and adding it to the dollop of scrambled egg on her miniature plate. "Five is such a great age—he's just starting to be interesting to me. So what about you? Seeing anyone?"

"Married for six years. Actually, we met senior year."

"Why aren't you wearing your ring?"

I hold up the thick gold band that belonged to Ryan's great-great-grandmother.

"Oh." She cracks up, touching my arm. "I thought that was one of those I'm-married-to-me thingies. I was looking for a real one. Will you pass me a piece of melon?" I do, and not by means of flinging it in her face. "Thanks, hon. Well, personally, I'm just so glad Citrine is finally getting a move on," she says conspiratorially. "Before Clark, I'd run into her every few years—I wasn't sure what the plan was there, you know? I mean, you can't tramp around with musicians forever, not while your capital is decreasing." She waves her fork with its stabbed chunk of meaty pink fruit. "You've gotta lock 'em in while you're performing at your peak." Which conjures an image of concurrently fellating her husband, playing killer tennis, and being measured on the NASDAQ. "How about you? Any baby plans?"

As Langly noodles her way down the other side of the table, I watch her drain her champagne and trade it for another from the circling tray while I figure out how to answer Alex.

"Well, I just finished my master's in December." I feel the need to have that on record. "So this is the first year it would really be feasible."

She looks at me blankly, as if she can't connect the two pieces of information. "Well, when you're ready, call me, I'm a wealth of information. I know where to find *great* nannies. They charge, like, next to nothing and go round the clock."

"Ladies!" Pippa calls from the dining room doorway. "Please come gather. Citrine is about to open her gifts!" She claps in excitement while behind her I can see the waitstaff carrying armfuls of packages in from the entryway.

Citrine nestles in and I take a seat on the piano bench next to Langly, who forgos food to sip her third champagne. "Thank you, Pippa, for organizing this," Citrine says, clasping her hands over her belly, "and to all of you for coming and being so enthusiastic, especially those of you I haven't seen in a few years—I'll be a better friend, I promise!" She gives a radiant smile and everyone twitters appreciatively, seemingly delighted to have her back. The first box is passed toward her like a crowd-surfing rock star. "Ooh, exciting," she murmurs as she shimmies her fingers under the maroon lid and pops it off, unearthing from beneath a mille-feuille of amber tissue a thick cashmere baby blanket. In she dives again to the elbow, surfacing with . . . matching pants . . . sweater . . . and booties. At this moment I am tempted to wriggle my bunny-wrapped gift from the pile and jettison it out the window.

"You like?" a voice at once little-girlish and smoker-raspy comes from across the room.

"Tatiana, it's gorgeous!" Citrine coos and I turn to see the flamethrower of yore leaning in the doorway. "Can I change the color?"

"You can change anything but the kid. The kid you're stuck with."
Everybody laughs. My eyes move up from the stiletto knee-high
boots to the skinny jeans wrapping her Core Fusion–toned body, visible through the diaphanous floral-print blouse. And then my gaze
moves up to the copious gold jewelry resting atop a chest so badly
speckled she looks like a giraffe. Finally I land on her face. A face that,
since childhood, always floored me. It floors me now. But because she
looks ... so ... fucking ... freaky. Unable to be alone with my raw
shock, I surreptitiously slip my phone from my pocket and text Sarah:
OMG! TAT HAD HEAD TRNSPLNT.

Tatiana catches me staring and I give a big smile and wave, as if
primarily what I do is miss her. She waves back while Citrine reveals
another teeny-tiny cashmere set. These people do know that babies
double in size the first year? Should I tell them? Tatiana tries to smile
back, but her eyebrows can't go up and her cheeks can't follow and
the effect is that somehow her face moves outward, as if muscles in
reserve that should never be called to active duty suddenly find
themselves on the front lines of having to make a smile. They give it
their best shot, but the result is only a Jokeresque grimace. She *paid*
for that?

She points to the grass cloth–sheathed dining room and I get up
and follow her in, grabbing another mini pain au chocolat from the
buffet. "Nan, it's so good to see you," she says warmly, planting a kiss
on my cheek, still coasting off the thin fumes of an affection born of
having grandmothers in the same building, who encouraged us to
play together. "How are you?"

"Great, thank you," I say, swallowing. "I've started my own HR
Consulting business, if you hear of anyone who might be in need.
And my husband and I bought a brownstone in East Harlem we're
trying to rehabilitate. We've done construction before, Habitat for
Humanity stuff, so we thought we had skills. No skills. We are skill-
less."

She blinks at me, fingering the bejeweled cheetah charm on one
of her necklaces. "I have sun damage."

I nod. She does.

"How are you?" I ask.

"Calliope's two," she says, as if this answers that.

"Oh, wow, yes, Citrine said you have a daughter—congratulations."

"And we're having our second—just as I get my body back, right?" She laughs, touching my arm.

"You look insane," I say, honestly admiring her abs as I reach for a second pastry.

"Oh God, well, you know I have to work at it. My husband's French, so he'll wander." She looks wistfully at the chandelier. "I left the magazine, I work out, I had my boobs done, I wear a lot of lingerie. I mean, yeah, he's fat, yeah, his teeth are black, but you know what? I just lie back and think, 'It's theater.' Am I right?"

Speechless. Sad and speechless.

"Nan, she's about to open yours!" Pippa calls from the living room.

"Oops," I say, clapping my hands enthusiastically, channeling Pippa. "I'm on!" I point into the living room with an apologetic smile—"It was so great to catch up with you!"—and scurry away.

I find Citrine wearing more than a dozen ribbons around her neck and tearing away my bunny paper to expose the plain matte white cardboard box below. "Where's it from?" she asks, lifting the lid.

"Babies 'R' Us . . ." I fight the instinct to say it with an accent as I reseat myself next to Langly.

"Oh!" She holds up the breast pump.

"You registered for it," I add lamely.

"They did it for me at the store—"

"Tah-dah!" She's interrupted by Pippa wheeling in a Bugaboo stroller tied with a gigantic red ribbon. "It's titanium!"

"Oh, darling!" Citrine leaps up to her feet to embrace her. "I wanted this one—it's supposed to be the best!"

"I was keeping it in the apartment and my husband was, like, twenty-four hundred dollars *for a stroller?* And I'm, like, since when do *you* care?" She laughs.

"I know, *right?*" Alex chimes in from where she leans against the bookcase. "You do your job at the bank. I do mine at home. You get paid. I get paid. Freddie Mac can bite me. Don't give me these excuses." The crowd dissolves in knowing hysterics.

"Guys." A woman in a pony-embossed cable-knit minidress over-rides the laughter. "If he gives you any trouble, pay for everything in cash—he can't trace it. Say it's for the 'tutor.'" She rabbit-ears her fingers.

Citrine holds up an envelope to regain the focus. "Ooooh!" The room is excited.

"What is it?" Pippa calls across the coffee table.

"Endermologie. A ten-pack," Alex squeals back before Citrine can even tear it open. Wow. A procrastinating hour of trolling the Web off the search word "cellulite" once educated me that Endermologie is upward of five hundred a session. "Trust me," Alex intones, "you'll need it. My stomach looked like a corrugated roof." As Citrine's face goes white, everyone nods in agreement.

"It's the *worst* thing we put ourselves through, right?" A woman leans forward, her plate nearly tipping its massacred contents to the carpet. I look around. Everyone has a pulverized quarter muffin on their plate. *Why?* Why take the carbs if you're not going to eat them?

"No. Nursery school applications are *the worst*." A murmur of assent.

"Just wait till kindergarten. Forty thousand dollars and they want to ask *me* questions. And it doesn't stop. My oldest is in first grade and they keep calling me, she's wetting her pants in school, blah-blah-blah. I'm, like, forty thousand dollars! Change her, for Christ's sake."

"Have any of you been following this Jarndyce thing?"

I straighten up.

"The helipad? They're launching it Friday, right? God, I wish our school had one—instead they put in another new science lab—yawn."

"No." The first woman leans in, her eyes bugging. "Not *that*. The *teacher*."

"I read about it on UrbanBaby."

"I heard the story from John Frieda."

"How does a teacher get so out of control? Reading the students' websites."

"Out of control?" I repeat, amazed to be hearing this sentiment out of mouths no older than mine.

"At Pilates," another woman adds. "We agreed. It's a total invasion of privacy."

"And you know it's all her," Pippa says. "Has to be. We *loved* our teachers. So many students wouldn't have created those sites if she wasn't a horrible witch. I'm sorry, but it's true."

I put my plate down on the piano. "But we have to take into account that the school controlled how the story came out—we should remember there are two sides," I say, careful, as there may be Jarndyce mothers in the room. "I've heard the students loved her."

"Remember," Langly says softly into her champagne, quieting the room, "when I shimmied under the desk and tied Ms. Conner's shoes together? She broke her front teeth."

My classmates break into hysterical laughter; Alex and Tatiana shake, eyes watering. And all at once Sarah's perspective doesn't seem so much unforgiving as realistic. As I look around the room I have to admit that when I started nannying for all those wealthy families, I absolved my classmates' wanton anger and frivolous cruelty en masse once I understood that behind the excessive privilege lay unjustifiable neglect. But sitting among them now, with the years and therapists and *Oprahs* that have passed and with every possible tool at their disposal . . . Is it that they normalize being mean for one another so they never have to address what they're really angry about? At? Never have to change?

"Citrine, you *have* to use my baby nurse," Alex finally says as she dries her eyes. "You know, you're recovering from a *major* trauma. You'll need rest."

"How long do I need one?" Citrine asks.

"Six months. Minimum." There's a murmur of assent.

"But be careful, they'll try to take advantage of you," Alex warns. "They are sneaky and snaky. Keeping an eye on them is a full-time job."

"That's so interesting." I'm done. "Because, you know, I was a nanny in college." All heads swivel in my direction as thirty or so women wish they could raise their eyebrows. "And I never met a woman doing the job who wasn't just trying to . . . do the job."

Citrine looks at me, all traces of warmth draining, and I have the strangest sensory experience of the room swirling away and the eyes in her thirteen-year-old face locking with mine as Sarah and I bring Ms. Conner a wad of paper towels.

"Cake! Cake!" someone cries with the mania of the underfed as Alex enters from the kitchen with a giant teddy bear–shaped confection. And not anywhere in the chaos of the big titanium carbohydrate reveal am I acknowledged for a gift I picked out with thought and consideration, to help someone I considered a friend on the journey she is about to embark on. Without me, it is starting to seem.

"Mom! MOOOOOMMMMMM!" I hear a young girl scream over the bleating cry of a baby on the other side of the door. The sickly residue of Splenda-sweetened teddy bear cake still in my mouth, I rest the box against the wall and catch my breath on the landing of Shari Oleson's third-floor walk-up. "Mom! Mom! Mom!" The girl rat-a-tats as the sobs get louder. I hear the clicking of the door being unlocked.

"Sorry, just a—Stand back, Chloe, so I can—"

"But you were going to get me my crayons!"

"Just let me get this open, please." The door pulls in to reveal Shari on the end of the energetic spectrum opposite her beatific wedding photo self. Her hair tugged haphazardly into a ponytail, she has a cloth diaper slung over her shoulder and a red-faced baby screeching in her arms. A three-foot blonde in a T-shirt and Dora the Explorer underwear peers up at me from behind Shari's legs.

"Are you sure this isn't a bad time?" I shift the weight of the box back into my arms.

She smiles wanly at this assessment, seemingly applying it to more than my arrival.

"I'm waiting for my crayons," Chloe informs us as she focuses on simultaneously unfurling the steeple of her fingers and kicking into a long split in the narrow hall.

"No, it's fine," Shari answers me over the screaming. "Please come in. Thank you so much for lugging this stuff up here. Sorry I never got back to you. And I'm sorry we're not really dressed."

"Oh my God, no worries." As I step inside, I glance at Chloe's shirt and panties, the cardigan half buttoned over Shari's leggings, and the diaper-and-sock-clad baby. "I think among the three of you, you actually have a complete outfit."

Shari laughs. Chloe eyes me suspiciously.

"Get it, Chlo?" Shari points down at her daughter's tummy. "You have the shirt, I have the pants, and Jake has the socks." Chloe looks from herself to her mother and brother and then breaks into hysterical giggles. "Thanks, we're running short on jokes around here."

I realize she is bouncing, has been bouncing since she opened the door, despite Jake's monotonous, irritated wail. "Oh, you can just leave the box there. I have to figure out where I'm going to put all that stuff."

"No problem. Sorry to seem so urgent this morning. I'm glad we finally connected."

"My husband will be back any minute, God willing, and we can take a walk."

"Great!" I lower the box to the floor and Chloe immediately sticks her little feet into my line of vision.

"I have purple polish on my toes."

"Gorgeous," I admire as I stand to smile at Shari, who stares at me foggily in return. Jake provides the soundtrack.

"I need my crayons." Chloe tugs heavily at her mother's cardigan.

"We've covered this. Pants, then crayons."

"But I don't want pants." Chloe despairs, dropping her head through her arms, dragging her mother's sweater to expose the top triangle of her thick nude nursing bra.

"How about a skirt?"

Chloe shakes her head forlornly.

"Shorts?"

"Pa-ja-mas." Chloe drops the sweater and slips to the floor, crumpling into a lanky heap.

Shari tilts her head at me.

"Long morning?" I ask.

"Long everything. Chloe, we've officially discussed this. This has been discussed from every angle."

"*Crayons,*" Chloe moans into the shellacked hardwood.

"You're on a warning, Chlo." Bouncing, Shari switches the baby to her shoulder. "Come in, Nan, please." She waves me down the long hall lined with framed family pictures. We pass a door to a small bedroom where a crib and changing table have been wedged in around the queen-sized bed. "Oh, God, please disregard the mess. Between the colic and the colic we've gone to seed." Shari talks up to the ceiling, pushing her voice over her son's to me.

"No! It's—This is a lovely spot. I've always loved the West Seventies, such a great neighborhood for families," I cheer as we pass the doorway of the next room, no bigger than an alcove but festooned in an explosion of Indian saris and stuffed animals.

"That's my room!" Chloe rolls onto her back beside the front door and extends an arm at me while her feet climb up the box I ferried.

I smile and turn to see we've arrived at a large space serving as kitchen/living/dining room, its three windows looking into the lush brownstone gardens below. "What a view!"

"Yeah, it's a special one." Shari darts her hand between piles of folded laundry covering the oval table, and reemerges with her phone. She hits a number as she brings it to her ear. "Where are you? . . . Oh. Hi!" she yells toward the front door.

"Daddy!" Chloe squeals.

"Chloe! Sorry, babe, the train took forever." I hear a man's voice as Shari walks around me and down the hall. I turn to see her hand the baby off in exchange for Trader Joe's bags, both parents still gripping their phones.

"Nan, this is my husband, Scott. Scott, this is Nan."

"Hi!" I give a little wave as Chloe wraps herself around his jeans and he theatrically walks her toward the living room like Godzilla, his upper body resuming the bouncing motion Shari's has at last dropped. Jake screams, keeps screaming.

"Hey there," Scott greets me.

"Okay!" Shari lifts the groceries onto the counter and swipes up a handbag, dropping her cell in it and simultaneously stepping into a pair of slip-on sneakers. "We'll be back in fifteen. Nan?"

"Yes! Nice to meet you, Scott and Chloe." I follow her as she pats each child's head and strides down the hall.

"Daddy, I need my crayons."

"Chloe!" Shari calls wearily as she opens the door and I step out onto the landing.

"I *need them!*"

"Bottoms on first is our deal, Scott. Warning two, Chloe."

"Nooooooooooooooo." Chloe's erupting cry adds a density to her brother's, chasing us down the steps and out the door to the stoop. Shari is on a mission. I scurry to keep up as we step into the afternoon sunshine and round the corner to West End. She abruptly stops to dig in her purse, producing a pack of cigarettes.

"Do you mind?" she asks, sticking one in her mouth and pulling a deli matchbook from where it's tucked between the pack and its ripped cellophane. I shake my head no; at this moment I'd allow her heroin.

She inhales deeply as she leans back against the building wall and then focuses in on me. "Okay. Hi!" she says, mugging greeting me for the first time.

"Hi."

"Please don't think I'm an asshole." She touches my arm with one hand and waves the cloud away from me with the other. "I don't smoke. I mean, I haven't since college. But I'm craving them like crazy. The smell is the only sign to my fried adrenal system that I'm off duty."

"I'm sure." I nod. "And with the colic—"

"Relentless. A baby's cry is nature's brilliant design to disturb you into action, but when there's just no action that will help him, *you* just end up perpetually disturbed." Her eyes tear and she blinks them dry. "And poor Chloe is so getting the raw end of the deal."

"She seems pretty terrific," I say reassuringly. "I mean, she's not crazy. Pants can be a downer. And it's great that your husband is around to help."

"Yeah, I'd rather his pilot got picked up, but no, it's good. With the writers' strike it's been a much lighter year for his work than usual. I'm sorry you had to stalk me, but he wrote your message on the back of a grocery list and then—"

"Yes, you mentioned that on the phone," I remind her gently.

"Shit. I'm saying everything at least twice these days. With the crying, I'm losing track of what's in my head and what's out loud." She lifts her cigarette-free hand to brace her temples. "Sorry, how can I help *you*?"

"Thank you—you are awesome to give me even five minutes." I smile. "So, it looks from your files that Jarndyce is in the process of building cases against some of the teachers, and neither Gene nor Tim seem to be able to have a straight conversation about it."

"Yes, straight conversation is not their forte." She takes one last drag and drops the cigarette, stubbing it out with her toe. "And now I feel like shit." She sighs, tingeing green. "From what I've been told it didn't start that way, but since Cliff and Sheila took over the board—first thing they did was push out the old guard by upping the donation ante into the tens of millions. So now it's all about brand and efficiency. They've been trying to wrestle the faculty into giving up all of their benefits in exchange for equity in the school. They've invested the endownment at some astronomical rate of return. And anyone who doesn't want to toe the party line, maintain 'flexibility' as they love to say, they're weeding out. Or as they prefer to call it, taking early retirement. Who did you axe?"

"Ingrid Wells."

"But she was so great! They had nothing on her." She makes a tsk-ing sound. "And they couldn't claim retirement. What did they hang it on?"

"They claimed she was 'fostering an inappropriate learning environment in her classroom' because some of her students were desperate for attention and when they couldn't get it from their parents they tried to get it from her."

"Oy."

I cross my arms, my head aching from some blend of disturbing cries, burning tobacco, and her sickening confirmation. "Is this why you really quit?"

Her cell rings and she digs in her purse with both hands, the brown leather strap flopping off her shoulder. I can hear the crying emanating from the device as soon as she answers. "Hey . . . How could you forget milk? . . . Okay, on my way." She clicks off and turns to me. "I'm sorry, I have to run."

"Is it?"

She smiles and lets out a short puff of air through her nostrils. "Chloe had a half scholarship to Jarndyce. We were moving up the wait list for a two-bedroom in Battery Park City. And I just ... couldn't stomach the job. I sort of switched into mission mode during the pregnancy—getting as much done as I could—logging as many hours. Gene's like a jackhammer. You get to a point where it's easier if you just decide it all makes sense—sure, we can save money by forcing out some of the older staff at half pension. Then once I went on leave, got some distance, the shit the board was hitting me with right up until the day I quit—take their health care?—it just started to feel more and more ..." She drops her head and runs her pointer fingers hard across her eyebrows before looking back up at me. "Isn't it crazy, the headaches come when I'm *not* with him. Anyway, even though the public school down the block has set up trailers in the yard and closed the arts programs to make room for the overflow of students from all the new Trump buildings, I was, like, fuck it, this is unconscionable work and I don't want my kids going here. We'll stay put in one of the three good public school districts in this city, I'll get some help, find new work, it'll be fine—"

"I'm going to quit."

Her phone rings and she glances at the number. "I *haven't* found a job. Bear Stearns has companies holding their breath. I mean, you know they're all too happy to save on the HR front. And they're saying I should check back in September, maybe things will have loosened up, but I can't wait until then. I need to work *now*. And I need to answer this, sorry." She tugs out her phone and clicks it on as she pulls it to her ear. "I'm coming ... So do you want me to run to Fairway or not? ... Milk, goldfish—got it. I'm just saying good-bye." She waves at me and darts down the corner at a half run in her half sneakers, turning back to call, "Look, no matter what you decide, someone's going to do that job." Her expression hardens. "And I wish to God it was me."

19

"I'm sorry, explain again why we're here."

Thursday morning Steve turns from the brownstone stoop to look at me, leaning his weight to his right Timberland resting on the first step. "You said you wanted an update."

"Because I need to move back in tomorrow. I thought we'd be able to go inside. I don't understand why you told me to meet you here if there's nothing to show. You made it sound on the phone like we were going in."

He drops his head to his flannel shirt, exhausted by me. "How can I do that when it takes seven days for the fungicide to clear? And that's *if* it works and we don't have to do a second treatment. With mold that bad there's no guarantees."

"Uh-huh, uh-huh, so there's no update. No progress has been made whatsoever." I take a calming breath and aim to begin closer to the beginning. "Weeks ago you promised me a timeline, Steve, a concrete timeline for a staircase, and two *livable* floors. That's including electricity and plumbing and a staircase to access them."

"And I'm gonna do that right now."

I dart my tongue over my upper lip and take a step back on the sidewalk. "Okay." I sweep my arm for him to enlighten me.

He clears his throat. "Once the fungicide lifts we'll get my men back here and get started. Get your stairs in, get the walls up, finish the electric. The works."

"Uh-huh, by *when?*"

"Well ... that's dependent on when my crew get off their other gigs."

"Other gigs?"

"Yup."

"Why?" My hand shoots to my brow.

"Well, we had this downtime—"

"No! No downtime, Steve! Work on the roof, work on the siding, work on the window frames. It's a top-to-bottom shit mess, there is *always* something to work on with this house."

"Yeah, well, when do you guys think you can pay me?" He squints as he crosses his arms.

"Pay you?"

"Yeah. Because you know that fungicide put you over another ten grand or so and that's coming outta my pocket right now—"

"Ten grand?!"

"Or so. Twelve, fourteen. I'm waiting on the final numbers."

"I don't—we don't *have* another twelve, fourteen grand." My phone rings and, giving him a pausing finger, I answer it with a dry mouth. "Hello?"

"Nan? Gene here. Any chance you can swing by in about thirty?"

"Definitely." Because Steve says this is *not* the time for stand taking.

"I'm on the roof, getting ready for the big event tomorrow."

"On my way!" I hang up and return to him futzing with the stoop railing.

"You know this concrete's pretty loose." He wipes his hands on his jeans. "You should add that to your list."

I stare at him.

He shrugs. "I'm just saying. I had to come in from Jersey for this, you know." He fans the back of his perspiring neck. "You're the one who wanted an update."

"The people who pay me so I can pay you—God, another *ten thousand dollars*—need me now. I need to go. Steve, you have a day. I need to be living somewhere in that"—I jerk my phone up at the stoop—"by tomorrow night. Friday night."

"Well, I'm still waiting for the fungicide to clear."

"Then put on gas masks. Hire a new crew. Get me a FEMA trailer. *Something* that makes me feel just the tiniest bit like you're in this with us, Steve. Fix the fucking concrete! *Anything.* Tomorrow night!" I call, hustling away toward the subway, BlackBerry primed to try Mr. X's office yet again. "Or my dog and I move in with you!"

As I jog into the white entry hall, Ingrid's report in hand, the Jarn-dyce receptionist instructs me to head under the sweeping staircase, through the newly unveiled arched doorway, and down the completed low-lit corridor to the back of the building, where a rhythmic pounding draws me forth. Every twentieth step on the glass mosaic tile, I lift my foot high above a roll of bound red carpeting waiting to be unfurled. I arrive at an elevator vestibule, where a cluster of carpenters crouch low, assembling green trellises. The elevator door opens, shining purple light on us.

"Sorry, I just need to . . ." I shrug apologetically and a team of what look to be young floral assistants squatting inside shuffle like ducks to make room. "Thanks!" I say as I step in, but they are focused on their manic insertion of fresh red roses into the trellises masking the pedestrian walls of the car.

I press for the roof and we ascend as the assistants weave and curse, the task too delicate for proper garden gloves, their latex gloves already shredding from the thorns. When the door opens I squint in the bright daylight and step out into a glass-enclosed landing. Even at this hour the trapped morning rays have heated it to hothouse temperatures.

Awash in a cloudless blue sky, I shield my eyes to look out at the vast space, ringed with a clear Lucite balustrade, and divided into two areas by the vestibule in which I stand. The flat expanse of asphalt, I assume, once the speaking platform and rows of folding chairs are removed, must be the helipad area itself, while on the other side of me is a small lawn ringed by manicured shrubbery standing only a foot high. I step over to peer out at a team of gardeners attending the tiny topiary with what look like actual Sally Hansen tools.

Overheating, I turn back to the helipad side and push the glass door open, its silver handle scorching to the touch. As I step onto the roof I pass a man beside the door in a blue jumpsuit muttering to himself as he installs a key-card reader, just one of the scores of workers hunkered at their various tasks.

I weave among them to see that behind the platform two men are hoisting a large painted scrim that looks like a Roman backdrop, its base dotted with villas nestled in rolling Cypress-strewn hills. Seven-foot-high kouroi flank the platform where a woman in sweat-soaked khakis is slowly pouring out bags of sand between the rows of chairs for the board.

I spot Gene in his shirtsleeves vigilantly overseeing the installation of can lights in the helipad's landing circle.

"Now, these will change color?" I hear him ask as I approach, his hands resting on the back of his trousers. The electrician nods, wiping his wet brow with the back of his gloved hand. "And that'll be visible in the neighborhood?"

"At night for at least ten blocks."

Gene nods, pleased. "And you'll be finished by five?"

"My boss wanted me to ask, we still haven't been covered for this overtime."

"We're a little overwhelmed with all the vendors for tomorrow, but we'll get everybody paid—"

"'Cause you're still, like, behind on what you owe us just for the building."

"I have a call in to accounting." He turns, seeing me. "Nan! Good you're here."

"Yes! With the report on Ingrid. I'm so sorry for the delay."

"Great, great." He sandwiches it and slides it into his breast pocket. "Things are a little chaotic getting ready for tomorrow. Oh, did you hear? Philip Traphagan's flying in from Stockholm to cut the ribbon. Little sendoff for all his years of service."

"I didn't know he was stepping down, but I'll look forward to thanking him in person for connecting us."

Gene slips his hands in the back of his waistband as he looks admiringly at the stage. "Great set, huh? We share a board member with the Met and he got us the scrim from Puccini's *L'ultimo giorno di Pompei*—it's so awesome. Referencing the pinnacle achievement of our founding civilization."

"It looks *amazing*. It's going to be a fantastic event. I sense great excitement among the faculty," I lie.

"Really?" He turns to me, so hopeful, as if I'd just told him I'd heard his stepchildren weren't cleaning the toilet with his toothbrush.

"Definitely. It's been a rocky spring, but I believe the faculty are eager to come back next year to a completed building and get everything moving in the right direction." Toward my paying off some fungicide. Gene spots something awry beside the stage and sets off. I hasten to keep up. "And me, too, I am very excited about this next ... phase."

Kneeling in the shade of the platform, three women are spray-painting bushels of white roses red with small airbrush guns.

"What are you doing?"

"There was a mistake in the order," one stammers through her surgical mask as she sprays. "We're fixing it."

"Red is the school color."

"These will all be red before they go in the trellises."

"And the Shakespeare garden is secure?"

"We rewired all the plants this morning. The rotors shouldn't pull up the herbs."

"Good, good." Gene moves us away from the aerosol fumes. "Sorry, where were we?"

"Excited. Is there a problem with the garden?"

He clasps his hands behind his back. "Well, half the board wanted the helipad and half wanted the roof designated as a green space." His voice trails off as he watches an abandoned balloon float over Ninth Avenue. "They shouldn't really be in the same area. We've had to go a little ... bonsai. But everything important is there: rosemary, pansies, fennel ..."

"Rue, daisies, and violets?" I finish for him as he holds the door for me, leading back into the sweltering silence of the greenhouse vestibule.

He smiles. "Nan, I wanted to ask you ..."

"Shoot!"

He eyes the closed elevator door. "You mentioned you're tight with Mr. X."

"Oh, no, I—" Fuck it. "Sure, yes, I am."

"Great. We need to get in touch with him." He fishes in his pocket for his cell phone. "What's his direct number." Huh?

"Have you called his office?"

"I'm not retarded," he shoots back impolitically, his accent thickening with his annoyance. "Cliff Ashburn can't get ahold of him and I said you'd probably have a private, a direct—"

"I—I don't think . . ." I struggle to be helpful, picturing my cell sitting in my purse, the number programmed into it that's taken me only to voice mail.

"Nan." He rises on the balls of his Docksiders. "*This* is the time to show allegiance."

"No, I appreciate that—"

"So the number?"

"I'm supposed to see him tomorrow, actually," I say quickly.

"Great! Fantastic!" He shoves his phone in his pocket. "Where?"

"Sorry?"

"Where are you seeing him? I'll swing by."

"Oh, I don't have exact plans just yet. Sometime around the end of business, I'm thinking, although we haven't finalized—"

"So just call me the minute you know." He pushes for the elevator. "I'm counting on you. The board is counting on you."

"Then I'll deliver!" I find myself saluting like a desperate jackass as he pushes back out into the relentless sun.

I'm the last customer that night at the Laundromat. The industrial dryer buzzes as the clothes tumble to a halt and, breaking my pacing loop around the folding counter, I beeline to the hot machine. Popping open the door, I glance over at my maddeningly dark BlackBerry sitting atop the fold station, the red light blinking from Gene's unanswered calls. God, why the fuck isn't Mr. X calling back?! We are twenty-four hours and counting. I am just going to take them out to Greenwich tomorrow, that's what. Gene can drive. It's pretty there. They have swans and lilacs. They'll be fine in that office. Hell, it's bigger than the corporate McPartment. And if they're in front of him, he will have to deal. I will make him deal. We will make him deal. And I will drop them off with clean clothes and strict bandaging instructions. And then Gracie and I are buying a whip and going pharaoh on Steve's ass.

Dumping the warm armful on the counter, I get a whiff of the nurturing aroma of fabric softener, with its suggestion of domestic order, and flash to how, when Ryan and I first looked at the house, I was so thrilled at the idea of having our own washer-dryer in the basement. The basement that might now have to be permanently sealed off like a typhoid ward if this fungicide doesn't do the trick.

He's going to freak when he hears about the ten-twelve-fourteen thousand. *If* he comes back to hear about it. Is he *not* stuck there? The thought occurs to me for the first time since he's been gone. Oh God, is he choosing to stay away, seemingly indefinitely, rather than come home and deal with me?

Scrambling up this tractionless mental slope, I flap out big T-shirts, small T-shirts, big boxers, small boxers. I raise Stilton's Batman tee to the fluorescent, feeling a flicker of pride that the remains of where Grace upended taco night have come clean.

I lower the piles into the large red tote standing in for a laundry bag and heave it to my shoulder. And I have to admit it's incredibly satisfying, in a fabric softener kind of way, making a dinner they wolf down, folding their stain-free laundry, helping them tackle their homework. Especially when everything else I attempted this week was an unqualified failure.

Before I even get the key in the lock, I sense Grace circling inside for her last walk. And after not barking when I got off the elevator with the laundry, she's earned it. I push the door, but it pushes back. "Grayer, you want to let me in?"

"Sorry," a man's voice comes from the other side. Startled, I shove it open and it hits the kitchenette cabinets, revealing Mr. X, who looks around as if appraising the place for auction.

"Jan, hi," he says distractedly as Grace waggles out to greet me.

"Hi! Oh, I'm so glad you're here—I've left messages." I step inside and drop the bag on the carpet. "So, what's the plan for tomorrow?"

"Hm? Oh, yes, yes, we're going to talk all that through tonight. Smaller than I remembered." His head torques from the stucco ceiling to the industrial carpeting. "But I've always liked the equestrian art. This was a good place." He nods to himself. "Ready, Grayer?" As he turns I see he's wearing a back brace under his jacket like a cummerbund.

"Are you okay?" I ask him.

"What? Oh, this, it's just . . . stress." He manages a dry laugh.

"We're going out."

I pivot to Grayer, face radiant, baseball cap and sweatshirt in hand. "Great! Okay, then you'll talk it through now and I guess Grayer can update me when he gets back?" I pat at Grace's pushy muzzle.

"Uh-huh." Mr. X smiles blankly.

"And where are you guys going?" I ask, fighting the temptation to throw the nearby leash around Mr. X's neck.

"Out," they say in unison.

At the word "out" Grace excitedly raises and drops her front paws.

"One minute, Grace." I look at the clock on the cable box—11:14. "Okay, um, well, I'll probably be asleep soon, so . . . have fun!" I cheer.

"Thanks. See ya." As his dad holds the door open Grayer slips his cap on, narrowing the arc of the brim with one hand.

"I'll get their things ready for tomorrow," I say. "For when you pick them up after work. Around seven, do you think?" I try on relaying Gene's message, but decide if he's planning to "swing by," it's better for me to look uninvolved.

"Sure, definitely, yes. Bye." Mr. X follows him out.

"Seven, then!" I call to the closed door. Right. Great—so this is great. After placing a pausing hand on Grace's nose, I reach in and pull out two possible school outfits for each boy and then go to their room, where, racked out from his field trip to the Bronx Zoo, Stilton sleeps deeply, curled next to the indent his brother left. From the doorway I turn to a waiting Grace, willing what is transpiring right now, between Grayer and Mr. X to be a declaration of a happy family plan over hot cocoa, or even a declaration of a happy family plan on Mr. X's Hustler Club expense account. Whichever—I'll take it.

I'm still lying awake hours later, my mind crackling among Gene's anxious face, Steve's impassive one, and the devastation that awaits me on Ryan's, when my door opens. "Grayer?" I sit up.

"Where is he?" Stilton asks, shuffling around the bed.

"He went out, Stil. He'll be back soon. You okay?"

Stilton lifts the covers on the other side and, without ceremony, climbs in and curls up, raising his bandaged hand on the pillow like I showed him. "I'm sleeping here until he gets back, Nan."

I look down at his small torso, his madras pajamas rumpling as he nestles deeper into the bedding. "Okay." I lie back, resuming my vigil of the ceiling and try to stay distracted from the separation that looms.

BANG!

WOOF!

BANG!

WOOF!

Squinting against the pink dawn reflecting off the glass high-rise opposite, I fling off the covers and run out of the bedroom with Stilton on my heels. We find Grace baring her teeth at the door.

"Hello?" I call, jockeying to get around her to the spy hole.

"Open up! Police!"

I peek through to see a man in an ill-fitting suit and an even more ill-proportioned mustache standing with a uniformed cop. "Open up, ma'am!"

Leaving the chain on, I crack it open. "Um, good morning. Can you please show me your badge?" He whips it out, wedging it to me under the chain.

"Nan, why are the police here?" Stilton asks from behind Grace.

"I don't know. Go wake Grayer."

"You're being evicted is why the police are here," the mustache guy says in a clipped British accent, adjusting his pocket square.

"Evicted? But this isn't my apartment."

"Exactly! I told you, officer, this has to end—"

"Hold on," I cut him off. "I'm confirming your badge." I bolt the door and step over to the phone by the couch.

"He's not here." Stilton runs from their room.

I turn to him, seeing his stricken expression as he tugs down on the hem of his pajama top. "Right, yes, not to worry. He actually was

out with your dad last night—isn't that great?" Pleaseohpleaseoh-
please. "He didn't want to wake you, but he told me to give you a big
hug for him. They probably had so much fun they lost track of time."
Is it lying if I'm not *entirely* sure it's not the truth? "So Stil," I say gently, "go pee and brush your teeth. I'm going to start oatmeal." I ruffle
his black Woodstock hair. "Don't worry, this is just some weird mis-
understanding and I have it totally under—"

BANG!

WOOF!

"I'm coming!" As soon as the desk clerk confirms the badge I go
and open the door fully, handing it back to Officer Velasquez. "Sorry,
but I read the paper."

"No, that's smart." He nods, returning his ID to his pocket.

"So what's the problem, exactly?" I wipe my hair off my face and
try to project authority in my pajamas, while Grace and Stilton push
against my legs.

Mustache raises his chin as if we smell. "The problem is that you
are behind on your rent and I have a notice to evict!" He snaps a thin
pink paper.

"Well, it's a mistake, a hedge fund owns this place. Maybe a mix-up
in the billing?"

"X Wealth Management has not replied to written notices, phone
calls, or legal summonses."

"I'm sorry, miss," Officer Velasquez says, looking it, "but you have
to leave."

"Of course I do," I sigh. "Can I at least have a few minutes to get
dressed and get him ready for school?"

Mustache straightens his lapels—he probably spends all day readjusting his readjusted apparel. "We will wait in the lobby. If you are not
downstairs by eight o'clock, I will have you arrested for trespassing."

By 8:01 I have finished packing for three, gotten myself dressed,
walked a dog, fed a child and readied him for school, all the while
projecting a calm vision of his future, smiling while I move into
full-on panic about his brother's whereabouts. As we sit on the duffel
bags in the lobby under the watchful and derisive eye of Mustache, I
give up on his cell phone and call Mr. X at work. "The number you

are trying to reach has been disconnected. Please check your number and try again."Wha? So I do. And the main number. And his private extension. And Connecticut 411. Disconnected. Disconnected. Disconnected.

"Grayer!" Stilton yells, leaping up.

"Wait here, okay?" I hand him Grace's leash and stride through the door and out onto the street. "Where the hell have you been? Is that your father?" I break into a sprint as I spot a town car pulling away into traffic.

Grayer catches the hem of my jacket. "That's not him."

I spin and take him in. He looks like utter shit. Which for a teenager could mean anything—at that age the best night of your life and the worst night look the same the next morning. "Where were you?" I follow him inside.

"I took the train—what the hell?"

"Grayer, Grayer!" Stilton jumps into his face while Grace sniffs at his calves.

"We've been evicted. What train? What happened last night with your father?"

Grayer gives a sardonic smile to their belongings strewn over the Buena Vida lobby floor. "Of course we have."

"What did Dad say? Are we moving to the gobble building now?"

Grayer pats Stilton's bobbing head. "No."

"What's the plan? What time is he picking you up tonight?"

"He didn't get around to that."

Stilton clamps his hands on the hem of his brother's sweatshirt. "So where are we going to live now, Grayer?"

"I have no fucking idea." Shit.

"Everything's going to be fine, Stilton. Okay!" I say, trying to confine this wreck to the tracks. "Grayer, let's get you a clean shirt and off to school." I reach into his bag and extract an oxford I ironed and a packet of Wet Ones from my overnight. "Strip."

"Here?" He gestures to Mustache.

"You'll make his day."

We pile everything into yet another taxi and I get out with all their worldly possessions and one dog at 721.

"Okay," I say, striving for an authoritative tone that couldn't be farther from how I feel. I look back into the cab as I hand them hastily scribbled late notes, propping the door open with my hip and holding Grace's taut leash. "So you don't have a key?"

"No," Grayer mutters from behind the driver. "I told you, it's always open."

"Right, okay, so I'm going to figure that out and, Grayer, you'll bring Stilton here after school?"

He just stares into the foggy partition, his eyes at half-mast.

"We're going home?!" Stilton throws his arms around my neck from the seat beside Grayer. He smells like cinnamon. I have to stay focused.

"Yes," I say, pulling away and running my hand through his hair. "Good luck with your Neil Armstrong presentation. Have a great day, guys!" I shut the cab door and watch it weave back into the flow of uptown traffic.

After tying Grace to the wrought-iron guard rail, I follow the doorman ferrying the bags through the bronze French door and gird myself for take two. "Hi! So those can go right up to the Xes', thank you!"

"Oh." He stops, the bags pinning his arms to his sides. "No deliveries. She's not in."

I blink up at the gilded ceiling. "She's not back yet?" I ask, even though I suspected as much, since every good-night call of Stilton's went to voice mail.

"Nope." He shrugs, lifting his gold braid epaulets. "She's still in the hospital. And I'm not supposed to accept any deliveries."

"Okay, well, this isn't a delivery, these are her sons' things."

He drops the bags to the floor. "Look, I can get you a cab."

"Except I don't need a cab, because these bags are staying in this building because they are the belongings of two residents of this building who'll be home this evening. So I can leave them here or bring them up, which I am happy to do," I say through clenched teeth.

"You have a key?"

"Don't you?"

"I do not." He circles back behind his desk.

"Well, someone must. What about plants?" A ridiculous question of a woman who wishes her own children inanimate. "Look, why don't I just leave this stuff in their vestibule for now while I try to get in touch with her at the hospital?"

He shakes his head. "No can do. Fire code."

"And why can't I leave it in the lobby or the package room?" We look at the towering pile of bags and sporting equipment. "Or just run up and check the door, because Grayer said it's usually unlocked, maybe she forgot to—"

"You arrive with stuff. Might be tenants', might not. I don't know you. I don't have a letter vouching for you." He points at a leather binder overflowing with such letters. "I'm sorry, I'll get in trouble. Excuse me." He opens the door for a delivery guy in a red and yellow windbreaker and I wish I'd had the forethought to bring a fake letter to slip in the binder.

"Mrs. X," the guy says. I whip my head up. "I'm double-parked." He practically flings the red and yellow envelope at the doorman, holding out his clipboard for a signature while hopping away on one foot. While entering the delivery in the building ledger, the doorman rests the envelope on the desk. I twist my head to read the mailing label—X Wealth Management.

"Why would Mr. X messenger her something all the way from Connecticut if she's not even here? He could mail it."

"She's picking it up," the doorman says as he scribbles.

"She's *what?*" I am now, I believe the kids would say, *in his grill.*

"It's not my business." He puts his hand up.

"Sir. I am folding her children's boxer shorts. We just got evicted from their dad's place. *Please.*"

He twists his lips and then lowers his voice. "One messenger drops an envelope off and another picks it up, to take to the hospital."

"In *Baltimore?*" Have these people never heard of stamps?

"That's what she said."

I walk over to the door, where I can see Grace's panting profile, and in full view of the frowning doorman, I plop down on Stilton's red duffel bag and tug out my cell. The president of the board can forcibly remove me by my hair.

Taking a breath, I call information for Johns Hopkins Avon Foundation Breast Center. At this point she has to appoint a legal guardian, authorize me to go upstairs, *something*. I'm put through to the hospital switchboard. "I'm sorry," the woman's kind voice comes down the line. "But there's no one by that name currently admitted here."

"Are you *sure*? Can you please check again?"

And she does. And nada.

?!?!?!?!

Brow scrunched, I call the Waldorf and speak to the events coordinator, pretending to be an unpaid rep for Cirque du Soleil, and get Saz's contact number.

"Oh, yes, Dorothy Hutchinson's daughter-in-law, of course I remember you. So sweet, yes, I want to send flowers, too, but had no idea how to do it in Baltimore. I read they have a lot of gang violence." Okay, I'm not crazy. That's where she's supposed to be. Maybe they changed her course of treatment? But when I call the other five hospitals Sarah suggests that specialize in treating breast cancer, it's the same story.

And then, with a glance at the time, I call Gene.

"Gene, hi. It's Nan." I aim for solid reassurance. "I just wanted to let you know that, unfortunately, I won't be able to make it to the convocation this morning because I'm just, um . . . just working on getting in touch with Mr. X for you, actually. He . . . lost his cell, so the number's been disconnected, but he's going to get the new number to me tonight. Okay, so, great. And good luck today, and thanks. Bye." I click off and drop my head between my bent knees.

"Nan?" I leap up. "What are you doing here?" Citrine asks, rounding from the shadows of the elevator banks and being tailed by a diminutive Filipino couple carrying a full set of T. Anthony.

"I'm waiting for . . ." I trail off, registering what "divine intervention" would sound like.

"Uch, don't look at me! I'm so fat." She holds up her hands, palms out, in front of her face. "I've been meaning to call you." She adjusts the camel cashmere shawl over the shoulders of her man-tailored cobalt blue blouse. "What're you up to for the holiday?"

"Holiday?" I say, the word making me slaver as if it smelled like popcorn.

"Memorial Day."

"Oh, wow." I nod vacantly. "This has been an *insane* week, with Ryan gone and my freelance schedule, it fell out of my brain."

"Listen, we're having a bunch of families out—you two should come! It's my first time hosting and I could use some support." I'm stunned. I thought between my noncashmere breast pump and domestic employee defense, I'd been erased from her phone.

"That's so sweet of you. But Ryan's still in Africa and I'm taking care of the X boys while their mom's in the hospital—and Grace."

"Well, Clark's allergic, but definitely bring the boys! We have seven bedrooms." She puts a hand on my arm, dropping her voice. "Listen, don't give up on me because I'm pregnant. We can hang out and really catch up. Shit, I have to go, the chopper's waiting."

"Chopper?" I glance out the window where Grace is being loved by a trio of toddlers.

"From the helipad on the East River. How great is that? Forty-minute flight and we touch down in East Hampton. Please please please come. We have a pool—it'll be awesome." She gives me a hug over her tummy, which I swear has grown since Tuesday. "And thank you for the booby thingy. It was crazy thoughtful. If I breast-feed I will *totally* use it." She wafts out the door, trailed by honeysuckle and the couple shuttling more luggage and a crate of wine to the waiting limo. Suddenly a sweaty guy with cargo shorts and Rasta dreads pushes in against their flow. "Manhattan Minute package pickup." He looks down at his electronic tablet. "Mrs. X?"

I grab my purse as the doorman hands the envelope over and follow the messenger outside. In one fluid motion he slips it in his bag, slings the bag over his back, rights his bike, and takes off into traffic.

"Yeah?" The dispatcher holds the phone to his chest and looks up at me through the scratched plastic partition.

"Hello. My name is Nan Hutchinson. I—God help me—work for Mrs. X." I run my nervous hands down the front of my skirt. "And I sent out a package to her this morning using your service, from her home, at 721 Park, but I think I had the address wrong. And I need to confirm the address."

"Why didn't you just call?" he asks gruffly, picking at a patch of flaky skin by his ear.

"I did, but I thought I might have better luck in person."

"They negged you, huh? Lady, you wasted your time." He pulls off a piece and flicks it away. "I'm sorry if that woman is fucking your what—boyfriend, husband—but if I gave up that information I'd be out of business."

I stumble back down the three narrow flights of stairs onto Thirty-eighth Street, dodging the smoke pouring from the Szechwan barbe-cue, playing through if the messengers come here on Fridays for their checks, maybe I could just wait for Rasta dude and beg and plead and bribe and— Catching my breath and brain, I dial. "Josh, hey, it's Nan," I launch in after the beep. "I am *so sorry* to be bothering you right now and *believe* me I exhausted every avenue before calling, but I need information and I pray that with your journalistic contacts, you might know how to get it." I squint as the sun tips over the top of the opposing building. "I've been totally left with the kids. Both parents are just . . . gone. She had a package picked up by Manhattan Minute today. And I need to know where that package went. It must be in the city. Somewhere bikable, obviously. It's only, I don't know what to do and I just need to find out . . . where the fuck is Mrs. X?"

20

Hours later, Stilton kneels on his seat and swivels his head around into the Jitney aisle to interrupt my racing thoughts. "How much *farther,* Nan-eh?"

I peer across the lap of my snoring seat companion and out the bus window at the row of buildings abutting the dark highway, Bridgehampton Plumbing and Heating, Bridgehampton Pool, Bridgehampton Hardware. I can also see Grayer's face in the reflection, sitting beside Stilton, staring into the night, ghostly. Taking a breath, I smile to his brother. "About twenty more minutes if the traffic picks up." He slumps back down with an exaggerated sigh and the woman across the aisle shoots me an admonishing look, as she does every time Stilton calls me "Nan-eh" in an exasperated tone. Which, with our pressed sandwiches providing the only brief entertainment on the holiday weekend traffic-choked journey, has been a lot. She's probably already logged onto ratemynanny.com on her iPhone to report me.

As the bus crawls I text Citrine that the last ETA I predicted was also ambitious, and another text comes in: GRACIE AND I HAVE PUT ON OUR PAJAMAS, BRUSHED TEETH, AND NOW SHE'S READING ME A STORY XO SARAH. Smiling, I add "Buy S thank-you gift" to my ever-growing BlackBerry to-do list.

I lean back in my chair and watch the leafy profile of lush trees inch by. Abandoned, these kids have essentially been abandoned. I shake my head. What the hell would Mr. and Mrs. X be doing if I *wasn't* here? Or—dear God—is my being here what's enabled this? I let my head rest against the back of the seat, unable, sickeningly, to explore the answer.

We eventually pull abreast of the Palms Hotel and everyone stretches up to disembark, folding pashmina blankets and pulling speaker buds from ears. Empty Starbucks cups in hands and limp *Financial Times* and *InStyles* under arms, they bend to look out the windows for waiting friends and family.

"Who's picking us up?" Grayer steps into the aisle, his finger looped in the back of Stilton's jacket to keep him close.

"Clark, Citrine's husband. How are you feeling?"

He shrugs and we shuffle down the steps before Grayer elbows in to wrestle our bags from the overcrowded hold. George Carlin's treatise on winnowing your possessions comes to mind as I look down at our three small duffels, which are now *just* the stuff we really need, the excess left piled in a corner of my parents' dining room.

I crane my head over the waiting cars till I spot Clark sitting in khaki shorts and an oxford on a vintage Jeep without its canvas top. I wave to him and he waves back, but doesn't move from his spot under the wrought-iron streetlamp. I signal to the boys and we drag our bags down the block.

"Hi, hi," he says, still tapping on his iPhone as he slides off the hood, his Docksiders hitting the pavement. "Apologies." He slips the device in the pocket of his fleece vest. "My first Chagall is arriving Sunday and I'm so pumped." He opens the passenger door and tilts the chair forward.

"Oh, wow, that's amazing. Clark, these are my friends, Grayer and Stilton."

"Hey." Grayer nods.

"Hi." Stilton waves as the boys hop up and wedge in the backseat.

"S'up?" Clark gives them a cursory glance as he passes them the bags to squeeze at their feet. Stilton looks to his left hip, then his right. "Yeah, sorry, no seat belts. Just hold on!"

"For you." I hand off the champagne I grabbed from the liquor store before we boarded. "Thank you so much for having us."

"Thank you," Stilton echoes.

Clark pops the passenger seat back into place so I can get in. "No problem." He comes around the hood of the car, patting it twice like a horse, before sliding in and starting the ignition. "Chagall! I'm so pumped." He screeches out of the spot and Stilton grabs the metal frame as Grayer clamps a tamping arm over him. I grip my seat.

"Congratulations on the baby," I say. "You must be so excited!"

"What? I like Bob Marley! You like Bob Marley?"

I can barely hear him over the air whipping around us as we speed off Main Street and onto a dark side road. "Sure!"

He leans forward to swipe a remote by his feet and then, steering with one hand, tries to aim it down between his legs. "FULL STE-REO!" he shouts. His phone lights up the breast pocket of his fleece and he anchors the wheel with his elbows, tugs it out with his left hand, and keeps punching the remote with his right. We swerve into the oncoming lane. "WASSUP?" he asks his caller as Shirley Man-son's voice floods the space. He punches the remote again as we clip a hedge. I glance back to see Stilton gripping the jeep, his eyes squeezed shut. Grayer has the impassive face of someone who's given over to a roller coaster. "CHAGALL, MAN! I KNOW, HOW FUCK-ING COOL IS THAT? NO, YOU HAVE TO COME OVER AND SEE IT SUNDAY NIGHT. BIG PARTY—" We hit a pothole and go flying. "GOTTA FIND BOB, GOTTA GO."

"CLARK, I THINK STILTON IS CARSICK, CAN YOU SLOW DOWN?"

"WE'RE HERE!" He floors it onto a circular gravel driveway, swerving to a stop, a wave of pebbles spraying to the lawn. "Awe-some!" He kills the engine, opens the door, and hops out, walking away to a massive, three-story modern beach house, all gray washed wood and oversized single-pane windows. He jogs up the steps and disappears inside while the three of us catch our breath. Through the open front door I can hear REM sending this one out to the one they love, and under that, the nearby ocean.

Stilton unwraps his knuckles and tries to stand. I open my door and step out. Forgoing figuring out how to flip my chair, I take Stil-ton's hand and help him climb down to the gravel. Grayer hops over the side and reaches back in for the bags.

"Sorry, guys."

"I think I'm dizzy," Stilton announces, letting out a long burp.

"Excuse you," I say, lifting my bag onto my shoulder.

"Excuse me."

"Well, let's get you a bedtime snack. I bet there is someone in there whose job it is just to bake cookies. I believe where there are men in Bermuda shorts there is sugar."

"Nan!" Citrine comes out through the glass door onto the portico and down the three gray plank steps.

"Hi!" I call as she crosses the driveway, arms extended to give me a hug.

"You made it! The ribs are finished, but there's still some chocolate cake."

"That sounds great! Thank you so much for having us. Citrine, this is Grayer and you remember his brother, Stilton. Guys, this is Citrine Cilbourne."

"Welcome." She waves at them, readjusting her dislodged wrap. "We had a little snafu. Clark went overboard saying children included, and I went overboard saying children included, so the boys are on the couches in the upstairs breezeway."

"I'm sure that'll be fine." I take my bag from the floor of the passenger seat. "I can't tell you how happy we are to be here. Stilton, you want to go in and Citrine will give you some cake?"

"Um, sure," Citrine says, her eyes widening before catching herself and touching her stomach. "I can do that. I can totally give cake." Nodding, she follows Stilton across the drive and up the steps.

Left alone with the surf and Grayer, I turn to see him tapping a cigarette out of a pack of American Spirits and sticking it in his mouth to light. He takes a deep drag and leans back against the side of the Jeep, duffel resting between his legs. I watch him in the sloping rectangles of yellow light that spill from the windows, waiting for a few drags to do whatever he needs them to.

"You're not going to say anything?" he finally asks, exhaling smoke.

I back away from the dispersing cloud, feeling the cold grass on the tops of my feet as I step off the drive. "It'll kill you." He squints at me. "But it is the number one activity for angst and if I said your parents never drove me to smoke I'd be lying to your face." He lets out a tired laugh, tilting his face to me, his hair flopping in his eyes. "Grayer, what did your dad say last night? What happened?"

"Nan." His face darkens. "I need to sleep. I have a headache like a fucking mosh pit in my brain, I've been awake for forty-eight hours and took a fucking history test today to boot. So can we please just let me pass out on my breezeway couch and talk tomorrow?"

"Of course. I just . . ."

"Need to know where the fuck to dump us Monday? I get that." He stubs his cigarette in the gravel and picks up our bags. "Believe me, I get that."

The next morning, I button my cardigan over my sundress as I shuffle through the canvas-upholstered, coral-accessorized, driftwood-adorned, double-height living room toward the smell of breakfast. Hungover from a night of exodus-induced coma-sleep, I try not to get diverted by the long white couches singing their siren song. Coffee. Coffee will help.

"Morning," I call as I scroll through a mess of spam on my Black-Berry in hopes of an update from Josh. I round the doorway into the kitchen, which is the size of most Manhattan restaurants, and look up to see the Filipino couple manning the professional cooktop, where bacon and pancakes are sizzling. "Good morning," I repeat, exchanging smiles with them as I take a thin porcelain cup from the counter and fill it with steaming coffee from the sterling urn.

"Morning," Alex says tightly from the glass-encased breakfast nook facing the ocean. "You've missed the golfers—they've already headed out."

"Oh, that's okay. I'm not really a . . ." I glance at her linen sailor pants and cable-knit cashmere sweater as I take a sip, still catching up to the fact that I seem to have unwittingly signed up for a high school reunion weekend. "Do you golf?"

"Well, not today, but I've been for a run." She smiles, closing the *Times* and refolding it.

"I'm so impressed. I woke up at seven, shut my eyes for a second, and it was nine thirty. The sound of the ocean totally knocks me out."

"Please, help yourself," the Filipino man says, gesturing to the tureens of three kinds of eggs sitting atop kerosene warmers.

"Wow, this smells delicious. Thank you." The coffee bean fumes jump-starting my hunger, I load my plate up and slide in opposite Alex, repositioning a double-C monogrammed throw pillow. "Have you seen the boys?"

"My nanny took Astin and the other kids to the farmers' market. Then I think they're going riding."

"Riding? Stilton has a burned hand."

"Oh, *that's* what that was." You thought it was a married-to-me bandage? "He'll be fine." She returns to her paper.

I bite my lip and look down at my plate. "Could I call your nanny? What's her name?"

"Gloria."

"It's just I'm not authorized to give permission for something like that." Alex looks at me askance, since she was already in bed with a headache when introductions were made last night. "They've been staying with me while their parents—"

"Well, I know who their parents are. Did you meet Carter Nelson? I didn't get a chance to talk to her at the benefit. What's she like?"

"Oh, she's really—I think she's very committed to her art."

"And you used to be these boys' nanny?"

"Grayer's, yes."

"Why?"

"I needed the money," I answer flatly.

She mulls this over as she rolls her ring so that the diamond is squarely facing out. "Well, I suppose it's nice for them that you all have stayed in touch."

Yes, it's just like that. "It's great. So if you could give me the number—I really need them in one piece come Monday."

She stands from the table, leaving behind her picked-over plate, patting my arm as she passes. "Then we have lots of time to break them and put them back together."

After inhaling a second helping of eggs Benedict, refilling my coffee, and getting Alex to reluctantly give me her nanny's number—WTF, like I'm unionizing?—I climbed back to my room on the third floor to resume my call station from my bed and fret in their Frette. Having been reassured that Stilton is contented feeding carrots at the stables, I stare down at the phone and try to figure out just who else I can reach on Memorial Day weekend to escalate the "Monday dump," as Grayer termed it.

Suddenly the little red light goes off and I press the button to see a text from Josh. CHINATOWN HOLIDAY INN.

Holiday Inn?

Chinatown?!

Mrs. X?!

I quickly type THNX!, dial information, and within moments the line is ringing.

"Chinatown Holiday Inn, how may I direct your call?"

"Hi, yes, I'm trying to reach a guest. A Mrs. X?"

"One moment, please, I'll connect you."

"Thank you!"

"Chinatown Holiday Inn, this is the operator."

"Hello, I'm trying to reach a Mrs. X, she's a guest at your hotel?" Or Josh is taking his life in his hands having the fun with me.

"One moment, please."

"Thanks so much." And suddenly I'm sweaty and shaking and totally blank. Just tell her to come get them—come get your kids, please! Comegetyourkidspleasecomegetyourkidspleasecomegetyourkidsplease—

"Hello?"

"Mrs. X?" I ask, though I would know that voice under anesthesia. Silence. "Mrs. X? This is Nan Hutchinson, I'm so sorry to interrupt your treatment, but Carter Nelson had to—" The line goes dead. "Hello? Hello?!" I check the signal bars—all five there.

"Chinatown Holiday Inn, how may I direct your call?"

"Yes, I am trying to reach a guest."

"One moment, please, I'll connect you."

"Thanks."

"Chinatown Holiday Inn, this is the operator."

"Hi. I'm trying to reach your guest, Mrs. X."

"One moment, please."

It rings. And rings. Finally: "Hello?"

"Mrs. X? It's Nan again, we must have gotten discon—"

Dial tone. Dammit! Oh my God . . . is she hanging up on me? She's hanging up on me. Oh my God!

"Chinatown Holiday Inn, how may I direct your call?"

"Yeah, trying to reach a guest."

"One moment, please, I'll connect you."

"Uh-huh."

"Chinatown Holiday Inn, this is the operator."

"Mrs. X, please."

"One moment—oh, yes, that guest has been asked not to be disturbed, but I can put you through to the message system, one moment—"

I hang up, my heart pounding. "Fuck. *Fuckfuckfuck.*" I pound the device into the soft white pillow.

"Nan?" I hear a man's voice at the door.

"Yes?"

"It's Clark."

"Sorry, yes, come in," I say, standing.

The door opens and he leans inside, toweling off his sweaty face from a round of golf. "I'm about to hop in the shower."

I realize I'm looking at him blankly. "Okay."

He grins. "Then we're all going to hang at the pool. You play poker?"

"What?"

"Poker, we could use one more."

"Oh, yes, but, I'm, uh, triaging a work crisis. Maybe later?"

"Cool." He spins around, slapping his hand on the top of the doorframe. "We'll have a drink waiting."

I stare after him, at a total loss.

Hiding from the smattering of poolside conversation behind Citrine's *Us Weekly,* I peer across the ruffling water to where Grayer is racked out on his chaise. His chest rises and falls under his sweatshirt, his Oakleys obscuring his eyes. A rumble of thunder rolls in off the Atlantic. "We may just have to go inside and drink," Bitsy Newhouse, a Core Fusion buddy of Tatiana's, announces chipperly, lowering her sunglasses, realizing the sky has clouded over their purpose. She slips them off and drops them into the whale-patterned tote that matches her kelly green hot pants. Probably a snub-nosed blue-eyed baby, Mary in the pageant, prom queen, sorority president. What happens to the Bitsys when our thirties give way to our forties, when we're supposed to start looking more like women and less like girls? "Does anybody make a decent Bloody Mary? My ex, he could mix a drink," she says, a little ruefully.

"Bits, you want a Bloody Mary?" Clark calls from the patio where the men are playing poker a respectable seventh-grade-dance-distance away. He picks up his phone.

"Well, yeah!"

He texts something. "Coming right up! Anybody else?"

"Pellegrino!" the other wives call. "Those seaweed chips!"

Grayer stretches, his glasses falling down. He sees me watching and pushes them back into place. Flipping up his hood, he sinks back into unconsciousness, or at least the appearance of.

Roger folds and pushes back from the table, as he has been doing every round. This time he wanders across the grass, down to the pool area, and sits himself on the edge of his wife's chaise. "What're you reading?" he asks.

"God, you're worse than Astin," Alex scoffs, not taking her eyes from her Candace Bushnell novel. "Why can't you just play with the other boys?"

He hunches his shoulders and stares at his hands. "Clark doubled the stakes to a thousand a hand and I—I—we—"

"We what?"

He looks around. I pretend I'm not listening.

"We've talked about this," he mutters.

"Oh my God," she says loudly. "You're such a worry wart." She lowers the book to her chest and leans in. "You got a two-million bonus last year," she says through tight teeth.

"In *options*," he whispers. "Clark's been saying some seriously scary shit. Doomsday shit."

"And he doesn't seem worried. He just bought a motherfucking Chagall, for Christ's sake."

"Alex." He pulls back to look squarely at her. "He's a short-seller. That's how he makes his money."

"Well, I don't know what to tell you. It's a nice weekend. Go have a nice weekend."

Dismissed, he lumbers back to the game, reluctantly taking his seat at the new rate.

"So what did you decide about your name?" Alex turns chipperly to Bitsy.

"Oh, I decided I'm keeping his," she says, fingering with one hand the large diamond pendant that looks like a converted cushion-cut engagement ring, and scrolling her BlackBerry with the other. "My mom pointed out it opens more doors—oh, the Jarndyce helicopter thingy was yesterday. Wow. Want to hear something disgusting?" She runs her thumb down the roller ball as she talks. Alex and Pippa nod. "It seems the event planner wouldn't leave without payment. Made some kind of stink. God, that's so gauche. My friend's saying we should all boycott her."

"Of course. Forward me that, would you?" Pippa sits up on her chaise, exposing the cushion's navy blue interlocking double C monogram—lest we go ten feet on this property without knowing whose house this is, as if Vicente was decorating for amnesiacs. Closing the *Vogue* in her lap, she swings her espadrilles to the slate rimming the pool and turns to Alex. "I'd better talk to the chef about lunch for the children." She gestures to the darkening sky. "They'll probably be back from the beach soon."

"Or not," Alex retorts, pressing her freckled lips together. "Gloria is very resourceful—she can keep them out there for hours." Except Stilton, who forsook the beach to trail Citrine since they got back from the morning's equine excursion.

"Good," Bitsy rejoinders. "My daughter needs to be worn out like a greyhound."

"I loved that little sundress you had her in this morning," Alex says.

"Well, I have to draw the eye down." Bitsy pulls a face. "Don't get me started. I'm counting the seconds until I can get her into Dr. Imber. Of course she takes after her father and looks weren't exactly the asset he brought to the party."

My cell rings and, all too ready for a break from these ladies, I swipe it from under my chair. "Hello?"

"Hey."

"Oh, thank God, hold on a sec." I slip my feet into my flip-flops and stride out to the base of the dunes. "Thanks so much for getting back to me. I'm going nuts. I tried calling, but she keeps hanging up on me. What exactly did you find?"

"Okay," Josh says, and I picture him flipping through his worn palm-sized Moleskine. "I schmoozed the front-desk clerk—Pepper helped—and she confirmed a blond woman checked in two weeks ago. Never leaves the room, but gets daily deliveries from Bouley— and a manicurist came twice."

"Wait, she doesn't leave the room?"

"Nope."

"So doctors come to her."

"Not that they know of."

"Then it's some sort of alternative outpatient treatment? An Asian healing retreat thing?"

"Not unless she finds coq au vin therapeutic."

"Are you saying—"

"She's a big fat faker? Yes, that is what I'm saying."

I shake my head, uncomprehending, as I look back to see Grayer stretched out on his chaise. "But *why* would you *do* something like this?" My mind reels. "It's monstrous." I hold my hand up. "Whatever, she can answer that Monday evening when I drag her by the neck back to 721."

"I want the blow-by-blow. I'll need the entertainment in Pough-keepsie."

"I'm *so* sorry, Josh. You know if I had a bank I'd hire Jen in a heart-beat."

"I'll tell her."

"You're awesome to do this, especially with everything else you're juggling. And tell Pepper she's a rock star. As soon as I get this sorted—"

"No worries. Good luck, Nan."

"Wait, Josh?"

"Yup?"

"What do *you* think I should do?"

"I dig the neck dragging."

"If that's not feasible."

I hear him sigh. "Fuck, Nan. Maybe ... maybe you really should just ask her if you can have them—oh, that's Jen, gotta go."

I hang up and cross my arms to take in the expanse of gray blue clouds moving in low from the water, an effervescence moving out from my chest. *Maybe I really should ...*

"Does anybody think it's going to rain?" Citrine comes around from the side of the house carrying gardening shears and wearing wellies, tiny black running shorts, and one of Clark's shirts open over a straining spaghetti tank top. Stilton follows on her heels with a basket full of fresh hydrangeas as I make my way back on the grass path.

"I love rain," Stilton says, gazing up at her. "Grayer, look!" Stilton puts the basket down and runs around the pool to where his brother is prostrate. "A baby frog." He opens his hand and places the gumball-sized creature on Grayer's chest. Grayer startles, leaping up.

"My frog!" Stilton screams.

"Dude, you scared the shit out of me, what the fuck?"

"Yo," Clark calls from the patio. "Language."

I hustle over as Stilton drops to where the slate meets the grass, manically looking for the tiny guy. "Stil." I bend down and touch his shoulder. "I bet he hopped off to rejoin his froggy friends. Do you want to play cards? Maybe they have an extra deck for us."

Eyes wet, he turns to Citrine, who now stands behind Clark's shoulder at the table like a fertility talisman. "What are you doing now, Citrine?" he entreats.

She looks down at the basket. "Putting these in vases?" she says testily.

"I'll do that for you!" He runs from me to her uncomprehending side, picking up the basket on his way. With a sigh, she lets him follow her inside and I'm torn between rescuing her and giving her practice.

"He thinks she's the new Carter," Grayer mutters for only me to hear as he sits back heavily on the chaise.

"I thought maybe he's now imprinting on real estate." We both stare after them for a moment before I turn to him. "Listen, do you want to go for a walk on the beach? I think we should talk."

"It's about to rain, Nan." He reaches into his sweatshirt pocket and pulls out his cigarettes.

"Ooh, can I have one?" Bitsy scrambles around past the deep end and plants her tanned legs before him. "You don't mind?" she asks me, pulling the pendant chain up over her lower lip. "Oh, right, he's not yours."

Grayer and I exchange a look. Despite Grayer's zoned-out state, or perhaps, because of it Josh's suggestion gathers momentum and I cross my arms in the gathering wind. "What do you think, Grayer?"

"What?" He tilts the pack at her and she sits down on the edge of his chaise for him to light the cigarette she slides out.

"So," she says, blowing out a strong stream of smoke through her nostrils like a baby dragon. "Your dad's the investment guru who swept up Carter Nelson."

"Yeah." He fixes her with a look that's not uninterested.

"What's Carter Nelson like?" she asks conspiratorially.

"She's a stuck-up cunt."

"Bitsy," I strain. "Actually, we were going to try to get in a walk before the rain starts."

"Cunt, huh?" Bitsy ignores me, laughing as she tosses her hair. "Ooh, we don't like those, do we?" Oh, God, no, no, no. This is how the Grayers become their fathers—the women who should be keeping them in check were someone else's neglected daughters and their reflex is to flatter and cajole, no matter what asinine offensive thing trips from the guy's mouth.

A tray of drinks arrives and Bitsy offers Grayer a sip from her Bloody Mary, which turns into a gulp. And another. While I stand there awkwardly—what—waiting for them to finish?

CLAP!

Fat raindrops splash down to darken the slate and everyone grabs their drinks and reading material and dashes for the patio. Grayer unzips his sweatshirt, throws it around Bitsy's shoulder, and, with his arm secured around her, runs her inside.

21

The cold evening breeze snaps the canvas awning as Bob Marley—which Clark put on with a wink to me—wails around us on the deck overlooking the dark dunes. "Di-vine," Tatiana pronounces, folding her CC-embroidered napkin beside her plate. Underneath the heat lamp I nod in agreement, mouth full of the foie gras bison burger prepared to decadent perfection by Clark's chef—amazingly sans an interlocking set of Cs seared into its bun. I'm now wondering if Citrine was chosen to match the monogram.

"Excellent meal, Clark." Pippa's husband, Stuart, pokes his finger into his mouth to pick between his back molars.

"See, he's *still* enjoying it!" Pippa lifts her glass of rosé to his roving hand. Everyone laughs, and Citrine, seated at the end of the cedar table, sends a text to the kitchen. The wall of glass between the deck and the house slides open and the couple sweeps out to clear. The plates lift past me, four of the nine burgers mangled but essentially uneaten.

Stroking his hands down the front of his shirt, Clark drums the table with finality. "Great," he says to no one in particular, pushing his chair back from where he sits at the end opposite his wife. "Who's up for a stogie? Just brought some Cohibas back from Geneva."

With a rousing chorus of "Hey now" and "Can't turn down that offer," the men grab their microbrews and excuse themselves—well, not so much excuse themselves as leave—to follow Clark down to the far side of the deck.

"And now we gather in the music room for cordials and singing?" I ask, thankful Grayer took off to hang out with some Haverhill kids who live down the lane and is missing this opportunity to diversify his lung cancer. Stilton is happily tucked up in the breezeway, studying the *Oceanside Gardening Essentials* he found on the coffee table. I take another sip of wine, returning to what has become a ceaseless playing through of asking his mother if she wants to give them to me. And what that will be like. And if we can afford to rent something little while the renovation is completed, something near their school. And if Ryan will get along with Grayer right away or they'll need to grow on each other. And if Sarah still sees that great therapist who I could maybe take Grayer to—

"Ugh, the smell of that foie gras is foul." Citrine twists her lips. "I'm so exhausted."

"Has anyone gotten a text from Bitsy? How's her date going?" Tatiana asks.

Pippa picks up her phone, taps it with her thumb, and then grimaces. "They haven't even ordered apps and he's already brought up his ex. Twice."

We wince.

"Mommymommymommy!" We collectively turn to the glass behind us, where Astin slip-slides in his pajamas into the illuminated living room. A red-faced Gloria rounds the staircase in hot pursuit.

"Christ," Alex says, sighing as if she fully expected this to be the next phase of what the evening held for her. As Astin paws at the glass, Alex stares into the night with her wine poised halfway to her mouth.

Astin moves his way across the pane, palms out, like a panic-stricken mime, until he finds the handle and flings it to the side, running out onto the deck. "Why is Gloria making me sleep?" He hurls his arms around Alex from the back of her chair. "I want to go swimming! I want you to go swimming *with* me."

"I'm so sorry, Mrs. Baxter." Gloria, out of breath, hustles onto the deck. Tatiana raises her glass and an eyebrow of disgust. Or attempts to. I think. Her cheek twitched. So sushi and soft cheese, no. Botulism and wine, yes?

"Go swimming with me!" Astin buries his head in the back of his mother's tan neck. "Go swimming with me!"

Alex's eyes energize to shoot Gloria a look that packs a slap before swiveling in her son's direction. "Astin, Mommy went swimming with you already today."

She didn't.

"And now Mommy was just enjoying her dinner."

She wasn't.

"Go upstairs and Mommy will come check on you."

She won't.

"Gloria?" Alex mutters with unmitigated annoyance. "Get him to bed so you can mix my shots."

Murmuring apologies, Gloria steps forward to unlock a screeching Astin and literally drag him back inside. "She always does that. Indulges him and then he's up until all hours and I have to do my shots at exactly nine fifteen. She knows I can't do them by myself. And he cries when he watches."

The men make their way back from the far side of the patio, stogies in mouths, lighters being passed.

"Shots?" I'll bite.

"IVF," Tatiana explains on Alex's behalf, making a syringe gesture.

"Conceiving Astin was disgusting." Alex grimaces. "It was, like, five straight days of watching porn. I was so full of sperm. But with IVF I'm just a fucking dartboard. Gloria needs to be more sensitive."

The breeze shifts and I wrap my sweater closer, shimmying my chair nearer the heater. "She did keep Astin entertained all day," I say tentatively, "even with the rain." I glance at Citrine, but she's focused on refolding her napkin exactly as it was in her napkin ring. "Plus Stilton, Calliope, Wendy, William"—the latter two Pippa's twins— "and Itsy Bitsy," I choke out the name. "She's a find."

"O-kay . . ." Alex says as if I'm taking it upon myself to explain to her how her toilet works.

"Astin's probably overtired, that's all. You know, big day in the country," I conclude, unsuccessfully trying to reroute into a "No need to be embarrassed" tone. About him. Green light on your miserable self.

"This is based on raising your own two sons?" Alex smiles tightly at me.

"Well, I had a big day in the country." Tatiana stands from the table, tugging at her Dior romper. "I'm turning in for my disco nap. Didier?" she calls over to her troll of a husband. "What time's the car coming?"

"Ten sirty," he lobs back as he strolls over to the table, the other men ambling behind. "And get your ass moving, eh," he says to her departing back as she slides the glass closed behind her. "You always make me late!" He smiles his blackened smile to all of us. "So fucking disorganized, right? Right, girls? My wife is a fucking mess."

The girls return his smile.

"You're going out?" I stand, eager to be out of Alex's rage range. Hoping if I sell it with enough enthusiasm, she'll go, too.

"We go to ze Pink Trout!"

"Shit, I haven't been there since it was the Banana," Clark says through puffs. "Those're days you can't get back, eh?"

Citrine blanches.

"I haven't been to a club since the twins." Pippa claps her hands together, the zest so palpable at the shower returning.

"We've been lying low," Stuart says a little too quickly. "Unwinding."

"He means dying on the vine. I call it parenting."

"C, let's go!" Clark grabs Citrine's shoulders as if about to massage them, but doesn't.

"To a *club*?" Citrine balks, twisting to look up at him, nauseous perspiration dotting her upper lip. "Clark, I can't."

"We already have ze table. My friend's ze manager." Didier puffs up. "Don't be fucking losers, come out!"

An hour later finds me pulling on a beaded filmy YSL tunic as Citrine stomps around her closet for a pair of matching shoes. "Here," she pronounces before emerging to slap a pair of glittering heels into my hands. "I knew I had them here. That fits you perfectly." She glares, her face drawn from throwing up dinner, her first-trimester morning sickness dragging on into second-trimester all-day misery. "You can probably just have it. I'm sure to be up three sizes when this nightmare is over."

"Citrine," I try yet again, tucking the shoes under my elbows to put both hands on her caramel forearms. "I'd really rather be here when Grayer gets back. We can watch a movie. Just hang out, catch up with you. Life has been plenty exciting and I would love some mellow—"

"Earrings." She pulls away from me and over to a chest of drawers to rifle through a Louis Vuitton case next to her makeup mirror.

"I don't need earrings. I don't need to go to a club."

"Nan!" She whips around, case in hand, as she drops her voice and steps away from the door to their bathroom, where Clark is showering. "Clark can't go out with a bunch of couples. He'll be totally bored. It's not fair to him. He'd have to find someone to keep him company. Just go and have fun. Can't you do that?" Her bottom lip trembles.

Socially depleted from navigating dinner's twists and turns of barbs and smiles, I make one last attempt. "Citrine, you're pregnant. And hosting all these people, *and* it's okay to have needs. Why not ask him to stay home with you?"

"Because I don't want to hear the answer." She tugs away from me and wipes at her eyes. "God, just . . . be a friend, would you?"

I sit on the bench at the end of their bed and obediently slide a four-hundred-dollar shoe onto each foot.

Our town car, one of the two ferrying our significantly prepartied crew, crunches onto the gravel lot of the Pink Trout and jockeys behind the other limos up to the white clapboard building with black shutters. If it weren't for the diminutive sign by the hedge lit pink and the line of people snaking to its unassuming door, this could easily be mistaken for the ice cream parlor down the lane. Or the bagel shop. Or the post office.

Eager to be released from the perfume crossfire, I watch the driver get out and circle round to open the back door for us ladies. As soon as it's unlatched, the frigid night air pours in and I rub my goose-pimpled thighs, waiting for Tatiana to squeeze out in her ass-skimming gold Hervé Léger bandage dress (is she actually using a surrogate?), followed by Pippa, "Woo!"ing in a Pucci print, and finally Alex, freshly pumped with ovary stimulants, care of Gloria, bringing up the rear in an apricot silk cocktail dress.

I take the driver's hand and climb into the cold night air, dense with the cigarette smoke of our queuing twentysomething Léger/ Pucci/Calypso manqués. Crossing my arms over the chiffon, I watch my riding companions size up these 2.0s, jaws clenching at the ample display of taut perkiness.

"I *would* have packed for this," Alex mutters, her ankles wavering as she navigates the tiny pebbles with her patent pumps. "Of course, I have the perfect Luca Luca just sitting in my closet. Now, when will I wear *that*?"

"It's a problem," I offer, and she takes it as we make our way over to the discernibly lit husbands being eyed as potential drink funders. Tatiana strides past the young'uns to grab Didier's fleshy hand while he chats up the guy manning the door.

"Oh my God, is this taking you back?! It's so taking me back!" Electrified, Pippa greets Stuart in his pink oxford.

"Back, yeah." Not meeting her eyes, he adjusts the lime green cable-knit thrown over his shoulders.

"I could have worn my Dior, if I'd known to pack it," Alex says, greeting Roger, who is intently following the offhand discussion of bottle service between Didier and the door guy. A slight ring of sweat glistens at the base of Roger's neck where the collar of his striped oxford begins. And as soon as we all step inside the blacklit room, I almost suggest Alex stick a Day-Glo name tag on his back because it's a densely packed throng of oxfords, moderated only by degree of gelled hair and orange tans. Tatiana raises her hand to lead the way, lifting it toward the low ceiling in time to the thumping beat. We weave past the crowd at the bar to a two-foot black cube with a "Reserved" sign tented on top. Our table?

Tatiana and her husband immediately sprawl on the crowded bench lining the wall. Having claimed the only seats, Didier slides his hand along his forehead and waves at us to make ourselves at home in the nothing that is our space. A waiter weaves over, a tray of Grey Goose bottles and decanters of mixers held high. The crowd parts all of a few inches for him to expertly balance it atop our cube. Didier lifts up on one hip to pull out his wallet and tosses the waiter his credit card, looking at the other husbands expectantly.

"How many more bottles you think he's ordering tonight?" Roger leans across me to ask his wife.

"I don't *know*." Alex recoils. Well, recoils as much as is possible when we're all stuck together like rush-hour commuters.

"I'm just saying I lost at poker and it's three-fifty a bottle, so don't rush it."

"Nice," she pronounces, then turns a big smile to the group. "I THINK WE'LL NEED ANOTHER BOTTLE. MOËT CHANDON?"

The ladies nod as Alex flags down the waitress, her eyes challengingly fixed on Roger. Pippa, already playing bartender, hands Stuart a drink and then pours herself a stiff one. They cheers.

"FUCKING AWESOME." Clark bends to pour himself a straight fifth and down it. There's something about watching adults play bartender with tiny glasses in a minuscule space that feels reminiscent of the Easy-Bake Oven. "IT'S LIKE SOUTH BEACH." He eyes the cube next to ours, where a pretty far along bachelorette party is getting their ya-yas out. Lobster skin and white strap marks cut unflattering lines out of tank and trapeze dresses. The girls dance on the banquette around their veiled friend with the penis necklace, hands braced on the ceiling and green palm wallpaper, their heels spiking deep valleys into the leather. Tatiana lists toward them as if on the brink of a whirlpool.

Stuart pours another shot for himself and Clark and the two clink glasses. "WAY BETTER ACOUSTICS THAN MARQUEE."

"WHEN DID YOU GO TO MARQUEE?" Pippa whips her head around.

"WITH CLIENTS." He shrugs, giving himself over to a house-base head-swivel as he goes for a refill.

"SO AWHILE AGO, THEN," she retorts, taking Tatiana's outstretched hand and following her up alongside the dancing girls on the banquet. Didier, jostled from the melee, types on his iPhone.

Stuart looks at me for a moment and I look back in the awkward opposite-of-silence. He leans into my ear. "PIPPA DOESN'T KNOW I STILL GO OUT EVERY WEEK. SHE WOULDN'T UNDERSTAND THAT SOMETIMES THAT'S WHAT WORKING LATE LOOKS LIKE."

I nod, wondering what he could have read in my expression that says please confide in me.

"LET'S DANCE," Clark suddenly says to me as he downs his shot and shakes his head hard.

So not drunk enough to be here. "THANKS, BUT I'M GOING TO HAVE A DRINK FIRST! YOU GO AHEAD!" I wave him toward the packed dance floor.

He reaches down and pours two shots. "TO CITRINE! LONG MAY SHE REST!" Cracking himself up, he hands me one. I down it, grimacing as it burns, and he takes the glass from me. "DANCE!" He puts both hands on my shoulders and turns me into the crowd, propelling me forward into unmoving people. I make a defensive breaker with Citrine's clutch and arrive into the nucleus of the sleepy-eyed flailing.

"YOU KNOW, IT'S A LITTLE TOO CROWD—" I pivot to Clark, but his elbows are already bent, fists already jutting, white man's overbite already bitten. Sigh. I bop my head back and forth. One dance. Then I'm pushing Didier off our couch and hunkering down. How long can this crew last? They're already sauced.

He drink-shakers his arms closer until there is one fist shaking on either side of my head. I smile as neutrally as possible, like we're passing in the grocery store. To no avail. His hips seek mine out, determined to grind. "YOU LOOK HOT IN THAT. C SHOULD GIVE IT TO YOU," he bellows into my ear in a smattering of vodka spittle.

I smile blankly back, willing the ceaseless beat to show signs of wrapping up. It doesn't. Instead, his grinding gets more pronounced. His eyes flash at my breasts, up to the girls dancing on the banquettes, back to me, to the girls, to my breasts, and more hard, and that's a— Okay! "I NEED SOME AIR." I point toward the main entrance and, hoping I've fulfilled my friend duty, swing my elbows like machetes clearing brush all the way to the door. "I JUST NEED TO ..." I indicate to the tan guy. He holds it open for me and I'm expectorated into the ringing silence of the scowling line. I click down the brick steps and take a deep breath of fresh air. *Yuck.*

"Good call."

I spin around. Clark jogs down the steps, sliding a cigarette out of a pack and sticking it in his mouth. He tilts the pack at me and I wave a demurring hand. "Insane in there." He lights his smoke and then slicks back his sweaty hair. "So you and Citrine were high school buds? Sleepovers and secrets?"

"No ... not so much." I look past him, weighing my options. Go back inside to angry drunks. Stand out here with sleazy drunk. Start walking down road, possibly get abducted by crazy drunk. Tough call.

"She said something about you having your own company?" He eyes me over the streams of smoke coming out his nose.

"I do."

"Nice," he murmurs, as if I had admitted to being pantyless.

"I'm just going to ..." What?

"Why don't we go sit in one of the cars?" He sidles another inch closer. "Get some air without all this noise?"

"Oh, I'm fine here, thanks."

"You should know." He leans in. "I still have my old place in the city."

Citrine's clutch blessedly rings. "Oh, someone's calling me!" I raise it theatrically to my ear. I pull out my cell while Clark's eyes wander to the line of giggling girls. Ryan! I flip it open, pressing the clutch to my other ear. "Ry?"

"Nan?"

"Yes! Yes! Hold on." I clasp the phone to my chest. "It's my husband," I inform Clark, but he's already wandering back inside. I teeter over to the hedge lining the lot. "Hi! Oh wow, it's so good to hear your voice!"

"Where are you?"

"The Hamptons. Stuck in the alternate version of the alumnae bulletin." I raise my voice to a perky register. "This year Citrine Kittridge Cilbourne's husband has decided to keep a spare apartment for extramarital affairs." I step one foot out of a heel and rest it on the cold gravel. "Where are you?"

"Standing on our front stoop."

"Ha-ha."

"Yeah, in that flew-four-thousand-miles-with-only-three-days-off-and-counting-to-spend-with-your-wife kind of way."

I freeze. "You're standing in front of our house? Seriously?"

"Sitting, actually, now." He sighs. "What are you doing out there? Where's Grace?"

"Citrine invited me. She's with Sarah. You're in the city?" I repeat.

"To a party?"

"No, no, to a 'relaxing' weekend that has turned into a tension-off between my high school classmates and their husbands. God, I miss you."

"What's with the music?"

I glance back at the house, where, now that my ears are no longer ringing, I realize the bass audibly thumps from inside. "Oh my God, I'm in the parking lot of some nightclub. Tatiana was going out and suddenly Citrine had this meltdown because Clark got so excited and she's five months pregnant so it's not really what she's up for and—"

"So can you get back here?" he asks so simply that all I want is to pour myself straight through the phone.

"Is the house even open? Does it look like anything's been done? I saw Steve on Thursday and he—"

"Let's not talk Steve, please. Do you need the house to be open to come home? I just flew all the way from fuck nowhere, Nan."

"No, babe, I know, and that's so awesome. Hey! Come out here! They have a pool and if you can squint past the exploited-nanny and sticky-rage veneer, it could be relaxingish." I can introduce you to your new kids . . .

"Nan . . ." And I know he's rumpling his hands through his hair. "Look, I'm shot and I just want to curl up next to my girl. Not really in the headspace for a house party. Can you please just come home? I only have three days—two and a half now."

"I can't." I bite my lip, preferring to navigate a horny Clark.

"I'll get a hotel! Just grab the first Jitney in the morning. We'll have breakfast in bed, take a bath—"

"Ryan, *I can't*." I stick my foot back into the heel.

"I don't understand. You said there are other guests there. Citrine will forgive—"

"I have the boys with me."

"What boys?"

I squint at the dark hedge. "The X boys."

"You have the X boys with you." I hear a long exhale. "Okay . . . so drop them off at *their* home on the way to meet me at the hotel," he says slowly.

"It's not that simple. Their parents are"—my voice rises—"I don't know *where* the fuck their father is. Their mother is holed up at the Chinatown Holiday Inn, I'm pretty sure faking cancer to save face, and the house was toxic and you were unreachable—"

"Text me Citrine's address," he says firmly. "I'm renting a car."

The sound of the slamming screen door startles me awake from where I passed out under my trench and a blanket on the portico's chaise, lulled by the rhythm of the Atlantic.

"Nan?" Citrine crosses her arms over the wrap sweater twisted around her nightgown. "You scared me."

"Sorry." I roll my neck and unstick my spine from the canvas. "What time is it?"

"It's after two. Waiting for Grayer?"

"He texted me his designated driver would be dropping him off by four." And if anyone thinks I'm going to start negotiating curfew in the middle of this *meshugas* they are mistaken. "I'm actually waiting for Ryan. He's driving out."

"Now?" She tilts her head at the darkness.

"He flew in for the weekend to surprise me and I ended up surprising him." I stand, enfolding the blanket around my shoulders.

"Romantic." Smoothing the thin cotton under her, she sits on the steps, patting the wood beside her, and I billow down.

"Can't sleep?" I ask.

"Clark stinks and he's snoring. He gets so congested when he drinks. Normally I'd sleep in one of the guest rooms, but . . ."

"Gotcha. Do you want to take my room? We can totally crash in the den . . . if he gets here."

"No. No, it's fine. Did you guys have fun?" She spreads her legs a little bit and rests her elbows on her knees.

"I took a cab back, actually. But, um, everyone seemed to be having fun, yeah."

She nods. "Did Clark seem happy?"

"Yes?"

"I don't know how Tat does it. I was so exhausted right away. And now I'm exhausted *and* fat."

"But her husband is disgusting," I say through a yawn. "Right?"

The statement hangs between us, gaining a dense harshness in the sudden silence. "Why are you so judgmental?" she asks.

"I'm sorry—"

"They're my friends," she says tightly.

"O-kay. But they weren't your friends."

"No. We went through a rough patch. But they were always my friends."

A ten-year rough patch. Gotcha. I inhale through my nose. "Which is totally fine," I say. "I'm sorry."

She pulls her hair to one side of her neck and stares out at the black outline of the hedge at the end of the drive. "What do you think of *my* husband?"

"Oh, I think—I think . . . you two seem to be, to make, a good couple."

"Bullshit." She turns to study me.

"I barely know him, Citrine."

"You look at me like you think I'm an asshole."

"I *don't* think you're an asshole."

"Right."

"But I just . . ." I trail off as she pushes the sleeves of her sweater up and for the first time it registers that her once tempera-stained hands are spotless. "I just have to ask, why are you—"

"What? Enjoying my husband's beach house? Having his baby?"

"*Your* beach house. *Your* baby."

She blinks at me. "Fuck you. Not all of us find someone who

comes back to surprise us from Africa—who 'works through' having a baby like some peace-summit love-in. I couldn't marry some skinny-jeans-wearing bass player from Bedford Street. That's not a grown-up life. You're a guest here. How dare you judge me?"

"Judge *you*?" I grip the edges of the blanket. "Because I didn't even care that you hooked up with that guy. You took one look at my house and never called me again. Not all of us get servants, Citrine. Some of us have to do the work ourselves."

Her face breaks in shock. "I don't care about *your house*! Is that what you think?"

"Yes?" I admit, feeling fourteen.

Her mouth hangs open. "God, you really do think I'm an asshole."

"Then why didn't you want to be my friend after you found out you were pregnant?"

"What are you talking about? I've been pregnant this whole time."

"You know what I mean."

She shakes her head in disbelief. "This is what I'm doing now, Nan." Letting out a short, dry laugh, she rubs her palm over her brow and takes a deep breath. "And unless you want to hurry up and get pregnant tonight to do it *with* me, these are the women I have to do it with. Your husband's here."

I turn from her to see the headlights pull into the drive, two blinding beams arcing across us. "Citrine—"

"I'm tired." She reaches to the railing to pull herself up and, without a look back, disappears into the house.

22

"Nan-eh."

"Yup," I answer from the deep pull of slumber.

"Nan-eh, Grayer threw up and it smells really bad."

"Okay . . . Can you flush the toilet, Stil?" Lifting up on one elbow, I crack an eye to see him standing at the edge of the mattress backlit by the sun streaming in from the hallway skylights.

"He did it in bed and I don't want Citrine to get angry and make us leave."

"Okay." I inhale.

"Okay." He nods like he can check this one off his list and proceeds to tuck in his shirt. "I'm going down to breakfast. Hi."

I look over my shoulder to where Ryan is stretching awake. "Hey." He waves at Stilton before his hand drops back to the sheet.

"Stilton, this is my husband, Ryan. He drove in last night."

Stilton eyes him. "So how much longer can we stay here?"

My fight with Citrine lands with blunt force. "Um, not sure. You go have some breakfast. I'll take care of the mess. Then we'll regroup and make a plan. Cool?"

"Okay. It really stinks."

"Yeah." I extend an arm at the door in the direction of said puke. "I'm getting right on that."

With one more look at Ryan, Stilton leaves. I fall back on the pillow. "What time is it?"

"In Khartoum?" He lifts his watch. "Four in the afternoon."

"East Hampton, Sudan, same difference." I sit up and scratch my hair, looking back at him as he wipes the sleep from his eyes. "So how are we?"

"Fucking tired." He pulls my pillow over his head.

279

"I mean, in the married sense."

He whips the pillow off. "I don't understand why you keep asking about our marriage. We're married. That's not changing. And we are exactly where we were when we passed out last night, or this morning, or whatever. Which is, you were going to explain this all after we got some sleep. So, hit me."

"First I have to clean up the puke." I swing my legs to the side.

"Right."

I walk across the pickled floor to slide my jeans off the chair and tug them on. I pull off my slip and feel in my bag for a fresh bra.

"Hey," he says. I look over to where Ryan has rolled onto his stomach, his face flat with the edge of the bed. He reaches out his arm for me to return.

Somewhat refueled just to have slept beside him, I wag a finger and grin. "I have puke to clean up." Feeling a vague sense of my footing from the grounding that only he can provide, I pull on my bra. "See, this is parenting! Hold that thought, honey, have to clean up the puke!" I reach for a tank top and slide it over my head, slipping my feet into flip-flops before I register he hasn't responded.

I turn back to see him sitting up, staring intently at me. "What are you really thinking here, Nan?"

I rub my lips together, adrenaline revving in a hot burst under my ribs. "Well, you met Stilton."

He nods.

"He is adorable and crazy smart and funny. And *so* aware of his surroundings it's heartbreaking. You saw how he came in concerned about being a respectful guest. So, I was thinking, and it's been impossible *not* to think this, given the circumstances of the last two weeks—I've been thinking maybe we could, because we have all this space, *will* have all this space—you really want to do this *right now*, and here they are, and Grayer will be going to school in eighteen months so he's in the home stretch, I'm not saying he'll be no trouble, he definitely needs real help, but with love and consistent support—"

"Nan."

"We could adopt them." I am breathless, feeling like I've been shooting toward this moment one way or another since I was twenty-one. "I mean, their parents don't seem to want them."

"*What?!*"

He jumps out of bed as I blanch, instantly enraged and relieved to have the decision out of my hands.

"Adopt them," I repeat, pivoting to the bathroom, where I twist on the water and grab my toothbrush, face beating. "You know, or maybe just be their foster parents, I'm not sure about the legal stuff. I was thinking I could go and speak to their mother tomorrow night when we get back."

He appears in the doorway as I jerk the brush over my teeth. "What happened here? Is it the fungicide? Do you think you're having some kind of breakdown? I never should have taken you back to that building—"

"Fugh ooo."

"What?"

I spit and rinse. "Fuck you!"

"Nan."

"I have been"—I jerk up my Mason Pearson and swipe it through my hair—"I have been—I have *followed*—your work has *totally* dictated our lives, my life, *for years*! You want a house and I am left to build it out of my bare fucking hands. You want children and I have to hurry up and get them for you." I clank my brush down on the porcelain. "Well, I got them!"

"Whoa. You followed me because *you* wanted out of New York and time to figure out what your life was going to be that wasn't working with kids. *We* bought a house because *you* wanted roots! And I want children that are *ours*. Ours, Nan. I want the honor of screwing them up ourselves!"

"See?! How can you possibly say this isn't about our marriage? It so fucking is!"

"Fine! We're fucked. Is that what you want to hear? Our marriage is totally fucked!"

"Nan?"

We both spin to the sound of Citrine calling cheerfully from the bedroom. Glaring, I step around him to peer at where she stands, smiling smugly in the doorway in a yellow eyelet sundress.

"Hi! Yes, good morning!"

"Sorry to interrupt," she says meaningfully, "but I thought you should know one of the boys got sick last night in the breezeway and there are crushed beer cans in the hydrangea beds."

"Yes, Grayer, sorry, I was just on my way to clean it up."

"I've had Lailai take care of it. Will Ryan join the guys for a round of golf this morning?"

"Um." I step into the room and continue to her, "Actually, I wasn't sure after last night. Should I—we—leave?"

"Don't be ridiculous!" She laughs brightly. But with dull eyes, she is nowhere I can get to her. "You have to stay for the unveiling party or Clark'll be devastated. Ryan," she calls past me. "They're leaving in twenty. If you hurry you can catch a ride in Clark's Jag."

"Oh, well, we're kind of in the middle—"

"Great." Ryan appears at the bathroom door. "Count me in."

"Not the two-pound hook, the four-pound!" Clark shouts to Citrine, who scrambles to find the right picture-hanging hardware in the Ziploc bag brought by the delivery men. Awkward and embarrassed, the female half of my fellow houseguests stare down their sorbet-hued laps on opposing freshly plumped canvas couches. I fidget with the beading on the YSL tunic Citrine insisted I recycle.

His dress shirtsleeves rolled up, Clark wallops another set of nails into the pristine wall and steps back to evaluate. "See, now if we move the furniture clockwise—I just don't want the Chagall competing with the ocean—I want it to have its own breathing space."

"Clark, the guests will be here any second." Clutching his cufflinks Citrine looks nervously past the white-jacketed servers lining the hall from the entryway to the kitchen, all holding trays of champagne. "You've been at this for hours." Four. Four hours. Since they returned from their postgolf boozy lunch and all the other husbands went directly to nap. Mine included. Clark, on the other hand, seems to have tapped into some repressed domestic well.

NANNY RETURNS

"It's not right! It needs space!" He points down at the draped painting awaiting its pending unveiling against the baseboard. Touching my finger to my forearm, I watch it turn momentarily white, then back to the burned color I acquired while hiding out with the kids and Gloria during their peewee croquet marathon. What I wouldn't trade to be downstairs for the movie viewing and pizzafest that has followed.

Alex purses her lips and twists her cocktail ring on her brown finger, while Tatiana stares longingly at the tray of caviar-festooned blinis symmetrically arranged to discourage early sneaking.

"Clark," Citrine tries again, stepping away in four-inch platform mules to the window overlooking the driveway. "You have a set of nails in every wall and the couch has completely scraped up the floor."

"Maybe not this room. Maybe it should be in my study. Maybe we need something else for in here—a Picasso or something."

"So where you buy that sing?" Didier asks as he descends the stairs, crosses to the coffee table, takes three blinis at once, and shoves them in his tobacco-drenched mouth. "Because, you know, I sink ze climate out here is shit for art," Didier adds his deux centimes.

"I know a guy. He helps people."

"What kind of people?"

"People who need to turn art into fast cash—quick and dirty." He smirks.

"Clark," Citrine entreats, clicking over to him. "I'll stand up there with you, we'll unveil the picture, everyone will love it."

"No, you stand with your girls," he says, reaffixing it to the wall again with his manservant, Aquino. "The pregnancy is too distracting."

"Oh my God, you won't believe what I just heard!" Pippa, wearing a pink lace shift, cell phone in hand, gallivants down the stairs with a freshly showered Stuart at her pink heels. "Oh, God, Clark, you're not moving that damn thing again, are you? It's a Chagall—it'd look great over a toilet." Tatiana and Alex have swiveled to her.

"Okay, so the first Jarndyce parents are choppering back now, early—"

"Early?" Alex asks in disbelief. "Why would anyone go back in the middle of a holiday?"

"Because," Roger says, coming in from the dining room, "some people are stressed out of their fucking minds right now and have to get back to work tomorrow."

"Anyway, get this." Pippa pauses dramatically. "They can't land."

"What?" I ask. "What does that mean?"

"The first copter was Julia Reid's from Morgan Stanley. She lands, but she couldn't get off the roof. She's got her staff and her kids and her yellow lab and the key-card door to the elevator wouldn't work. So she's freaking out and calling the board. So then another helicopter shows up. But it can't put down. Because Julia's pilot isn't going to leave her stranded. Then another shows up. My friend's at the Soho House pool and she said everyone's watching."

"That's mortifying. The alumni must be committing ritual suicide up and down the shoreline. Let's see if it's making the news." Alex claps.

We all leap up and follow Pippa to Clark's 1930s ocean-liner study, complete with porthole windows and curved zebra veneers. Pippa skibbles around to the Mac's front and opens Firefox.

"Holy shit," Stuart says as NY1's home page loads up. There it is. A massive aerial clusterfuck stretching all the way to Penn Station.

Roger takes the mouse from Pippa and scrolls down into the story. " 'The building is locked up and the board can't be reached for comment,' " Roger reads aloud.

"What do you mean, locked up?" Alex asks, and I jostle to get a better view. Roger points to the photograph of the padlocked front door. My mind reels at the implications. Padlocked?

"So who's accountable?" Stuart asks.

"I'll call my friend at the mayor's office." Roger tugs out his phone.

"The guests are arriving," Citrine frets from the doorway.

I shimmy past her, wanting to call Ingrid, Gene, Josh, my mother. I jog up the staircase and arrive at the third floor just as Ryan steps from the bedroom. "Oh my God, Ry, Jarndyce is padlocked."

"What does that mean?" His brow drops.

"I don't know," I acknowledge, hearing how crazy it sounds. "But it can't be good."

"More not good. Terrific." We stare at each other uncertainly as he straightens the knot on his tie, his face sunburned from the morning on the green. "And these people," he pronounces, "are assholes."

"I know," I say as he walks toward me. "Now you see why I want to rescue the boys."

"Nan, yesterday I was in *the Sudan.*" He starts down the stairs and pauses. "And Grayer is about my height with blond hair?"

"Yes."

"Yeah." He looks up to me. "I think I heard him being 'no trouble' on the floor under ours. I saw him head in there on my way up to change. Just an FYI to his new mother." He continues down and I run into our room, grabbing my cell off the bureau. I dial Gene's office number. "The mailbox you are trying to reach is full." I hang up and take off down the stairs, cornering onto the second-floor landing. I peek in the open bedrooms, which are empty, except for the back guest room, where I spot Calliope, Wendy, and Itsy Bitsy playing Barbies with Gloria.

"Gloria?" She raises her head and I see she's been heavily made up by two-year-old fingers. "Have you seen Grayer?"

She shrugs apologetically. Downstairs I can hear Citrine greeting the first arrivals. "Thank you."

Not seeing any more vomit or, say, drug paraphernalia or firearms, I'm about to take the last flight down so I can find Roger when the bathroom door clicks at the far end—the one just below ours. Grayer and Bitsy emerge, her face radiant, his impassive but flushed. She giggles, pulling him into her for a sloppy kiss. They startle when they see me and Bitsy straightens her skirt and smoothes her shag-tousled hair.

"Bitsy," I sputter, *"seriously?"*

"What?" she says, looking at me like I'm crazy. "He wasn't a virgin." With a wink to him she rolls her shoulders back with self-possession. "See you downstairs." She descends the pickled planks.

I turn incredulously to Grayer, who is throwing his looped tie back over his head. "Party time?" He says grimly, shimmying the knot up.

"Grayer?" I reach out and grab his arm as he tries to pass. "If you're testing me—"

"Yeah, Nan, it's all about you." He tosses his bangs off his face and jogs down the stairs to the filling atrium below.

Collecting myself, I slowly descend to see through the front hall's plate glass window a steady stream of cars arriving as Clark hangs the painting back in the first spot he tried this morning.

Couples flood into the living room, the wives in gossamer-thin shawl cardigans over dresses short enough to expose formidably toned thighs, the husbands in seersucker blazers that cling unflatteringly on their arms and that they couldn't button if they tried. I fin my way through the crowd, looking for Ryan in the sea of slicked hair.

"You won't believe this—look." People with iPhones hold them out to their drinking companions to watch this afternoon's footage of tiny helicopters hovering above Jarndyce as if it were carrion.

Roger comes into the room, phone in hand, and announces, "My friend said when they got the police over there they found the front door chained up with a sign that says 'Closed until further notice.'"

Everyone looks at one another, stupefied.

"An official sign?" I ask. "From the school?"

"Ladies and gentlemen!" Clark suddenly shouts as Aquino takes his cue to ping a fork against a crystal glass. "Thank you all so much for coming to my little viewing." Clark claps his hands together and the crowd quiets while my mind races, skin prickling. I surreptitiously scroll for Josh's number. "Now, as many of you know, I have had a great year." Chuckles ripple through the male half of the crowd. "And I've wanted a Chagall since I can remember." I look for Ryan. Across the room, adult attention diverted, Grayer swipes champagne from a tray and knocks back a gulp. "Many of you scoffed that I couldn't pull this off, that it could not be done without paying outrageous auction block prices. But that's not how I roll. Tom, I believe you owe me a few bucks." A balding man raises his glass. "So, without further ado ..." He whips the white cloth from the gilt frame, revealing a blue-toned painting of a family in front of a tilting house.

Smash!

A glass shatters and all heads turn to where women in open-toed shoes leap away from Grayer's doused loafers. He mumbles an apology for dropping the flute and backs out of the room as people clap for Clark's acquisition. I move to follow, but Ryan steps into my path, blocking me. "Let him be," he says, voice low.

"I can't. I know how that sounds, but I can't." I put my phone in his hand. "Can you please call Josh and see what the official word is on Jarndyce?"

I loop through the crowded ground floor, coming to a stop at the sound of sniffing from Clark's study, and hesitantly push the door open. Grayer leaps up from behind the desk, wiping his hands over his wet eyes. "I can't deal with you right now."

"Okay . . ." I nonetheless shut the door and sit on the edge of a club chair.

"Just—" He braces either side of his head with his hands and paces. "I need to—Where's Stilton?"

"Watching the *Pirates of the Caribbean* trilogy in the media room with the other kids, why?"

"Because I need to—we need to get out of this house. I can't be here anymore."

"Just one more hour. As soon as people start leaving we'll drive back, I promise."

"You *promise*?" He spins to me. "What the fuck is your deal?"

"Can you be more specific?"

"Specifically, you're not our fucking mother. You *do* know that, right?"

"Of course I know that, Grayer."

"Then stop bullshitting me."

"I'm not—I have never bullshitted you." I stand.

"Never?" He gapes. "You mean like the nine months when I was four?"

"Yes! God, why are you so angry at me? Grayer, where is your dad? What's happening?"

"*What's happening?*" He takes a step back. "Thursday night Dad says we're gonna hang out—wanted to take me to Greenwich— suddenly had an *interest*. And it was a fucking lie. His back was out.

He just needed a pair of hands. He used me . . . used me." His voice thickens, his head dropping to his chest as he lets out a choked moan.

I step tentatively over and reach out my hands to his shoulders. "I—I don't follow, Grayer. I want to help you, but I can't unless you ex—"

"You can't! Exactly, Nan-*ny*. Write it on a card, stick it in a bus pass. *You can't help me.*"

"But maybe I could, Grayer," I entreat. "Maybe you could come, with Stilton, and live with Ryan and me. Maybe we could be your—"

"*You?!* Why would I want *you?* You're a fucking mess," he sneers, his nose dripping, his face contorted, ugly. "God, do the world a favor, would you? Don't have kids."

"Listen to me, you ungrateful shit." Before I can stop myself, I've grabbed his chin. "I have beaten myself up for years and do you know why? Because I let your sociopath of a mother fire me. *Fire* me. Because you ran to me and not her when you hurt yourself at a party. I always thought if I'd just *handled* her differently, somehow I could have changed it for both of us." My mind's eye flits to Gloria upstairs, covered in makeup—standing as much a chance of handling Alex as Ingrid did of handling Grant—and then to those last hours in Nantucket. "Your narcissistic shit of a father drove me off an island in the middle of the night. They wouldn't let me say good-bye to you, explain, even though you were screaming, *screaming* for me." I drop his quivering chin to wipe at my wet cheeks. "I don't know how they could do that to you. I don't know if I'll ever. But I do know your father has disappeared and your mother is most likely faking a terminal illness at the Chinatown Holiday Inn and I am the last man standing, trying, at the risk of my own marriage, to do right by you, and if you *ever* so much as breathe a word disparaging my maternal potential again, so help me, I will drop you like the guilty favor you are." I catch my breath, shaking uncontrollably. His eyes saucer and he steps back, his face white. Tripping over the garbage can, he keeps backing up and I, oh God, realize what I've done. "Grayer . . ."

He spins around, grabbing the decanter of Scotch off the bar and flinging back the patio door.

"Grayer!" I scream, chasing after him as he runs into the darkness.

The party finally winding down, sometime after midnight I misera-
bly descend the flight of stairs to the basement media center, where
Ryan slinked off to join Stilton and the other kids, now passed out
after watching all seven and a half hours of the trilogy. Stilton stirs
next to William, a napkin tied over one closed eye. "Argh," he mumbles, "who goes there?"

"Argh," William echoes in his sleep.

Careful not to wake Astin, who has fallen asleep in his lap, Ryan
shifts him onto the leather recliner, removes his own napkin eye-
patch, and stretches up to join me. "Still not back?" he whispers, hitting the power button on a muted ESPN.

I shake my head. "Any word from Josh?" He shakes his. "I said horrible things about his parents."

"But it's the truth. And he's going to find out eventually."

I drop my forehead to his chest.

"Look, you pack them up and I'll go out and drive around, check
the beach, see if I can find him."

"Nan! Nan!" We both jerk up to see Citrine hysterical at the top
of the stairs. "Your Grayer just stole Clark's Jag!"

23

The sun is rising, orange and agitated, as we pull off the I-95 expressway at the exit for Greenwich, Connecticut, following not so much Clark's Jag, which we lost sight of half an hour ago when we slowed past a parked cop, but a hunch. The minute one of the party's panicked valets stammered, "The kid said something about Chinatown," we threw our stuff in the trunk of Ryan's rental car, tucked Stilton in the back, and took off, hoping that, even with his lead, Grayer's inexperience navigating back to the city might give us a chance of catching up. And we did—briefly—near the Holiday Inn.

I cannot believe we've driven through the night. I place my hands on my face and close my eyes for a moment, digging my ring fingers under the ridge of my brow bone to ease the prickling feeling behind my eyes. "Take that left," I say, breaking the tense silence. I orient myself with the Metro-North station to give Ryan directions to Mr. X's office building. I glance to the backseat, where Stilton is slouched out cold, head lolled, mouth open, held up like a scarecrow by his seat belt. "*What* is Grayer's plan?" I ask quietly, while digging in my bag for gum I know I don't have. "Confront them both? Get them to confront each other? You don't think he'd do anything violent, do you?"

Ryan stares at the empty street, one arm extended to the wheel, the other elbow propped on the door as he grips his temples. "I don't know this kid, Nan."

"I might not either," I admit for the first time, tossing the bag at my feet. "Twelve years is . . . long."

As soon as the squat black building comes into view, it's blatantly apparent the parking lot is empty. I crane my head to see if Grayer is approaching from the other direction. "Maybe he stopped to get gas or pee?" I postulate. "Maybe he got lost?"

"Maybe he shot his mother and is now looking for the perfect bucolic spot to bury her. Maybe by those swans."

"You're helping." I rub my face, watching the explosions behind my eyes. "So he hijacks his mother from the hotel . . ."

"Hijacks? Nan, we saw her get in the Jag."

"But we were three blocks away. And it was dark. Her son shows up in the middle of the night, less than sober, and asks her to get in a Jaguar that isn't his and she *does*? What the fuck?"

"It's not like he had a gun."

"He stole a car! And you just said shot!"

"It was a joke." He clenches and unclenches his jaw. "They walked out together. She got in the *stolen* car of her own volition."

"Whatever. He hijacks her, drives her up the highway to Connecticut—"

"Nan," he cuts in sharply, swerving the rental to a stop in front of the pond. "They might not be here at all."

I twist to him. "So then what next?"

He squeezes the wheel.

"I *can't* just drive home and forget this, Ryan! That you could even—"

"Nan, I walk out of situations every fucking day where I want to strip myself to the bone to fix things. *I get it.* You're just way too close to see that you've done everything you can for this kid—"

"I have fucked this kid up! *Again!* Again, Ryan!" I lower my voice, darting my eyes back to a snoring Stilton.

"I'm not adopting him, Nan."

"I know that."

"And you're not adopting him."

I stare at him, unable to answer, Grayer's backing away from me in Clark's study replaying itself over and over.

"That's it." He lifts up and tugs his cell from his pocket. "We're calling the police, telling them about the Jag. We'll drop Stilton off with Boozy or Ditsy—"

"Bunny."

"Whoever. And they can go back to being a family—"

"They *aren't* a family, they *never were* a family. Just generation after generation of disappointment and—" I slap my hand over his. "I know where they are."

As directed by Ryan's iPhone white pages, minutes later we drive the length of a long, high brick wall until we come to an imposing fourteen-foot wrought-iron gate open on its hinges. Far up a rolling lawn, I spot the Jaguar parked like a silver slash across the drive. Ryan cuts the engine and we both get out on the lilac-lined road, gingerly shutting our doors so as not to awaken Stilton. The temperature has only begun to creep up from its overnight low and I shiver reflexively, buttoning my cardigan over the thin dress.

He approaches the call box, but I grab his arm. "Don't. I'm just going to go up."

"Nan," he says firmly.

"What?"

His hands find his hips and he drops his head. "You're acting like a crazy person."

"See, Ryan, that's what parenting is—if the baby climbs a fence and runs six hundred miles, you climb a fence and run six hundred miles. You keep saying you want this. But I don't think you get what *this* is."

"Most people don't! Unless you have twelve younger siblings, most people don't have your level of experience—they just dive in. I get for me this will be on-the-job training. I also get that's somehow not enough for you."

"Because how are you going to get the training if you don't show up for the job! You left me. For almost a month, Ryan. And there's still no end in sight."

"I'm sorry. But if you're going to—"

"If I'm going to what?"

"Make the most important decision of our marriage based on four weeks out of the last twelve years."

"It's not even about us. Or you. It's about me." I pound my fingers into my solar plexus. "Me."

"Jesus, Nan." His eyes drop to the reddening mark.

"What?"

"I give up." He raises his palms.

"What does that mean?"

"Just what it sounds like," he says simply, his face flattening with hurt. "I'm not going to force you to want a baby. I'm not going to force you to anything. We'll just . . . be us. In a big house that we'll rent out and our old dog and that can be our lives."

And as he articulates this alternative that I had somehow completely overlooked, the opposite of becoming a mother—not becoming one—I feel sadness clamp my heart. "I have to get up there." I gesture to the redbrick mansion.

He waves for me to go ahead and I pass the open gate to jog up the sixty or so yards to where the drive splits off toward a multiple-car garage, or maybe a stable, and, as I stop to catch my breath, I realize Ryan hasn't spun around back to New York. He's rolling the rental slowly up the gravel. He parks behind Clark's car—left at a haphazard angle, the passenger door still open—and gets out, leaving his window ajar for Stilton. As we approach the house birds chirp from the oaks towering overhead, the sun slanting in bright rays through the tree line. Glancing uneasily at each other, we step onto the veranda, where the flagstone is in desperate need of a sweep and the plantings in the urns languish brown and papery.

"Nan." He points at the black front door, also left open.

Confused by the disrepair, I push and it gives into a grand entrance hall. Across from me, two staircases sweep up opposite sides of the room to join on a landing one floor above, visible through white balusters. Under the balcony is an archway to the rear of the house, conjuring servants scuttling back and forth with coats and galoshes, the husband's ironed paper, the wife's contribution to the parish's charity lunch. But now, the room is cold and barren. I look down at the sole furnishing, a pedestal table, its dust-free center circle suggesting an object recently sat there. Ryan touches my back and we step fully inside, taking in the walls bearing numerous dusty outlines where paintings must have hung. Has Elizabeth X died?

I round through the wide arched doorway into the formal double-height living room, its wood-paneled walls empty, the floor bordered with a ring of scuffs demarking a rug no longer present. Chintz couches sit guard beside family pictures piled on the floor, assumingly divested from occasional furniture.

"Grayer's grandmother lives here?" Ryan asks from the doorway.

"Lived, I think. So of course Mr. X's been MIA—his mother passed away and he's obviously been undone by it and clearly this family navigates grief with as much health as they do love. Let me just see that he's okay, get the Jag's keys and we'll go."

Nodding, he follows me into the chinoiserie dining room, where, above the table large enough to comfortably seat twenty, raw wires dangle and a massive Chippendale breakfront is empty of whatever treasure it had displayed.

Then voices. We follow, turning through a gallery of undressed china cabinets and back into the entrance hall, where they get louder—coming from the second floor. I jog up the stairs, Ryan beside me.

Stepping onto the floral-wallpapered landing, I see, at the far end of the hall, Grayer's back outlined in a doorway.

"No my fault," I hear a woman with a Latin-American accent state defensively as we pass a framed photograph of Elizabeth as a young bride, her son seated in linen bloomers by her spectator pumps, her cigarette smoke blowing out of frame.

"Grayer?" I ask and he looks over his shoulder, barely registering me before whipping his attention back to the once glorious room, now just dotted with indelible marks in the pile carpeting where furniture must have been. We step in behind him to see at the chamber's other end, past the string of lead-pane windows overlooking the garden, Mrs. X standing in front of a marble fireplace in silk pajamas and a barn jacket. She stares up at a large rectangle on the wall above the mantel, a reverse shadow in the faded yellow paint.

But then a raspy haggard breath turns me to where, between us, buried under blankets, Elizabeth X lies in a hospital bed, hooked up to a feeding tube and heart-rate monitor.

"He sold the Chagall?" Mrs. X asks, her small fingertips to her lips.

"I never knew it was Chagall," Grayer says quietly. "Not until last night."

"Is no my fault," the agitated home health aide repeats as she huddles in a quilted coat by the bed. "He take the pictures and rugs and makes rules. No heat. Last summer no air conditioner. The winter I afraid she die, no heat. Sometimes I plug in space heater I bring for her and hide it when he comes."

"Dad brought me up here last week to help him take it, *steal it, sell it.*"

"Shit," I hear Ryan murmur behind me. Oh God, no wonder he was so—

"He drained her trust. I'm over him, Mom, done. Stilton will be, too—"

Her head oscillates from side to side.

"So, okay, Mom?" Grayer crosses to her, his loafers leaving a trail of sandy prints on the buttercup carpet. "I'm sorry. I'm saying I'm sorry—I thought how you were kept him away, but I just—didn't get it." He throws his arms around her from behind, squeezing her tiny frame tight as she stares above the mantel. "So we can come home. And we'll just forget Dad. You don't have to be sick or pretend or whatever or any of that shit anymore because I believe in you now. We'll be cool to you, okay? *Okay?*"

Her arms flattened at her sides, her gaze remains riveted by what isn't there. "Where are the dogs?" she asks.

"The pound," the aide answers with a melancholy tsk-tsk, unzipping her coat as the morning sun starts to warm the room. "They make missus so happy, but he no want to feed them."

"But why?" Mrs. X asks, tugging her arm free from Grayer's hold to touch a crack in the exposed yellow paint.

"Because, he's bullshit, Mom." he says, desperate for her to get it. "His hedge fund never took off. He started using investor money to pay off other investors. He's done some seriously illegal shit. He only proposed to Carter because he thought her Hollywood friends would give him a few million fast to cover his debts. We have to go to the police and—" Her hand flies to his face. A slap. A sickening sound. "He's your father." She bores into him. "He's been having some cash-flow problems this year—getting some new ventures off the ground—"

"He's a fucking con man." Grayer stares at her, his cheek reddening. "Charities. Museums. Schools. Did you watch the news last night? *He's* the reason that school closed." I look to Ryan.

"Stop distorting things. He does what's *required*. I've had to spend the last two weeks holed up in some intolerable hotel room, faking an illness, for God's sake, because that's what was required. People will not tolerate failure."

"So let's find new people."

She draws herself up. "You think you don't like your friends at tennis camp so you'll make some new friends at sailing school?" she asks, her voice soaked with sarcasm that shifts to outright contempt. "They're the *same* people, Grayer. Your life has been so easy. When I was your age I was cleaning toilets at Swensen's. Don't stand there in the clothes he paid for and tell me what I can and cannot give up."

"But he *left* you."

She turns to the bed, crossing her arms. "This is between him and your grandmother. He can handle it."

"*Handle* it?" Grayer repeats, his voice thickening. "We don't know where he *is*. He may already have left the country."

We all watch this land as she whips back to him, the veins in her neck in sudden relief. "They will seize *everything*—*do you understand?* The apartment, the bank accounts, *everything*."

He grabs her hand. "I'll get a job. You'll get a job. We'll find a place, the three of us."

She yanks it back. "I don't want that."

A breeze lifts the branches outside the window, one of them scraping the glass, and somewhere in the vast house a remaining clock ticks steadily. "I've suffered enough. *None* of this is my fault, Grayer. It's not my fault."

"It's not," he finally speaks and, despite the tears breaking, his voice is flat, emptied. "And when that's you"—he points a finger at the bed—"it won't be mine."

She goes white.

"Nan?"

"Yes," I answer him.

"Can I get a lift to the train?" he manages.

"Of course," Ryan answers for us both.

Tucking his head, Grayer darts past us into the hall and down the stairs, Ryan and I only a few steps behind. He stops at the round table, planting steadying palms in the dust, his shoulders rising with each audible breath. I suck in my lips and walk tentatively over.

"Wait!" Ryan and I lift our heads to see Mrs. X on the landing balcony. "You can't just *leave* me."

The words hang in the air.

"Fuck. You."

Ryan and I exchange glances.

Blanching, she touches her sternum. "Grayer, there's no need to—"

"Fuck." He draws out the syllable. "You." He lifts his gaze up from the table. "I have spent my *life* getting left by you." His rage echoes off the bare walls, sending her head flinching back.

She swallows, squinting in the light streaming through the glass transom above the front door onto her quivering frame. "Grayer"— she attempts to strike humility—"I'm sorry you think that. I mean, perhaps, it's possible, in the last year, with the challenges in my marriage, my focus may not have—"

"Stop! Just fucking stop. Stop talking." He lifts both hands into his hair and, with a quick huff of air, drops them. Squaring his frame, he raises his gaze to her once more. "When Dad goes down—and he will, Mom, whether I'm the one to tell or not. Because look around— he hocked everything in this house except his own mother." He twists his lips. "And when he does, I'll still have my trust from Dad's family. So will Stilton."

"Yes," she acknowledges, her voice caught.

"So, I'm out of here in a year. But Stilton . . ." Grayer turns it over in his mind. "Stilton needs things."

"Of course." She knows things—acquiring is her forte.

"No fuck, Mom. He loves cooking. Hang out in the kitchen with him. Eat a meal with him. Can you handle that?"

"Yes, I can—"

"Find out what sport he plays and then go to every game. *Every* one. So he never has to look into the bleachers and see that you were too busy shopping to show up." He gathers momentum. "And Christmas."

"I do Christmas."

"Fuck you."

She takes a small step back.

"Not Rosa making eggnog. Family fucking activities: bake something, sing something—Christmas is not your nanny taking you back to her house in Bed-Stuy because she feels sorry for you."

"Who did that?" she asks, alarmed.

He ignores her, and I watch as he runs their life behind his eyes, narrowing in on his demands. "When he starts boarding school—and we can wait a year, now that you're sober—send him daily e-mails. Take him out every weekend for family visits. Mother him. It may not be what you *want*. It may be more suffering than you *deserve*. But as long as he's happy—"

"Yes?"

"You'll get an allowance until Stilton turns eighteen." He studies her reaction.

"An allowance?" She perks up, walking down a few steps closer.

He tilts his head out the open door to where his brother sleeps in the driveway. "And if Stilton hears so much as a word, gets one fucking look from you explaining your transformation, the money stops."

She shakes her head.

"What?" Grayer throws his hands out.

"Yes. Yes, Grayer, I agree. Thank you for—wanting to take care of me."

He takes her summary in, probably the only version she can hold in her mind—not that she's being blackmailed into being a mother, but that her older son has promised her a soft landing. And I sense from the almost imperceptible lightening of her features that this revision somehow makes her feel, perhaps for the first time in his lifetime, safe.

He nods, every ounce of animation draining, and he seems more

weary than even the ninety-year-old prone a floor above. "Fine.
Okay. See you at 721, Mom." He follows Ryan outside.

I lay the car keys on the table and find my voice. "Stilton is asleep
in our rental car with the boys' things. Why don't you drive him back
and we'll pick it up when we get back to the city?"

She nods and, passing the table, grabs the keys to follow me outside, where Grayer is helping a groggy Stilton out of the car. He
speaks to him in a low voice and points up at the veranda. Stilton
follows his brother's finger, his face breaking into a smile as he spots
his mother behind me. He races up the stone steps to throw himself
around her waist. She flinches, but stays in his grasp.

"Mommymommymommy!" His enthusiasm is manic. "You're
back! You're back! You're back!"

"Yes," she answers stiffly, her arms raised as if being mugged.

"At Carter's my friend had a newt—then I burnt my hand and we
were at a hotel. Nan's dog was barking every single time the elevator
came, it was a racket!" He rocks from foot to foot, jostling her. "Then
this guy with a mustache said we had to leave and we went to this
house on the beach that belongs to Citrine and Clark. Citrine gave me
chocolate cake—she's Nan's friend—and I watched all three *Pirates of
the Caribbean* movies in a row and . . . and . . ." His frantic locution loses
steam as he checks her withdrawing gaze. Uncomfortable on both
their behalves, I walk down to join Ryan and Grayer on the gravel.

"Now you're here," she fills in ambivalently.

He nods, releasing her, rushing to calibrate. "Yeah, yup," he says
casually. "Now we're here. Where are we?"

"We're at Grandma's." She allows a hand to find his hair as we all
watch her think. "Daddy's going to be selling this place, so we wanted
to come say good-bye."

"Should I go say hello? I can if you want me to." He turns toward
the front door, prepared to run into the house.

"No." She puts a pausing hand on his shoulder. "She's on vacation.
And I'm going to drive you home. Although my license is in my
purse, back at the hotel." She looks to Grayer. But he just tucks his
head and pointedly gets into the passenger seat of the Jag. "So . . . then . . .
um . . ." She recovers her enthusiasm. "After we get unpacked, maybe

we can see the Indiana Jones movie? Kathy Lee said it was good for boys your age." The things we learn trapped in an HI. "And I can ... make dinner." She squints as her mind picks up speed. "Sloppy Joes."

"Sure. What's a Sloppy Joe?" he asks, finding his cue.

"It's a sandwich. Like a hamburger. I'd make them for my dad when he got home from work."

"Are Nan and Ryan coming?" he asks hesitantly.

She looks past me as she steers him down the steps and toward the rental car. "Stilton, Nan has to go."

"You'll have fun with your mom," I hear myself say, feel myself willing it to be so.

He steps from her grasp and wraps me tightly in turn. "Please tell Citrine I said thank you for teaching me about hydrangeas' care and presentation."

"I will. I'm sure she'll miss you." I smile over the tingle forming in my throat.

Stilton and Ryan exchange good-bye waves and Ryan gets into the backseat of the Jag. "Stay cool, Stil!"

His mother holds open the back door for him and I realize I am frantically trying to memorize his face, his sweet scent, his slip-sliding. "Oh, and Nan?" he says as he climbs in.

"Yes?"

"My birthday is next month. June fourteenth. It's a Saturday. Will you and Ryan come as my personal guests?"

My breath catches. "We'd be delighted."

"I have your address," Mrs. X says as she shuts him in and opens the driver's door for herself.

I lean down to the window so Stilton and I are at eye level. "And you have my e-mail." He nods intently. "So let me know how you did on your Neil Armstrong presentation." I touch my hand to the glass and he matches his palm to mine.

"Nan?"

I turn and she looks up from the driver's seat, eyes fully on me; they flash for a moment and I don't want to know what she's thinking, but all she manages is, "Thank you."

"You're welcome."

I twist off the engine of Clark's Jaguar and turn to Grayer, quiet in the passenger seat beside me. He stares out his window, squinting up through the sun to the Metro-North tracks empty of their usual Monday seersucker and khaki-clad commuters.

"Grayer, we can seriously drive you back in." I look to Ryan in the rearview, who nods in agreement.

"Thanks, but I want to take the train. I just need to zone, make some plans, figure things out."

"But you don't even have keys—"

"I do, actually."

I turn to him in disbelief and his eyes dart away, cheeks reddening.

Ryan opens the back door. "I'm gonna grab some water. Anyone want anything?"

"No, thanks," we say together.

"Do you think I'll have to wait long?" Grayer asks as Ryan walks away.

"Oh, I don't know. I can go in and check the holiday schedule. Or check on Ryan's iPh—" I shake my head, still stuck on the keys. "Grayer, I meant it, you know." He meets my eyes. "That I wanted to take you guys."

"I know."

"I guess now that seems kind of . . ."

"Yeah." He nods down at his lap. "But thanks." He clears his throat. "I mean, thank you."

"Are you going to be okay?"

"Sure. A descent into alcoholism, a moment of clarity, a few years of therapy, a conversion to Scientology, and I should be fine."

I laugh. "Listen, what you did back there was crazy brave and whatever rolls out, I'm here for you guys."

"Here?"

"Yeah, e-mail me. I want to know how it's going. *I* want to come to the school plays. And if, for some reason, you find yourselves at loose ends for Thanksgiving, we could pull out some extra chairs."

"At your 'house'?" he rabbit-ears.

"It's going to be beautiful."

"Right. No, I think"—he nods—"it'll be good—for Stilton. To stay in touch."

"Cool." I match his nod.

He turns away from me to look out the side window. "Listen," he says to the glass, "about what I said back there—you should totally have kids. Jesus, if anyone should, it's you."

I glance again into the rearview, where I see Ryan leaning against a low metal barrier, not getting water, just giving us a moment to talk, and a solid, grounded warmth rises from my chest, replacing what heretofore has been effervescent and flitting. "Thanks, Grayer." And instantly I know it's the benediction I've been waiting for.

"Okay." He opens the door and steps out.

"Wait!"

"Yeah?"

"I don't want you to go." I grab his arm, irrational panic washing over me. "I feel like I should go with you."

"Nope."

"How about, um . . ."

"I gotta go."

And suddenly I know. He climbs out of the car. I grab my bag from the floor of the passenger seat and dig for my keys. I slide off the charm and unlock my seat belt to reach it out to him. He looks down at the little gold cone, so tiny in his grown-up hands.

"Just to remember." I smile, letting him go through wet eyes. "I never stopped."

The day has bloomed into full-blown summer by the time we've returned the Jag to Clark's garage, collected the rental car from 721 Park, done a round-trip loop to retrieve the boys' bags from my parent's, returned the rental, swung by Sarah's to collect Grace, and finally made it back in front of our own house. Grace hops onto the pavement and, extending her leash taut, climbs the stoop as Ryan pays the taxi. Achingly tired and emotionally drained, I shield my eyes from the noon sun and stretch my back before digging in my bag for the keys, perceptibly lighter without the charm. I grip the warm metal, hoping this Memorial Day finds Ingrid roasting marshmallows over a bonfire of her now meaningless unrenewed contract. But as I put the key in the lock, I acknowledge the equally likely possibility that she's cursing me right along with the rest of them—that were she to rant her griev-ances into a teddy bear, I would warrant a shout-out.

"Nan, is this ours?" His hands full with our luggage, Ryan gestures with his chin to the "Poison" sign that has fluttered from our front door to the sidewalk.

"Yup." I shrug. He hustles up the steps as I turn the final lock and Grace barrels between our legs. We both stop short as we step into the dim light of the space that is, minus the plastic sheeting, as I left it.

"Wow," he murmurs, dropping our bags and blowing dust off our answering machine before pressing play.

"Hey, ladybug." My mother's voice fills the room. "Sorry we missed you. Your father took me to see *The Children of Huang Shi*. I made him buy me an ice cream cone on the way home to cheer me up. Anyway, I would have loved to share this in person: guess whose apartment is for sale—the Schwartzes'! How crazy is that? They spent over a million on the reno alone. Anyway, we got a letter on Saturday from the co-op's lawyers saying they want to revisit this in six months. So we're saved! Hope you're having a great holiday weekend, even without Ryan—he'll be home soon. Love you, bye."

"Yey, they're saved." Ryan smiles.

"Until November. When I'm sure their apartment will be worth even more to the board." I squeeze my face in my hands again.

"Hey, you don't know that."

Nodding, I unhook Grace from her leash. "Okay, listen, it'd be great if we could set me up downstairs today before you go, like, if we could tag-team on the ladder to bring down the microwave and my clothes and stuff. I have a lot of hustling to do now that Jarndyce is no longer."

"Sure, of course." He bends down to examine the gauges along the floor where the walls had been. "I just need to check in with work."

"Fine," I say, pulling the ladder from the wall and leaning it against the third-floor landing. "What time do you have to leave?"

"I could take a morning flight?" he asks hesitantly.

"Sure." I smile in an effort to right the energy that is awkward and defeated between us. "Okay—well, I'm going to just . . ." I gesture at the ladder.

"I'll be up in a few." He tugs his phone from his pocket.

I nod and begin my ascent, one hand over the other, feeling the climb zap what's left of my reserves. My head clears the landing and I clamor up to the hall, righting myself and passing the rooms currently warehousing all our boxed possessions to mount the last flight to the top floor.

"Hey, John, it's Ryan . . . yeah, it's been a great break, thanks. How 'bout you?" His animated work voice grows fainter and I hear his footsteps tread back into the kitchen. I roll my neck as I walk, thinking maybe a nap before we dig in, wondering if we should splurge on going out to dinner—I stop.

Then step into the light pouring into the hall, onto me.

I gasp to see the most beautiful treetop, our treetop, which I am looking at through my brand-new window, its Andersen stickers still plastered on each pane of glass, the bright wood of the frame crisp against the faded wallpaper it's been sunk into.

"Ryan!" I scream. "Ryan, come here!"

I hear him running and then the clanging as he climbs the ladder. "What's wrong? You okay?"

But I am smiling too hard to get out an answer as I walk toward the streaming light, wiping at my sweaty face with the shoulder of my cardigan.

He runs in behind me as I put my palm to the warm glass. I turn and he tilts his head. "You got your window." The sun is bright on his face.

"Yup."

He crosses his arms. "That contractor knows how to keep a girl interested."

"Yup." I laugh.

"So I did a lot of thinking on that drive."

"Which drive?" I crack.

"Nan, I'm asking to be transferred to something with less travel for a while."

"Ryan."

"But don't think I'm paying off this loan myself. I'm expecting *this* office to be extremely productive. Now that you got your fancy-pants window."

I tilt my head. "*If* it's an office."

He nods slowly, smiling deeply. "If it is."

WHOOF!

"Coming, Grace!" Ryan yells over his shoulder. "I'm going to pull up the report on the well systems that just got passed around. I'm thinking I could rig some pulley-basket thing to get her up and down, that way we can stay up here for the rest of this mess."

"We?"

WHOOF!

"Yup, we." He reaches out and squeezes my hand before heading out to calm the dog. "Think of the upper-body strength we're going to have after a few weeks with a pulley, we'll wow 'em at the beach," he calls.

I turn back to my window, feeling a tremor of anticipation, of curiosity about this little person we haven't met yet, this relationship yet to be forged. Here. Because it seems Grayer's benediction was inextricably linked to my own. I reach up to turn the lock and raise the bottom pane high, the breeze washing over my face as I take in what to some may be a string of dirty roofs, a smattering of graffiti, a lacing of telephone wires, but to me is a view that, in the freshness of its revelation, rivals anything I've seen yet.

ACKNOWLEDGMENTS

We are grateful to . . .

Judith Curr for her continued support and enthusiasm. Our phenomenal editor, Greer Hendricks, for her humor, patience and insight. Her wonderful assistants, Sarah Walsh and Sarah Cantin, for always getting everything where it needs to go. Our dear friend, Suzanne O'Neill, for guiding us for take-off. Our fierce agent, Suzanne Gluck, the only lady we want out in front, for her faith and foresight. Her rockstar assistants, Sarah Ceglarski and Caroline Donofrio, for triaging our 5 p.m. phone calls. Alicia Gordon and the entire William Morris Endeavor Entertainment team for their unflagging commitment. Sara Bottfeld for taking us with her and her assistant, Tarika Kahn, for all her help. Ken Weinrib and Eric Brown, our favorite men in midtown, for their debonair vigilance. Katie Brandi for once again lending us her brilliant mind. Joan for the perfect porcelain polar bear. Our husbands, Joel and David, for cheering us on every day and giving us a reason to turn off the computers. And finally, and with full hearts, Emma's grandmother, Francie, for finishing in style.